Kim Scott is a descendant of people who have always lived along the south-east coast of Western Australia and is glad to be living in times when it is possible to explore the significance of that fact and be one among those who call themselves Nyoongar.

Kim Scott began writing for publication shortly after he became a secondary school teacher of English. His first novel, *True Country*, was published in 1993 and he has had poetry and short stories published in a range of anthologies.

In recent years he has received grants from the Literature Board of the Australia Council and the Western Australian Department for the Arts to enable him to devote more time to writing. He lives in Coolbellup, a southern suburb of Perth, Western Australia, with his wife and children.

Benang

from the heart

Harley, a man of Nyoongar ancestry, finds himself at a difficult point in the history of his country, family and self. As the apparently successful outcome of his white grandfather's enthusiastic attempts to isolate and breed the 'first whiteman born', he wants to be a failure. But would such failure mean his Nyoongar ancestors could label him a success? And how can the attempted genocide represented by his family history be told?

Oceanic in its rhythms and understanding, brilliant in its use of language and image, moving in its largeness of spirit, compelling in its narrative scope and style, *Benang* is a novel of celebration and lament, of beginning and return, of obliteration and recovery, of silencing and of powerful utterance. Both tentative and daring, it speaks to the present and a possible future through stories, dreams, rhythms, songs, images and documents mobilised from the incompletely acknowledged and still dynamic past.

Winner, Miles Franklin Literary Award
Winner, Western Australian Premier's Book Award

Cover image: Terrence Shiosaki, *European Subjugation*, installation.

Benang

from the heart

KIM SCOTT

FREMANTLE ARTS CENTRE PRESS

Many Nyungars today speak with deep feeling about this wild, windswept country. They tell stories about the old folk they lost in the massacre and recall how their mothers warned them to stay out of that area. One man describes how Nyungars will roll up their car windows while passing through Ravensthorpe, and not even stop for food or petrol. The whole region has bad associations and an unwelcoming aura for them. It is a place for ghosts, not for living people.

(Eades and Roberts, 1984, submission
to the Seaman Land Inquiry)

The Half-caste: Means of Disappearance

The modern world has many problems to face. The half-caste is not one of them. He (or she) is merely a passing phase, an incident in history, an interesting event in what we call 'progress', a natural transmutation in what we know as cultural evolution. He will solve himself and disappear. That much is certain; it is not problematical. The only problem that enters into it, though it is a palpable misuse of the word to call it that, is how long it is going to take. A few centuries maybe; perhaps much less.

… on the ground alone that he is a nuisance to us, we should hurry on his disappearance.

(*West Australian*, 22 July 1933)

Black May Become White: Work of Elevating the Natives

The black will go white. It is exemplified in the quarter-castes, and by the gradual absorption of the native Australian black race by the white.

The position is analogous to that of a small stream of dirty water entering a larger clear stream. Eventually the colour of the smaller is lost.

(*Daily News*, 3 October 1933)

from the heart

I know I make people uncomfortable, and embarrass even those who come to hear me sing. I regret that, but not how all the talk and nervous laughter fades as I rise from the ground and, hovering in the campfire smoke, slowly turn to consider this small circle of which I am the centre.

We feel it then, share the silence.

Of course, nothing can stop a persistent and desperate cynic from occasionally shouting, 'Look, rotisserie!' or, 'Spit roast!' But no cynicism remains once I begin to sing.

Sing? Perhaps that is not the right word, because it is not really *singing*. And it is not really *me* who sings, for although I touch the earth only once in my performance — leaving a single footprint in white sand and ash — through me we hear the rhythm of many feet pounding the earth, and the strong pulse of countless hearts beating. Together, we listen to the creak and rustle of various plants in various winds, the countless beatings of different wings, the many strange and musical calls of animals who have come from this place right here. And, deep in the chill night, ending the song, the curlew's cry.

Death bird, my people say.

Obviously, however, I am alive. Am bringing life.

People smile at me, say:

'You can always tell.'

'You can't hide who you are.'

'You feel it, here?'

And, tapping their fists on my chest,

'Speak it from the heart.'

But it is far, far easier for me to sing than write, because this language troubles me, makes me feel as if I am walking across the earth which surrounds salt lakes, that thin-crusted earth upon which it is best to tread warily, skim lightly ...

Quickly.

The first thing is the first thing is that we always knew it was not the best way, but that there was no real choice and we had to keep moving if only to get past the bad smell of it all ...

And it is thus — with a bad smell — that I should introduce myself; even if such an aroma suggests my words originate from some other part of my anatomy than the heart.

Sadly, I can begin only so far back as my great-great-grandparents, for it is they — Fanny, Sandy One Mason, and their boy, Sandy Two — who limp by the government water tank, trying not to breathe at all rather than have this stench invade their nostrils.

Phew! Phew!

Something dead. Sandy One cursed the bastard who'd

dumped a carcass by the edge of town. A dead kangaroo, he thought.

Well ... No. In fact, it was the body of a child. A boy. My family may not have even realised this, although I see Fanny — discreetly, indecently — sniff the air.

The poor boy had been only a few years old. His name? His name was ... I'm tempted to give him my own name, but his was that of a famous man, an explorer, a pioneer, a politician, and although I intend to write a history, it is not one at such an exalted level.

However, it is true that the explorer — a Premier Man — had travelled this very way, some years before. Before the gold rushes, and even before the telegraph line which sprang up in his footprints. A very strange thing it was, that telegraph line; such thin wire, trembling with unseen unheard voices, looping from pole to pole across the country.

I admit I am not absolutely sure of the boy's name, or even why the body was left there. I merely happened upon the incident in my fitful attempts to supplement Grandad's research and my Uncles' memories. Kylie Bay's Board of Health had written to the Aborigines Department asking for funds for the disposal of the body of said child which, having been deposited within the town area by *blacks*, posed a hazard to the town's health.

I feel a certain kinship with the boy, but my kinship with Fanny and the two Sandies becomes all the stronger with the realisation that, when I began this project, I too breathed in the scent of something discarded, something cast away and let drift and only now washed up. It was the smell of anxiety, of anger and betrayal. Of course, it may equally have been the rank odour of my grandfather, his puke and shit. Or perhaps some olfactory nerve was triggered by the thought of a boy, left limp and lifeless and more like me than I care to admit.

But I anticipate myself. I do not wish this to be a story of me — other than in the healing — but of before me. I wish to write nothing more than a simple family history, the most local of histories. And to make certain things clear.

As reluctant as I am to face it, I may be the successful end of a long line of failures. Or is it the other way round?

So ... So, by way of introduction, here I come:

The first white man born.

the first white man born

As I see it, what we have to do is uplift and elevate these
people to our own plane ...

A O Neville

As the first-born-successfully-white-man-in-the-family-
line I awoke to a terrible pressure, particularly upon my
nose and forehead, and thought I was blind. In fact, the
truth was there was nothing to see, except — right in
front of my eyes — a whiteness which was surface only,
with no depth, and very little variation.

Eventually, I realised my face was pressed hard against
a ceiling.

I pushed out my hands and shot rapidly away from
it. Thus, I fell. Still groggy from the collision with the
floor, and once more floating toward the ceiling, I
kicked out and managed to hook my feet in the
wrought-iron bedstead. It was an awkward and
clumsy process but I succeeded in securing the

bedsheet (which must have fallen from the ceiling), and inserting myself beneath it. And there I lay, secure but trembling, staring at my hands which gripped the sheet so tightly.

I couldn't stay trapped like that. Summoning my courage and tentatively experimenting, I discovered that I merely had a *propensity* for elevation. I would rise in the air only when I relaxed, let my mind go blank.

I felt so weak but, obviously, it was not from the effort of supporting my body's weight.

Hovering before a mirror, I saw a stranger. It was hard to focus, but this much was clear; he was thin, and wore some sort of napkin around his loins. Dark blue veins ran beneath his creamy skin, and his nipples and lips were sharply defined.

The image shifted, and changed shape as I have seen clouds do around granite peaks above the sea. But it was terrible to see the shapes, the selves I took.

I stood motionless against a setting sun; posture perfect, brow noble, features fine.

Saw myself slumped, grinning, furrow-browed, with a bottle in my hand.

Was Tonto to my grandfather's Lone Ranger. Guran to some Phantom.

There appeared a footballer, boxer, country and western singer.

A tiny figure, sprawled on the ground in some desert landscape, dying.

And then I saw myself poised with a boomerang, saw myself throwing it out to where the sky bends, saw it arcing back again but now it was my tiny, cartwheeling mirror image which was returning, growing, merging with other crowding, jostling selves into one shimmering, ascending me.

I closed my eyes, and when the crown of my head gently nudged the ceiling I must have looked like some elaborate light shade. Perhaps that was what my grandfather meant when he said I was brightest and most useful in an uplifted state.

It was easy enough to come down again. I kept my eyes closed, and let the voice in my skull run through what I now realise was the thinnest of narratives, my father's few words. Thus, it was anger which returned me to earth. Well, to the floor at least.

I dressed myself carefully, opened the door.

I wanted to be bold, but walking felt very peculiar. Had I ever known how? I held my shoulders back, placed each foot precisely and, flicking my toes and flapping my arms, desperately tried to propel myself forward. It was very difficult to maintain balance, and although perhaps it should have been laughable I was, in fact, desperate and tearful because — more than anything else — I wished to appear as normal as possible.

I mastered a way of walking, and my light tread — despite being little more than a series of soft touchdowns — sounded the floorboards like a drum.

It must have been morning, because I was blinded by light as I opened the last door.

Blinking, I saw my grandfather's back, and we were both looking out over a view of ocean, island, headland reaching in from the right of the window frame. The old man turned his pale and lined face to me.

'You're back,' he said.

He stroked my jaw with the back of his hand, ran his finger along a scar there.

'My son. You look so much better. You still don't remember, do you?'

His face shone with relief. Or was it the reflection of success?

Oh, I remembered all right, and I get better all the time. But I kept quiet. You might call it my *native* cunning.

In the window's frame I saw the ocean pulse against the tip of the island. It blossomed, disappeared. Again. Again.

My heart was beating calmly, my own pulse lulled me.

I was between the sheets of my bed, and my grandfather's eyes, in that face so close to my own, were brimming.

He moved his lips, trying to speak, then reached out and patted the back of my hand. He was fighting back tears. I stayed mute, did nothing.

'You'll be all right,' he slurred. 'We'll get you back on track. Everything that's mine is yours, you know that.'

Oh.

I let him hear my voice.

'Thanks. Thanks, Dad.'

I knew that would get to him. He smiled, and a tear ran down his cheek. It was like one of his beloved bedside scenes.

I had come back from the dead. Obviously, I was not in the best of health; I was pale, my memory was poor, and it was as my grandfather's child that I sensed an opportunity. The old man wouldn't last long. Well, I've been raised to this, I thought. *It is survival of the fittest, and let the fittest do their best.*

raised to this ...

When I was seven years old my father gave me to his own father to raise.

My grandfather owned and managed a gentlemen's boarding house. He and my father shook hands at the rear of the building to finalise the transaction.

Hands parted, and I followed my grandfather between walls of corrugated iron, teetering crates, empty glass bottles. Struggling with my plastic bags of clothing and breathing the air of unwashed laundry and indifferent cooking, I followed him up rickety and creaking stairs until eventually we emerged from gloom and into a wash of light. Before us an array of tables, set with cloth, cutlery and condiments, patiently awaited the arrival of those who would be served.

Grandad thought this would be a good place for me to start.

A doorway to my right led to a room with a desk, filing cabinet, television and bed. My grandfather introduced me to his business partner, Aunty ... I can't remember the name. There was a succession of them over the years. She sat up in bed, wearing a thin dressing-gown, and with receipts, money, accounting books and magazines scattered across the bedclothes. The desk was beside the bed and supported a worn typewriter, a box of chocolates, and an ashtray overflowing with cigarette butts and chocolate wrappers. The solemn visage of the Queen observed a crucified Christ pinned to the opposite wall. Aunty looked at me from between the two of them, and gave a very quick smile.

I was led to an old verandah enclosed with glass louvres. My room. There was a bunk-bed with a desk beneath it, and three walls lined with the books I was to read in the long weekend and holiday hours before me. How familiar I became with them, their smell, the way words can blur, and shift, and welcome you among them.

In that room I always woke with dawn light on my face. One step brought me up against the louvres, and a view of the shabby, flaking backs of other tall buildings. Below, in the middle of a small concrete enclosure, a tiny, stubborn rug of buffalo grass defied the cars which nosed up to it. A tap hung over a little drainwell.

'We all have to make our way in this world,' Grandad said, 'on your own. I want to give you an even chance. You will never get that with your father.'

Grandfather — Ernest Solomon Scat — told me that my father had agreed it was for the best.

At first, adjusting to the new circumstances, I had an unfortunate run of bed-wetting, but once cured of that — with an ingenious system my grandfather designed whereby an electric shock was administered to my penis each time the sheets became wet — I was off to the very best of boarding schools.

I suppose it was effective enough.

In the school holidays Grandad trained me in all the tasks required to run a boarding house, and ensured I did extra studies. He made up a timetable. I served our gentlemen guests, and cleaned up after them, and made their beds, and washed their dishes, their clothes, their sheets ... Except when it was a necessary part of my duties I tried to avoid the boarders, many of whom were alcoholics.

I accepted the books Grandad had mailed from this or that book club; classics, instructive manuals of one kind or another, best-sellers ... I read them all.

There was nothing else to do. Like many isolated youths, reading was a great comfort to me.

I knew Ern was a reader, but it was only in the later years of his life that I became aware of his interest in local and family histories, and realised he had always kept notes, worked to a plan, documented his activities and research.

Grandad was very insistent that I achieve well at school, and I was still very young when I brought home a report which indicated that I was not achieving to my potential, was somewhat lazy. Grandfather said nothing as he stood beside me reading it but, having accomplished that, he suddenly struck me to the ground and delivered a kick which sent me sliding across the floor. It was a startling violence, and as I lay there curled up in shock he told me I was to stay in the room and study for the duration of the school holiday. I was relieved to be left alone.

It was many years later that I crept through Aunty's bedroom/office so as not to wake her, and into the dining room. White plastic tablecloths, stainless steel, grubby lace curtains and grey light. The old fellow, Uncle Will — who I dimly remembered from a time before I came to live with my grandfather — was the only one in the room. Grandfather had told me I was not to call this man uncle.

The old fellow motioned me over to where he sat very straight, eyes twinkling, and with his damp hair combed back along his scalp.

'How those girlfriends of yours?' he asked.

His comment caused me some anxiety. I had been sneaking out in the evenings to see a girl. She had an adopted sister, and the two of them were remarkably close and supportive of one another. One or the other of them had said, 'But just imagine, what if we were twins.'

'But,' I said, 'you look nothing like each other, and ...'

They laughed a little, were patient with my dim-wittedness.

'But just imagine, Harley, if we were twins.'

We did more than imagine. Perhaps I was merely following in the steps of my grandfather and father. It was the stuff of male fantasy, but I have come to believe — despite how I strutted and flattered myself at the time — that there was far greater intention, passion, and — yes — even love implicated in our intimacies than the three of us knew. And I remain exceedingly grateful, because since then ...

Well, all of this will become clear.

Uncle Will said, 'She looking for her family, is she?'

I did not reply. Will was smiling, but he seemed nervous.

I was at what Grandad referred to as *a most dangerous*

age, and can't say what caused him to become so lax over those long summer holidays. Perhaps he was preoccupied with his latest business partner, who I recall only as another new 'Aunty so-and-so', or it may have been that Uncle Will covered up for me. Whatever the case, had he known the extent to which I had freed myself from the timetable set for me, my grandfather would have said I was like *an oarless boat adrift on a wide sea.*

But, at that *most dangerous age*, I in fact had an oar — or something very like it — secreted away in my trousers. In return for accounts of my exploits Uncle Will had made himself a wonderful accomplice, and when I let him know — after all, I was isolated, I was proud, and I had to tell someone — that the girlfriends and I were ...

Please forgive my coyness, but how can I summarise all this, having now started?

Uncle Will, with a knowing smile, said, 'No wonder you look so tired.'

I asked for his help!

And it was in the subsequent search for the biological family of one of my girlfriends that so much trouble began, and led me to reconsider who I am.

Raised to carry on one heritage, and ignore another, I found myself wishing to reverse that upbringing, not only for the sake of my own children, but also for my ancestors, and for their children in turn. And therefore, inevitably, most especially, for myself.

funerals

How lonely I was at my father's funeral. Gravel rolled from beneath my feet as I skidded and stumbled toward the grave. I remember thinking that there should be more bodies, there were not enough bodies. Why just the one? There should be more.

I was full of self-pity. Is that normal for a murderer at his victim's funeral?

A small crowd circled the grave, heads down. The breeze plucked an orange flower from a tree and, setting its tiny propellors spinning, carried it toward where I saw the distant blue ocean, and an island with the sea blossoming white against its edge. A few faces I recognised floated before me. Glittering, brittle stars fractured my vision.

How is it possible for me to say how I feel, how I felt? I can say that the chain on my wrist was heavy and uncomfortable. I can say that I remember trying to place it over my shirt sleeve to protect my skin. I can say that I felt the shame of it, and that I wanted to ignore the man at its other end, but if he pulled me one way then of course that was where I must go. And my grandfather was there, at my other side. Showing his support, you think?

When the first of the real aunties reached for me, those two men pushed and pulled me away from them.

And so it is very curious — oh yes, it is curious, it is paradoxical, it is strange, it seems all wrong in every way for me to say it, but ... that chain may have helped pull me back from the edge of our grave.

Driving back to the remand centre the road dipped suddenly where there had once been a creek, and my stomach lurched. At the time there was only that gut feeling, but now, initially, I might explain it by way of dusty archives.

The Inspector for Aborigines and Fisheries' diary describes the pool where that creek once joined the river: *Acres and acres of mullet*, he said, *their tails sticking out of the water*. He wrote of how the dew saturated both banks, and how the fish seemed to move from the river into the milky mist which lay over it. The river, said the inspector, was very full, and rushed to and from this pool in its bend on the way to the harbour. The inspector also wrote that he was after *a gin* who, with a bunch of *very fair children*, had been reported as camping and hunting along the river. It was the nineteen twenties, long decades before I was born. It may well have been my family, generations back, out of their territory, running to escape.

That river still feeds into the harbour, but how little I

knew of my ancestors' tongue then, how that river had dried up. But not completely.

The Nyoongar name for that harbour is Merrytch. Meaning dew, or dewdrop. But the word is similar to a word for penis, and also very similar to the word for mullet. Mullet, penis, dewdrop; they share the same root-word.

There are no more acres of mullet there. But there is still dew, and the sea still breaks over the island I saw from the cemetery. The river still flows, although it now floods the shallow harbour with pesticides. And what of my penis, its dewdrop?

I appreciate your concern, and that you remain with this shifty, snaking narrative. I am grateful; more grateful than you know, believe me.

As I was saying, the remand centre. There was a court case, certain charges were withdrawn, and I was acquitted of the death of my father and once again handed over to my grandfather's care.

We moved to the quiet and tiny coastal town of Wirlup Haven. Uncle Will helped us make the place comfortable.

Grandad had his plans. What he would bequeath me. The house I would renovate with him, the local and family histories we would write. Your forefathers, he said …

I was still ill. It is difficult to appreciate the way a cultural and spiritual uplift can affect one. And then he had his first stroke.

success

Uncle Will, Grandad, me at sixteen years of age. It was like ... things had suddenly finished for me. Scarred, fragile and empty, I was still recovering from what I realised was no accident. My grandfather was observing me in such a way — *scientific* he would have said; lecherous, say I — that it was impossible for me to feel at ease.

At times, I confess, I just wanted someone to be proud of me. Anyone. I felt defeated, and guilty, and even wondered if it was Grandad I'd betrayed.

We drew up a timetable. He was always pragmatic, my grandfather. Of course he was not without vision — I'm thinking of his lofty ambitions for me — but he had always stressed the value of timetables and a systematic approach to problems. The setting of goals. The importance of his heritage.

So, as I said, we drew up a timetable. First, my recovery. Then later, the renovation of the property. He was going to retire here, he said, and wanted to leave me something.

'Try to think of your father's death as an unfortunate necessity.' Really. That's what he said.

From the way he talked I knew he'd already begun drafting advertising leaflets. 'What we want here,' he said, 'is a small bed-and-breakfast place for the well-heeled, for those who wish to escape the hurly-burly, to relax and forget. We have pristine beaches; turquoise waters and white sand. Granite outcrops. We can offer the history of the place's pioneers, explain how once there was an unofficial port where the enterprising Mr Mustle welcomed the whalers, sealers and other adventurers in the very earliest days of settlement. They used rum for currency ...' And so he went on. Adventure, enterprise, vision.

Tap tap. I began chipping the render from the stone walls of the old house. I hesitate to mention it; in the context of this story it may seem so dreadfully *symbolic*. But what can I do? It is the truth. Tap tap. There were many walls to do, and I was doing only a very little at a time. I was very listless, but the task, the tools I was using, and the fragments of render I stuffed in my pockets kept my feet on the ground.

Grandad disappeared into his study each morning. Uncle Will visited occasionally, and I tap-tapped on not knowing, even then, what to say to him. He cooked our meals, and afterwards I watched television.

I worried that Grandad was right. That I was a success.

Tap tap. Uncle Will tapping me on the shoulder, interrupting my reverie. I carefully put down the hammer and chisel, shook the hand he offered me.

'I'm going away,' he said, softly. I didn't like the way he was looking at me. 'I left something in your room.'

I watched him walk away; his tall, thin body held so very straight, and each foot lifted and placed so very precisely. He walked like some sort of bird. He was not really my uncle. He was only my father's cousin. A hand waved from the car as he drove away.

Tap tap. Fingers on the keyboard now. Long after then.

After some time (weeks? months?) of that tap tapping, of house cleaning, of meal preparation, of working in the garden and performing all those necessary domestic chores; after some time of this I found myself drifting along the passage to my grandfather's study. I lacked the confidence to even allow myself to think it, but I wanted evidence of some sort. I wanted confirmation of my fears, what my father and the girls had told me that last time.

The room was neat and well organised. Quite apart from anything else I did it was probably my lack of order, and how I disrupted his, that made the old man rage so in the months to come. Well, as best he could anyway.

I found myself hovering over sets of documents, things filed in plastic envelopes in rumbling drawers and snapping files. Certificates of birth, death, marriage; newspaper clippings, police reports; letters (personal; from this or that historical society); parish records; cemetery listings; books, photographs ...

Photographs. As before, I shuffled idly through them. I was careless, letting them fall to the floor. Various people, all classifiable as *Aboriginal*. There were portraits arranged in pairs; one a snapshot labelled *As I found them*, the other a studio photograph captioned *Identical with above child*. There were families grouped according to skin colour. And, sudden enough to startle me, my own image.

A boy. Wing-nut eared and freckled, he wore a school uniform, a tie, a toothy grin. He grinned like an idiot, like an innocent.

Captions to the photographs; *full-blood, half-caste (first cross), quadroon, octoroon*. There was a page of various fractions, possible permutations growing more and more convoluted. Of course, in the language of such mathematics it is simple; from the whole to the partial and back again. This much was clear; I was a fraction of what I might have been.

A caption beneath my father's photograph:

Octoroon grandson (mother quarter caste [No. 2], father Scottish). Freckles on the face are the only trace of colour apparent.

I saw my image inserted into sequences of three or four in which I was always at the end of the line (even now, I wince at such a phrase). Each sequence was entitled, *Three Generations (Reading from Right to Left)*, and each individual was designated by a fraction.

I was leafing through the papers, letting them fall.

Breeding Up. In the third or fourth generation no sign of native origin is apparent. The repetition of the boarding school process and careful breeding ... after two or three generations the advance should be so great that families should be living like the rest of the community.

A cough. Grandad at the door, leaning in its frame.

Such an inadequate memory. What had my father tried to explain?

I turned away from the old man and in a sort of controlled tantrum — oh, no doubt it was childish — I plucked papers from drawers, threw them, let them fall. I made books fly, index cards panic and flee.

Occasionally, rising and falling in all that flurry, I paused to read from a book which had passages underlined on almost every page. There were a couple of family trees inscribed on the flyleaf. Trees? Rather, they were sharply ruled diagrams. My name finished each one. On another page there was a third, a fourth. All leading to me.

Question marks sprouted in the margins of those diagrams, and I was sowing my own.

Books everywhere, with strips of paper protruding from them like dry and shrivelled tongues.

The need for both biological and social absorption. Dilute the strain.

My grandfather was still in the doorway, now on his knees. One hand clutched his chest, while the other waved feebly at me. I remembered a similar scene, but this time did not flee from him but picked my way among the sprawling books, softly slowly stepped through rustling pages, so sharp-edged and so pale.

Uplift a despised race.

'Well, old man, fuck me white.'
I helped him to his feet.

I would like to say that I remember slowly falling, and how rectangles of white curved and moved aside as if they were sails, and I a great wind. But it was only paper, sheets of paper strewn about me.

And it was there, in a dry and hostile environment, in that litter of paper, cards, files and photographs that I began to settle and make myself substantial. A sterile landscape, but I have grown from that fraction of life which fell.

I understood that much effort had gone into arriving at me. At someone like me. I was intended as the product of a long and considered process which my grandfather had brought to a conclusion.

Ahem.

The whole process — my family history, as it turns out — appealed to Grandad's sense of himself as a scientist who *with his trained mind and keen desire to exert his efforts in the field investigating native culture and in studying the life history of the species, supplies an aid to administration*. He just got lost along the way.

It was the *selective separation from antecedents* which seemed most important, and with which Grandfather was a little lax. It was one of the areas where he had erred with my father.

It was a part of the system used at the settlements and missions.

Of course it is impossible to completely retrace the process. A hundred years is a hundred years is a hundred years … Following my grandfather's dictum, as with such an inheritance I am bound to, I will provide documents where I can. Let me assure you that I have been diligent. But remember, I had to look after an old man and — at least in the beginning — I wasted time on the house.

So, I was busy. And then, as my awareness of my historical place grew, so did my desire for distraction.

I had not wanted to write a book. It was Grandfather's idea. The pleasure I first gained from it was through reading my efforts to him, sharing intimacies. He did not like it. And although disabled by his stroke, his eyes could still bulge, his face turn red. I would wipe spittle from his chin and, after putting him to bed and smoothing his pillow down, re-read the sections that had elicited the most satisfying — for me — response.

Really, I wanted to prove myself his failure. Or, at the very least, a mistake.

People should learn from their mistakes, right?

I tried to explain that I needed time. After all, wasn't it his own estimation that it would take generations for the plan to succeed? I had far less time than that.

'You have me,' I would smile at him. 'Your living proof. Study me, Grandad, your conclusive evidence. Another *one without a history, plucked from the possibility of a sinister third race.'* (In Grandad's day, apparently, there were only the two!)

I want to stress that I am not proud of my behaviour, but nor can I deny that I was very angry. Angry with my grandfather, his rigour, his scientific method, his opportunism, his lust. And so I am reluctant to begin with my grandfather, as if all I can do is react to him and his plans, as if I have nothing else.

But even if that were true, is it such a bad thing, to begin with anger and resistance?

ernest solomon scat

My grandfather used to listen, awaiting the entrance of his younger self as I read to him. Knowing his impatience, I shook papers at him, flapped my arms and moved about the room which was already beginning to show the evidence of my fitful renovations. Mocking him, I waved his will, his titles and deeds, and hovered just beyond his feebly swiping arms. 'What have I done to deserve all this?'

The old man's speech came slow and croaking. He told me nothing new, and there was no comfort in any of it.

He snarled at me, his jowls shaking. *A most dangerous age*. I had spent months looking after him, and no sooner had he regained some fluency to his speech than he uttered those words, trying to manipulate me once again, grabbing at power whichever way he could.

He lifted himself from his chair and took a few steps toward me, and I wrapped my arms around him. It gave me a weightiness which increased my strength. Laughing,

I returned him to his chair and did not succumb to the temptation to let him fall.

Despite the power and strength I felt at such times, I nevertheless felt impoverished, weakened, reduced. It appeared that in the little family history my grandfather had bequeathed me options had disappeared. It seemed an inexorable process, this one of we becoming I. This reduction of a rich and variously shared place to one fragile, impoverished consciousness.

Once I would have insisted this little story represent nothing other than its grumpy, unhappy narrator. This fuck-me-white and first one born. This drifting lightweight who so wanted to be his grandfather's failure. This (let me do away with all vanity) faceless, empty-scrotumed, limp-dicked first man born.

I began, I believe, with how I found the seed of myself (but never, alas, my seed) in Grandfather's study. He had fallen ill. He fell. I did not push.

Ernest Solomon Scat fell seriously ill. He was not pushed. His grandson was staying with him, and was himself in convalescence, recovering from a serious accident in which ... Well, it was not a happy time. His injuries were what, depending on your priorities, you might call superficial. That is to say, the damaged and missing parts were not at all large.

The grandson discovered his patriarch's study. And although the boy had a timetable of tasks his grandfather had given him, he was forced — not so reluctantly, but oh most nervously — to alter it.

There was the grandfather to take care of now. And,

having found his grandfather's life's work — and seeing that it seemed incomplete, and seeing, moreover, how it so directly led to the grandson himself — the aforementioned boy wanted to help. He wanted to play a more active part.

It was necessary to go further back, but within those walls I could go only so far. It was not something I was able to articulate, but even then I wished to pick up a rhythm begun deeper and long before those named Fanny and Sandy One Mason. But my grandfather's intentions deafened and blinded me, and so I began with where the paper starts, where the white man comes. I thought, trapped as I was, that this was the place to begin.

Whatever the confusions of my genealogy, there seems little doubt that my grandfather intended to be my creator. It was he who, if not indeed forming the idea, applied it as Mr Neville was unable to do.

For Ernest, it was a rationalisation of his desire. It was a challenge. It was as if he — a little too late to be a pioneer, and not really cut out to tame the land — could still play a role in taming a people into submission.

Whereas for me it was contrition, it was anger. It moved from one to the other.

Old Ernest watched me as I wrote; brow corrugated with anxiety and doubt, his eyes followed me as I drifted — scribbling, rising and falling — around and around that paper-lined and littered room.

At first I tried to study and write for a couple of hours

each morning. What was it? A family history? A local history? An experiment? A fantasy?

What kept me at it? Malice? Perversity? To achieve against Grandad's failure? To better him? I think it was simply that, in such isolation, I had nothing else.

In the afternoons I worked, as instructed, on the house. It was fitful and poorly planned. I had no strength, no skill. I tapped a hammer and chisel, hacked feebly at the garden. Chip, hack, destroy.

I prepared meals. On washing days I discovered the pleasure of letting myself flap absently on the line, with only my fingers gripping tight. I was successfully assimilated to the laundry, washing machine, a used car.

I used to take him out in the wheelchair but, pushing him, my feet scrabbled to remain on the pavement. Even after I had crammed my pockets with rubble, earth, and loose change I still needed to keep a firm grip on the wheelchair or risk drifting away.

On one downhill run the wheelchair suddenly picked up speed so that, my feet having left the ground, I trailed behind it like a banner. We coasted well out onto the flats before I was able to regain sufficient composure and gravity to drive my heels into the earth and bring us to a stop.

I decided it was better for Ernest to walk, and so I sat in the wheelchair and pushed the wheels at just the right speed to keep him stumbling along behind me. Weighed down by the wheelchair, I could relax and not have to concentrate on remaining earthbound. I often arrived home with an exhausted Ern on my lap which, given the nature of our earlier relationship, both amused and repelled me.

It required no concentration, once a month or so, to drive Grandad and his pension into Gebalup for our shopping. Of course it was I (safely belted to my seat) who drove, and then the old man at the periphery of my vision sometimes became an echo of my father on our last long screaming journey. I had to turn to him, to make sure it was indeed just old Ern.

We hummed along the black top. On either side of us trees, dying, turning white. Once there were many, many more of them, and they were alive, and they drank the rain and returned it to the sky. Now their roots shrivelled in salt water and — thus betrayed — they raised bare and brittle limbs to the sky.

Vast squares of yellow, or sometimes rippling green, stretched away from the roadside. The sun shone through glass, our air was stale, and when we opened the windows the wind roared and tore at our hair.

Gebalup was a garage, a hotel. It was faded green, yellow, dark red bricks and — despite the pervasive smell of diesel — the wheat and barley pollen in the air made me sneeze. From the centre of the main street I could see dark rectangular signs, advising how far it was to elsewhere, and which white line you must follow to get there.

We parked. I unfolded the wheelchair, pushed it to Grandad's door. Then I seated myself and led him slowly across the shimmering rectangles of concrete.

Flies swarmed around me, buzzing irritation, and crawled into the corners of my eyes. Various small birds landed in my path, and flapped away at the last moment. Each time I went into Gebalup this happened, and each time I ignored it and pushed on.

I grinned at whoever I met, and said whatever they

wished. Crossing the road, I caught our reflection in a window; my arms thrusting at the wheels, and Grandad stumbling behind, straining to keep hold of the chair.

Such an arrangement with the wheelchair helped keep me grounded, but I did not present us in this way when we first visited the lawyer and bank.

I had taken care that Ern's clothing concealed the scars I'd given him, and held lengthy rehearsals to overcome the difficulty he had speaking. Nevertheless, I was nervous.

The bank manager glanced sympathetically at the youth tucked up in the wheelchair. I was silent, concentrating, gripping the arms of the chair. Imagine then, how mortified I felt when I found myself drifting upwards. However, to my surprise, the bank manager did not change the direction of his gaze. I studied the little threesome below me — for threesome it was. The bank manager. The grandfather. The youth in the wheelchair who, apart from the marked and mottled skin, could be anyone, except that — as an astute observer would have seen — his breathing was very slow, very shallow.

My grandfather's success. Absorbed, barely alive.

'You're sure, a joint account?' the manager asked. Although his eyebrows rose in a query, his smile was one of acceptance.

I noted my grandfather's nod, and how suddenly fluent and quick his speech had become. 'He will be taking over our affairs. Despite what you see, he is very capable.'

It was a victory, I suppose.

We shook hands and I swung the wheelchair around,

and waited for Grandad to position himself before I hauled him through the door held open by our banker.

My elation carried us across the carpark. I accelerated, stopped, turned; and Grandad stumbled repeatedly. But I did not let him fall.

For a time, in the evenings, I shared with my grandfather what I had compiled.

I read to him, and as the work developed it became obvious he was not impressed. I thought it was the ease with which I did it that infuriated him. I had written pages and pages, and all he had ever achieved were notes, references, and immaculate indexes.

Question marks sprouted among his words; witness, for example, those genealogical diagrams. But I simply knew, and used my imagination.

'How could you?' I patiently plucked these words from amongst his bristling tangle of superfluous consonants. 'What proof?' He was furious. Why, he seemed to enquire, did I trust whatever it was my father had told me.

He snorted when he read of my ancestors floating from the pages and up, up, up among clouded peaks. I hope for more respect when I share the incident with you.

'Language,' he would say. Croak, stammer, cough stutter sniff. 'It's a f-f-f-fence that keeps you out.'

I knew that.

'Even Daniel,' he said, determined to have his say, although he need not have rushed, I left him yawning gaps. 'Even Daniel Coolman spoke some Nyoongar. It was all curses, mind, a black tongue. That's the sort of language it is. And now there's no one left to tell you what you want. You can never know.'

But I knew, and I said … I wanted to say …

How could I dispute him, this man expelling his words at me, his face growing into an almost permanent snarl?

I wanted to strike him, but knew — because of my own lack of substance, my own weightlessness — that if I did I would be the one sent hurtling backwards across the room.

It was still his story, his language, his notes and rough drafts, his clear diagrams and slippery fractions which had uplifted and diminished me.

I wanted more.

I dare say he was all the time thinking, When and how will I appear in this history? Hoping. Worrying.

Oh, I promised I would get to him.

I did not continue the readings.

It may have been a desire to transform myself, or even self-hatred, which suggested I slash and cut words into my own skin. But I soon turned to my grandfather's flesh. I wanted to mark him, to show my resentment at how his words had shaped me.

And now I pluck Ernest Solomon Scat from my memories of his insecure dotage, and plant him with his arm inserted in the filing system, up to the elbow in the documents of the very respectable Auber Neville's office. My grandfather, so recently arrived from his own country, had come to his distant relation Mr A O Neville, the Chief Protector of Aborigines, no less, and — until recently — chief of a department representing the odd combination of the North-west *and* Aborigines *and* Fisheries.

Ernest Solomon Scat, a thin and pale young man,

earnest by name and nature. Consider him with his hand deep in the filing system, among shelves he'd helped construct. See him staring — as certain members of his future wife's family continue to do — down a corridor of words. Unlike them, Ern does not know to be wary, does not need to prepare to flee. He walks toward us; confident, comfortable, awake to an opportunity.

Yes, that's our man. He helped construct the shelving — he and his distant cousin both being accomplished amateur carpenters — and was now temporarily employed in clerical duties with the department.

'He's been reared as a white man! He does not speak for the *natives*.'

At first Ern thought he was the one accused. Auber Neville, Chief Protector, was furious, and the shelves and filing cabinets quaked with a violence the figure at their centre could not contain. Ernest, not well acquainted with the man, could not have known how rare was this fit of anger. Having so boldly approached Auber's desk, Ern now thought of stepping backwards through the door. But then what? Left-right-left backwards through streets; the train, clickety-clack back; a quick glance over his shoulder to judge the leap from wharf to ship and then steam stern-first back home? He couldn't. Ernest couldn't even think like that, let alone act in defiance of all he knew.

For a moment Auber Neville looked directly at him in so habitually superior a manner that Ernest, even as a white man, felt like an intruder.

'Ernest? Ernest. I'm sorry. The newspapers,' he indicated one on his desk. 'They delight in this of course.'

Ernest was relieved to become an accomplice. 'And what of this one? *Quadroon*. Strictly speaking, he does not even come under the control of the Department. Unfortunately. What right does he have to interfere in its affairs? Who does he speak for?'

Auber Neville's voice was very quiet, ticking its regularity and reason. 'If anything, our powers should be increased so that we can provide further protection and see that justice is done.' He pulled at his jacket, briskly rubbed his hands together, studied his fingernails, and then apologised for his rudeness.

Ern, sensing his own calloused hands and grubby fingernails, suddenly felt a little embarrassed. But his embarrassment was also because Mr Auber Neville had obviously not reached so high as the family believed. The entire department was a verandah and two small rooms. Clearly, it was an impoverished and unimportant one, regarded as such because of the status of the people waiting to see its chief. Both the building and the queue at its rear door were tucked away in the shadow of a modest cathedral. Auber's staff consisted of a secretary, two clerks, and a travelling inspector, with numerous 'Local Protectors' — usually police, not answerable to his authority — scattered everywhere.

'Tsk.' Auber glanced down at the newspaper on his desk, and Ernest's eyes followed his. Yes, Ernest was such a reader — even then — that he could read upside down just as easily as upside up.

A unique deputation of Western Australian aboriginals, well spoken and in some cases well educated and well read men, waited on the Premier yesterday morning and received from him sympathetic consideration for the remedying of a number of disabilities under which they labour ...

Ernest looked up and saw that Auber Neville, his eyes intently focused, appeared to be reading *him*. 'Nothing will come of it,' Auber said, glancing away and indicating the newspaper. 'I know these people, I know what is needed.' The papers on his shelves were still. Not a rustle, not a sigh. Genealogies, personal histories, court cases; requests for marriage, employment, and exemptions from the Aboriginal Protection Act. And now — about to be shelved — one deputation.

'Perhaps you could help us,' Auber went on. 'The trouble these *natives* who have been raised as white men can manufacture.' He asked Ernest to accompany one of his department's officers on an investigatory visit. The ANZAC club had contacted Auber regarding a particular fellow, who — as a returned serviceman — had applied to join their ranks.

'What I really want to find out is, since he is a coloured man, whether he is a *native* in law, or a person of, say, Negro or Maori extraction,' said Auber. 'Naturally I do not want this fellow ... er, Sandy ... Mason, to know that I am making this inquiry. I am told that he is a *half-caste* but I do not know him under that name.' Auber was offended, not only for himself and his department, but in particular on behalf of his filing system.

'We wish to know his caste,' continued Auber, 'because it has a bearing upon whether he is entitled to join the ANZAC Club.'

Perhaps I am not being quite truthful here. Perhaps Auber did not use these exact words. I take the language from the file of the man the department's representatives went to 'visit'; my Uncle Sandy (Two) Mason.

EXTRACT FROM THE FILE OF SANDY MASON

I have been to Greenmount on three occasions, accompanied by Mr Scat, but failed to contact Mason until yesterday, when I called at his residence and found him at home.

Mason, in my opinion, has the appearance of a half-caste, but is certainly lighter in colour than usual. He is a man of only about 40 years of age, tall and very thin. His hair is completely white and he has quite a refined appearance, although he looks a sick man, and this may account for lightness in colour.

He lives in an ordinary house which from outward appearances is in good order, but no attempt is made to cultivate the ground surrounding the house.

Bearing in mind the Chief Protector's injunction that any inquiry must be made without Mason's knowledge, and in any case not having the powers of a Protector, I could not question Mason as to his antecedents, and try as I would I could not turn the conversation on the matter of his family connections.

Later, however, I managed to get into conversation with a neighbour of Mason's named Mustle, who spoke very highly of Mason's character and behaviour in the district. Mustle told me that Mason has been living at Greenmount, immediately behind the Blackboy Hill camp, for some six years. To his knowledge, Mason has never had a woman living with him in the house, although there was a time when he contemplated marriage to a white woman. He further told me that Mason was suffering from lung trouble and never worked, but that he was a war pensioner and that the house he was living in was rented from Mustle's own family.

Mustle, who seemed to know quite a lot about Mason's sisters at Gebalup and their children, told me that Mason claims to be quarter-caste, and that he had never heard him make any reference to having Maori blood. Mustle talked quite freely and I requested him not to make any mention to Mason of enquiries being made about him, which he promised to refrain from doing.

I made further enquiries this morning of a friend of mine in the Repatriation Department as to:
1. *The illness from which Mason is suffering*
2. *The prospective expectation of life*
3. *The pension.*

31/7/29   *C Proud*

Ern had listened to the approach of light and measured footsteps, and was standing slightly behind Mr Proud when Sandy opened the door to them. Observing the exchange between the two men, Ern thought that something about Sandy, his distracted air, his surprisingly fair complexion, his soft voice — it was hard to say what it was really — reminded him of a ghost, some sort of phantom.

Sandy kept one hand on the door and seemed unsettlingly attentive, almost as if he was studying them whereas, as Ern well knew, it was actually the other way around.

This was the beginning of Ern's entry into our family, the first of many entries, I might say. Sandy Mason, as further investigations revealed, was not — whatever his own beliefs — the equal of any white man. There was his proximity to Blackboy Camp, for one thing. And Auber wanted no more trouble with spokespersons petitioning the Premier; he wanted this man under control. He need not have worried, because before too long Sandy Two Mason — having escaped the department's detection almost all his life — no longer presented it with a problem.

Ern was a shrewd man, see. Newly arrived, and he had already contacted his cousin Auber, found employment with him in construction and information storage, and become acquainted with — if not yet enthusiastic about — Auber's expert opinions on the need for both social and biological *absorption* of the Native Race.

I like to think of Mr Ernest Solomon Scat stepping off the boat; that initial moment when his leather-clad foot touched the dock. A small sound, but it set up resonances, and those resonances, admittedly diminishing all the time, were picked up by the railway and ran all the way to where a very last vibration rolled into the sand. It was, and is, a long way from that railway's end to the tiny town of Gebalup, but the land holds all things — even such trivial events as my grandfather's first footfall — from which we may later select, amplify, and consider the resonances.

Yes, my grandfather was a shrewd man. A rat-cunning mind, dear reader, mark my words. (And here I must interrupt myself to record my grandfather's response to having such words read to him. His mouth went even tighter, his nose and cheeks began to twitch. At the time

I was encouraged by such behaviour.)

So who was Ernest Solomon Scat? A Scotsman, with a trade and education enough to pass himself off as a clerk. The youngest in his family, he understood the necessity to make his own fortune, and how patience and information would help him do so. He needed to prove his superiority, and trusted no one.

He left his home town and the scrawny women of its streets and brothels and, stopping off in South Africa, discovered young and *coloured* women. The differing hues of flesh. Various entrances.

So how much was all of this a factor in his interest in Sandy (Two) Mason? In the man's attractiveness? In the power he could gain over the likes of him?

I am not yet comfortable to pursue such an inquiry.

Ernest Solomon Scat's professional investigations, on behalf of cousin Auber's department, into the aforesaid Sandy (Two) Mason — invisible *half-caste* — not only first put my family tree on paper, but also revealed to Ern an isolated and tiny railway which stitched its brief way from Wirlup Haven to Gebalup, at which point it promptly stopped, as if it was a small scar in the earth. To the west, still days away by horse, a vast railway network reached, and wheat fields sprang up and ran away from each of its lines.

It seemed logical. Get there. Buy land in between the railway tips. Then, just as soon as those lines connected ...

Ernest accompanied the Travelling Inspector of Aborigines, a Mr James Segal.

James Segal, perceiving the impression he made on the young man, indulged himself. He had opinions, liked to talk, was an expert. He waved his hands at the bush, pointed to farmland either side of the train, and told Ern he had taken up farming himself, for a time, after working on stations in the north-west. 'The only people making money now,' he said with considerable contempt, 'are speculators. They buy up land just before the railway reaches it.'

Ern grabbed at this information. Filed it away under O, oh, an Opportunity. Cross-referenced to C, for Confirmation. And made a mental note to ask James, at a later date, where he thought the railway might go next.

James continued; His Life. He'd worked closely with Auber Neville since the opening of the first Native Settlement in 1915. He'd been the superintendent there. And at the other one, which had since closed down under the instructions of an Incompetent Oaf who'd stood in Auber's shoes for a brief time.

'The Settlements,' he said, 'give the *natives* a chance. They're a Child Race. It's our duty to train them for Useful Work, and keep them from harm, from causing harm. They can be an Embarrassment.' He hesitated, as if considering the varied causes of such embarrassment.

'An ideal camp,' he continued, 'is near enough to town to allow the *natives* to call for rations when they are indigent, to come under surveillance by police and other local protectors, and to provide a ready labour force when necessary. However, it must always be far enough from white habitations to avoid complaints and to discourage unwelcome visits by white men.'

Ern blushed, remembering the night of his arrival in this country.

James, like the train, had gathered momentum. 'They have no place in the scheme of things, and have simply become a nuisance. Many otherwise gentle folk secretly think and openly say it were better that they were dead, were dead, were dead …'

The rhythm of the train and his words seemed to have overcome James, he was pounding his thigh with the palm of his hand. Ern waited patiently while he regained his composure. 'There seems a clear choice,' James continued. 'Let them multiply in wretched camps, let rations cost more, let them be useless and untaught, keep them out of sight; or absorb them into our population.'

Absorption, he said, it's possible. *Assimilation*.

For some reason the words aroused Ernest; perhaps because he was still struggling to free himself of certain erotic memories and guilt. Indeed, his erection threatened to intrude into his mental note-making, as if wanting to prove that there was plenty of lead in this pencil.

James, unaware, made things worse for my grandfather. He began to speak of breeding. 'Auber is going to write a book on it,' he said. 'How we can absorb these people into our community. We know how, but the law needs to be made more rigorous.'

And, to the various rhythms of train, horse and cart, motor car and the occasional footfall, James Segal spelled out the plan, and having already provoked a reaction he did not see, provoked another he could not have foreseen. He showed the young man what he called 'paper proof'. Part of a draft of an article Auber had given him to read. They sat side by side, and he showed the younger man photographs.

They must have impressed my grandfather because so much of his own writing and photographs are modelled upon them. But it was the older man's life which particularly won him over. Ern savoured James Segal's story as he never did mine; tales of courage and the treachery of the outback; of the *blacks*, both good and bad; of *full-bloods* dying out; of the despised and destitute *half-castes*. He listened to stories of the confidences and velvet skins of the women; of the scientific rationale behind his talk of breeding. And saw how good could be done, and power won.

Perhaps it was with James Segal, perhaps another time with Auber. Whenever, with whoever, the fact is that the photographs were numbered, and there were notes pinned to them. I know their kind well.

A finger — red and lined at the knuckles, flesh sagging from the bone — hovered over one portrait. 'Now, here, you see? This woman is *full-blood*.'

A solemn face. Eyes lifeless and bored.

'And here,' the voice of authority said, sliding out another photograph, 'her daughter. *Half-caste, first-cross*.' The older man assumed Ern's knowledge of eugenics and theories of breeding matched his own.

Ern studied the photograph. 'Rather attractive, really,' he said, tentatively, quite prepared to be dissuaded. He remembered the family gossip; Auber had once written brochures to attract British migrants to this country, and was even thought of as a purveyor of brides.

'It depends on the genes, you see,' said James or Auber. At another time it might even have been Ern. 'Theirs is recessive.'

And, as if once again flourishing that ace, the dealer produced a third photograph.

'*Quadroon*!' he exclaimed. 'The freckles, you see, are the only trace of colour.'

'This woman's eyes must be blue, or green!' Ern was

beginning to understand such enthusiasm.

Ern had to admit he was lonely, the more so when he remembered his first night in this country, its conclusion at one of the aforementioned camps. 'There,' his companions had said, 'now you're initiated.' The squeals, the glass breaking, the silence at their backs as they staggered away.

But Ern was receiving a lecture. 'This is what the Department should be promoting. This is the way to help. This is the answer. Sometimes we have to bend the rules.'

In a tone which signalled a detour from such lofty concerns the voice said, 'I know of some eighty cases of white men marrying *native* girls.'

'But, aren't there *throwbacks*?'

'No.' Decisively. 'No. That's clear. We know that as far as the colour is concerned — and that's what matters most, after all, that's what chiefly disadvantages them — as far as the colour is concerned, atavism is not in evidence.'

The voice fell silent for a moment as if redrafting its set piece as the end approached. 'Perhaps, perhaps it is not so much a question of the colour of the skin as the colour of the mind … No, no, that will not do.'

Ern spoke quietly. 'You're a clever man, James.' He felt a deep respect for the ideas, if not the man. After all, it could have been any one of a number of clever, progressive men of the time.

See, already, he was forming plans. Seeking a future, aiming at me.

Yes, Auber — with all that information at his fingertips — knew of some eighty cases where white men had married native women with whom they now live happy, contented lives.

And another? An eighty-first, which, in fact, James Segal knew of but Auber didn't? Daniel and Harriette Coolman, my great-grandparents.

Even James Segal thought that the Chief Protector sometimes became too zealous, so that people might need a protector to protect them from The Protector. James said as much to Ern, having been sufficiently flattered by the younger man's attention to take him into his confidence.

'The policeman here is a good friend of mine. This used to be quite a town. He's seen it boom, and seen it bust again.'

'You're a carpenter?' Sergeant Hall asked, and Ern saw the publican's gaze meet that of the sergeant. Sergeant Hall's fleshy hand embraced his beer. If you're always on duty, how can you not drink on duty? Because you have to drink.

Ern felt a heady elation. He knew he could make something of himself in this country, and that he was surrounded by the very best of men. James; a pioneer, no less. Daniel Coolman was present at the founding of this very town. Sergeant Hall ... All of them experts on the poor Aborigines, and on their situation. All experts on this country.

The men bent together at the bar, shoulder to shoulder, except for Daniel. He was a very big man with an unpleasant smell about him, and so he was kept at a little distance.

My true ancestors, those of my blood-and-land-line, the women I must call Harriette and Fanny, sat by a very small fire at the rear of a hut. Unlike myself, they were distinctively of a people, and this fire of theirs was deep among overturned rainwater tanks, wagons, and stacks of timber in the yard right beside the police station. They peered back into their hut, smiling, speaking softly. Kathleen, who has slipped from the policeman's wife and home, helps bed down the youngest children. But first the one who goes to school must go through his lessons with the others.

The town would not stand for more of them at the school. They all know the stories of school.

There was no room for more children at the school, as there is no room for them in this town, and they will all have to go out into the bush again tomorrow, packing themselves into boxes and beneath blankets on the back of a wagon. Soon, it might be time to try another child at the school.

Someone asked Ern, 'Have you seen the camps?'

'No,' Ern said, quickly, remembering the first night. The dirt on his bare knees, and how she turned her head away as her body took his thrusts.

'So, you're a carpenter?' the publican said it again, and offered Ern a job.

Ern drew plans with fine black pencil on clean paper, sat all night over just one pot of beer. Somewhere in his mind, as if tucked behind his plans and paper, he weighed the gamble he was taking. How long could he wait? He'd studied maps, had listened.

Ern judged the rainfall as about right for wheat, the soil adequate. Transport was a problem. If only that bloody railway reached a little further, or if the ships were subsidised to the same extent as the railway. Ern noted the town's economy: mines (working fitfully); some mallet bark (going by horse-drawn wagon to the sea); a little work with horses (stables, fodder, farrier ...); a general store; a photographer (the displays in the window yellow and curling); two pubs; a bicycle shop ...

Ern paused, he was on the roof. Conscious of the sky around him, he looked out over decaying buildings which ceased barely a block or two from the main street.

The height, and the solid wall beneath, gave him confidence. He felt important; up in the sky, and with a gentle breeze caressing his resolute jaw, he again thought of possessing land in this place, right here, and then — as soon as the railway connected — Yes! Not just future farmland, either.

But first he needed money, and to continue accumulating it.

The railway, he could see, would have to detour around the northern side of the ranges where there was enough of a pass for it to sneak through.

He identified the properties before him. Shabby houses — huts really — many deserted and already collapsing.

The police station, with its stables. Nineteen twenty-nine, and they still used horses. Why, even the mail run was by motor car.

There was a large yard beside the police station, with a small hut positioned at the furthest corner. Not only was it as far as possible from the police station but it seemed that the hut, with its vine-covered enclosure, was intended to be hidden among the many rainwater tanks which surrounded it.

Ern considered the yard from his vantage point as a

newly elevated and self-employed carpenter. There was a lot of old timber there. The gate at the front of the yard was only partially open, and the path from there was overgrown, and apparently rarely used. Within the yard, however, an extremely well-worn path formed a perfect circle. There was a cone-shaped object at the centre of this circle from which a long wooden pole extended. Ern guessed this would be attached to a horse — or horses. The long shaft running from the centre of the circle and into a roofed area near the police station's fence drove a saw.

For a moment Ern's mind moved among the intricacies of the cogs that must mesh somewhere in that central cone. There was timber, there was timber milling technology.

A movement at the back of the police station next-door caught his attention.

It was a woman. Young. Slim. Dark? Or was that the glare?

She leaned against the wire fence separating the police and timber yards, and called into the roofed space just the other side of it. Then she strode to the rear of the police yard, swung her legs across the low fence there and, winding her way through the water tanks, disappeared into the sagging enclosure of wire and vines at the rear of the little hut.

Ern thought of what Travelling Inspector James Segal had said about the *natives*, and of Auber's photographs. He thought of the timber yard, and the railway.

Opportunity?

Ernest Solomon Scat was up in the air, back then, and

looking around. He had touched jetty, railway, electrical and telegraphic wires, sealed road. He had rarely touched the land. Ernest Solomon Scat floated all his life, in a different way to myself, and never even realised it.

Although he rarely touched the country it is nevertheless true that in Gebalup — riddled as it is with death and abandoned mines — his footsteps resonate. Oh, it is a subtle thing, and he is one among many, but the rhythm of his steps is peculiar, very particular, and it was this which alerted me to other rhythms, to other memories held there.

hairy angels

Ernest Solomon Scat looked to his pocket-watch, looked at the sky, and climbed. Once again he saw the woman step into the night cart's lane, pushing the wheelbarrow before her.

He saw Daniel Coolman leave the shed. The woman wheeled the barrow into position behind him, tilted it, and took his weight in her hands as he slumped. Coolman sat as if in a too-small bath. An easy-throne. The woman pushed him to the lane and into the police yard.

Ern saw her glance toward him and he lifted his hand in a tentative greeting. Her head moved slightly. She is returning my wave, he thought. The possibility that it might be a query, or even a gesture of dismissal, never occurred to him.

At the rear of the house she tilted the wheelbarrow again, and the big man waddled into the shadows. The woman put the wheelbarrow to one side and followed, and because she had her back to Ern, who was slyly watching her even as he swung the hammer, she did not see him toss the hammer aside and curse. She missed her chance to laugh at him baby-sucking his thumb.

The gates to the street were closed. Ern went to the lane at the rear where there was sufficient space for a single horse and rider to squeeze through. Or — of course — a wheelbarrow and a very fat man.

A tall grey horse plodded the circular path at an irregular pace. When it was furthest from the shed it moved very slowly, and the saw was very quiet. But each time it approached Coolman it sped up until the saw was screaming like a siren. A whip, thickly coated with dust, hung on the wall at Daniel's side.

Ern had spent hours listening to the rise and fall of that saw.

The horse's circular path was so deeply worn the poor animal, in rushing past the shed, had to almost hurdle the saw's drive shaft.

A very high chair supported Coolman in a half-standing position, and his hat was low and angled so that it concealed most of his face. His clothes — which he had insisted his wife stitch, belt, lace and pull so tightly — appeared to be all that prevented him from becoming just another mound of rotting matter and bristling hair.

Daniel Coolman worked in the shadow cast by a large stack of dressed and very well-seasoned timber. Clearly, business was not brisk.

Smoke hung about him as if he was slowly combusting. But even the smoke could not disguise the smell of something bad; something that had gone off, some dead and inadequately buried thing.

'I een etrayed,' he kept repeating. 'Tricked eye an old cheater. Deserted eye a ruther.'

He turned to Ernest, took a halting step, his outstretched hand quivering with the effect of that footfall. 'And now I rely on a coufle o *gins* to dress ee each day.' He laughed, blasting stale air into Ern's face. The old man's whiskers fluttered across the hole of his mouth like a curtain. There was no upper lip, and yellow teeth hid behind a damp curtain of whiskers.

The saw sometimes called to Ern, and he would visit Daniel and his timber yard. His pocket-watch and vantage point helped him avoid the young woman, and he sometimes noted an older woman leaving early in the mornings with a horse and cart.

My great-grandmother, Daniel's wife — Harriette Coolman — used to go hunting. It was she who supported the family. For the sake of the town's mental peace — Harriette, after all, was a *black* — Daniel provided the appearance of working while Harriette smuggled children to the bush and back each day, wanting them to learn what she knew, and hunted and gathered most of their nourishment. Each time she did her shopping she took her shuffling husband with her for support and security against an insecure town which might suddenly turn hostile. She kept the house as clean as anyone — lest they ever doubt — and she washed and stitched, organised and sheltered those that she could; we survivors.

Knowing nothing of this, Ern kept returning. The stack of timber continued to grow. Coolman was maintaining a habit.

'Can't stot irking now, you know.'

Rheumatoid arthritis had made him so swollen and distended, he said (although it took Ern a little time to realise his words); and his pipe had given him cancer of the upper lip. Ern was grateful for such rational explanations.

Daniel Coolman wheezed as he spoke, and the missing lip fluted his breath in strange ways. But once you adjusted, Ern found, he was easy enough to understand.

'Isness is ad,' he said.

And clever Ern could see what he meant. He'd not seen a single customer enter the yard. Although later, recalling the conversation, Ern wondered whether in fact the old man had been suggesting something about the relationship between accounting, or accumulation, and a state of being.

'I used to cart oughter, ut now ...' Coolman shrugged his shoulders, and for an instant the bootlaces which held his coat across his chest loosened fractionally. His age, his health, his problems. It was difficult to put it all into words, let alone words he could pronounce.

On one visit, the circling grey horse suddenly fell over. There was a thump as it hit the earth, and then an eerie silence. Ern and Daniel looked at one another, then walked over to the corpse. It took them quite a time; Daniel was only capable of a slow shuffle. He used the journey to explain the death. The horse must have inherited a weak heart, he said. He'd thought the weakness had been bred out of that line. It was difficult to know, was always a surprise, he said — pensive, soft, sibilant — how some characteristics can throw back right across the generations. They looked down at the dead animal, its imprint a little wider than its body. Already it was shrinking into the land, leaving only its mark, its one true record, before being rushed away.

Ernest eked out the work on the stables. He had his savings, was getting food and a bed. In the short term he didn't need much else, and he loved this work. Well, it was hardly work. He loved it, loved constructing things. He had always enjoyed the building of something from nothing; straight wood, iron, a stack of bricks. But it surprised him to so enjoy a reconstruction.

Ah, so perhaps there is something my grandfather and I have in common, after all.

The publican would shout him a beer or two. That was enough.

Ernest Solomon Scat went up on the roof whenever he thought the woman would be in sight. 'That roof is taking a long time,' the publican shouted from below.

The young woman's name, the publican explained, was Kathleen, and she worked for Sergeant Hall who had as good as adopted her. 'Must've been a couple of the old people survived, after all,' he said. Ernest did not ask for an explanation. Did not say, 'Survived what?' Even then it was obvious. It was not the sort of question anyone bothered to put, and very few people wanted it answered.

He asked Daniel, 'The father a white man?'

'Oh es,' wheezed Daniel. Sometimes, listening to him, Ern thought he could still hear the saw, somewhere away in the distance. Although no horse circled, the circle remained. Perhaps the old fella's fluting hissing speech merely enticed the memory.

'Look at her, you can tell. Sun tines, they're verry fair. Vy children, sun o then, you oodn't know. Girls varried viners and farmers. Ee don't see dem now. Vy voy is ere ...'

Ern let the details wash over him. They soaked into him. He let a lonely old man talk, and speak of when he first moved to the area, was a teamster, built roads ...

Ern was thinking of the information he could add to Auber's diagrams, and of grand theories. How he could help.

He stayed longer, choosing some timber, waiting for the girl.

Half-caste, he thought, as if the language gave him the authority to verify Daniel's words.

Of course, Ern needed a woman. Daniel and he spoke of this. 'I have a wonderful wife,' Daniel would say. After all, Ern agreed, what do you want a woman for? Such a wife would be beholden to him. They would see the treatment the *natives* get, and be grateful. 'She looks after me, know what I mean?' said Daniel. 'A wonderful mother.'

And then one day, approaching the yard, Ern saw a stranger handsawing timber, over by the water tanks. Daniel Coolman's disembodied arm, floating in the sunlight, emerged from the shade and pointed at the stranger. 'Vy nephew,' said Daniel. 'Jack.'

My Uncle Jack Chatalong. Once more I realise what a curious name it is. As a boy, apparently, it suited him well. Yet when Uncle Will first — so generously — introduced us, it seemed singularly inappropriate; Jack was so quiet. However once he recognised me, he began to speak, and the words flowed as if they had been dammed-up too long. It was a deluge of words which drowned my grandfather's own, flooding them so that

Grandad's filed notes and pages seemed like nothing so much as debris and flotsam remaining after some watery cataclysm. It was rubbish, for sure, but I clung to it for so long because it was all I knew.

Jack Chatalong's home was a hut — you could not call it a humpy — and the very piece of land that Sandy One Mason had once held as a Miner's Homestead Lease. 'On the coast?' the warden had asked. 'That's my business,' Sandy One told him. Chatalong lived there, but had no lease. He kept himself apart, believed he kept his independence. He heard the sea as he woke, and through a gap in the dunes could see the tiny beach.

Stand on that sheltered beach and you find yourself on a thin strip of weak and riddled limestone, which rises from the water's edge for a short distance before diving under the dry dunes. Still further up, there grows a grove of peppermint trees.

The sea rolled small pieces of limestone at Uncle Jack's feet and, bubbling from the sandy shallows, a quite different sort of rock raises itself. Hard, smooth boulders, grey and brown; and further out the same rock, mixed with coral, trips the waves and keeps the water between it and the shore calm, but forever trembling.

Ten minutes walk along the beach to the right, to the west, and near a tiny spring-fed creek, is what you feel obliged to call an island, even though it is so very small and close to shore. A small swell lunges against its back. Then the beach curves out of sight, reappearing in the distance as a smudge of land reaching out to the sea. Chatalong used to walk around that curve to reach the shelter of Wirlup Haven.

Shelter, at least, from the sea and winter gales.

Jack Chatalong had taken some trouble with his hut, even though it was an irregular and secret home, he being so often away and working on the farmers' land. It was made of materials gleaned from other people's rubbish, and timber pilfered from Daniel's huge stockpile. It was a sturdy hut, walled with hessian and flattened kerosene tins. A bit of maintenance and care, he thought, and it would easily outlast him.

He did various work for local farmers and householders; a lot of things with horses, and equipment. Sometimes carted wood, or water. He occasionally spent a day at the tiny store; mending bicycles, helping cart and stack supplies. Regularly, still, there were consecutive months of work on Starr's property.

Starr had kept his long-ago promise, and arranged for Jack's education, after a fashion, and fed and clothed him in return for his labour. But when Chatalong found he could get paid for the same work, and that his skills were valued ... Well, of course he moved away when he could. He was good with horses. He kept to himself, just an occasional visit to the camps of those who cleared the land for the farmers. There was less and less clearing required, and the people became protected, and were kept away from the edge of their traditional runs.

There were no police stationed in Wirlup Haven, and Jack was known by the few residents, had been since he was a child, and was still remembered as Sandy One's young boy who went wild for a bit. He'd go to the pub most evenings for a few drinks with the few regular working men that were there.

Then one day, the pub had a new owner.

what reason

Gebalup October 26, 1929
The Chief Protector of Aborigines

Dear Sir,

   In regards of the Aboriginals Act has it I am a half-caste and I Don't mix up with the Blacks and I work Hard and Earn a living the same as a white man would my mother was a black woman and my father was a white man and I can Read and write But I have now Been barred from going Into a Pub and having a drink because I have got no permit so Could you do any thing in the way of granting me a certificate of exemption.

   Yours faithfully,
             Jack Chatalong

The Officer in Charge
Gebalup Police Station

Re. Aborigines Act, 1905
Section 63 — Exemptions

I have received a communication from Jack Chatalong of
Wirlup Haven asking that he be exempted from the
provisions of the Aborigines Act, and in order that I may
be in a position to decide the matter I shall be glad if you
will supply replies to the following questions, and to
return the form to me as early as possible.
> *Yours,*
>> *A O Neville*
>> *Chief Protector of Aborigines and Fisheries*

ABORIGINAL ACT, 1905
SECTION 63 — EXEMPTIONS

1. What is the full name of applicant for exemptions:
> *Jack Chatalong*

2. Alias (if any): —

3. Age: *approx. Twenty-eight years*

4. Parentage: Mother — Aboriginal (woman named
> *Dinah)*
> *Father — unknown*

5. Where does applicant live, and what is his mode of
living?
> *As a child lived with Sandy Mason (deceased) and a*
> *black woman, Fanny. More recently lives quietly by*

himself. Clean and respectable, although it is believed he may have been involved with some disreputable native persons in his youth.

6. *Is the applicant married?*   No.

7. *How does applicant earn his living?*
   General labour, farrier, teamster, shepherd etc.

8. *Does applicant in any way consort with other natives or half-castes?*
   Applicant is seldom seen with other natives or half-castes, other than his mother and half(?)-brother and sister. He has been warned regarding supplying liquor to natives travelling in the vicinity of the town. Natives are believed to have visited the senior Mason's camp, when he was alive, and particularly in his absence.

9. *Does applicant have a good character?*   Yes.

10. *Is applicant addicted to drink, or likely to introduce liquor amongst other natives or half-castes?*
    Not addicted to drink, always a big chance of supplying natives etc however we are usually able to keep natives away from this town.

To Under Secretary
Aborigines and Fisheries

The attached application for exemption under the Aborigines Act is submitted for the Honourable Minister's consideration. In view of the fact that the application is only made in order that the applicant may enter hotels, and that there is a chance of his supplying liquor to natives if the request be complied with, I recommend that the application be refused.

    A O Neville
    Chief Protector

Mr Jack Chatalong
Half-caste
Wirlup Haven

Sir,

  With reference to your letter of the 26th October last, applying for a certificate of exemption under the Aborigines Act, I am directed by the Chief Protector of Aborigines to advise you that your application cannot be granted.

    I have the honour to be
        Sir
    Your Obedient Servant …

Wirlup Haven
Dec 17, 1929
To the Chief Protector of Aborigines

Sir,

On the twenty sixth of last October I applied for a certificate of Exemption and Received a letter stating that my application can not be granted. Please can you tell me for what Reason my application can not be granted and another thing I would like to know am I under the Aborigines Act or am I not and if I am under the Aborigines Act I don't think it is right that I should be under the Aborigines Act Because I do not mix up with them nor live with them and I am always with white people.

I am yours
faithfully,
Jack Chatalong
a half-caste

Jack Chatalong
Wirlup Haven
Jan 3, 1930

Sir,

In reply to your letter of the 17th ultimo. I beg to advise you that the reason you have been refused a Certificate of Exemption under the Aborigines Act is that insufficient evidence has been submitted to show why the privilege should be granted to you. Being a half-caste you come within the provisions of the Aborigines

Act though half-castes are not specifically referred to in every section. In this connection however I would point out that there is a penalty for supplying liquor to aborigines or half-castes.

I have the honour to be

Sir

Your Obedient Servant ...

strictly routine singing

Sergeant Hall walked into the space Ernest had almost finished enclosing, complimented him on the work he had done on the stables, and asked whether he might consider a similar sort of job at the police station. They were getting a motor car and could sell off their horses. Nineteen thirty. So it was not before time. If he could do it for keep, plus a little extra?

Ernest agreed, having formed, if not a plan, then the beginnings of one. And he needed more time in this place.

He made a small camp in the shed where Daniel sawed the timber. Sometimes he thought he heard children's voices coming from somewhere deep among the water tanks. He reasoned that it must be all those tanks detecting, altering, amplifying other sounds. But there seemed so many voices, particularly when he awoke in the very early morning.

It was dark, and Chatalong stood in the doorway. Daniel

would have preferred him to stay right where he was, would have kept him there or tossed him clear out. But he was unable to get himself upright. Harriette joked him out of his fit of pique, said she'd tickle him like a belly-up crab, and then explained to Chatalong that Daniel was worried. The government had written to Policeman Hall about us, and Daniel didn't want any trouble for his family.

Harriette and Chatalong sat on the ground amongst the water tanks and lumber. Chatalong seemed reluctant to speak. He spat, looked at the ground between his feet as if expecting something to grow from his spittle, despite the cold and darkness. He looked across at the policeman's house, its corrugated iron roof gleaming like a slice of the sea in moonlight, its lines of swell frozen, and being tipped up, tipped away. Similar surfaces, curved, tilted this way and that all around them.

Chatalong was reluctant to talk, didn't want to say what kept running through his head but at the same time he wanted to speak it, release it, not hear it again. His own humiliation. This continuing betrayal.

He had been across to Kylie Bay.

'Oh! Again.'

There were still no kids at that school. No. There was the camp, the reserve, between the tip and the shit pit and hardly any water for the people who were pushed all together like that. Yeah, they were huddled under thin, scraggly trees in tents and humpies, which was okay, but it was such an awful place to camp. He hadn't wanted to go there but had been told that was his place.

He'd taken some horses across for Starr, see. When he got there he was sick, something. He went to the hospital, so weak he could hardly stand, hardly talk, and they put him in a room with a sandy floor. The Aborigines Section. It was just an iron shed, with holes in it, and well away from the rest of the building. Someone came, a nurse, maybe once a day. He was out of there in a couple of days, quick as he could. He had nothing. Not the strength to walk back.

Now he was here. You know, he was wondering. About that mine we had … You remember? Yes, old Sandy had actually started a mine one time, and got a fair way down. Maybe they could work it again. If Daniel was interested?

Morning. As if everything had been washed by the darkness, and light was returning its colour. The water tank wagon was hitched up nice and early, and most of the space between the tank and the wagon's sideboard had been covered with hessian.

Harriette, Daniel's wife, stood beside the wagon, seemingly nonchalant and admiring the new day. She stood very straight, a blanket hanging from her shoulders like a cape, or folded wings. Suddenly she hissed, Shh! and tapped the side of the wagon. Nothing moved there, no sound came.

Chatalong was at the horses. He turned his head toward the police station. Daniel, in the shade of the hut, cursed.

Sergeant Hall was walking toward them in that way he had, with his head forward on his shoulders, and his arms held out from the sides of his body and swinging stiffly.

'G'day. Who's this then?' He spoke to Daniel, indicating Chatalong with his head.

Because, really, there should have been a permit — if he

was working for Daniel. And it was best if he was not here on a social visit. 'He's not family, is he, Daniel?'

'No. No, he's not. Sandy and the old girl just vrung him up.'

'Yeah, well, seeing as how he isn't family. He shouldn't be in town. Even if he is family, really.'

'It's okay, Jack,' said Sergeant Hall, but then, because he was a good bloke, because he was teasing them, because of course he knew this fellow, he slapped Jack Chatalong on the back. 'Heading back to Starr's?'

'Yeah. Yes.'

He was seething. Daniel had just discarded him, hadn't he?

'And help collect some water?'

Daniel held a cup up to Jack, raising his eyebrows and widening his eyes by way of command.

'Yes,' said the sergeant, and moved over to sit with Daniel by the little fire at the rear of the hut. As Jack walked away from them, having delivered the drink, Hall said, 'Does he know who his father was? Should we tell him?'

Sergeant Hall was himself an unusual man, as I realised when I tried on his prose style. By now the diligence with which he had begun his Police Occurrence Book had withered somewhat, but his fine script retained its elegance. In fact, perhaps it was a tribute to his diligence that he now had so little to write: *Did Patrols*; and, *Strictly Routine Work*. As the town dwindled so had those patrols, and his routines became smaller and tighter. Occasionally there was a kerfuffle at the hotel with a stranger passing through town. Apart from the difficulties — the nuisance, really, was all it was — Sandy Two Mason and friends had given him in the early years of the town, his time had been most sedate. He had married one of the Starr girls, and helped make this town the peaceful place it was. *Everything correct and in order.* He even told himself he'd performed his duties of protection admirably, which was something not every policeman could say. No, not by a long shot. Why, he even had *natives* living next-door. Their children had joined the community. That was tolerance. It showed what could be done.

Take Kathleen, for example. She was practically like a daughter to his wife and himself. Almost. Perhaps if they'd had children of their own, they might not have been able to save her, as they undoubtedly had. Daniel Coolman was fortunate his family had grown by the time he developed his terrible illness. And whatever he might say about his long-gone brother, if not for Patrick, Daniel would not have had a house and a business — such as it was — and it would have been much harder for Sergeant Hall to have allowed his presence in the town with such a family.

Sergeant Hall was proud that there was no *nigger* problem in his town. He'd seen that trouble off long ago. Not that there had ever been many, what with the Mustles, and Starrs, and Dones doing all they could to tame and pacify the place.

With Coolman's family, and even with Kathleen ... well, you had to watch them lest they regress and revert to less civilised ways. He was grateful to have been fortunate enough to help enact an answer to such an onerous, yet strangely engaging issue; the *Native Problem*.

Ern seemed deeply absorbed. As she approached him Kathleen studied his shadow; head forward on the neck, back bowed, and one hand working rapidly to and fro between the legs. All this with just one foot on the ground.

Ern was sawing, yet again.

'Mr Hall said would you like a cup of tea?'

Once again, Ern thought to himself: she is slim, she is young. A *native* woman, of course, but she wore shoes, and her faded dress was clean. Her hair shone. Ern sniffed, and believed he could smell the soap and fresh water on her. He breathed all the more deeply because of it.

It's hard for a white man here, poor Ern thought.

He admired her as she walked away, savouring the sway of her hips beneath her dress, how thin her ankles were. Perhaps he did not yet think of it as admiring, but whatever the case, he ate her up with his eyes.

Yes, only a *native* girl, of course, but there were few white females in a little place like Gebalup.

Sergeant Hall and his wife called, 'Kathleen, Kathleen.' They wished to talk to her. 'Sit here,' they said, the sergeant speaking first and then the wife repeating it. 'Sit here.' She sat with them, at the same table. The same cups. The same best china, although hers had chipped at the rim so that one blood red rose was completely missing. The same dark, milky liquid from the same one pot.

'This builder. Ernest. You've been talking with him?'

Sergeant Hall had conversed at length with the likes of James Segal, was familiar with the ideas of Auber Neville. Sergeant Hall was remarkably progressive in his ideas, particularly for a policeman. He understood it was necessary to raise the level of debate.

Raise it? Raise it from the level of troublesome indigenous fauna, of vermin control, of eradication and slaughter; raise it to the level of animal husbandry.

A submission to yet another Royal Commission, a few years later, would reveal how progressive were the people surrounding my family:

> *In regard to aborigines and their multiplying <u>too much</u>, which half-castes are prone to do, I should suggest sterilising them and preventing them breeding, because they will get as numerous as rabbits, and we do not want them and something ought to be done to them at once.*

So should I be grateful?

And need I repeat radical, progressive thoughts of the time?

> *Their English, being reconstructed ... a firm hand ... boarding house and breeding ... cut out the sore spot ... absorb and dilute like a small dirty stream into a large and clear one ...*

No.

'You like him?'

Kathleen saw that they wanted her to say yes.

'Yes.'

'You're a sensible girl, Kathleen. You can make a life for yourself. For your children.'

She didn't know where to look.

'You could have a home of your own. A house like this. Cups like these.'

It was Mrs Hall who said that the sergeant would be

retiring soon, and they would be moving. Far away. They would not be needing her any more.

Kathleen knew that Sergeant Hall was trying not to look at her. And then, having succumbed, he would not look away again. 'It's for the best, I think. It's the only way.'

Ern's work was nearly completed. Kathleen brought sandwiches, and for Ernest and the sergeant, a bottle of beer and two glasses.

The white froth rose, the glasses tinkled their pleasure. Sergeant Hall had asked Daniel to join them.

They spoke of breeding and uplifting. These two hairy angels wished to seize people in their long arms and haul them to their own level. Their minds held flickering images of canvas Ascensions, with pale fat cherubs spiralling upwards into the light. They saw steps leading up stone pyramids, and realised that some creatures were simply unable to continue higher, even though the steps were there for them. Their noble selves sat at the top and no, they did not see themselves as leering, as guffawing, as throwing scraps to those below.

These hairy angels, scratching at their groins. Belching. Drinking beer.

'No *throwbacks*. Except to a white man in there somewhere. Genetically stronger, you see.'

'I'm confident. The women'd back me up. White father. *Half-caste* mother. Harriette's sister. Very fair, all of them, civilised and well-mannered.'

'Often a *quadroon* may appear southern European. You know? It's the sun.'

'There were different genetic types, you see. Species, almost.'

Daniel's wife helped Kathleen. Brought tea and cakes

until Mrs Hall left. Then brought beer. The passionfruit vine reached through the wire mesh into the shade. The little stars of sunlight grew and faded.

Whatever rationalisations Ern played with, the truth is that his loins were tingling, and — especially when alone in the evenings — he played with more than computations. He thought of a reversal, of small white streams entering black. He saw fractions sliding up against one another, the lower numbers growing larger as a single digit skipped from one to the other, always on top.

Sergeant Hall, his smiling quiet wife, often went on picnics with Kathleen. Kathleen knew a lovely place. Sergeant Hall invited Ern along. They sat by a stream in the shade of paperbark trees. There was a grassy plain, just like a park, and wildflowers to pick. Kathleen showed them the Qualap Bells, but understood it was wisest not to mention the sweet yams that were there for the digging, the eating, the singing of.

well-meaning friends and that
entrepreneurial spirit

As a youth I had known only the middle Ernest; he was cunning, and a man of sly lust. (I remember winking at him as I wrote that. He grinned his dementia. Lust, cunning; all gone.) Later I came to know him better than he knew himself. After all, not only had I pored over his writings, but I had been very intimate with his little probings, his 'investigations' to see the colour of my skin where the sun had not reached. He used to part my hair to see the scalp beneath and — when I was older, and recovering under his care — run his fingers through my curls, and all over me. 'Looking for traces of colour,' he'd mutter, stretching my cheeks apart. 'There (mumble, mumble), a purple tint where we are pink, and that bluish tint to the whites of your eyes.'

He would begin this way, clinical, but — soon enough — was shouting, urgent with power.

'Keep your eyes open. Eyes open,' he would say, one

hand clamping the back of my neck, the other my shoulder. 'Keep them open.' At least he accepted that I could not look directly at him on such an occasion, and so I stared at the wall as he thrust, in his stilted way, trying to get deeper within me, and if that was not violation enough, wanting to remain there even as he shrivelled.

Having tucked into me, and tucked himself away, he primly fussed in his efforts to smooth the bedclothes and pillow.

Of course it is difficult to forgive him; I was at his mercy, and weak, and grieving the death of my father.

Need I write of Ern's self-deception, his scheming? I could not trust him, but he was family. 'He's family, that's all you've got,' my father had said. 'You can't change your family.'

And he was all I had, back then.

The younger Ernest had found himself in a backwater, and a salty one at that. He did a little work here, a little there.

He worked on a salt lake close to Wirlup Haven. When the breeze came up of an afternoon, the sea came gurgling and chortling with it. Thick salt water lapped at him, tonguing little nicks and scratches in his skin, opening them into clean raw ulcers which grew alarmingly.

In the early days of sharing our stories, I helped him revisit this memory. I bathed him in salty water, was slow and gentle with my touch. The wounds I'd given him grew, and in unforeseen ways. Letters I'd taken so much trouble with changed shape, and the words became hard to decipher.

Ernest talked to Sergeant Hall, revealing very little except the reflection of the sergeant's ideas. As if the sergeant was a client, and Ern was about to build for him. Inevitably, perhaps — one being a Protector and proud of his patch, the other introduced to the country through a parish connection to the very *Chief* Protector of Aborigines — they spoke at length of the Native Problem. Generously, distantly; after all, it was not their problem. Ern, if he considered it at all, would say his interest had been aroused by Auber Neville and the words of the Travelling Inspector. He would never admit to the way his thoughts curled back to the memory of his first night off the ship, and — stiff and obstinate — returned to his present loneliness.

How he had spurted his ecstacy on that night. And he had felt so powerful, even as he turned his back and returned to the light.

Sergeant Hall's face was pained as he stressed his concern for the welfare of his domestic, Kathleen, who'd been like a daughter to him. He felt a genuine love for her, he said, blushing at having expressed such sentiments. A father's love. She's not like most of them, he said. Never been in a camp, not that she could remember anyway. We've brought her up, really, like a white girl.

And so they had. She worked for them, yes, and hard, but they let her eat with them, taught her the niceties of etiquette, and she attended the church as one of their family. At picnics it was Sergeant Hall, wife, and domestic. Ernest was invited along.

There were nights of cards, when Daniel Coolman came, and Ern — despite the difficulties demanded by the conversation — would shepherd things along, listening attentively. He was exhausted at the end of such evenings.

Sergeant Hall was a good policeman, the whole town knew this. People would beam at the girl, the policeman's girl. She showed them that they were tolerant, that the ones they kept away from town were indeed wasters, deserving their poverty and exclusion. If they tried harder, they would be accepted. By arrangement, they could be allowed into town for shopping, providing they first notified Sergeant Hall of their intentions.

Ern was almost openly courting Kathleen. He was taciturn, and awkward; fingers clumsy at her elbow. They danced in the living room, from one wall to another, and Ern was careful to keep his body away from hers. He moved stiffly.

Ern was proud of himself; of his daring, his open mind. But — we must be frank — he was also thinking of the wood yard, and Daniel's health. When the big man died, what would happen to all that timber, and the land? They'd talked, see, Ern and Sergeant Hall, about the danger of leaving any property to Harriette. At present, because of the marriage, she may legally be a white woman, but once Daniel went … Well, it was risky. A matter of interpretation.

Daniel would point out to Sergeant Hall that he was not the only one who regarded Kathleen as a daughter. He felt the same, more so. The two men competed as to the strength of their paternal feeling.

And Ern's dreams of property ('dreams' sounded more innocent than 'plans') were more humble than they had been, certainly. A salty backwater? He had to start somewhere. He saw it as a place where he could become someone. He had plans — dreams — for all that timber.

There was no market for it in this town. He was the only one who would be able to use it. He could build several houses on that block of land, he could build this town. Just as soon as that railway connected ... There would be wheat. Industry.

Of course he realised that the economy had slowed. He understood. A bad year for wheat prices. An aberration.

Ern applied for the contract to collect and dispose of the town's *nightsoil*. 'Go on,' Jack Chatalong said in an aside to Kathleen. 'Go on, the Goona man on the goona cart!' He said it quietly, but Ernest and Sergeant Hall heard their laughter. They put their heads together and arranged that Jack take on the job, for appropriate wages.

Ern had his first employee.

Jack Chatalong and Kathleen were brother and sister. Perhaps that helps explain what Jack did. Perhaps Sergeant Hall told him of his father's identity. Or his anger may have been of a more general kind, and never intended to achieve so final a result. Quite likely he did not think at all, but simply acted on the spur of the moment.

Slowly, they made their way to the mine shaft. Slowly, because it was a long time since Harriette had been there, and how the bush had grown. Slowly, because there was no hurry. Slowly, because of Daniel. 'No,' he had insisted, 'I can walk.' He wheezed, stopped to lean against some thin tree. 'There can't be anything here, this isn't much more than dunes where the creek used to finish.'

There was a small, spindly looking construction above the shaft, which was itself very narrow, once you got past its opening. Jack told them he had left something at the bottom.

He descended while the others waited at the top.

As he came creaking up again he thought of Daniel's continuing rejection of him. Of Kathleen, what she had told him.

He changed his mind. They would not wish to see these old bones he'd hidden, would not wish to be reminded of all this. What for? What good would it do? Jack Chatalong dropped the small burden he carried.

It was not a deep shaft but still, coming up, he saw its entrance as a fissure in the darkness. He saw a wound bleeding light, and imagined inserting his fingers in this opening. The backs of his fingers would be together; and then, opening his arms slowly, in an arc, as if they were wings about to launch him, he would thrust them down. He would pull the world inside-out. It would be another world.

He resumed the pulley, and his jerky, mechanical ascent.

To Harriette and Kathleen it seemed he was materialising from a diluted wash of light and bottomless darkness. And Jack Chatalong, looking up at his sister and aunty, seeing with their eyes as well as his own, saw both himself rising from the dark earth and their silhouettes dissolving in the wound of light.

He had reached where the ladder should be and remained standing in the bucket, bemused and blinking. The ladder was not there.

A few feet above him, his aunty and sister lowering the ladder. And Daniel's voice muttering, 'Yes all right all right. All right.'

As he came up the ladder Jack Chatalong took Daniel's outstretched hand and squeezed it, hard, as men do. And leaning backwards, still holding tight, he hung all his weight on that hand. Jack Chatalong imagined geometric shapes — squares and rectangles and diamonds — suddenly exploding, suddenly being blown apart. He pulled on Daniel's arm and, despite their relative weights, Daniel's body came arching over his own. Clumsily, flailing, a balloon body and bloated tongue arms legs brushed Jack's back. Who would have thought Jack had such strength?

Daniel's echoing scream was abruptly muffled. Stopped.

Jack saw awe, something like fear, and even relief in the faces above him as he took on the light of day. What? They had not seen him pull. It was as if Daniel had dived in. They looked down upon the man jammed head down in the shaft. A last kick from the legs. Some strange plant that would not quite wilt.

Daniel's coffin was huge.

And so, finally, Sergeant Hall — although uninvited — wound his way among the overturned water tanks and timber to what he thought of as the dead man's shed. He was surprised to see a small crowd gathered under a sort of lean-to at the back, the adults drinking tea. Hall had expected to see merely the members of the household. But there were children playing, so many children. Although startled at such numbers, Sergeant Hall was composed enough to survey them with a professional eye.

There was:

The tall, old woman, Fanny (*Full-blood*. Widow, married an Englishman. Must be sixty, seventy, years old or more). Daniel had said she'd gone.

Her daughter, the dead man's wife; Harriette (*Half-caste*. Recently widowed, married a white man. She'd be, what? fifty-ish?). Sergeant Hall saw the woman glaring at him and, uncharacteristically, he turned away.

His own Kathleen (Old Fanny's niece? Granddaughter? *Quadroon? Half-caste?* Patrick Coolman presumably the white father. Aboriginal mother, Dinah; deceased?). Kathleen was no longer a girl. Yes, he was fond of her and wouldn't want to lose her, and nor would the wife.

The boy, William. How old? Twelve? (*Quadroon*).

And that fellow Jack Chatalong, the shit-cart driver. He'd be late twenties, surely (*Half-caste?*).

And children. All looking at him, all suddenly quiet. So many of them, from toddlers to teenagers. His calculations faltered. He had to call them all *half-caste*, and ignore the range of hues. One — there — the backs of his legs covered with weals as if from an old or inherited whipping. Another with feet so long and thin they might have been worn flat from running, from being repeatedly chased from town to town. A third with a skin evidencing a startling range of colours; black, brown, tan, red and white and even blue swirling together in scars formed from burnt flesh. Hall's eye was caught by a girl staggering as if drunk. The child was somehow damaged, unable to stay still or move properly. She rolled her eyes at him and held out a hand. A fifth had a shock of red hair, and freckles like spattered blood. He recognised a strong jaw, and saw youthful caricatures of people who lived, had lived, in his area. Mustles, Starrs, Dones; even Coolman. Hall? His memory flickered.

There was such a lot to keep track of. Sergeant Hall hoped he could avoid having to write all this up in a report. It looked almost like one of the missions, like one of the settlements. Here in his own street. His mind buzzed, settling into its rhythm of calculations. *half-caste*, *quadroon*, *octoroon*. What word next? One-sixteenth. No. It was all too much.

And there was Ernest, with his tongue practically hanging from his mouth. His face flushed and unable to keep his eyes off Kathleen. His hands, too, seemed to be blushing, or was it that they were scrubbed raw?

Sergeant Hall was due to retire in a few months. What would his successor think? What would he say?

The older women tried to explain, their fathers had deserted these kids, the mothers didn't have a chance … Where else? Who else? Fanny and Harriette hesitated, fearing they'd said too much.

But Sergeant Hall hadn't noticed. Sergeant Hall waved her silent. All this, next-door to the police station. Where did they keep them all? The rainwater tanks, the shed …

It's a wonder there hadn't been more complaints from the townsfolk. His brain ached from the mathematics.

He saw Kathleen look at him from under her brows, behind her lashes; shy, like she did. He'd thought … For a moment he wondered if he'd been made a fool of.

He was a policeman. He was the Local Protector. He reminded himself — and it came as a relief — that these people needed his help.

Had Daniel been deceived?

Officially, he was off-duty. He said his goodbyes gruffly, and left.

Ernest guessed … Ernest thought about what could happen. He'd looked into the law, had listened to Auber and James Segal. There was every chance the policeman would sell the property, transfer the funds to the Aborigines Department, and send the lot of them away.

That was what usually happened, and this case was only a little different from the majority because of the husband being — having been — a white man.

Ern had got on well with Daniel. He had understood the man, which was no mean feat when confronted by a speech impediment like that.

It was a gamble, whichever way you looked at it. But Ernest had plans, and did not yet suspect that he may have erred in reckoning on the railway coming across this far.

Auber had sung the praises of these native women. James too, more intimately. Ern had seen the results himself, those children of Daniel and Harriette's, for instance; they were practically white. Should be free, he thought.

Ern, already, wanted to make them as I am; free to drift away like bright fair flowers, free to float out to the islands.

And Ern elaborated to himself what Daniel had implied. After all, what do you need a woman for anyway? There's no trouble, they make great mothers, great wives, and it's easy to let 'em know they'd be in the shit without you. Ernest did not dwell on his choice of metaphor, did not think that it might one day be he who crept up behind the white townsfolk as they turned their backs on him and squatted.

It was a matter of who he was going to save, and where the best investment lay. Course, he was getting lonely. Know what I mean? I know all about loneliness.

And yes, I felt lonely, even in writing that, as I hovered over the keyboard, my fingers tap-tapping and my heels in the air. I feared I was losing my people, that options narrow down all the time. That I was losing. Even when family welcomed me back, they did so warily — but it became easier when I no longer carried my grandfather on my back wherever I went.

I was frightened, I remain proud.

When I first began to sing around the campfire, my body rising and falling with my voice, a cousin to whom I had been introduced offered to accompany me on the didj, but we could not get it right. He cried out, 'Relax, loosen up, you be singing like a wadjela next,' and stomped away. Almost weeping at that I let the song come, and my hovering body resonated something like a didgeridoo itself, except that the notes were so high and varied, and then my cousin came back into the campfire light.

But my singing still makes people uncomfortable. It is embarrassing I suppose, someone looking like me, singing as I do.

But ...

Sergeant Hall looked at Ern warily. This was some proposal; he was not sure what to make of it.

It bettered his own plan, and it would hurt Kathleen less. Yes, again, he had to admit he'd grown very fond of that girl. It seemed a fair plan. All things considered, it seemed best for all concerned. *Everything correct and in order.*

Sergeant Hall said there was no need for permission from the department. 'I am the Local Protector. And I judge Kathleen, unequivocally, a white girl.'

Sergeant Hall was a good policeman. He could only blind himself for so long, could only bend the rules to a limited extent before bending them back the other way. His successor was about to arrive, and Ern and he agreed that this much was clear;

1. These people weren't white.
2. There was no hope for them now with Daniel gone. (And surely he had never known that they gathered like this.)
3. It would be unfair to burden Kathleen with them. They would drag her down.
4. The townspeople would not like it, and the children would never be accepted at the local school.
5. It was necessary to act for their own good.

Sergeant Hall hired a good solid cart. He couldn't get anything too luxurious, the Aborigines Department was not a wealthy one. And, anyway, there was nothing else available, not for so many. Although in fact, there were less on the cart than there legally should have been because Harriette had remained, subject to Sergeant Hall and Ernest's goodwill. The two men had assured her, had assured them all; things were different now. This place the others were being sent to had a school, it was like an agricultural college. It was a place to learn, to gather skills, to equip oneself for life.

Harriette had no choice. She wanted to believe them.

Sergeant Hall tried to reassure them. 'I have a friend,' he said, 'who will care for you.' He handed them over to another policeman, and gave them one last (unreturned) wave.

At the siding there was a man to guard them. He made a little sign, and wired it to the carriage. *Niggers for Mogumber.*

The farmer told himself he was affable and egalitarian, leaning against the fence post like this, and speaking to Jack Chatalong.

'You got a job lined up after this one?'

The farmer leaned very hard against the post as he spoke. He was looking for a discount, but the fence post did not move.

Jack shook his head, tightened the last wire.

'I hear they found a mob at Daniel Coolman's place, they're moving them all.'

Jack was on his bike. He slewed through sand, through alternating shadow and light, concentrating on the path his wheels must take, and it was as if the shadows were of people, silently willing him to maintain balance and momentum.

There was no one at the yard and there was only quiet among the water tanks. A couple of late magpies danced before him. He looked at the ground. How far to the railway?

As the night closed in around him, his breathing grew ragged. He rode until he was exhausted, slept, and rode again in the morning.

It was dark before he got to the siding. He heard the train shriek. And then he was rushing past the siding; the train moving away, trailing its plume of steam. He moved in steam, or was it now mist?

The bike twisted under him, and he was running, stumbling on sleepers, chasing the train, knowing even then how foolish he was. He called out into the darkness, his thin voice joining the giant hissing and panting, the rumbling of metal on metal. Then his hand got hold of something. The train dragged him, and his breath had been left far behind, when he saw a figure leap stiffly from the carriage, hit the ground and roll, and roll, and roll. He saw this even as the train dragged him. Fanny?

The train slowed, stopped.

The guards pulled him to his feet, counted those in the stock car. With this one, who had obviously tried to leap off, there were seven. Okay.

Those on the carriage were thinking of old Fanny, somewhere out there in the bush. She would not have been able to survive such a fall, surely. Should not have even been able to leap like that.

The train continued on, its unhappy passengers in the stock car now a little less sullen, and strangely cheered even though Jack Chatalong had his hands cuffed. Just in case, you know. It would look bad, now that it had been decided, if anyone were to escape

Some of these are heading, inexorably, toward the first proper white man born. The others, irrespective of caste or fraction, will mostly make a different future. I fear I have lost them. I fear it is being proved once again, I am so much less than I might have been. I fear that once were we, and now there is only I.

Nevertheless, I can offer a further glimpse. In some ways it corresponds to my own experience, the treatment I took at Ern's hands. This is from what I have been told.

Someone at the carriage, opening it. The sand felt luxurious at first, and you let your feet sink into it. Earth.

'Someone will be here for you in the morning.' What could you do? You didn't know where you were. Some of us were about to find out we didn't know who we were.

In the morning you saw a series of unconnected carriages

which had been released of their human cargo. Not just your family's. You were rounded up by a few fellas in half uniforms; a jacket, a whip, a spear tipped with glass, sticks and waddies.

'This way,' they indicated. 'This way.' You were driven to the settlement like animals, really, but of course it was not for slaughtering. For training? Yes, perhaps. Certainly it was for breeding, according to the strict principles of animal husbandry.

And one, of pure but rejected strain, must have been absorbed into the earth further back along that long railway.

The children were distributed variously.

Wire mesh on the windows. As soon as the sun falls you were locked into a dormitory. Insects in the mattresses stung your shivering body. You heard bare feet padding across the floor. Muffled cries. Whispers. Other bodies slipped into your bed, to investigate the newcomer.

Small children shat on the sandy floor of one room, and like cats they covered their heap.

If you were very lucky, a woman who worked in the kitchen said, 'You call me Aunty. Aunty Dinah.'

They ran a comb through your hair, speaking of your scalp. 'White, really.' Someone jerked at your clothing. 'See, where the sun has not been?'

'Elsewhere. We need somewhere else for the lighter ones.'

They kept you at the compound for a few days.

In the schoolroom the teacher was shouting across the room at a girl. A thin web of spittle trailed the words, and fell as short of the mark as the words themselves. The girl was dragged from the room.

A young one on the floor, tied to the leg of her desk.

A girl returns to class with her head shaved, wearing a sack for a dress. Those who quietly snicker nevertheless suffer with her. Because you never knew. It might be you.

The evening meal. You sat together at long benches, and did not talk. Cold. A thick yellow skin formed across the bowl. You tapped something solid at the bowl's centre. It bobbed, and the yellow skin broke apart.

Eyeballs floated across puddles of greasy soup, and crusts of bread showed signs of having already been gnawed by tiny mouths. If you were lucky there was a dull spoon.

Locked up of an evening, wire over the windows. Things in the mattress bit you, and you welcomed the others into your bed. Because of the warmth, see, and the company.

You dreamt that you were punished, like the boy you'd seen put into a bag and suspended from a rope tied high in a tree. Swinging. Trying to keep your head above your feet. Feeling that you were not quite drifting, but released; set free, thrown out and abandoned. It was dark, the weave of the hessian making rectangles of light. You could not distinguish trees, but only sky and earth.

Cut down, crawling out of the bag. You could not walk, and fell, kept falling; the earth had moved away, rolled away and left her behind.

In daylight you were bundled into a train again. A proper carriage this time, and a man in a suit watched you. A woman dressed in stiff white clothes receives you at the station.

You walked, almost breaking into a trot at the woman's

side. It was very hot. The sky blue. Heatwaves everywhere, rippling the air above road, red brick. So many lines against the sky and rumbling trams reach up to them.

And yes, the children here were all paler, as you must've realised, taking the cue from your inspectors. It was all so much nicer here.

So do you disappear from me, from us? Accept this kind of death? Keep secret your many miseries, your joys and laughter too?

I laugh at the reports of the visitors to the settlement, just as some would have at the time. But it is a peculiar kind of laughter. The Ugly Men's Association sent a delegation there. I am sure some of our white uncles and fathers were among them. It was written up in a church newsletter:

> A visit to a native settlement is always a joy to me. Any place where they are caring for the original inhabitants of Australia should receive the sympathetic support of all who have made this country their home.
>
> In company with the supervisor we drove in a sulky and tandem across the sandplain which brought us in sight of the settlement. Delightful people with black skins were running about, and great was the excitement at the arrival of a visitor.
>
> Lunch was ready on our arrival, and after refreshing the inner man, we set out on a long sandy walk to visit the cemetery, accompanied by about one hundred and fifty natives.
>
> What a blessing for the natives that they have got a

sympathetic superintendent and self-sacrificing staff.

Segregation is the only thing for the Aborigines. But let their segregation be Christian, and the natives taught to be useful ...

I do hope I am being useful, I used to say to Ern. I do hope I am being useful.

At least they were together, and sharing. Things are never so bad when you're together, or so I have been told. It was what made Uncle Jack strong enough, eventually, to lead me back. Whereas my closer family — say, Harriette's children — were weak and floating, and becoming free.

Uncle Jack Chatalong?

The supervisor accompanied him to the camp. Too old for the compound. Male. Too dark to be sent elsewhere. It was tents, huts of packing case and flattened drums, and snotty-nosed kids. The adults watched him. A few welcoming grins.

'You can put him up,' the supervisor said to an old couple. Jack wanted to apologise, and his expression must've shown this. 'They're blind, you can help them.' He wanted to refuse, felt quite numb. 'We'll try you at the kitchen. Charlie here will collect you in the morning.'

Uncle Jack learnt many things in the kitchen, and there was an awakening, just as there have been many awakenings. There was much Dinah, his mother, could tell him.

So suddenly; death, and then a wedding. The soil still settling in the grave, and Daniel and Harriette's daughters were hurrying their white husbands from various small towns around and beyond our traditional country.

Sergeant Hall, having decided Kathleen was unequivocally a white girl, said there was no need for permission from the department. And even though Kathleen was sick in the morning, she glowed at the wedding.

Yes, Kathleen glowed. Wore white. Sergeant Hall insisted that he give her away. With great respect to the recently departed. The sergeant stood beside her for so long in front of the priest that his good, quiet wife was forced to hiss at him and give Ernest a little shove into position.

I hovered over that wedding. A wedding. A white wedding. A couple of photographs of it exist, and I inspected them with a magnifying glass, wanting more, more. I used to hope that they loved one another. He married her. I wanted some help, some support for the fact that I stayed with the old man.

There was even a reception, a few presents on the table. A tablecloth, white, and patterned in a lace of straight lines and right angles which gives its edges teeth. Teeth which saw at the shadows beneath the table. On the table there is a clock, which I recognise as the one in Grandfather's study. There is also a cake, of two tiers; a china teapot; cups and saucers; a vase, with roses in it.

I concentrated so fiercely upon that photograph, and yet was otherwise so often floating and drifting toward the ceiling, that it must have appeared to my grandfather that I balanced upon an eyeball, upside down upon a lens of glass.

Deep in that photograph, there is another photograph, of a couple. White man, black woman; it must be Daniel and Harriette. The man stands at the rear and one of his hands is on his chest, the other on the shoulder of the woman seated before him. I can make out only the shape of her dress.

The man's hands are so pale they glow, and look like mittens or even paws. He is probably wearing gloves, and I imagine his hands ineffectually and clumsily groping, perhaps wishing to cling to something or someone always about to leave.

The clock chimed an hour.

In the clock's face there is even the reflection of the photographer, bending at his tripod. Ern had hired the photographer. It seemed only right that he contribute to the costs of the wedding. Other than the photographer's reflection the only indication that anyone other than myself admired these presents is the hem and cuff of someone's jacket, and part of a pair of trousers. There is — of course — a body inside these clothes, and indeed there is a hand protruding from the jacket, holding a celebratory glass. Ern told me the hand was his own.

In another hour the clock chimed beautifully, its sound all the purer because there was no one there to hear it.

There is a photograph of what I assume to be the wedding party. Ern is surrounded by women; Harriette, and her daughters. The women are frozen in a moment between glancing at one another, but their faces reveal that they are sharing the occasion. They hold their chins high in what seems an extravagant manner. Kathleen has flowers in her hands. There is another, smaller, woman beside her who I cannot account for. A darker woman, plump and grinning. Who can it be? It cannot be Fanny, surely? Knowing the conventions and equipment of the era, she must have had to hold that grin for some considerable time.

A magnifying glass reveals that she is looking straight into the camera, is defiant, and that it is a very serious smile, intended for me.

Ern is also staring intently into the camera, but he looks a little anxious, as if trying to read his future.

Following branches of my family tree, I discovered a series of white men who — because they married Nyoongar woman and claimed their children — were exceptional. But their children grew in a climate of denial and shame that made it difficult for even a strong spirit to express itself. And there were other children those same fathers did not claim. Witness Ern's first spree on arriving in this nation. What came of that? He dismissed it; a moment of weakness only. Another aberration. And another, another, another, regularly repeated. Ahem. And Kathleen, my almost-grandmother, was rejected by her father which, whatever foster-father and policeman might say, hurts. He was a white man, like them. And then there is my own father ...

Once again, I am confusing things, not following an appropriate sequence. I wish to note that at this wedding there were other white men, those who had married Daniel and Harriette's daughters. After the wedding, these white brothers-in-law shook hands with Ern, grabbed their wives, and rushed off in different directions.

Searching the archives I have come across photographs of ancestors which have been withdrawn from collections, presumably because evidence of a too-dark baby has embarrassed some descendant or other.

My family, my people, we have done such things. Shown such shame and self-hatred. It is hard to think what I share with them, how we have conspired in our own eradication. It was my Uncle Will who taught me something of this.

But I was writing of when he was still a very young boy, and of how my grandfather first married a Nyoongar woman, despite the law. Why was it Kathleen? Because she was there. Because he was advantaged. Because of greed. Because it was the challenge of a long-term plan, spanning the generations. Because of the power it would give him over her. Perhaps it was because his brief experiences of drunken sprees in *native camps* had excited him, and Kathleen promised similar excitement — with the added attraction of greater control of personal hygiene. Oh, and perhaps it was love. Perhaps it was love.

Ern and the policeman protector had a long talk about this. Or rather, as long a talk as was possible, given the pressures of time, and impending retirement. There were many and various pressures. The policeman protector — the Local Protector of Aborigines — worried as to Ernest's motives. But, as Ern assured him, if *that* was all he was after then he needed only to make a short trip to the *native camps*. Nudge, wink. As men of their world, both knew it happened all the time. And, of course, legally she was a white woman. Parents married; a white father. Living like a white person, of course — goodness — right next-door to the policeman and working for him. (Hall, once again, felt a moment's unease.)

Perhaps Ern felt guilty, having bought the house, the wood yard, all business contracts, and split up the family. But, as he explained to Kathleen, he had little choice. He paid a fair price, and otherwise the Aborigines Department would have it all. That'd be worse.

At Mogumber Settlement, Jack Chatalong cut and carted wood for the old couple. He took them water. They knew him by his voice. In the evenings he sat stoking their fire, seeing its reflection in their blind eyes and listening to words he may not have understood, but which reached deep within him, made him feel like an instrument being played. But such a poor instrument because although he felt the humming alive within him, it was more like a struggle to breathe than articulated song.

Inside his head he tried the sounds, attempted the rhythm, felt the vowels slipping together.

Chatalong had been struck dumb. What happened to that easy way with words, the easy launching of them, the unthinking way he could set them into flight?

Strange, that the first words for a long time were, 'No. No, no, not me.' Jack continued to refuse. A corroboree, at the camp, but he would not dance. He wouldn't do that stuff, couldn't do it, it was strange to him.

But he watched. From a distance, in darkness veiled by leaves, he watched. The dark bodies marked with the river's white clay making these people he recognised from the camp, these strangers, stranger still.

Sometimes, even the superintendent came to watch.

The old couple sang, their voices searching out the silent Chatalong, refreshing some other 'inner man', and dismantling an outer one.

Chatalong saw the superintendent staggering into his house in the evening. Saw him sleeping face down on the floor. Saw.

A great feathery bird was trapped within the little crowd

that had gathered, perhaps attracted by its calls. The people watched its clumsy distress, its stumble from a doorway and out among them. Beyond the silence of the large bird standing among them, Jack Chatalong heard the mocking voices of the white women.

Small feathers spiralled behind the bird. Not a bird. Not a bird, but a man. And his calls were strangled ones of frustration and fear. He ran to the centre of the yard, moved in a few small circles. He stopped and turned, sagging at the knees. The feathers were in bunches, this way and that, stuck to the black tar which covered him and stretched in long drops from his eyelids and nostrils. Tar must have filled his ears.

His eyes and mouth looked so vulnerable.

The bird boy was sobbing. Head bowed. Chicken feathers and tar stuck all over him. Silence. Snorting from where he had come.

Being taught a lesson. Something about being uplifted?

Our Jack Chatalong was learning. It was whispered to him as he spooned his watery soup, grateful that he could serve himself, and pick the choice bits. His mother, beside him, said softly, 'Whatever you think about, you keep it to yourself. Careful what you do, you might end up someone else otherwise.' Tilting his cup to drink, Chatalong saw the reflection of his nose, eyes, long lashes within its closed circle.

They heard the bird man talking in the little hut of corrugated iron. It had no windows. There was barbed wire on top, and a big iron door locked with handcuffs. A tracker in a shabby military jacket led Jack from the kitchen across a dusty yard which had been swept of all footprints. He motioned with his head for Jack to leave the small battered can of water, the heel of stale bread, at the door.

'Want me to lay them an egg, that's what they put me in here for. I got no time for chooks. I'm no chook.'

Jack looked into the hot darkness. He saw the stakes on the inside walls, the small holes in the walls growing tiny stars of light, and how barbed wire slashed at the bellies of the clouds rushing overhead.

Leaving, Jack softly dragged a hand along the corrugations of the iron wall.

'You wanna keep out of here brother.' It seemed a different voice.

In the afternoon a flock of cockatoos flew over the compound, screeching. They flew low to show how their glossy black feathers, so neatly side-by-side, felt the wind. Seeing the white tail-feathers, Jack remembered the clay on the dancers' bodies. The birds flew in, over, showing themselves off and Jack realised that this was a dance too, and how wonderful it was.

The bird man heard the birds, must have seen them through some pinhole in the iron around him, arcing twice across the little sky above him. The birds, in turn, would have heard him.

He kept up his screeching even as theirs faded.

Jack had heard others in the little prison hut, when they first went in, singing, 'You are my sunshine ...' They came out, dressed in hessian, heads shaven, squinting and with a hand shading their eyes. It might have been that they tried to smile.

But no one saw the bird man emerge in that night's heavy rain. He got away.

Dinah said, 'See? You can get away.'

Jack let his skills be known. Good with horses; handling them, caring for them, and he could mend wheels and wagons. Yes, he could even drive a car.

He'd be valuable on a farm, if they sent him to one.

Some of these, my people — let us call them 'characters' — are distributed variously. Some gathered together and gained in strength. Others ran to where they could.

My grandmother. Plucked from our family tree, falling toward me.

ern to close

To the Chief Protector of Aborigines:

There is an Aboriginal woman name of Fanny Benang ...

Benang? Consider the spelling of hard-of-hearing and ignorant scribes: Benang, Pinyan; Winnery, Wonyin. It is the same people. We are of the same people.

Fanny? It was really a no-name, a mean-nothing name. Not a name used to distinguish between people. We cannot depend on such names put down on paper. I think it was Dinah who had accepted what her mother bequeathed her and now had a baby in arms and a young girl walking at her side like a sister. But it may have been Fanny herself, rejuvenated by her escape and Sandy's goodbye. Or perhaps, even, that the two of them had come together so close to their home to make yet another effort to keep the spirit they represented alive in the face of continuing betrayal.

Constable Blake, temporarily stationed at Gebalup, was

merely doing his duty, part of which was to report on the activities of people such as this *Fanny Benang*, however that name might be pronounced, or spelled. He was passing on information received:

> ... *Fanny Benang, who wanders about the country between Wirlup Haven and Dubitj Creek. She has two half-caste children with her; one a little girl between nine and ten years old and the other I am informed was born at the Dubitj Creek about four weeks ago.*
>
> *The woman I am informed is at present at fifty miles from Wirlup Haven. From what I can learn from stockmen and others she is a notorious prostitute. It would be exceedingly difficult to say who is the father of the children. I would suggest arrangements be made to have her and her children removed to an institution when opportunity offers.*
>
> *Mr Ernest Scat of Gebalup, a reputable and kindly person, informed me that he would willingly adopt this eldest half-caste if you give your consent.*
>> *PC Blake*
>> *1/7/1930*

> *To Const Blake:*
> *Gebalup*
>
> *I have no objection to the child being adopted within the town. Police will of course be required to keep an eye out for the child's welfare.*
>> *A O Neville*
>> *Chief Protector of Aborigines*

To Chief Protector Neville:

In reply to yours of 1/7/30 the Aboriginal woman Fanny had left Wirlup Haven with her children before your news arrived and until recently I have been unable to ascertain her whereabouts.

At present she is about eighty miles from Gebalup and I am informed is coming in this direction.

November 17 1930
Const Blake

Report of Edward Blake PC Reg No 939 relative to Aboriginal woman Fanny and half-caste children

Inspector Segal

I respectfully forward for your information completed file relative to Aboriginal woman Fanny Benang and half-caste child Topsy.

This matter was perused by you during your last visit to Gebalup, but was only completed this date. The delay was due to the woman Fanny being induced by other natives to go to Barren Peaks and Munglinup, ninety to one hundred miles from Gebalup, last August. I seized her and the children at Wirlup Haven on 27th November.

The girl Topsy is an extra fair skinned half-caste, perhaps ten years of age, but the baby (six months) which was reported to me as being a half-caste, is, in my opinion, not a half-caste at all, but is the child of a half-caste father, and is very black.

Relative to the removal of the woman and remaining

child I am informed that she is willing to mate with a rather respectable black fellow named Ted Cuddles, who is the sole native employed by Done, twenty miles from Gebalup. If so, I think she should be allowed to remain. The baby is still at breast and could best stay with her for the time being at least. The child was handed to Mr Ernest Scat, in the presence of the visiting R M Mustle, this date, and will, I am satisfied, receive every care and attention.

Edward Blake
Constable

To Commissioner of Police

Despite your officer's report and the advice of members of the Gebalup community I have serious objections to the woman remaining in the Gebalup district instead of being removed to the Native Settlement. I enclose the necessary warrant for her removal. Also the child; if it seems to have a preponderance of white blood it would be best to also have it removed unless we can be confident of no reversion to type, or unless we have someone close at hand to tend to its welfare. In this case we have, and what a pity we do not have more people in our community like Mr Ernest Scat.

Deputy Chief Protector 22/12/1930

My dear grandfather knew the Inspector, knew the Chief Protector, knew the neighbourly policeman and — being of a kind — he trusted them. His kindly heart had him take in the poor waif, and Kathleen and her mother and this last adopted child were photographically captured together on the verandah. Ern was struck by how frail and thin the young girl was, and how good it felt to be able to help her.

Together, at least the women were together.

Even in my youth, after I had gained some idea of who I was and when I had my grandfather under my care I had moments of ... hesitation. Moments when, perhaps, I almost admired him. After all, he took Kathleen as his wife, which was more than many would have done.

Ern arrived from nowhere, knew no one; and so he had pluck, you might say. Well, I could respect that, and even — to a degree — his opportunism.

I was very aware that the organisation of his 'local and family history', and the documentation of his social engineering, were so much better than my own feeble efforts. He was a very rigorous and well-organised man; consider how he shaped my life, recaptured me after my car accident, and then took charge again.

He pushed me back to physical health, and gave me a plan. He moved us to this little isolated place on the coast, this property. He gave renovation instructions, prices, contact numbers for tradesmen. Said what to do with the garden.

This tree by my window, where the children climb, once again casts cool shade and lets the wind whisper in its leaves. It is a tall and pale gum. One of those whose bark peels and falls in strips. It towers over the house, and Grandad believed its roots threatened the foundations. He was right in that, they have cracked one wall.

Grandad wrote: *Cut down the tree. Burn it, dig out its roots.* He might also have written: *Displace, disperse, dismiss* ... My friends, you recognise the language.

He gave me the instructions on the day of his stroke, and long after that — but before my uncles came to save us — I trimmed the branches which grew close to the window. I was pleased to see Grandad's grateful smile when he peered through the window frame and saw no hint of tree.

I was even more pleased to see his reaction when I carried him outside, and he realised I had trimmed only those limbs which could be seen from the window, and left others intact. The tree still lived; it would grow again. I lifted him from the ground, nestled his neck and chin in the fork of two truncated limbs, and let him feel the burden of his own weight. It was still a tree you could hang from, or hang some other from.

Which — of course — I didn't do. I don't know, perhaps his vulnerability softened me. But it was only the strength I gained after Uncle Jack Chatalong and Uncle Will Coolman came to live with us that allowed me to feel anything like sympathy for poor silly old Ernest.

I used to look at how the heavy stones of the house fitted against one another, the small pebbles and dust which collected where they touched. The stones were roughly rectangular and between each one, where I had picked out the mortar, the darkness crept in. Cold air moved about me, and I sat within a stone grid, oozing light.

Not a fire. Not a family. I rubbed at the words I'd written so fastidiously. The pale, thin stuff felt cold and damp beneath my fingers. Mine and my grandfather's skin, my only kin, these pieces of paper.

The walls were strong, despite my continued picking and probing. The timbers of the ceiling sat strong upon them. I had peeled back the roof above some of the rooms, and there the joists showed like ribs against the stars.

Nyoongar language. Culture … I thought of all the things I did not have. Unsettled, not belonging — the first white man born — I let myself drift. I gave up, and drifted …

As far as the joists. I hooked my toes beneath one, and stayed. I thought I was the only one. I thought it was just me — a solitary full stop.

Or a seed. I know now there are many of us, rising. Like seeds, we move across and dot the daytime sky. More and more of us, like stars we make the night sky complete.

But back then I felt only the silence, and saw how the roof joists made yet another grid.

They told me afterwards. Uncle Jack and Uncle Will had stood together (at least I achieved that!) below the old house on the hill. They saw how rectangles of thin yellow lines described each stone, the light showing through the gaps where there had been mortar. There were stars in the space which had once been roof. They saw a dark silhouette drifting across the windows, loudly declaiming some nonsense, rising and falling. Rising.

A big yellow moon rising behind the house showed the figure in silhouette as it rose, and paused, and seemed to stand within the roof.

A thumping at the door. Uncle Jack pushed in. 'What the fuck, Harley! What you done around here? You practising for the circus or what? Gunna run away?' I saw him look at Ernest, huddled and scarred in the corner. I rose a little further toward the cold and glittering stars, but the moon was warm and low and reassured me. I saw Uncle Jack crouching beside Ernest, patting him on the shoulder as the old man wept and blubbered. I saw — just over the wall, just outside of the house — Uncle Will, looking up at me.

'Harley,' he said, so softly, but the voice carried. 'We're all sorry. But, think of us. Your people. Your kids. I'm the one was wrong.'

I didn't take in the words, heard only their intent. I kept my feet hooked beneath a roof joist. He would have seen me silhouetted against the fat moon, and I, in turn, looked at that same moon, and the path its light made across the sea to where the island was a patch of coagulated darkness, at one end of which was a continually flickering, a continually growing and shrinking, a small and continually reforming white blossom. That white and visual pulse.

And so then there were the four of us, all men. Sort of.

I had almost destroyed the house. The wind whistled between the stones, the floorboards were gone from most of the rooms, and so was the roof. I had hacked at the trees, leaving only a large limb out from each to support a rope and a heavy weight. I don't know what I was thinking. I don't know that I was thinking.

Stupid, they said. But they were gentle in saying it.

No point doing this, they said. They kept looking at me, with curiosity, with sympathy. With some sort of respect even, for the strange way I sometimes drifted, and the way I shimmered and trembled and sang in the evenings.

'You wanting to find out?' said Uncle Jack, and I told

him something of what I knew. 'Old Ern, eh? Yeah, he's a bastard. He's a bastard all right. But, you know ... You're not like him, eh?'

Uncle Jack put an arm around Ern's shoulder, squeezed him roughly. He observed me for a moment. 'You look a bit like him but.'

It was the last thing your sulky narrator wanted to hear, and I saw that he regretted saying it. He held his tongue between his teeth, and looked away.

I showed them the photos, and Uncle Jack was angry. 'Yeah, well this is just to make you sad, reading and looking at things like this. It's just a wadjela way of thinking, this is. You should just relax, feel it. You gotta go right back, ask your spirits for help.'

Despite those words there was something like gratitude in Ern's expression. And perhaps, after the way I'd treated him, it was understandable. Now I reached over and wiped his nose.

Uncle Will seemed to always be a little further away, to hold himself back. I would look over Uncle Jack's shoulder, and see Will running his finger along the gaps between the stones, or staring up at the ruined roof, or — at a distance from us — standing with one hand on the car door as if considering whether to get in and drive away. He was a very thin man, something particularly evident when you saw him standing in that way he had, with one knee bent and his hands pushing into the small of his back.

They continued to speak of Ern. I remember that, initially, Jack did most of the talking, and Will would nod, add a word here or there. Our heads tilted to Ern at intervals, and he would drop his head, look up beseechingly, and drop his head again with shame. He was silent, knowing there was nothing he could even try to say.

Uncle Will, Uncle Jack, they understood. But I know best. And I also know I have to work right through this white way of thinking, it is the only way to be sure.

When the girl was born Ern had said, 'I don't want her going into the sun.'

Harriette looked at this man, who had not yet picked up his child. Kathleen sat propped up with pillows, the baby in her arms. Dark wooden furniture, a white lace doily beneath a clock. It seemed to Harriette that Kathleen, after all the lonely effort of the birth, had moved away from her. But then, herself borne along on a current of regret, she realised that Kathleen was imprisoned by this tight-lipped man who stood by the door. She understood it was not his child, but did he? Harriette remembered bitterly what her own father had promised. The best of all worlds.

It was easy, after all, for Kathleen to keep the child indoors, since Ern refused to let her leave the house, except to hang out washing or some such thing. He allowed her a small garden which she and Topsy tended in the early morning and evenings.

Vegetables, Ern advised. He gave Kathleen gloves to wear, and her fingertips flapped as she handled the pegs, and kept her from the soil.

She dressed carefully to place orders at the shops. Had the floor shining when the food was delivered.

As soon as it was possible to do so Ern bundled the mother into his truck. Kathleen looked across the bonnet at him as he swung into the crank. It was a novel experience, she found herself thinking, being out with him. And in daylight even, although it was not quite that yet. And he was the one cranking the motor, rather than it being her out there pulling her arm away to save it from being broken when the motor suddenly fired. She turned to wave goodbye to Topsy. The young girl's face was touchingly serious.

It was a long drive. Ern parked off the main street. He knew the registrar here. 'We can't be too careful,' he said. For the future.

When they had completed the details (And this is the mother? Beautiful handwriting, the man said to Ern) they returned to the car.

'Stay here,' he said to Kathleen, and he took the child from her.

Kathleen watched him walk away. She stared at the point where he had disappeared, the corner of the building. Men appeared there. They were red-faced, loud, stumbling. She saw them glance, then gaze more openly. They called out to her that they were going out to the reserve, but could she save them the trouble? Perhaps it was the car that kept them away.

'Photographs,' Ern said. 'I had some photographs taken.' He had also bought a small camera.

I once put it to Ern that he married Kathleen, and tried to keep Harriette, as some sort of display. His watery eyes goggled at me, and I heard Uncle Will coming so I did not pressure him any further. He wished to keep her as a display, as a domestic, as a tamed tribute to himself, but Harriette was too accustomed to independence and was known as Daniel's widow. She came and went as she chose.

Ern insisted that Topsy, like Kathleen, did not leave the confines of his yard except to go to school.

Ern knew that Harriette would not be allowed in most towns. But here, she, Kathleen, Will and Topsy ... Ernest expounded his progressive views to some of the individuals in the wary town. The mother, the little girls; they are not like those others. See how Topsy does at school. It's the white blood. Such a shame about the measles, the weak constitutions, such a shame that more of their descendants had not survived. But there were never many here anyway. He sighed, and was gathering a reputation as something of a soft-hearted expert.

At home, sometimes, noticing the baby, Ern worried that perhaps he had been too ambitious, perhaps he should have married someone lighter, some other *quadroon*. Look at Harriette's son, Will. You wouldn't hardly know. Not when you saw him dressed up, at places where you would not expect any *native* to be. He spoke like a young gentleman, almost.

But, as Ern soon had to admit, his child may as well have been born in police uniform. Yes, of course it was a girl but there was Hall's jug ears, the same hair and the freckles. He believed each peal of laughter he heard was directed at him.

Poor Ernest. Yes, although it came as a surprise to him there is no need to delay the truth any longer. He had been cuckolded by the cop. He did not mention his realisation to Kathleen, and tried to dismiss it from his mind. But once, trying to help his wife, the child slipped from his arms and cracked her head heavily on the stone steps.

Harriette and Kathleen carried the child around for

days. She became flushed and listless, and her limbs moved loosely, like a rag doll's. Ern saw that they could do no good for her, it was something beyond their resources. He reasoned that it was not his child anyway, and that she was better off in professional care. Ern drove her to a hospital in another town, at the terminus of the rail network, and abandoned her with a note explaining her condition and that the father was a policeman. He gave no name, and no address.

It toughened him. He thought, you can't trust people, whatever they may seem to be. Sergeant Hall! He studied Topsy, *observed* her, looking for resemblances to a father.

After he had disposed of the child, Ern told himself again that it was up to him to make his life the way he wanted it, and he could not include someone else's sick child in his plans. Ern would make a mark; he would leave something of himself. Of himself only. He had property already. A business. The railway and the wheat farms were almost here. Soon. He would sit tight, and hold on to what he had.

Ern set about preparing himself for when things picked up a bit. Ernest Solomon Scat; he wanted to make his mark, and that was that.

He had Kathleen's young cousin Will working on the sanitation cart. The boy needed a job, and it would be good training for him. Ern was pleased to help his wife's family in this way.

The publican advised him, and — with all that timber he'd inherited — Ern was getting enough work as a carpenter. Usually it was in nearby towns. As soon as he was able, he bought himself a motor truck.

He slept in the truck, in a room if offered, spent his

evenings cannily nursing a beer. He liked to return to Gebalup, where he lived cheaply, so that he might survey his assets. A yard next to the police station, he thought. Couldn't be better.

Except — if he thought about it — for the wife. And the mother-in-law. Topsy. Will. The whole bloody family. He would have to be careful. He explained to Kathleen that she — and Topsy — were to care only for him now, to only look after him, no others. Her family could stay, but they were his guests. If he threw them out, they'd have no one. He spoke of missions, settlements, of the friends he had and what legislation could do with Aboriginal people. They might end up anywhere, with anyone, and hounded from fence to fence.

But Ern found himself having to travel farther and farther to get work.

Dry winds, sun, no water. Ern rattled across a land rapidly becoming desert. Cleared of trees, its skin blew away in a searing wind. The land's fluids rose to the raw surface, and they were thick and salty.

Farmers turned their backs on the dying and wounded, because suddenly no one wanted the little they grew there.

The miners had left, the farmers left ... Were they leaving him? Ern, alone, bounced along rough and sandy roads at a speed which forced him to focus on the narrow track ahead and nothing else, and he understood that he was going backwards. The farms and farmers; receding. The railway line; shrivelling back to some centre. He was surrounded by cleared land, by sand; but there was always, somewhere, some tight and curling bush, and still-secret waterholes.

He had a *native* wife. A *native* family, back in Gebalup, pulling him back.

Gebalup, the town there, was dying. With no new people arriving and hungry to impose themselves upon this country; with no railway, no telegraph, and with only shifting, sandy roads to connect it to the rest of the new nation, the town seemed about to dissolve, to sink back into the sand.

Ern held to his vision, even as it shimmered and shifted. He blinked. A temporary setback. Be patient, he told himself, because when the railway reaches this far! The rainfall is sufficient, there is land here. He dreamt of railway lines retracting as he pursued them, leaving him stranded just beyond their reach. Even with such dreams Ern kept to his plans, still believed.

At least the shrinking town kept Constable Blake — a young fellow who Ern had cultivated, but whose Occurrence Books bored me in my research — free of the pressure that towns elsewhere were feeling. The *native* camps at their edges always threatened to spill over their boundaries. Threatened to unsettle, to intrude. But Gebalup, for some reason, had so few *natives*.

These people of the land, said citizens everywhere, they are like the land, they are treacherous. Something to be tamed, subdued, harnessed, made to work. Something to be improved, in order to fit our ways. But in those towns, in all the towns, crops failed. And the citizens' far-away markets failed them also. Citizens had made sacrifices, had worked themselves to exhaustion. Now, facing failure, they saw some of us looking in from the edge of the town, at corners, crossing streets within the very town. They measured themselves against these

117

original inhabitants, and consequently wanted them pushed further down. Controlled.

Ern found himself needing advice, reassurance, further security. He returned to the city, for a few short weeks, and did a little work for that good friend of the family, Auber Neville.

When, reassured, Ern returned to Gebalup he was surprised — amused even — by young Will, who, in what Ernest thought a disturbing lapse from his usual gentlemanly demeanour, told Ern he could stick the whole shit-cart right up his tight arse.

Public sanitation, collecting nightsoil ... the goona cart became the mainstay of Ern's business. After all, even in an economic depression, even in a dwindling town ...

Ernest crouched behind the white bums of the town and took what they left behind.

For Uncle Will it was a matter of pride, see. Of self-respect. He had done a lot of work, alongside the Starrs, delivering horses, carting sandalwood, clearing, doing all sorts of general farm work. He was an enterprising young man. His fair skin, his education, his isolation made it easier for him. He knew he was as good as anyone.

Young as he was his ambition was to buy himself a block of land in the town. It was what Mr Starr had advised. But, having turned his back on Ern and the town's sanitation, he found — suddenly, the same as so many others — that there was no work. Same as everybody, he went to apply for the 'Susso'. The clerk hardly looked up from his sheet of paper. There was a queue of men behind young Will.

'Sorry. Can't help you here. Anyway, too young.'

Will said nothing. Was struck dumb. He remembered this clerk, one of the older boys at school. His desk was a few boards slung across trestles. The flimsy hall sounded with shifting feet.

'It's no good coming here,' the old school chum smiled at him from behind the desk, from behind his pen, from behind his sheets of paper. 'You'll have to see the Aborigines Department.'

But. But. Will was a man as good as any. His father had named him the first white man born.

Ern offered him his old job on the shit-cart, explaining that — because things were bad for him, too — he could not offer wages, only food and keep. Will could live among the tanks down the back there.

Harriette, seeing Will's ambition, reminded him of his Uncle Sandy Two Mason, who had gone to the war. He had made a place for himself here, but policeman Hall had squeezed him and made it impossible to return because of all the trouble. It wasn't just silly men's stuff; Sergeant Hall had wanted to make himself Uncle Sandy's protector, which was intolerable for Sandy Two.

Uncle Will liked to talk of his uncle, Sandy Two Mason. Uncle Will was a reader, and he could place Uncle Sandy in the stories he had read, in even the local histories he later devoured; all those roles for daring pioneers, for explorers of new territory, for men who were innovative and adaptable, brave and proud.

He told us how his mother, Harriette, spoke of her brother, Sandy. She was proud of him. Uncle Sandy had his own block of land, she said. He has travelled everywhere. He can do anything, just like a white man.

He is going to marry a white woman. This last troubled her, at once some sort of balancing of her family history. But would such a wife help keep our children alive? Or perhaps she thought, at last, revenge.

If so she may have been a long way behind a great many others, a little late to arrive at this way of thinking.

'Listen,' said Uncle Will. At the time he was charged up and full of steam.

Listen … The train rattled, sounding like an ailing thing. Framed, fleetingly: brick, rusting iron, smoking chimneys. The sound changed; they flew across the river. Uncle Sandy Two's feet hit the ground before the train stopped, and he charged at the city, thinking to take it with his boldness. He had the address on a piece of paper, had consulted a map beforehand but even so he reached the river almost before he knew it, and realised he had come too far. Relax. He had not come so far. Follow the river, turn back toward the railway. A hill. A big church. He walked down the side of a house.

Remarkably, there was a queue at the back verandah. Calmed by the walk, and feeling safe among his fellows, he took his place in line. His fellows? Yes, they were people out of place. As he, were he not so careful and so proud, would also feel. The others looked around; up, down, not at one another. He saw a hat held by its brim, sheltering a groin; saw that some pulled at collars, turtle-moving their necks. A woman contorted herself; she looked over her shoulder, and then raised a foot to inspect her heel.

He walked away, and watched from a distance that precluded conversation.

Sandy joined the queue when it had dwindled, its

members having entered the doorway and slumped back out of it one by one.

Just as Sandy reached the door a face appeared diagonally from behind it, and Sandy quickly checked his fist from rapping.

'Lunch,' the face smiled. Door closed. Lock clicked.

Sandy's fist remained clenched, inches from the door. He let it drop.

He sat on the verandah and lit another cigarette.

'My mother. I believe my family is at Mogumber, and I want to get them out. They can come live with me.'

The man opposite had a pen in his hand. There were rows and rows of small drawers behind him, and files which insisted that you tilt your head to read the tiny vertical labels, balanced as they were on redundant full stops.

'I am Chief Protector Neville, as you would be aware,' the man smiled. 'And your name is?'

Sandy Two saw that his answer meant something to this Mr Neville, whose mouth remained open as he began to form the sentence: 'Ah … Ah. You are a returned soldier, are you not? Wooloomooloo Road?'

The Chief Protector's pen hovered above the page, describing little circles in the air. A hawk watching, waiting to fall, to grasp, to take away.

Chief Protector Neville's focus shifted. He went to a filing cabinet. Sandy looked around the room. A portrait of the king. The man's attention was upon him again, and he held a bulky file in his hands.

'Ah, yes. Your mother was Fanny Mason?'

'Yes.'

'She was a *full-blood*?'

'Yes.' And then Sandy Two saw where this devil Neville was leading him. 'I don't really know. My father was a white man.'

Our Chief Protector wished to study the man before him. He agreed with Mr Proud's comments. *Half-caste*. And what eye was more informed and respected than his own? *Half-caste*, he repeated to himself, *but unusually fair*. His very fine mind recalled the relevant diagram. *First-cross*, he believed. *Remarkably fine features. Very well-spoken.*

A younger man entered the room. Sandy Two recognised the curious visitor of a year or two ago. The young man looked away from Sandy's gaze.

'Yes?'

A further bundle of papers fell onto the Neville desk.

'Thankyou.'

'Oh. She's passed away? I should have gone to see her, even if Hall …'

'You are jumping to conclusions. And let me assure you that you need never worry about funeral arrangements. The Aborigines Department has …'

'No. I don't want the department having anything to do with this.' But it was already done.

'This is no affair of yours. The department is running the children's affairs, and you have no business here.' The Chief Protector looked up from his desk, from his papers and his card indexes. 'Sandy, you have to come under my laws, you can't get away from them.'

'I'm not an Aboriginal. I defy you to call me one.'

The Chief smiled, and his ears rose fractionally with the effort. He flicked at the raised corner of a piece of paper with his fingertip. Papers and small cards surrounded him in neat stacks.

'What do you call your common-law wife?'

'A white woman.'

The undeniably white man shook his head, and tut-tutted softly. 'No. She is a *half-caste*.'

Uncle Sandy Mason would not be denied. 'Her father was a white man, her grandfather was a white man.'

Family trees, and odd diagrams of genealogy appeared as if floating in some dark sea. And himself hanging from an upturned branch, like precarious fruit, about to fall.

He knew the law. 'I am not an Aboriginal but I am treated as if I am one. I want to be exempted. My family and myself not being Aboriginals should not be pauperised and kept under the act.'

The Chief Protector held his hands in front of him with their palms up. 'The proof is to the contrary, Sandy. And it is I, or my representatives, who decide who is or is not Aboriginal. I'm thinking of your family, Sandy. Did you ever hear the yarn about the needle and the camel?'

Uncle Sandy wanted to look at something in the room, anything, anything but this man.

The Chief, devil Neville, allowed himself a grin. 'Well, on account of your police reports, you have as much hope of getting an exemption as a camel has of getting through the eye of a needle.'

Constable Hall's reports, deviating from *all correct and in order, strictly routine patrols* ... Constable Hall's reports from all those years ago now stopped Uncle Sandy right there dead in his tracks.

Well, not quite dead, not literally. Not yet.

what jack and kathleen built

After the noise of the motor, the wind tearing at the metal and canvas of the car; after the jolting, the shifting, the being thrown together and the final slewing of the car that brought them to this stop it was silent.

Silence.

Ern uttered clipped and strangled sounds. Barely audible curses.

Kathleen looked into the distance. She might have laughed, but she knew his anger. He had wanted to get her away from Harriette, and to himself. Now this.

The sound of insects, the earth moving. She breathed the light and the heat.

Ernest returned from his inspection of the car.

'The front wheel. I knew it. Soon as we lost the spare.'

The wheel was no longer a circle.

Kathleen lit a fire a short distance from the car to boil a billy, and sat in the shade while Ern removed the wheel. Even after replacing some of the spokes, he was unable to return it to its original shape.

Kathleen watched him. Occasionally she stood and turned around in a slow circle, her eyes following the horizon. The sandy track they had been following curved in the middle distance, and then she could see only mallee scrub. But there, in the far distance, something a little taller, bobbing in the heatwaves.

Ern's shirtback was dark with sweat. He bumped and grazed his knuckles. Each breath, each curse, was louder than the one before.

The shade had grown to embrace the two of them before Ern sat back, and placed his wrists on his knees. Even in relenting, his mouth remained tight. He couldn't fix the wheel, and without it they might never be able to roll away across the flat land which surrounded them.

'I can't unbuckle it enough to tighten the spokes,' he said, half to think it through, half to complain of the injustice. He might perish, shrivel, be forgotten.

'Look,' she said, 'I could sit on it. Like this.'

She did so, and her weight held the rim so that it formed something more like a circle.

Kathleen saw the relief in Ern's face. She bounced up and down on the wheel.

'Stop.'

She waited, patiently, until it was all but done, and then began to bounce again, lightly. Bouncing, she looked over her shoulder at him, at the patch of pink scalp at his crown, the grazed knuckles. The concentration.

He was aware of her buttocks bouncing on the wheel, her back, the twist of her neck and her throat. He thought of that policeman, and squinted up at laughter which fell upon him as if from the dazzling sun, the vast pure sky.

Kathleen stood. Ern held the wheel. He ran his fingers

around it, felt the weight of its circle. He clung to the technology of hub, of spokes and the arch of a rim from which the weight of a car could be seen to hang. Civilisation.

He replaced the wheel.

'Yeah, well,' he said. 'What about you show us what you're made of, be a good *darky* and find us a camp and some water.'

But she was already in the cab, and pointing ahead.

The sun was low, and it was as if the earth had tinted the sky. A pink light bathed them as they approached a crowd of trees.

These trees stood tall, and their reaching trunks and limbs were a creamy white, were mottled; in places their limbs were the pink of the sky.

Ern saw limbs of flesh almost like his own; a little warmer in colour, and so lithe, so long, so slender. The trees' flesh swelled as the sap moved in them. There were folds, and clefts where limb and trunk met.

'I came here with my mother, once,' Kathleen said. 'I think, she brought us here.'

'Your mother!' Ern snorted.

'Harriette. I mean Aunty Harriette.'

Ern was thirsty.

Again they sat in a relative quiet. The engine creaked as it cooled in the shade of these surprising trees. There was a lot of good water underground.

'This is a good camp,' he said.

Kathleen smiled, still looking at the trees, not at Ern.

'Now,' Ern grinned. 'What about that fresh water?'

'I think ...' Kathleen walked in among the trees.

'How do you know this stuff anyway?'

'I don't know. From when I was a little girl, and Harriette always … You need a big knife, or a little axe.'

She was circling a tree.

Ern, head down and stepping toward her with the small axe in his hand, looked up and saw a *native* embracing Kathleen. Ern saw two *natives*, embracing. It was a man, a *black man*. And his own wife.

Kathleen freed an arm and beckoned Ern to her.

'This is my brother,' she said. 'Jack, this is Ern. You remember. He is my husband.' Again there was a little silence as they all adjusted themselves.

Jack dug around the tree to expose a root. They cut one off, and Jack held it above Ern's mouth. Ern knew it was the coolest, the clearest, the purest water he had ever tasted. But he couldn't savour it. It seemed somehow tainted.

'I had to get away from there,' said Jack. 'Find somewhere where no one knows me, maybe then I'll be all right.'

Like a sister, he had said, *like* a sister to me. Not a sister, not really.

Ern thought they had been very slow to take their arms from one another. But Kathleen had returned to him and taken his hand.

She knows me. He had looked over her shoulder and seen, even as his glance slyly swept on, Jack grinning. At him. At them.

She wants me. Me.

Jack could not help shaking his head and grinning, and

was still doing it even in the light of a campfire late that night. He had only just got here, he said, after being sent to a wheat farm. But ... You couldn't go into town. They set one day aside for Aboriginal people to do their shopping, and told him that was his day off. Not that he had money, most of it was banked for him, somewhere. He never saw it.

And had they heard what that Mogumber place was really like? Anyone can be put there, just about (unless, maybe, you got yourself married to a white man). Criminals, black trackers with whips. They chase you down. It's a prison there, it's like a dog kennel.

He was just trying to get away, find some peace. But he needed work, really. Keep to yourself, that's the way, if you wanna live.

They drove off with Jack's bicycle roped awkwardly on top of a neatly interlocking stack of boxes, tools and luggage behind the cab.

Ern had a job in Norseton, building, for the publican. It was verandahs, some further rooms.

The publican's voice and belly introduced the man an instant before the rest of him came out into the sunlight, with Ern at his back.

The man said he had a room, for Ern and ... his missus.

His eyes stayed on Kathleen as she came close to him; as she brushed past him, through the door, into the gloom of one of his own rooms. His gaze swung back to Jack, who still leaned against the truck. The man scratched himself, and Jack did the same, for his own amusement, but was grateful the big red man did not notice the mockery.

'The woman, yeah. Long as she doesn't cause any

trouble. But not him. Haven't got room. Yeah, I know, I've heard that some of these *coons* are all right but I haven't met any.'

It was convenient, Ern said, that Jack sleep on the tray of the truck.

Ern had no dog to guard the vehicle, and he worried for his tools.

Jack wrapped himself in a blanket and canvas, and lay with his head pressed against the locked toolchest. He listened to the voices in the pub, felt the cold night air on his face. And now the voices were close, suddenly intimate. He heard glass clinking, and slurred boasts were murmured, it seemed, into his ear.

'See that builder? Taking his about with him. You reckon he really married her?'

Jack's hand roamed his body, found the stiffness, relaxed himself.

Ern, conscience clear, rocked to and fro upon the not-his-sister's body.

Most of the building materials were on site. Ern set up a small bandsaw and cut planks from the seasoned logs the publican had stored away.

There was a claypan near the edge of town and, not far away, an assortment of humpies and tents. Women and children came to the far edge of the claypan and, scooping the clear water from just above the mud, slowly filled old kerosene tins. Some balanced a stick across their shoulders, and hung a bucket from each end.

Not our people, thought Kathleen, watching from the corner of her eyes. Jack, remembering the camps, was not so sure. There were larger groupings, and what was that saying? There, but for the grace of God …

Jack and Kathleen made a crude kiln to bake the bricks, and then spent days culling the surrounding scraggy scrub of firewood. They used picks to break up the clay and, pouring in more water, set a horse to working the earth. Kathleen walked at its bridle, around and around in a small circle, and the clay was stirred to a thin, muddy consistency which would swallow anything placed in it.

They poured the soft earth into a mould, shaped it into bricks.

The fire glowed day and night until the tangled pile of wood became a few straggly remainders, and there was only white ash; soft, fine, and somehow soothing. The wind lifted it, and spread it across them.

Jack and Kathleen stacked the bricks as high as they could reach. They put handfuls of fine sand between each layer and the wind blew grit into their eyes, nostrils, ears, between their teeth; dust coated their skins, changed their voices, settled in their hair. The sun rose over the wall and, tired and dry and irritated by the dust, Kathleen and Jack turned away those who came visiting from the camp.

Kathleen and Jack heard Ern's motor as if from the sky, or from somewhere else altogether. They could see only bricks, a high wall before them. And when they turned away from the wall there was only the sloppy-holed earth and the blackened kiln, already crumbling.

Jack dug trenches for the foundations in the earth behind the pub, while Ern and Kathleen began carting the bricks and soon the great stack of bricks was only a neat and diminishing ruin which they drove the truck between.

Kathleen kept to the room they'd been given while Ern and Jack built the walls, and then she was enlisted once more.

Jack slept on the ground inside the walls. In the evenings he heard the men leaving the pub in small groups, and heading out to the claypan on the edge of town.

Jack slept inside a doorway so that the sun fell upon him as soon as it rose, and he let the light draw him up. He splashed the sleep away at the rainwater tank, and made tea on a little fire in the yard. The publican sent a meal out to him; bread, tea. He and the girl snatched at one another's words before she hurried back.

Waking with the taste of metal in his mouth and his jaw tight, Jack heard Ern's voice among the others escaping the walls of the pub and — to the accompaniment of bottles clinking, a motor coughing, a couple of horses clip-clopping — disappearing in the direction of the claypan at the edge of town.

Jack wondered if Kathleen was awake.

Now that Will had gone to be with his Uncle Sandy, Ern had Jack and Harriette collecting the nightsoil. Topsy was finishing at school, and Ern was reluctant that she take on domestic work, and thought it would be a shameful waste if she was to assist Harriette.

Since Kathleen seemed unable to bear him children, he took steps to have her earn some income from cleaning, washing and ironing for the townspeople. If not enough work came that way, then she could assist Harriette. 'We certainly don't need you going off into the bush with Harriette, hunting.'

Although he took no notes, Ern was — discreetly — observing Topsy, and — doubtless — did so as dispassionately as the scientist of whom Mr Neville wrote:

with his trained mind and keen desire to exert his efforts in the field investigating native culture and in studying the life history of the species, supplies an aid to administration.

Little Topsy, he noted, was no longer so little; breasts budding, hips altering the way she walked.

He bought her books, and English magazines, and even engaged a tutor for her. It was obvious to him that she had outgrown what the school could offer.

Harriette tried to reassure Kathleen that Ern, in this way, was doing little more than what Daniel had done for his own daughters.

Ern took to buying Topsy articles of clothing and having her parade for him. He wanted, he said, for her to learn *deportment*, and how to dress like a lady.

A different policeman was stationed next-door, and Ernest was quick to advise the man of his part-Aboriginal wife and Aboriginal domestic. He gave the policeman the benefit of his own, progressive ideas on the best means to *uplift and elevate the natives* and of the manner in which he intended to raise his own children. 'My wife ...' he began, and the new constable, staring at something behind Ern, finished the sentence for him: '... is very young.'

Ern noted the envy and admiration on the policeman's face and, turning to introduce his wife, saw that it was not Kathleen who was the object of the official gaze, but Topsy. Never one to lose an opportunity, Ern said, 'She is older than she looks,' and introduced Topsy as his wife. 'This is Kathleen,' he said, looking directly at the girl, determined that she should not contradict him. Ern was thrilled, and just a little frightened, at what he had begun, had seen he could do.

It made sense. Kathleen's child had been fathered by Sergeant Hall. Kathleen was too attached to her Aunty Harriette. Kathleen was tall, and Ern was already having to instruct her as to her diet. She had changed, and not to Ern's taste. But Topsy ... Topsy was young, and small, and as fine-boned as a bird. She looked exotic, her hair sometimes seemed almost golden, and she spoke and moved with remarkable elegance given the limited tutoring he had given her. She seemed, my grandfather-as-scientist told himself, almost a new *species*.

When Kathleen found Ern embracing Topsy, bending her over their matrimonial bed with her skirts all bunched up, she could only give a little noise of surprise. Ern looked up and saw her. He pushed Topsy's face into the bedspread, hissing, 'Just a moment. Don't move.' Topsy lay still, her face hidden and limbs splayed like a discarded doll. She was so small. Ern straightened up, adjusted his trousers, and — walking across to where Kathleen stood in the doorway — closed the door in her face.

Kathleen did not slam doors, did not stamp her feet. She was in the dusty street, near where — so many years ago — her Aunty Harriette had run toward the violence, not understanding her own terror. Harriette had been only a toddler, and her father, Sandy One, had chased her, caught her, thrown her to Fanny who had quickly hidden her away.

Now it was Jack, who — seeing Kathleen striding into the distance — ran after his sister.

My grandfather, Ernest, stepped from the front door of his house. Jack Chatalong was striding toward him. The way Jack was moving would have alerted Ern to danger, and — indeed — Ern's own nagging dissatisfaction had quickened his perception. But for all that he would not have expected to be hit, so hard, so soon.

Sprawled on the steps, Ernest put one hand up as the constable rushed toward them from next-door. 'No, no, it's all right. As long as he goes, I'll make nothing more of it.'

To be able to speak and behave in such a controlled manner made Ernest feel deliciously superior.

Harriette returned almost surrounded with the bodies of rabbits. They were heaped up behind her, and hanging from the sides of the old spring cart ready to be sold to the people in town, at three to the shilling.

'I don't know where Jack is, or Kathleen,' said Ern, which was the truth. Harriette worried for them. Ern did not say that the policeman had taken them away. What else could Harriette do, other than stay near home? Topsy did not say anything of what had happened. She was very young. What difference could it have made, anyway?

Ern told Harriette he would allow her to live among the old water tanks in the yard, but she mostly stayed away, camping along the coast. Ernest, at least, was pleased because he realised Harriette could only be a bad influence upon the girl, Topsy, who he now called his wife.

a menace in our midst

My dear grandfather Ern had reason to be grateful for that goona cart. Even in a financial depression there remain deposits; liquid, firm, soft or hard.

Topsy, a growing swelling girl, cooked cleaned washed, and invested small portions of the above deposits in the vegetable gardens. Ern was always trying to train the girl in various useful skills; to help her know her role; to look after his needs.

He took her on a long drive, and parked where they could look down over a rough clearing beside the rubbish tip on the edge of a nearby town. Ernest pointed to various things below them, informing and educating Topsy about such things as *native reserves, settlements*, and *missions*.

There were little huts, tents, bush shelters.

You could see people milling around the one bush toilet, or making the long walk to the horse trough in the street to get their water, and carting it back in old kerosene tins.

Topsy recognised Jack and Kathleen as just two of the many people who did not look in her direction.

The residents of nearby houses — some of which had windows facing the reserve — believed the place shameful; the idle people, the little children, the shabby huts and tents, the untidiness and squalor of it all. You could see their whole life just about, if you wanted, said these poor townsfolk. It should not be like this. They wanted the situation improved; the reserve must be moved out of sight, and the children sent to some school of their own.

Jack had built a hut in bush just the other side of town. He used old timbers, hessian, flattened kerosene tins. He found a little farm work, but then fell out of it, and someone from the town complained about him and Kathleen living like that, on public land. A policeman and a public health inspector arrived together. The inspector reported that the hut was not fit for human habitation.

They were moved onto the reserve where, having been permitted to salvage the materials from his previous hut, Jack rebuilt it. Within a few short weeks the hut had suddenly not only been deemed fit for human habitation, but was used by the Local Protectors of Aborigines — a policeman and a priest — as an example of what others could do if they only showed a bit of initiative.

Being introduced in such a way immediately put Kathleen and Jack at a distance from their fellows in the reserve. Kathleen wanted to keep a little distance anyway. It was important to her, for instance, that they have a table; she didn't want to eat on the ground, watched by the people up in those houses.

Some people in the camp said she was stuck-up, toffee-nosed, that she thought she was too good. 'She thinks she's white!' It was only ever the people in the camp who said this; never those in the town, who either glared, or ignored her completely when she came into their sight.

And it was true that Kathleen wanted to be like a white woman; to have rights, and respect. She dressed as well as she was able to for the long walk to the water trough.

Someone might see her leaving her hut with a makeshift bucket in each arm, and they'd sing out.

'Hey, look at this white woman coming along this way.'

And Kathleen would say, 'Don't be silly.'

'Well, true. True, sister, we thought you was a white woman coming down to visit us boys.' And they'd laugh and laugh.

Kathleen and Jack's hut had an earth floor. Kathleen would wet it, stamp it down, make it just about shine, and sweep and sweep and sweep it with a ti-tree broom just like everybody in the camp used.

She dug out some little grasstrees, young ones, and stuck them in the ground to make seats around her table. She fashioned cushions from scraps of hessian stuffed with grass and leaves.

Jack read old newspapers he had collected, and — in the very act of doing so — dispelled and disproved what those very same papers said about him and his people. But it was hard for him to be aware of this, and it was a lonely battle because he felt as if the print was a wall advancing at him, pushing him further and further away.

A Menace in our Midst: the Aborigines Camp in our Town.

It was very hard to get past such a headline. Such words made it hard to even remember how to read.

Kathleen made trip after trip to the water trough, preferring to do so on her own. She would look out for others returning, and then head off. It would be best of all, she thought, to fetch water after dark, but there was the curfew.

She read the labels on bottles, tins, old magazines. She and Jack tired of reading old newspapers they'd retrieved from bins, or snatched from the wind blowing through the camp.

Kathleen stripped the bark from trees and burned it to a fine ash which, once cooled, she rubbed on her knives, forks, spoons, her pot and pan, until they shone like mirrors, almost.

Like mirrors.

Separately, neither speaking of it to the other, Jack Chatalong and Kathleen Scat would face their gloomy and distorted reflections. They considered their noses, lips, skin, wondered at the lesser brain capacity — according to what they read — allowed by their skulls. I also have studied my features in the mirror, searching for resemblances to my own people and, growing increasingly bitter at my grandfather's apparent success, I have wondered what else has been taken away, and what remains.

Jack found he could earn a bit trapping rabbits. It led him away, sometimes for days at a time.

Kathleen began to collect water at night, curfew or not. It was a long, mad walk.

So mad, in fact so mad that when you felt a hand on your shoulder as you leant on the trough you might think that, well, you had it coming. It was your own fault. The man wore a uniform like Sergeant Hall had, and if he even looked like Sergeant Hall, this man leading you into a cell, unbuckling his belt? Well, maybe that was the way it had to be for us, the same thing happening over and over again.

Kathleen had kept to herself so much that it was days before it was confirmed that she was missing.

I followed a trail of old Aborigines Department papers; Mogumber, domestic service, a number of children taken away from her. Like Fanny, like Dinah and Harriette, like Topsy and like even my own mother, Kathleen exits this story too quickly. You wonder how we can continue.

Jack felt that way, too, when he returned. How to continue. He went to the police. Dunno, they said. Oh yeah, they'd found her in the street. She was scrubbing the water trough. They'd sent her away, she was crazy. Some nervous trouble the doctor had said. He might be able to get permission to see her.

Jack arrived back at the reserve a considerable distance behind the sound of his very own voice. They were all useless, he was shouting, a dirty bunch of no-hopers, who didn't even try to stop them and one of them had dobbed in Kath out of jealousy. If he found the one did that …

So it was just another fight, and Uncle Jack ended up pretty sore, in his house of kero tins and old bags with tree-stumps for chairs. Looking into the mirror of a spoon, looking back at himself. Thinking, a menace in his very own midst.

heartbeats in the grass

Within the dunes, the scent of salt and the only peppermint leaves of our country, there you can sleep. You hear the many heartbeats among the rippling grasses, the many whispering voices, and your own is somewhere among them.

Harriette's camp.

'Oh, people pass through you know, sometimes.'

And, 'If you would be quiet and stay still enough, relax, they are still here you know.'

Jack wasn't so sure.

'Topsy,' said Harriette, 'should be with us here now. All of us should be, even that Ern if he could remember who he is, who we are.'

They lived easily. Jack loaded the old cart with rabbits, swapped things, sold skins and carcasses where he could. Harriette might go into Gebalup on the horse. She tied it up and walked through neglected streets. The wind skipped and spun on vacant blocks, slapped at the houses shedding iron warping boards. Some of the buildings leaned, and fell to the ground very slowly, one corner at a time, as if dropping to their knees first.

That new policeman never challenged her.

my sandy heart

The old men talked to me, or at least the two of them did. We propped Ern up in the shade, and he listened; he was forced to, really, and even though he must have wanted to have his say, we could make no sense of his groaning and spitting, his gnashing of teeth. Uncle Will and Uncle Jack suggested this or that. Occasionally, one of them took up a tool himself. But really, they saw it as my initiative, and my job. Under their erratic and shifting direction I repaired the roof, and re-mortared the walls although quite often, when, say, the gaps between the stones provided an interesting pattern of light, or fluted the air in a pleasing way we left the walls as I had altered them.

'When Uncle Sandy died ...' and here Uncle Will digressed, by way of characterisation, you might say. 'He was your great-grandmother's brother, and he was born at Dubitj River, and went to the world war and was going to marry a white woman, but ... I ran away to live with him. I went all that way to live with him.' Uncle Will was leaning against one internal wall, and the sun shone through the roof and between the stones of the wall so that he sat among grids and planes of light. He looked across at Ern, who we had propped in a corner, but I knew he was not seeing my grandfather ...

'Uncle Sandy was in the main street, up in a little town among hills. It was a long way from here, he'd got so far away. He had tried to get back to Gebalup but, well, there was always trouble for him. It was hard enough just to get a ticket for a train, let alone get off and walk through some towns. Uncle Sandy was not someone who liked to feel shame, or to have to slink about. So he didn't get out very much when I went to live with him. He was sick, and I suppose, having made a habit of keeping his distance, he had no one to help him. He was trapped.

'He was such a brave man, you know,' said Uncle Will. And it was right in town there, the place he would've least liked, that Sandy Two collapsed. The police came rushing. They were first — maybe they'd even been following the man and his nephew — and it was as if it was a big joke for them. Someone walking past tut-tutted, muttered, 'Take him to a cell to sleep it off.'

Uncle Will was on his knees beside Uncle Sandy who was fast becoming a corpse, and the police were standing around talking to passers-by. Uncle Will told them off, shouting at them even from down on his knees like that.

'I was just a boy, really, you know,' muttered Uncle Will, shaking his head. And then, surprising me, he suddenly said, 'I hate myself, know that?' The thought seemed to come from nowhere. 'I hate myself. I should have been like that more often, more angry.'

We both looked at Ern, toppling very slowly to one side, as if in an extreme slow motion. We caught him before he fell, and stuffed him in a chair to keep him upright.

'Should have been more like him maybe.' Uncle Will indicated Ern. 'Have things to aim at. Something. But, I can't hate him, even knowing what he's done. I'm too soft.'

Will said he watched them drag Uncle Sandy away, drag the body away. Will remembered the soles of Uncle Sandy's shoes, how each had a hole in it, and together they reminded him of a pair of eyes, staring at him as they retreated.

Then Will got up and bolted.

He came into the post office the next morning, intending to send a telegram to Harriette. He thought, just send it to the post office at Gebalup.

There was a policeman, and he said that Will need not worry about the funeral arrangements, that the Aborigines Department would sort everything all out and had it in hand.

Uncle Will said he wanted to say no, that they did not want the Aborigines Department having anything to do with this funeral whatsoever. But he didn't. He just didn't know.

And he didn't send the telegram because it occurred to him that to do so would be to provide a target for the Aborigines Department to aim at, and that target could be his mother, sisters ...

'What happened, see, is that I have always tried to keep away from Aboriginals because I knew the people would

144

try to bring me under the Aborigines Act. And they took your children, hunted you down, moved you for no reason.

'I didn't want any "assistance" from them. All I wanted was for them to leave me alone, and to be free of them.

'It has made me very lonely, all my life.'

I felt reassured somehow, hearing him say this, looking at him ... Of course we feel very lonely. Look at us, stuck out in the sky like branches from which the rest of the tree has been cut and carted away.

So, for a time we were all working on that old house. The two old men told me I was doing fine, and what I should do next. I don't believe their hearts were in it, just then, but they encouraged me for my own sake, I suppose. They thought I seemed interested in the job.

In fact, I felt very insecure. I didn't know who to trust. After all, I remembered what my father had told me of Uncle Will, how he had kept right away from even his own mother.

I knew that I had been uplifted. I knew I'd been ill. But what about these old men, how did they see themselves, how did they see me? And how could they be so, so ... So kind to Ern. So kind. They knew how he was, surely. I could not bring myself to tell them what I knew about him.

So what was it made me, with a mortar in one hand and a small trowel in the other, tremble so? I hoped it was only fatigue.

I kept telling myself that I had been given another chance, and that I too had to seize every opportunity. The way it was, I had nothing. This place still seemed strange to me. My grandfather had reassured me, told me he knew me, told me my place. I knew, already, the bullshit of that.

He'd be all right. He was comfortable enough. Plenty to drink. Books. Radio. He was gunna die soon.

But what about those other two old fellas? And me?

From up on the verandah I could see the sea. I saw the swell rippling right to left on the horizon, continuing its way around the planet. Closer in I saw how the headland to my right caught it, and swung it around to break on the island.

Each time I turned from the slow, irregular, and fragmentary exposure of the wall's rigid pattern of blocks, I would see a white blossom appear at the right-hand tip of the island, as if from that thin line where sea met sky met land. All day, blooming and dying, blooming and dying.

I turned to it more and more often, eventually letting my tools fall and resigning myself to the rise and fall of that distant rhythm. I was thinking of what I was learning about my family.

I was feeling light-headed, of course, and so made a little commentary of what I was doing, and what I intended doing, and that seemed to settle me. But as I turned the corner of the house a gust of wind blew me against the wall. My head bumped the eaves, and then I was beside the roof and heading ... well, further up. Who knows where?

The cuff of my trousers caught on the guttering, and there I was; uplifted and spread out to the wind, which whistled through me, and in and out of orifices, singing some spiteful tune.

I could not concentrate on any sort of story, no narrative. My trousers ripped a little more.

Desperately I tried to get some words flowing through my head. Fuck fuck fuck fuck fuck I gotta I gotta gotta I must must must I will will will oh will will Uncle Will what he had said and my father and what I guessed, remembered, imagined?

I got a hand to the guttering.

I was worried that someone might see. An embarrassment, such an abuse of reason. I was a freak.

I worked my way, hand over hand, around the guttering to the other side of the house where I found some shelter, from the wind at least. In relative quiet, and safe from such a buffeting I began to ease myself to the ground.

But suddenly, there I was again, spread out against the sky like a banner.

Uncle Will came hobbling as fast as he was able in response to my cries for help. He stiffly ascended the ladder, reached out his hand ...

And then he was suddenly up in the air with me, with the guttering in one hand, and a kite-like me in the other.

Uncle Jack's turn. And for some reason, which I could not comprehend at the time, he was able to get hold of Will, and was both weighty and strong enough to pull the two of us in like spent fish.

Will's eyes were wide. 'I thought that had all stopped,' he said. 'It's a long time since I ...'

They suggested I remain inside the house.

'You can write? That helps?' They looked at one another quizzically. I would have to return to writing. It apparently helped knot and tie me down. Even now, writing, my hands stay easily at the keyboard and I loop my legs to settle in the chair.

If I am to be so light, well, so be it. But let me at least learn how to adopt a certain weightiness of manner, and not always approach things with levity.

I am serious when I complain of the time it took to develop these small calluses on the tops of my toes so I might hook them under the sill and hover at the window, watching that island and how the sun and the wind shifts, and the sea's coat changes.

I remained there, throbbing.

I had listened to my grandfather roar.

Now it was the voices of these other two old men, and Uncle Jack, tapping me on the chest (as, more and more, others would later do). 'You feel it in your heart? Say it like you feel it.'

in white and black

The central clause in the 1936 Act was the definition of persons to be deemed 'natives' within the meaning of the Act. It embraced a wide range of Aborigines of part descent in the south who had been exempt from the 1905 Act. Briefly, it included all persons of the full and part descent, regardless of their lifestyle, with the following exceptions: all 'quadroons' over the age of twenty-one unless classified as 'native' by special magisterial order ... and persons of less than 'quadroon' descent born before 31 January 1936. They were prohibited by law from associating with 'natives' regardless of the nature of their relationship.
Proclaimed April 27 1937
(Haebich, 1988, p 349)

It was Ern's ambition to have the first white man in the family line. And he was almost quickly successful, because Topsy gave birth on 30 January 1936 to a child, Ellen. Unfortunately, from Ern's point of view, Ellen — though *legally* white, was not a male. Consequently, Ern

149

— a stickler for detail, and a very rigorous man — felt somewhat cheated. And to Ern's mind, my father, born a couple of years later, would never have the unequivocal legal status of a white man, even if Ern could control how he was raised, who he associated with, what he thought and might become ...

The 1936 legislation was the result of yet another Royal Commission, and Ern had followed the reports closely, nodding sagely as he read of Chief Protector Neville and others expounding their views on The Native Problem and its Solution.

There was a problem, experts agreed, with those people of Aboriginal descent who *are half-castes in blood, but who claim they do not come under the Act, yet they consort with the natives. They run with the hares, and hunt with the hounds and no one can stop them ... Time after time, knowing we have no legal power in the matter, we take action because we know it to be absolutely necessary.*

These words could almost have been Ern's own, and although he had agreed that it would be best that the new legislation applied to all people of Aboriginal descent — no matter to what degree, or what their lifestyle — he nevertheless was disappointed.

He needed a son.

No one need ever know how the law defined his future son. And there were other ways for him to continue his good work.

As it turned out his son, my father, Tommy had only been born a matter of months when Ern was distracted from his grand plans by a world war, and went off to defend his home country.

Tommy was a healthy baby, but the girl, Ellen, had become a disturbingly pale and sickly child.

some tiny inlet

Soldiers came limping back throughout the war years, and Will Coolman came limping back to Gebalup and Wirlup Haven with some companions. His friends were not Nyoongars. Once again, they were men who were a bit dead inside. They flirted with Topsy, when she and her children went to Harriette's camp outside of Wirlup Haven. Watching from the jetty there you would see them walking along the beach from town, and then quite suddenly disappear.

Tommy had only just started walking.

Harriette continued to tell her old story of what the cry of the curlews meant. Remember, she would say, hold yourself proud. You are as good as anyone, better.

Two Nyoongar women, and sometimes a third or fourth who had made their way to visit Harriette, once again welcomed even these maimed men; one with a leg missing, another an arm, most with an absence of love or sense.

In the mornings the women fished from the reef, the shore, the jetty. The kids crushed and scattered shellfish for bait. Sometimes the shellfish were the tucker; abalone, mussels, periwinkles plucked from the rocks and prised, with a pin, from their boiled black shells.

The kids glistened with the sun and the ocean. Some were always dark-skinned; some — like the toddler Tommy and his sister, Ellen — merely had, um ... a propensity to tan. They all swam, had to learn early. One of the cripples grabbed toddler Tommy with a lone arm and threw him from the jetty. Topsy, fully clothed, leapt in and swam him to shore.

The men laughed at her. Observed how her clothes clung.

The men went to the pub in the afternoons. The publican, first time, questioned Will — not for himself, you understand, but because there was a law, and a policeman in Gebalup. There was a law, yes, about Aborigines and drinking. The men bullied him until he relented. But, he told them, the less he knew about those women the better thankyou very much.

They lit a fire around the corner of the beach; sang. There was sherry from the pub.

Three or so free years Topsy spent with her Aunty Harriette. Jack Chatalong — who had no interest in going to such a war — saw more of them, and some of Harriette's long-lost daughters, with their white men also away, came to visit Harriette.

Harriette's camp was among the few peppermint trees behind the dunes around the beach from Wirlup Haven. Tommy swam, walked the reefs, ate of the sea's abundance.

His sister was inclined to cling to their mother.

Watch toddler Tommy and Jack walking around the beach. A small blond boy, the thin man … disappear. A tiny inlet tucked out of the winds, and in among the dunes there was home.

Dolphins waved from the sea. Salmon traced the coast, the wind calmed, the ocean flexed with distant storms.

Topsy moved back to Gebalup when those storms came to stay, because Ern had returned. He trembled, and clenched his jaw more than ever.

hazel eyes!

'They had some good ideas, those Nazis,' Ern said. 'But they went a bit far.'

'You should think yourself lucky,' he told Topsy, after he had asked Harriette not to vist. 'Some towns …' he began, but he did not need to go into the details of how Nyoongars were treated, the power of the legislation.

Tommy had hazel eyes, and Ern — who had not seen the boy since he was a baby — looked into them as if they were desert waterholes from which he could drink. 'My own father had hazel eyes,' he said, as if assured that his own heritage would continue.

Three of them — mother and children — stayed in the house all day.

It's true, it's true I'm sure, thought Ern. You will never know them from white children.

He asked his dear to keep her face powdered when she must go out.

Ern took the children to a photographer. Topsy wore gloves, the powder was thick on her face. She was still very young, very thin, and moved with the precise steps of a bird.

'Stay in the car,' said Ern. And he carried the children away.

Flash!

Flash!

Ern thanked the photographer, and returned to where Topsy was waiting.

He handed her the children. 'I'll be back,' and walked briskly away.

The photographer looked up, politely querying his customer's return.

'I'd like ... that is, I've seen photographs with the colour in them, like a painting. Can you do that?'

'Certainly sir. I can colour them, subtly, with a brush.'

The photographer showed Ern some examples.

'You see, said the photographer, 'the cheeks, the eyes, the hair and clothing. But, I'm afraid. It would be helpful if you could bring the children so that I may take some notes. It's busy today, and I've had several children already. My memory ...'

'The boy has hazel eyes, you would've noticed. Their hair is fair. Rather like that.'

Ern pointed at one of the photographs.

'Rosy cheeks?' the photographer queried, sizing up the situation.

'Yes, a lovely effect.' The photographer complimented Ern's taste.

'Lovely children. Very like you in looks, sir, if I may put my opinion. And the clothing, sir?'

'The boy in blue, of course. The girl, in pink, or perhaps in white, her ribbon was pink.'

The photographs sat proudly upon the small mantelpiece. The children, playing with their warmly laughing mother in the gloomy house, liked to look at them. They wanted to share their father's excitement. This was who they were, he said. What they had become.

In fact, it was what Ellen remained. In the few weeks since the photographs had arrived she had sickened, and been put to bed. The doctor could not provide a confident diagnosis, and suggested hot and cold baths, various medicines and unguents, compresses and vapours. When she suddenly died he was astounded.

At least, thought Ern, it was not my son, not the boy.

The boy that was saved to beget me. The hazel eyes which I closed for the very last time.

mirrors

Our policy is to send them out into the white community, and if the girl comes back pregnant our rule is to keep her for two years. The child is then taken away from the mother and sometimes never sees her again. Thus these children grow up as whites, knowing nothing of their environment. At the expiration of the period of two years the mother goes back into service. So that it really doesn't matter if she has half a dozen children.

(A O Neville)

Yet again I stood in a doorway, listening, trying to understand.

Or rather, what I mean to say is that the child, my father, Tommy Scat, stood in the doorway and listened to Ern dealing with Topsy, his mother.

At Tommy's back the maid moved through the house; sweeping, billowing sheets, patting pillows. His mother usually moved with them, but right now Ern was shouting into her face.

Ern poured bleach into the hot water, placed his hand on the top of Topsy's head and pushed her under. Her glistening belly stood out from the water like an island, and little rivulets ran down it.

Tommy knew that Ern liked to hug all the maids, to help them pat the pillows and turn back the blankets. Every so often, Ern took a maid to the railway station and changed her for another one.

Grim Ern, tight-lipped and frowning. Ern at his books, in his shed, Ern drinking in the evenings, Ern's footsteps going to the enclosed part of the verandah where the newest maid slept.

Could Ern possibly have believed that his was a selfless task? That he did not think of himself, or if he did it was only insofar as he was helping these other people become more like himself? He wanted to remake us in his own image, uplifting us to that.

So many of us have considered ourselves in my grandfather's various mirrors, trying to see what Ern and his others see. Perhaps Harriette also, since she could read and write, but perhaps never enough to become contaminated by it.

Yes, reading about ourselves can be just like looking in such a mirror.

The mirror, that mirror mirror ...

Who's the fairest of them all? Well, it was me. Obviously. Though my father, Tommy, was fair also. Ern discarded all the others. And only he and I remained to see, with appropriate rigour, his experiment through to the end.

But could I trust any mirror?

Floating through the house towards the room with its window and mirror, I revised my work so far. How heavy I was with words, with notes quotations journals year-books newspaper cuttings archives scribbles. The squeezings from my grandfather's hand. How burdened I felt with all this, and yet I drifted and floated.

And now Uncle Will and Uncle Jack were back, talking again.

I had studied the mirror, familiarised myself with the selves revealed there, and seen myself teasingly revealed as I descended, feet first. I have seen my feet as prehensile. I have seen a foot nuzzling its partner's ankle, and my body weight balanced on a single stem like some wading bird frozen with concentration.

I saw how I shimmered, just like the aliens do on the television, and although a variety of images were shown, they were all of a kind.

I turned away, turned away from the mirror. I turned my back, showed my black hole, that last aureole of my colour, my black insides. To think this lured grandfather! I had repeatedly taken him inside me, in different ways, and it was always easy, like a joke, but it terrified him now because he understood what it meant that he shrivelled while he remained there.

My births took longer, were different; not something he could discard and forget. I gave birth to all these words; these boasts. Grandfather, they spew you out. Me and you both, transformed too.

You see, some things insist. Some things persist. Your plan needed more than a few generations.

But then, I know in some cases it succeeded, within my very own blood line.

It is hard to know what to think.

Ern's mentor wrote:

> *Their thought processes must necessarily be in English*
> *where their own tongue is forgotten, and as their English*
> *is restricted their thinking lacks cohesion, is slow and*
> *often leads to incorrect assumptions … He must not be*
> *rushed, he is not a quick thinker, and you on your part*
> *must seek to find out what he really wants, which is*
> *often very difficult.*

Did Ern return to such words when I cut and made him sting? When I poked and prodded him in return?

We were lucky, both of us, that my uncles returned.

I am not the only one to have used a mirror.

Uncle Jack told me how he used to have one hung up in the boughshed he and Harriette shared among the peppermint trees, not long after the war years. He told me he even used to pinch his nostrils together. He would wet his hair, and flatten it with the palm of his hand.

In that mirror he could see the blue sky, a few leaves. And that mirror was like a pool amongst the rough bark. You sometimes saw a bird, a shadow. For a short time during the day it blazed white fire from the sun.

As a young man he used to study his face, look for someone else looking back at him.

When he went out setting his traps there was a place where, close to sunset, he could see the mirror winking at him.

Topsy used Ern's mirror, just as Kathleen had. It was patchy, and so their faces were incomplete. There were flecks and spots, and there were pieces of themselves missing, and yet each believed that it showed how others saw her. There were increasing areas of blackness, more pieces missing and making her invisible.

I studied myself, looking for Ern or Will or Tommy or any family. I was looking for a likeness to Harriette, whose photograph I had. I held my gaze. I tried turning away, turning back, as if in surprise, to see what I looked like when caught unawares.

I looked for ancestors in the mirror. I posed with Grandad's artefacts. And when Uncle Jack walked in on me I looked at him in the mirror, looked at myself, and tried to hold my expression as it was. That look of surprise.

'You need to throw that away,' he said. 'You know, a mirror — or even if it's water — a mamari, a little devil man, he sees himself in it, that'll stop him. Make him think too much, dance around, not know what to do. It's not that different for some of us.'

we move ...

I had a new game. I had never been one for games, but I was unusually thrilled, I was giggling like a child with the pleasure it gave me to share this one with Uncle Will. I could see, even within the composure and dignity he liked to feign, that it startled and excited him.

At the same time — and this helped his appearance of composure — he was I think stunned, and in awe of such freedom.

Previously I had performed it solely for the pleasure of seeing the terror, and — later — the *indignation* it aroused in Ern.

I simply indulged in my propensity to drift. In the mornings I would attach strong fishing line to a reel on my belt, anchor one end of it to the house and, stepping out the door, simply let the land breeze take me. I rose and fell on currents of air like a balloon, like a wind-borne seed. The horizon moved away so that the islands no longer rested on its line, but stood within the sea, and it seemed that the pulsing white at the island's tip was not a mere transformation induced by collision, but was a blossoming and wilting at some fissure where sea met land.

It was indeed a very long time after this — but it may have begun here — that I realised that I had come back from the dead, was one of those few. I may well be djanak, or djangha — so much so that I stumble at what is the correct dialect, let alone how I should spell it — but even then I had not completely forgotten who I am. I floated among the clouds, and even with a bleached skin, and an addled memory I nevertheless saw the imprint of the wind upon the turquoise ocean. I remembered the call of quails in the dune grasses, and thought of curlews crying from moonlit chalky paths, and the footprint such a bird would leave.

It was as if sunlight told me of the sameness of granite and sand, and — in the evenings — flickering firelight fed the fire of my life, of my breathing.

But I was telling of when Uncle Will and Uncle Jack had returned for me, and of when I was accustoming myself to this experience of drifting. I studied the pathways and tracks which ran along the coastal dunes, and saw the white beach as the sandy, solidified froth of small waves touching the coast. I noted how rocks and reef and weed lurked beneath the water's surface, and saw the tiny town of Wirlup Haven and how Grandad's historic homestead — as if shunned — clung to a road which was sealed and heading inland.

So it was not purely mindless, this floating on the breeze. It required a certain concentration, and I chose it not just for the fun, but also because I wanted to view those islands resting in the sea, and to get that aerial perspective. I couldn't have said why.

The wind ruffled my hair as I rode its currents toward the islands. At first I worried when I saw boats or any sign of human life marking land or sea, but such sightings were rare along that isolated stretch of coastline and, after a time, I realised that I could not be seen at all, except by my family.

Grandad used to stare in shock. It scared him. I loved that.

Uncle Will said he envied my unburdened existence. More pragmatically, he suggested I take another line, and try fishing as I drifted across the ocean.

I liked it best when the breezes were soft, and I watched whales, dolphins, the schools of salmon moving below me. Late in the day the breeze blew me back to the house.

The very first time he found me so tiny and out of earshot in the sky, Uncle Jack hauled me in like some sort of airborne fish. A sharp tug upended me, and then I was bent double, my limbs flapping with the force of such a retrieval into the land breeze.

'Shit, you made a mess of the line,' I said.

He snorted. 'You fuckin' silly little shit. What? You kartwarra, that it? You're something special, you know.' He was insistent and angry. 'I tell you you gotta go right back, you got something special there coming out. I can see where you come from all right. You oughta give away that reading and all those papers for a while.'

He wanted to take *all* of us?

Uncle Jack wanted to take us all driving. He wanted to

show me some places. We could drive, and camp. We'd take Ern with us.

'Will?'

Uncle Will nodded.

Uncle Jack reckoned that the main roads more or less followed traditional runs; along the coast to where his Aunty Harriette had been born. The roads went inland from there, up to Norseton, and back to here. It's the waterholes, see. They used to follow the waterholes.

Rain still falls, water still gathers.

'Bring your papers with you if you like,' he said. 'Do all that. You can even fly yourself high as a kite, if you like, if you still wanna. No matter.'

'The main roads follow a traditional run,' he had said. 'And, you know, we showed all those white blokes.' He looked at Uncle Will. 'Your father, he was shown by your mother, and her mother. And there you were wanting to be a pioneer.'

It disturbs my clumsy narrative even more, of course, this sudden and contemporary journey. It disturbed me at the time also. I was scared, but seeing the reluctance in Ern's face convinced me it was the thing to do.

We drove for the afternoon, humming along the sealed road. A 'run', I kept thinking; we once walked where now we skim? The wind roared outside our small and stuffy capsule.

I remembered the little Uncle Will had written — it was not much more than notes scattered among Ern's well-organised papers. It was all about his father, as, perhaps, is my own.

Uncle Will had begun a little history of this region, and of his family. His motivation was the publication of a little booklet, a feeble local history, to which he had taken exception. He had written:

> We may see how greatly facts are distorted and these people are most misleading in their trying to put the arrival of their parents in the new field before many others, for the sake of being known as descendants of the first pioneers.

It was incomprehensible to me: Uncle Will, who had been refused 'Susso' in the Depression and told, instead, to go to the Aborigines Department for rations; Uncle Will, who had barely escaped being sent to a Mission or Native Settlement. Uncle Will desperately wanted to name his father as among the very first to 'settle' at Gebalup, and he scarcely wrote of his mother. Yet it was she who gave him his rights to be here.

He was of 'the first'.

I thought of how Uncle Will walked. Proudly, cautiously; like one provisionally uplifted, whose toes barely gripped the earth.

Grandad had written very little, yet he had organised and collected an array of material. Uncle Will had written a few pages from memory, and that was all he had. But I saw the evasion, the desire to compete and to say he was as good as anyone and that this seemed the only way possible. In his rather formal, affected language, there was this hint of an alternative:

> Can you understand, dear people, why I'm rather diffident about discussing the early history of Gebalup as I knew it as a boy? The descendants have given their forebears images which they wish to see and present to the public in

their most favourable light. It would be a continual source
of acrimony were I to join in their discussions. So I think
it much better for me to write all my thoughts down for
the perusal and study of my younger relatives.

But then he'd faltered, and after a few hundred words
had stopped.

My father had written nothing, and had just begun to
speak to me when I killed him. Uncle Will was family, my
father had said. Even your grandfather. That's all you've
got, your family. Even if, sometimes, it hurts to have them.

Of course, this was not in any of the material I had read
to my grandfather, the so-close-to-smug-in-his-victory
Ernest Solomon Scat.

We camped close to Uncle Will's birthplace on our first
night away. It was among ancient sea dunes, and nearby,
behind a fence, there was a dam which, Uncle Will
informed us, collected fresh water from a small spring.

The four of us sat around the campfire, sipping beer. It
was a cold night and I was clumsy with the vast bulk of
my clothing. I had wrapped a long scarf several times
around both myself and a log, partly for the warmth, but
also because, as Uncle Jack reminded me, drinking grog
inevitably set me drifting off 'something cruel'.

'Somewhere here, eh? I was born somewhere around
here,' said Uncle Will, suddenly.

'It was a hot day,' he said. We allowed him the
authority to tell us of his birth. We assumed the story had
been handed to him and not that he was possessed of a
most remarkable memory.

When Uncle Will was born the sides of the tent had been lifted and tied to catch any movement of the air.

Fanny and old Sandy One arrived at the camp, and then Sandy One went to find the other men and left the three women to attend to the birth.

What other men? *Three* women?

Uncle Will and Uncle Jack had to explain to me who all these people were. Be patient, have patience, their sighs said.

Harriette and Daniel? I knew about them, Will's parents. Daniel Coolman of the missing lip and great bulk who was sown in a mine. Harriette, a shadowy but already powerful figure in my little history.

Dinah and Pat? I didn't know them. Uncle Pat, they told me, was Daniel's twin brother. Dinah was Harriette's sister. Aunty Dinah was the other daughter of Fanny and Sandy One Mason.

I worried, as any reader must also do, at this late and sudden introduction of characters. Except that for me it was not characters, but family.

'Yeah, well, there's lots all of us don't know,' said one of the old men.

And then it was definitely Uncle Jack who spoke. 'It's hard to know where to begin — except with each place we come to, really. Where we are right now.'

It was hot, back then, by the tiny pool, here; the heat snapped twigs from the trees, and they bounced off the heavy canvas roof of the tent. Fanny and Dinah murmured to Harriette.

Deep and rasping breaths. The soak's water is still. Campfire smoke grows straight to the sky. The women's breath is very warm, and there is so much moisture, all this liquid pooling beneath the trees.

The place's spirit continued to billow. Fanny felt so grateful.

As the wet child took its first breath they heard the leaves above them clacking and rustling. Will was rolled in white sand.

'This sand is so fine,' Uncle Will said, looking into our faces and letting it run through his fingers, 'it's like talcum powder.'

When Daniel took the child in his arms the women could not help but smile, he so thick and burnt and gnarled and the baby just a bundled heartbeat, mewing and clutching.

Daniel was happy. 'Now, this is the first white man born here. No doubt about that.'

Uncle Jack was smiling at Uncle Will, teasing him.

So where was Uncle Jack born?

He said he'd tell me that later. When we got back to the other side of Wirlup Haven. He hadn't been lucky enough to know his parents like Will had.

Harriette, Daniel, Dinah and Pat had come across from Dubitj Creek way (as you can imagine, I spent a lot of time consulting a map as we drove), where they had been carting goods to the goldfields. There's water all through there, the old men told me, and it was true that my map showed many small and temporary waterholes to which the main road clung. But a new railway line from the capital city had depleted the need for teamsters, and there was various troubles to get away from.

They tried roo shooting which — in those days — gave

them enough cash for what they needed.

The truth is, the Coolman twins were happy. It was a decent life. Moving slow; hunting, drinking. There was always the chance of gold. They had wives who knew the country; who found water, food, a place to camp. The women could do everything. They could work like men, feed off the land, embrace their men and make them strong. And Sandy One Mason, their father-in-law, that enigmatic fellow they laughed at between themselves, was known by people all around this way; pastoralists, old miners, carriers, all of which could prove helpful when and if they needed to get work again.

There was no fear of attack, as was prevalent with some travellers. When the Premier Man John Forrest had come this way less than thirty years before, he and his party had kept a rostered watch each night. A publication of 1900, *In Darkest Western Australia*, devotes several pages to the threat of attack by the *blacks*. But when Daniel and Pat met any who were not like themselves they stood close behind the women. It was what Sandy One had advised them. Their faces would echo the expressions of those speaking this peculiar language, as they half-listened and tried to understand.

They gathered kangaroo skins. Or rather, the women gathered them. A trip back to Kylie Bay every few months meant they were making money. Do you wish to hear how they suffered; of their endurance, hardship, deprivation? In fact it was almost too easy a life. It was practically a relief to run out of grog and so they purposely deprived themselves, brought less of it with them — and even that they sipped with their wives.

They moved between the coast and the goldfields; between the old and the new telegraph lines; between the railway to the north and the ocean to the south. Finding where they could take a heavy cart. And, always, there might be gold.

Drinking. Fucking. They wandered, following gossip and getting Harriette and her sister Dinah to take them as far as the goldfields, where they thought they saw their women's people slumped in the dust, rotting from the inside out. The women brought them back, always, to no further than a day or two from the ocean.

No gold. Then suddenly you needed a license to sell roo skins. They found themselves 'Gebalup' way, near the outer limit of the women's country, and fell in with the Mustle and Done families. The *landed gentry* of this story.

The four of us sat around the fire until late in the night. Perhaps it was the beer, but I felt very heavy, as if burdened. Old people surrounded me.

'Listen to the voices in the trees,' said Uncle Jack.

In the firelight the three men looked exceptionally old, ancient beyond their years. Grandad's face glistened with the tears which now so often came to him. Uncle Jack and Uncle Will's arrival had given him some protection from me, and I had not harmed him for months.

The intervals between Grandad toppling, and being propped up again, grew longer. The eyes of my uncles reflected the fire. I remember noticing my own hands, and being frightened at how old they looked in that light.

'Daniel was my father,' said Uncle Will.

'Our mothers, Harriette and Dinah were sisters,' said Uncle Jack, 'and Patrick might have been my father,' he continued, 'but probably not.' The two men looked at one another, hesitated. 'The Coolman brothers mined with the

Dones and Mustles, even took a contract building the rabbit-proof fence with some of them. They shared a contract hauling goods between Gebalup and Wirlup Haven.'

'They worked with the Mustles and Dones,' Uncle Jack went on, 'and this is a very hard thing for us to understand, and forgive. A very hard thing for us to accept.'

'No doubt about it, they were partners with the killers all right. But I dunno that they helped with the killing, that was long before they got here.'

The words were coming out — Uncle Jack had started it — but I could see that Will knew the story too. Grandad fell over yet again, groaning as he did so, and this time Uncle Jack — without seeming to take his eyes from the fire — reached across and absently pushed him back into a sitting position.

Did those two Coolman ancestors help toss the bodies, haul the timber, burn it all? See the limbs crooked and dangling in firelight, the limbs akin to our own but lifeless?

No, of course not. All that was years before, at the Done's station. Harriette was only a tiny child.

'Sandy One and Fanny were our grandparents,' said Uncle Jack, waving his thumb to and fro between Will and himself — 'and that is going no time back, not really.'

They were to take supplies back to the new lease at Dubitj Creek, and had almost finished loading. Sandy One left Fanny and their child, Harriette, and went to the stables.

Fanny glanced about, thinking of how the women she knew had got away at sunrise, and how these Dones had no respect for who they took, or how they treated them. Such thoughts left her, suddenly, when she saw an old man at the woodheap. He must've been lying there the whole time, in the sun, among the timber, and had only now raised his head. Less than a dog, he had no bowl of water, and a chain was looped around his throat. Like Fanny he would have been able to look down the slope of paddock to the bigger trees where the creek ran, and that strange outcrop of rock.

Little mounds of earth showed where he'd covered his shit.

Fanny and the old man knew one another. Perhaps he called to her.

Fanny saw all the ropes in the stables where the women had been tied, and one of the men — either a Done, a Mustle, or Moore — working at a grindstone with his back to her. She studied his vulnerability, and retreated. She stepped over more ropes on the verandah, and into the gloomy house. The air was stale, and she pulled the child closer to her breast as she crossed the cold stone floor. An even darker room, and the smell of gunpowder. Another, a bedroom, but nothing like keys nearby.

Back to the kitchen. Above the fire, a shelf.

The keys were heavy, and jangled their malice. The child grabbed them, and Fanny — holding the child's hand in her own to keep the keys silent — slipped back into daylight. The house was like a deep cave which faces away from the sun.

Fanny unchained the old man, and he embraced Fanny and the child as one. Then, indicating that she must return the keys to the house, he moved toward the stables.

Fanny heard the scream as she placed the keys back on

the shelf. It was a scream which froze everything, and it seemed a very long wait before that moment moved onto the next and she was able to rush outside and see an agitated Sandy One at the wagon.

Their eyes met across the space between them, and they turned together to see the old man Fanny had released hurrying away from the shed. The old man glanced across at Fanny, and then at Sandy standing with the horses. Although he held the axe in only one hand, he did not wave but simply veered away and disappeared into the scrub by the creek.

Sandy waved Fanny across to him, and she hid herself and the child among the wagon's load. Sandy continued to fuss at the horses and Fanny listened. The voice of one of the Mustle brothers called out to Sandy, who pulled up the horses. 'Nah,' said Sandy One Mason. 'Didn't see anything. Nah, haven't heard nothing.'

Fanny heard other men arrive, rush away again.

The wagon creaked and shifted. Not far from the homestead Fanny — cautiously peering from the load, peeking over bales — saw a small group of men women children, running and falling before station men on horseback.

And suddenly the child, Harriette, had somehow fallen from the wagon, and was stumbling toward the distant violence, calling something in her shrill voice. Sandy One leapt to the ground, and ran after her. He threw her up to Fanny, who once again concealed herself and the child amongst the load on the wagon.

My family left and did not return for many years. It was such a sorry place. Fanny and Sandy One huddled within small campfires, and talked of how the firelight changed the look of them, how it made them appear aged and sacred. Fragile and forever.

And so it was that we — my uncles, my grandfather and I — turned back toward Gebalup the next day and deviated from a humming and stale journey along bitumen roads which, Uncle Will informed me, my father had helped build.

Uncle Jack took us through a neglected farm gate somewhere between the townsites of Wirlup Haven and Gebalup.

'They got a permit,' I said. 'From the police. To kill.' I had seen a reference to police permission for a revenge killing among my grandfather's papers. 'Eighteen, they were allowed to kill eighteen.'

Uncle Jack snorted. 'More than that, they killed just about everyone around here. Most Nyoongars still won't come here, just wind up the windows and drive right through Gebalup.'

Perhaps it is most exciting to gallop and shoot and blast holes in people as they turn and fumble with whatever slight weapon they might carry; to keep the horses stomping and rearing, to turn around and around, to reload and shoot; to think these which the dogs seize and fling about are not humans, these are not men women children.

But it is afterwards that the words come. *Oh, they are not really human. Not like us. We are superior (and here is our proof).*

Forget it.

But there has been such a lot of suffering. Again and again.

The bodies were dragged away from the creek to

prevent contamination and damage to stock. A fire. Maybe heap the bones together.

We stopped the car and walked to an old mine shaft, the construction above it seemingly frozen in the act of falling. Little gullies showed the ground in cross-section. 'I had the bones hidden away in there,' said Uncle Jack, 'for a time.' Large ones, small ones. Skull, hand, the tiny what-names bones of a foot. Jack Chatalong did not know the names. Fanny would have, in her own tongue.

There would have been femur, pelvis, tibia, spine, vertebra even, and many funny bones. Is there pleasure to be found anywhere in this pain?

They had all been collected, and placed together among the granite rocks, high where the water would not reach and the sun might bleach them pure. What could be done? Bones white like the skin of the young ones will be, the children flowing from these, the survivors growing paler and paler and maybe dying.

Well, Fanny had collected the bones, and sung here. Uncle Jack sang once again, when he took us there, and Uncle Will muttered some prayer or other.

registering romance

I asked it of my two uncles, even looked to my
grandfather as I did so. 'How come Sandy One and Fanny
registered their children? Why did they marry, that way?
There must have been some others did that.'

'Yeah,' Uncle Jack nodded. 'Some. But that meant
another sort of death, for our ancestors, because some of
us tried to forget about them altogether.' He looked long
at Uncle Will.

'But not me,' I said. 'Anyway, why did Sandy and
Fanny do all this? Did it mean protection?'

'Yes.' Clearly Uncle Will thought so. 'Sandy even sent
the kids to a mission, for a bit.'

Why? For my sake? For your sake. For our sake.

For someone's sake ...

And when I eventually came to write it up, I was still
not sure why I was doing so. Was it for my children? For
me? For all of us? I had thought I was an end, and had

wanted a beginning, but that is to think of it in the wrong way. It is a continuation. It is survival.

Fanny and Sandy One.

Some would call it a romance.

Simple names: Sandy, Fanny.

They followed the telegraph line. It was newly completed. Sandy had come this way on the boats, just before and after he took up with that last mad, whaling venture. He had tossed long posts into the ocean, and left them to float to shore and into the hands of men constructing their own line of communication across the country.

Many of those straight and upright posts were raw and red, the life smell still clinging to them. Looking from beneath, Fanny and Sandy saw how the wire divided the sky, how clouds crossed it, not faltering. Birds rested, then flapped randomly away. Lines such as these carry messages; and they listened to this one sing in the wind.

Sandy wanted to follow it all the way to Frederickstown to register the child's birth. If he registered his child, then it would be murder when they took, used, killed like they did. Because there would be the certificate. It'd be written down, there'd be words saying who there was. Then it couldn't be just for fun, just to feel the power, just to try to make up for being like nearly dead that people were killed. Some people wanted everything for themselves, and if you got in their way …

The boss had smirked at him. Would have said something like, 'What chance, eh? Look at its father, a black mother. Where's it going to live? What sort of education? Send it away, send it away to give it a chance.'

It was a long way to travel. Sandy had only journeyed this far by sea, but had heard the talk of shepherds, prospectors, teamsters. Horses ate the poison, and died along with scores of the sheep. You walked — behind boss horse sheep — across grazed and broken ground, through different kinds of shit. There was never enough water.

The diaries and journals tell me that there was nothing but plains of sand and sharp rolling stones. Impenetrable mallee. Salt lakes, and brackish streams. You ate tinned dog, listened for the croaking of the green canaries, slept at the Star Hotel.

Now, him and Fanny, the child in the wheelbarrow. There were flowers spread across the undulating plains. Pinks, creams, yellow white and blue; delicate little things, looking so fragile, but so hardy, it seemed. The sun did not mark them, nor the wind tear.

The mallee was in flower, brazenly red. In the mornings the wind pushed at their backs, and in the afternoons they felt a breeze on their faces. Or was it that they moved with an effortless speed, gliding along like the soft white clouds?

There were kangaroos all about, keeping an eye out ears up. The animals looked at them and scratched their chests, thinking. Then bounded away with such exuberance.

Fanny and Sandy moved across grassy plains. Sandy thought of all the books he'd read, yet understood that it was people and fire had made this parkland. You could look across, and yeah it was green and soft and undulating; it was what was called hill and dale, with running creeks and tall trees here and there. They were Yate trees, their high crowns glistening in the afternoon sun. And their yellow sap; that yellow sap it tasted like sugar.

There was another tree. Sandy broke off a twig and smelled raspberry jam. Or his senses were deceiving him, his memory muddled.

'Possums like these flowers,' said Fanny, glancing around and high. Her finger traced scratches down a tree trunk and, where they ceased, it was a mere possum's leap to the ground. No possums here today but. Sandy ate the flowers.

Black cockatoos kept rising from trees, screaming and calling as they spiralled up. Their black feathers, the white-tipped ones at the tail, might have fallen down about the couple, soft and congratulatory. A celebration.

There were more and more peppermint trees, and growing closest to the coast and near deep creeks, variations of the banksia they knew.

Fanny ripped flowerstalks from the banksia. The flowers were golden, tiny and ticklish, and she put them into Sandy's mouth. She penetrated him with golden-downed stalks and he sucked at the honey he tasted there.

Fanny led him into green rushes and they pushed and parted the close and sharp-edged green, their feet feeling the water long before it created the sudden space before them. They drank, and whenever Sandy — in the long future before him — remembered this his senses became confused. He would see a surface of dark water, and recall the taste of a pool brimming with daytime stars and tiny, pale blossoms.

In fact, the water was crowded. There were green floating creepers, insects, themselves, and the nodding dark heads — ringed with petals — of the tall rushes behind them. And then the occasional rippling of the air showing its breath.

There were leeches, too. Fanny searched for the words. That one-who-sits-on-his-face-and-drinks-blood. It was another part of the world she was returning him to, and he had to smile for it.

He never remembered the midges, hardly noticed them at the time, except that he thought they were the reason for moving on a little further and camping near a stream which fell onto rocks, grumbled a little, and changed its direction.

Sandy spat it back. It was salty. But later in the night, when the face in the sky was at its most distant, Fanny took him to a crevice in the rocks to one side and below where the salt water tumbled. At the bottom of the crevice, there; water, rose from between the rocks, growing like the moon and its beaming. He tasted sweet water from her hands, heard the faint roar of water beneath the ground.

They looked at it again and again throughout the night, and the water at the little spring rose and rose until it became a well. In the morning it had gone.

There was a harbour at the bottom of a muddy street and a cold wind crossed from the hills at its far side, buffeted the stone buildings, ruffled itself over the cobbles, and swept irritably up the street to meet the descending man, woman, wheelbarrow and child. The wind eddied around them, as it had in the dark entrance of each cold building it passed, and lingered a little longer at the church. Perhaps because of the ceremony.

Water was poured over a soft skull, and ink swirled within the grids ruled on thin white paper.

Name: Harriette Mason.

Father: Sandy Mason, Shepherd. Mother: Fanny, An Aboriginal.

It is flamboyant handwriting, yet its bold flourishes do not quite transgress the lines. Names are disposed of. You would think this no place, and that there are no words here, from which to continue.

Harriette. They called the girl Harriette. A good English name.

Fanny, Sandy, the baby Harriette; they headed east, and rather than skirting around the ranges they went through a pass, which led to an old port, where the whalers and sealers used to trade their catch for rum. Sandy knew it from his childhood, shepherding with his own mother and father, and hoped to find work on a boat, and thereby transport them back to Dubitj Creek.

But first they came through the heavy stone bluffs which were defined, dark and sharp, against the soft colours of the early sky. On some of the slopes there were tall trees, on others masses of weathered stone with extrusions of grey-green leaf and a red blooming.

They detoured, climbing, exchanging the child's weight, until they stood surrounded by cloud and what could only be sky. The rock named, you might say, Drizzle-carrier. Fanny stamped her feet on the small flat surface beneath them. Again, there was a spring. It brimmed, water trickling across damp rock and into the mist.

Coming down, emerging, they looked out over the tops of great and ancient trees. Fanny and Sandy called to one another, their voices echoing, again, again. Many times. The child listened, eyes wide mouth open. And so the parents felt compelled to shout pleasant things at one another, because offering, because the voices repeated so.

As they may do still. If only I had the ears, memory …

A tongue to speak.

I remembered my grandfather's words, almost as if they had emerged again in the night, in that bush, around that campfire when the other three of us felt so frail and bitter.

The words which had come clear from among Grandad's spit and bubble, from among his buzz and groan.

'Sandy Mason. He spoke some Nyoongar. Even Daniel did. Not you. Not your dad. So how can you ever ...'

His words cut deep. I had inherited his language, the voices of others, his stories. That history whose descendants write:

There was never any trouble. Never blood spilled, or a
gun raised in anger.

Uncle Jack laughed. 'Don't need guns when you got poisoned flour, poisoned waterholes.'

Even Uncle Will, 'Yeah, that's not right.'

'No.'

'That's what they'd like to think.'

'Yeah. There must've been death everywhere, for us, for Fanny and Sandy.'

I surprised myself, not only with my attempt to be balanced (which is so important when you're up in the air, and — after all — I was always fair), but also with my recollection of Grandad's references. I said that it is sometimes admitted that the pastoralists took up firearms:

They crept to the natives camp deep in the night, gently
raised their weapons and fired an earth-shattering volley
over the heads of the sleeping natives. The natives rose as
one man, and as one demented man they screamed and
fled through the bush with more frightful roars following
them. Their bewildered pet dingoes yelped and ran in a
wide circle — one of them was shot dead to show what
these noisome weapons could do. Some of the terrified
natives in the rear saw the incident and, screaming

again, they left their weapons and ran as fast and far as their slender legs could carry them.

After the shooting, and chuckling like naughty schoolboys, they wandered about the deserted camp and chose the best of the native weapons for their collections! The rest were put on the smouldering fires and left to burn.

Thus all attempts at uprisings were frustrated in such a way as to leave no bitterness but just a quiet sense of mastery on the part of the white man, and a good lesson to the primitive mind.

It was east. East. Where tomorrow may be.

There was a tree, and they saw it from far away, standing tall and alone and casting a long shadow at them. Sandy and Fanny felt that shadow reaching for them first thing each morning after that day, and it would only fall back as they came fully awake, and the sun rose higher, burnt stronger.

They had camels hitched to a cart, but it rained and they would have been better off with horses. The wheels turned with a sucking sound, and the mud filled the space between the wheel spokes.

It was rare rain; and they came to a new day with the moisture still in the air, and the sun before them. Fanny couldn't hear the voices, not over that distance; not over the creaking of the wheels, the slap of the harness and traces, the shuffling of the beasts. The sucking sound, still, of the earth's resentment of turning wheels.

The crack of rifle shots.

There was just that one tree, tall above the tufted scrub which stretched away in all directions. Hanging from it, what seemed assorted shadows. But these were too solid for shadows, and although too heavy for the desert breeze they nonetheless swayed, and shifted, and probably spun on their axis if ever you got close enough to look.

After each new movement, the sound of a rifle shot. There were only a few shooters. My family, the shooters; they stared at one another across a space. Well, you would want to keep a distance, wouldn't you?

Fanny, Sandy One, their tiny children my ancestors, saw several thin columns of smoke as they approached the homestead. Signals. To hear the bosses talk it was as if they were lost in a forest of charred trees which had suddenly popped through the earth's crust. Yeah, they were worried.

'Well, she heard anything then?' a boss asked Sandy One, tossing his head in Fanny's direction. Fanny was untying the load. The boss said there'd been fires on and off for days.

The station *blacks* had told him that the *blacks* were gathering to attack the station. The women he kept were sick with anxiety.

'They're going to kill us,' he said. 'That's the word.' He indicated the people gathered at the woodheap. 'But you can't trust them, any of them, *niggers*.' Sandy held the man's gaze.

The sudden coming to consciousness frightened Sandy One. He was being roughly shaken. The children stirred like larvae. Even in the darkness he could see the liquid of Fanny's wide-open eyes. Again, the staring.

'C'mon, c'mon get away from that *gin* for once. Come with us, we've got you a gun. There's a horse ready.'

It was dark, and cold enough for him to be grateful for the warmth of the horse. There were several men, all on horses, and all with guns.

They rode without speaking. After a time they halted, and one man dismounted and disappeared into the night. He returned, and whispered for them to follow him.

The gun metal was cold against Sandy One's skin. He touched the barrel with his tongue, still tasted its bitter tang as he pressed the rifle against his shoulder. He thought he might fire upward, into the sky. Fanny's words of ancestors — those bright and ferocious stars, isolated yet pulsing still — returned to him. Her warm breath.

Now.

Shots roared in the vast canyon of night the little hollow had suddenly become.

Perhaps the stars had brightened; he could see figures leaping to their feet, helping one another up, running. And there were voices calling, calling. People fell, were shot. Were shot. A woman running at Sandy jerked, and was flung to the ground. In the little space between gunshots there was the sound of running feet, other bodies hitting the ground, screams and shouting. Small voices, too.

Flame and explosions leapt from beyond the outstretched arms of a man beside him. A Winchester, almost the very latest thing. The man bent over bodies, lunging and hacking, faceless in the grim darkness.

'They understand this.'

In the glow of dawn, Sandy at first saw only his own breath, fogging his vision. But as a red stain spread upwards and across the sky the waxen faces of the other riders were bouncing all around him, seemed to be floating above their shadowless bodies. Small trophies of flesh were strung together and dangled from saddles. Sandy's horse slowed. A darker face, beside him. Sandy kicked his horse after the others.

When the wagon passed the tree the next morning, the bodies still hung from the tree. Crows sat on the shoulders. Some dingoes, licking the ground beneath and rearing on their hind legs, stared cheekily at the distant passage of my family.

The shadow of that tree reaches toward us still. Its stain grows larger, darker; is deep in the earth.

Even in darkness, and after, and even when it no longer stains the crusty skin, blood continues to seep down and down to water below. The paths we took have disappeared and been sealed, and yet at the very least we still skim, humming, along the scar tissue.

That is not quite how I told it, then. But my two uncles were staring up at me, open-mouthed. Grandad's eyes were closed.

'How did you do that? How do you know that?'

They shook their heads. The sticks around the glowing heart of the fire looked like thin limbs to me, like Uncle Will's wrist even as he poked and rearranged them. The smoke rose, and I hovered within it, still awkwardly attached to the long scarf which held me to the log.

Uncle Jack came back from having a piss. 'Too much death; of course they were hemmed in by it. But tonight, we talked all the way west, then all the way east. We should stay here for a bit, for our stories. They came back here, anyway, when their children were grown-up. And Will was born, remember?'

We drove back to our house the next day, and it was several days before we set off again. We rarely drove very far at a time, a few hours at the most, and Uncle Jack took us from camping place to camping place. We did this many times before he ever took me to visit my people.

sandy two

We went in among the trees and made a little fire, and smelled the sweet smoke, the salt in the air. We listened to the waves, and the leaves, whispering.

I was thinking how when I was a little boy my father used to come home from his fortnight on the Main Roads. The first morning he was home we'd leave, come out this way.

Uncle Will remembered it from his own childhood, and being here with Sandy Two. 'Uncle Sandy,' he said. 'My mother Harriette's brother.'

'We been here forever, all along this coast. This is our country,' said Uncle Jack, and then, turning to me, 'For your family history, what story do we need next? Who do you wanna hear about?'

'My father, Daniel,' said Uncle Will.

'With all due respect, Will,' Uncle Jack was looking right at him, 'you never mixed that much with blackfellas, eh? Not as a man. Your father, Uncle Daniel, he was almost the same as Ern. No disrespect, you know what I mean.'

Ern was with us, mute as always in his latter days, with that hangdog look he'd developed.

'Even Sandy Two, what would he have told you? There's things that are hard to say.'

'Yeah, but Uncle Sandy, he was some horseman,' Will said. There were things Will wanted to say, he wanted to be positive, he wanted to give praise. 'An athlete; tall and wiry.'

We used to yarn all night, then, me and the three old men. Well, it was Uncle Will and Uncle Jack, in their different ways, and me and Ern listening. Ern must've been learning all the time. I know I was.

As we all relaxed I'd ease myself into the air, and hover like a balloon anchored by a fine line. I was more comfortable that way, but I feared to think what it meant: that I preferred to be let drift, and that it came so naturally to me.

Drifting in the warm smoke, I looked down upon the fire far below me, its shape continually shifting. The moonlight showed paths leading through the dunes, and pale sand glimmering; that fine sand which holds the prints of anything, even a bird which might alight — just touching down, as it were — with one foot.

The sea, like the fire, formed and reformed and out by the island — even at night — there was that blossoming; white, gone, white, gone white gone. Like what? Like ectoplasm, like breathing.

Here.

Here.

Here.

Sometimes the sky lightened so suddenly as the sun appeared out there that I felt as if my skull had opened, been peeled back, and I was gone, merged with that sky.

Of course, a lot was empty vapid yarning. Familiarising ourselves. After all, I had brought them together after a very long time apart. But — this empty yarning — you might call it characterisation.

So, Sandy Two? 'Yeah, he was a horseman,' said Uncle Will. 'He was my hero. Is. Even when he was not much more than a boy he was better with horses than most men.'

The teamsters gathered at Wirlup Haven. Sandy Two accompanied his father, and although just a boy he already worked the animals better than the old man. He had a … a special skill. You could see it best when he was on horseback. His riding was more than the result of his athleticism. It was a measure of his sensitivity; he listened to the horse, and worked with it.

When Mr Alexander Starr landed in Wirlup Haven with two fine buggy horses, and wanted them watered and exercised, he asked at the teamsters' reserve.

It was young Sandy Two's job to drive the mob of team horses out to Done's Swamp, and Starr opined that his horses should go also. They were expensive animals, he said, and he warned Sandy not to ride Maestro; the horse liked to chase kangaroos, and it would take the bit in its teeth and be away.

Sandy, kicking an old Clydesdale along, glanced across at Maestro. The horse pranced, kicked, shook its mane. Sandy changed horses.

They were almost at what had become known as

Done's Swamp when three kangaroos popped their heads above the scrub; they may even have winked before turning their backs and bounding across the sand plain. Maestro immediately took off after them, and what could Sandy do? The horse had bolted. Sandy Two laced his fingers in the horse's mane, and — floating on its back — enjoyed the gallop.

Sandy at last turned Maestro, sweat-drenched and winded, back toward the swamp. He took the horse into the water and washed it down.

Old Alexander Starr was so pleased with the condition of his horses, and the care Sandy had apparently exercised, that he presented him with five shillings. A good day. At that time sixpence would buy a jug of beer, a packet of smokes or a good cigar.

A Sunday. The teamsters gathered at the Wirlup Haven camping reserve. Horses munched at their feeders.

Someone bet Sandy Two — in the way of people, when they gather and time is slow — that he could not put a bullet in a hat thrown into the air. While Sandy went to get a rifle, the others found a rock of the right size to tightly fill the hat. It seemed obvious, and they chuckled; a weighted hat would be much harder to hit than one gently floating to earth.

At the report of the rifle the hat disintegrated. The exploding fragments of rock had blown it apart.

The hatless one should have bought two hats, and given one to Sandy instead of just replacing his own. He complained that the boy wasn't old enough to use a gun in such a public place. Isn't there a law about them having guns? Especially here ...

Uncle Will used to yarn that way, trying the style of all the stories he'd read. All those westerns, those cowboy novels and the country and western music he'd immersed himself in, showed up again and again. It was what had failed him in his attempts at history, at helping Ern with the history. The impossibility of it. The difficulty of that style, his truth, and such a collaboration.

I preferred Uncle Jack's more circumspect tales. I knew of Sandy Two, from Hall's Occurrence Books. I was particularly comfortable with the policeman Hall, because I knew his style and all his accounts were there on paper.

Police Constable Hall, the very first policeman at Gebalup, liked to get away from the office. Office? It was a tent. I was ... He was ... It was all a bit intimidating, if you let it affect you. So he went out on the horse, on *patrol*. He intended to integrate that dutiful patrolling with some socialising. It was necessary to *get to know* people. And you never knew, it might be possible to pick up some tips, some hints, some advice; might even find some gold for his very own self.

Of course there were not only miners living here. There were the old pastoralists: the Mustles, the Dones. There were the shopkeepers (why, there were more and more of them all the time, but the Starrs were still the shining lights). There was the telegraph office staff, and the harbour workers down at Wirlup Haven. And, of course, there were the indispensable teamsters, moving between here and there. Now, they really had to know the country. He'd met some, and he quite admired them. There were those twins, Daniel and Patrick Coolman. And an old man who dropped off a load of forage for the police horses (the Mustles had the contract); he seemed an interesting and likeable character with his kangaroo skin shoes, his clicking tongue, and that sandy-coloured hair and beard. The aptly named Sandy Mason. Or, Sandy One, as he appeared to be known. The constable would have to ask him about his relationship — his *arrangement* — with that *half-caste* lad who helped him unload. There might be trouble there. There had been new legislation hinted at which would require that he take out a permit to employ the boy.

The constable did his rounds. He attended meetings in the town, and was occasionally invited to soirees, and various entertainments that genteel folk arranged. He did not, however, present recitals or such himself. It would not do, given his public profile and duty. After all, a certain distance is required for the proper exercise of authority.

Secretly, however, he fancied that he might become a writer. He was practising the habits of a writer, with each daily entry in the Occurrence Book. In this, however, he was restricted to an official role. He wrote *as* the police constable, *about* the police constable. *Constable Hall* ... he would write.

This strange third person, always present with any writer and reader.

Whatever the intricacies of the writing and reading situation (Where and who were all these people when he re-read his own work?), it never failed to give him a particular joy to write *Everything Correct and in Order*. After public meetings he could not help but smile as he formed the words, *a good number of persons were present and all past quiet and orderly*.

They were lovely words. At such times it was a lovely world.

Of course he was lonely, and sometimes full of doubt. But it would not do to dwell on it. There was too much to be done. It was what they were all engaged in here, in various ways; taming, controlling, elevating the whole bloody country so that it might achieve its potential and become part of the civilised world.

When he dismounted for an interview, friendly-like, or exited his hessian office, he would discreetly turn his hands so that his finger pads touched the cuff of his uniform, and he would give the gentlest of tugs, tidying its set on his heavy shoulders. He was like a cockatoo preening itself, adjusting its wings. And, it's true, although the good fellow did not know it of himself, he did like to move his arms about as if he were flexing his wings, and he would glance about as he did so, tilting his head and looking along his nose at what captured his attention. His eyes were small and round, and rarely blinked. Constable Hall's hair had greyed prematurely and his beard, despite being well-groomed and shaped quite square, always seemed rather dirty and stained. Perhaps it was nicotine, or the careless eating habits induced by solitary meals.

He liked his rounds to include the public houses, especially the Federal, just out of the townsite and a staging point between Gebalup and Wirlup Haven. And he found that he liked to visit some of the teamsters' camps.

Sandy One Mason's was furthest out, closest to the coast, and on the Mustles' pastoral run. He got there infrequently, but it was always a novelty to listen to the old man. The old fellow's voice clicked strangely, and he worked his tongue between his teeth whenever he paused for breath. Constable Hall was glad those

194

Coolman twins had moved into town, although he worried there would be problems with their wives. Two *half-caste* sisters.

At least Mason stayed out of town. A strange fellow. His woman was a *full-blood*.

Constable Hall knew he had been posted to Gebalup as the first-ever policeman because of concerns about the enthusiasm with which the Mustles, Dones and others had dealt with the *natives*. Even he had heard of the zealousness with which they had gone about their licensed and official task of punishing resident *natives* after the murder, many years back, of one of the town's pioneering brothers.

There were very few *natives* in the area now, except for these women and their children. It was a worry, obviously; the potential nuisance of them.

'My tracker's done a runner,' Constable Hall told Sandy One.

'Oh.'

'There's no one else, not yet.'

'Look,' said Sandy One, 'is it you I see about a miner's lease, and whether I've made the improvements or not? Whether I can renew it?'

'Yes,' Hall spoke slowly. 'I have influence, that way.'

'Look, take the boy. He can track as good as anyone around here. His mother and the mob at Dubitj Creek, they showed him how when he was a littl'un.'

Constable Hall didn't glance at Fanny but her image — dark, and featureless — came to him with the words — *Fanny: Aboriginal* — inscribed beneath it. His trained mind, see.

'How much you pay?' asked Sandy One.

Constable Hall hesitated, which was very unlike him in the course of his duties. But this was a most novel situation.

'Usually, trackers,' he said, 'well … they're black.'

It was awkward, this reluctance to acknowledge that the boy was a *black*, like any other *black*.

'So … he gets nothing.'

Constable Hall noticed the woman (Fanny, wasn't it?) staring at him over the shoulder of her boy. What was she at? Even her stare was in a different language.

'We'd like to help you out,' said the old man. 'Take him.' He spoke from within that flamboyant beard. Hall could tell the man believed it was a generous act. 'Take Sandy,' and he gestured at the boy. 'That's his name, remember, same as me. We call him Sandy Two!'

'I'll be in in a few days, I'll pick him up then.'

'We wanna help you out. He can go with you now.'

The boy looked keen and seemed ready to go immediately. He moved away to gather a few things. He was about thirteen years old, the constable guessed. A wiry, thin boy. His hair was light, almost blond, but he was undoubtedly *half-caste*, whatever his father might claim. Still, it just showed you. How quickly they could adjust.

See, with some things, Constable Hall was quite free of doubt and not at all alone.

'It'd be good for the boy,' said Sandy One, seemingly speaking to the constable. Hall guessed, however, that he also spoke to the woman and boy.

'You might even learn something yourself.' The old man broke in on Constable Hall's thoughts.

'Snails good ones for learning,' said the woman. Constable Hall stared at her. Fanny. It was what they were all called. She held herself very straight and erect and returned his gaze, the constable thought, with defiance. Or something very like it.

'Oh,' he said, thinking, 'What?'

She dropped a piece of gristle into the fire, and crouched before it once again.

'Morning time is best, when their trails are nice and glistening.' She was smiling. At him? With him?

The boy had rejoined them. He placed a small bundle behind the saddle of the constable's horse.

Constable Hall had an uncomfortable premonition. It was merely the uncomfortable part that registered with him at the time, and that only faintly. The boy might be difficult. He was not at all shy the way most of them were. A white boy indeed.

He (Sandy ... Two?) was pointing to a group of trees. His finger was not quite straight, as if it were echoing the arc of a small throw.

'Look, there, in the shade. See? You follow that one.'

Sandy Two led the constable over to the spot. Constable Hall bent at the knees. Yes, he could see it, a barely opaque trail running across some pebbles and a few blades of grass. He followed the glistening line, moving very slowly, his eyebrows low with concentration. It was a tiny path all right, already losing moisture and fading. He had that sense of the excitement you feel when your perception is suddenly enlarged. The trail went this way, that, went among some small rocks in the still moist undergrowth beneath a tree. There were no further signs of it. The constable lifted a hand slowly, placed it upon the rock, and

'Alliwah! Aiee! Look out!'

Jesus!

The constable jumped back, his head swinging, hands raised as if he had the memory of wings and was about to take off.

'He behind you. There! There he is.'

He had thought, you know, snake! Or something. But it was just a snail, a snail's shell, because the creature had withdrawn into itself.

They were laughing at him. All of them. Mongrels.

Still, he would take the boy. If something came up, it would cover him. He'd followed recommended procedure. He would keep the small allowance for himself.

As the constable was about to leave, the boy, without invitation, swung himself up behind him.

Constable Hall was relieved when, after half-an-hour or so, he told the boy to dismount and was obeyed.

'The horse needs resting,' he said.

The boy nodded, and easily kept pace behind. He was still there as they entered Gebalup.

There was a spare horse for the tracker's use. The boy could use that. For now, he must see to this one. It would be part of his duties to care for the horses. He could sleep with them.

Sandy Two did not know what to do, was already learning doubt and indecision. He stayed a few paces back as the constable shouted and swore at a small family group. They didn't seem very interested, and only occasionally nodded, as if in agreement with the constable's stream of words. He'd had enough, he roared. He'd had a gutful of their begging; and he lingered over the word 'gut' to express his contempt. He didn't want begging, not in his town. And the townspeople … He'd

had complaints of harassment! The town was bothered —
and here the constable hesitated so that his own sense of
justice, as well as his disdain, would be clear in the
emphasis — by *people* coming onto private property and
trying to sell clothes props, or firewood.

The constable kicked at a couple of bottles by the
campfire. 'I could arrest you, send you away. There's to be
no drinking.'

Constable Hall stopped speaking. He looked at each of
them in turn. They were all standing, and looking
elsewhere, glances occasionally touching. A couple may
have rolled their eyes at one another.

'You can't camp here. I want you out of town.'

Constable Hall got back onto his horse.

They had little with them. No horses, no tents. The
crude shelters they'd erected held a few bundles;
blankets, rags, pieces of glass and billycans. They began
scooping up these meagre possessions.

'Out. Out of town.' Constable Hall dug his heels into
the horse so that it took a few steps at them and at least
that made them hurry along a bit. An old man stepped
aside, keeping his eyes on Hall, and swept his hands
about on the ground to snatch a last few things. A woman
tucked a child under her arm and jogged to the furthest
side of the group.

The Constable and Sandy Two followed them, drove
them as if they were just another flock of sheep, and
indeed they did fall into an orderly pattern as they
moved. The constable warned them not to come back.

Sandy Two told himself he had not taken part in any of
this. It was just that he was there. Some of those people,
they could have maybe been a sister, a brother. A mother.

Sandy Two and the constable entered a row of houses. Sandy was listening to the different sound of the horse's hooves, and reflecting upon what a fine thing it was, to be riding around like this. He shifted slightly in the saddle, enjoying the height of the horse. A horse was not as good as a camel for height, but he liked the gait better. Downhill, a bicycle was best, and Oh! to be mounted on one and whizzing along a camel pad with the wind at your back.

Two Nyoongar boys came running from between the houses and into his daydream of modern technology. Sandy recognised one of them, Corrigin, from some of the teamsters' camps. He thought of the younger boy as a little brother. Same people.

Sandy heard the bellowing of Mr Starr, the shopkeeper, before he saw him come running clumsily around the corner of a house, and his first impulse was to cheer for the boys. He grinned to himself. Starr would never catch them, even though each boy was handicapped by the big watermelon wrapped in his arms. The boys were laughing, and then they saw Constable Hall and his tracker. His tracker? Sandy Two was close enough to read the recognition on their faces, and then some other expression.

The boys changed direction, their bare feet sending the little stones of the new road flying, but others had arrived, what with the shouting and all, and everyone so watchful that the *blacks* not make a nuisance of themselves and what have you and just how were you supposed to make a town a place a community anyhow?

Constable Hall collected his wits enough to shout.

'Halt!' He rose higher in his saddle, his legs thrust straight into the stirrups, and his lips protruding like a howling dog's. Sandy Two dug his bare heels into his horse and, as if in response to the Constable's shout, was in motion. It was a reflex action; he rode as if he was mustering and so it was he who cut off the boys' path of retreat.

He didn't think what he was doing. It was just wanting to be part of the pleasure of a chase.

Starr and his neighbour got to them. Starr clouted the smaller one across the head. The blow lifted him off his feet, and he rolled up only as far as his hands and knees. The neighbour grabbed Corrigin, and clamped an arm around his throat.

One of the precious watermelons had split. Red flesh and black seeds were strewn across the bone-hard road.

Sandy Two moved his horse to shoulder the man who was choking the struggling Corrigin. The man stumbled so that his grip on Corrigin's throat loosened, and he snarled up at Sandy Two.

Constable Hall slid from his horse, and handed the reins to another man who had just arrived and seemed eager to have a swing at one of the boys. It seemed most probable that the cheeky little half-uniformed bastard on the horse would be first.

Hall wrapped the reins around the fellow's bunched fists. 'Give him the reins,' he said to the man, gesturing at Sandy Two as he did so.

The man looked at the constable, at Sandy Two. He dropped the reins, and walked away, muttering.

Constable Hall and Mr Starr gave the boys a good strapping. Sandy Two got himself out of sight, but he could not close his ears, and he was reminded of other strappings.

Fanny and her very young son Sandy Two had stood at the door of Mustle's stables. They had been searching for the girls, since there was a *spree* on, and that was always a dangerous time. Mustle had taken a stirrup iron from the wall, and its leather was fastidiously looped around his wrist. He was using it to beat one of Fanny's countrymen. He swung the stirrup, and the iron made a dull, muffled sound as it ripped bare flesh. The man was curled on the ground, and exhaled heavily with each blow. No other sound left his lips.

Mustle suddenly turned and Fanny and her boy saw his flushed face and how his throat, where the shirt had unbuttoned, was bright red. He patted the pistol at his belt and walked right past them.

They heard his voice at their backs. 'Eh, Fanny. Where you keeping those daughters of yours?' He gave a little snort of laughter.

Sandy Two had always liked to sit up on horseback, and get a good view. He liked the way objects, the horizon, shifted in your vision with the horse's gait.

He saw a man, still quite distant, wobbling toward him on a bicycle. The fellow could ride a bike, that was clear, but his balance was affected. Ah, he was drunk.

A cart rushed out from behind a building, busy busy hurry hurry. A two-in-hand. Frisky horses. Mr Starr was driving. Gunna give that fellow on the bike a fright. Sandy Two was interested in this.

The bicycle had remained on course for a good while, held by a deep wheel rut, but now it lurched and its rider fell, sprawling as a drunk does. The skull made a popping noise as the wheel of Starr's cart ran over it.

Starr reined in his horse. The man lay still on the

ground. It had happened so close, so all-of-a-sudden. Sandy Two saw Starr's angry face looking into his own, and the fallen bicycle, and the man splayed across wheel tracks which continued irresistibly into the background.

Starr looked down. So did Sandy. There was the body with its limbs lifeless as a doll's, and its crushed mess running into the wheel ruts of the street. Sandy and Starr looked at one another. Starr's cart had done it, but Starr glared at Sandy Two, wanting to blame him, wanting that black face to be the crushed one.

Well, Mr Starr was furious. At the fool for doing this to him, at Sandy Two for seeing, and staring so vacantly.

'Get the doctor,' he said.

Sandy Two was already away, and heading for the hospital. He raced at its steps with that crushed skull, those floppy limbs bouncing in his brain. He only dimly saw the bulk of the matron standing at the entrance.

'Go away.'

He tried to explain: the crushed head, the bicycle, the wheel ... How he had met Mr Starr's eyes.

'Go away. I will not listen.'

And she no longer needed to, because Constable Hall was approaching with Mr Starr, and a body in the cart behind him.

The matron waved her hand dismissively at Sandy Two.

'Be off.'

The townsfolk held an Indignation Meeting. Everybody was there; the members of all the clubs, including the newly formed Australian Natives Association. Daniel Coolman, as a new member, was among them. Some people had to listen from outside the building. You could crawl under the floorboards, or stand beside a window.

There were a number of concerns. The way the mail was delivered, for instance. At the post office, they just opened the window and tossed it out onto the verandah. Then it was elbows up, hip-and-shoulder stuff. It was rough-and-tumble when the townsfolk gathered to collect their mail. Women and children had been jostled and pushed aside. The secretary of the football association, in his excitement, almost interjected that — yes! — his members particularly enjoyed it.

Well, you know, it was an Indignation Meeting, but it was also a social occasion and they didn't get enough of these, not as a community.

Mr Mustle, the president of the Australian Natives Association — those citizens (white, of course) born in Australia — suddenly called out across the meeting, challenging any other club to a tug-of-war. It caught people by surprise a bit, and no one likes that. The Oddfellows and the two football clubs answered his challenge immediately. Men were laughing and jeering at one another across the room before the chair had time to interject and point out that their discussion was inappropriate.

And then the mood suddenly turned, because someone called out, 'What about the people — yes, these *niggers*, but there's plenty of white men among them too — who are camping on town lots?' Mr Starr pointed out that the Roads Board, of which he was a member, had resolved to request the police to remove campers from town lots to the area set apart for same. It was at the edge of town. They had even resolved to write to the warden — who was also of course the resident magistrate — to request the police to take action to this end.

And the roads! Well ... Voices were raised. Shocking. Shocking, a disgrace, shocking, abominable, shocking. Shocking.

What about the water! They needed a new dam built, that was for sure. What was the government doing? And who was to ensure that the teamsters refrained from camping on the catchment areas above the reservoir just out of town? Shouldn't they also be utilising the designated camping areas?

Those teamsters, some of them like to live with the *blackfellas* anyhow.

Daniel Coolman was not thinking of himself as a teamster anymore, that's for sure.

Constable Hall was put under considerable pressure at the meeting. Nevertheless, his Occurrences Book merely noted that the gathering was *lively, well attended,* and that *everything past correct and orderly.* He had underlined these last words. The date was particularly beautifully written.

Of course there were other would-be writers in an expanding town like Gebalup, with so many new arrivals each day. Most, like other newcomers, began prospecting alone, and then worked for one of the companies. So although there were other writers, it was really a town preoccupied with matters of commerce.

Commerce, and writers; the Chamber of Commerce in the nearby town of Kylie Bay joined forces with Gebalup to write to the Aborigines Department regarding:

> ... the position of the unfortunate aborigines that are at present in these towns. For the past years we have been free of them, but owing to various causes they have

returned again and threaten to take up their abode in our midst. It is a pitiful thing to find them as they are here now begging for bread, rations only being allowed to the children.

I saw the police ordering them off the town as they become a nuisance to the people.

The Chief Protector, predecessor to Mr Neville, replied:

It is clear that before long something will have to be done towards gathering the natives onto reserves. However, we must wait until the enlarging of the law enables us to act towards the natives with more parental authority. There is a new bill being proposed which will give us the power to locate natives on certain areas.

The Dones and Mustles had been writing ever since the Travelling Inspector's report several years before, when they had uncharacteristically felt compelled to argue for justice on behalf of the Nyoongars residing on their leases:

... you will see the unfairness to us of maintaining any of these natives who follow us here from our other properties when a fund is set aside for some at any rate of them.

We shall feel compelled to turn a number of unprofitable natives adrift with recommendations to apply to the local Resident Magistrate for their maintenance. We absolutely refuse to keep them at our expense when we are already taxed to provide a fund for that purpose, which the constitution prescribes must be spent upon the natives, and which our natives in equity should receive their proportion ...

Part of the long-ago Travelling Inspector's complaint had been that the Mustles and Dones were claiming rations disproportionately, and using them as wages. The pastoralists knew how to threaten a department, and the town. It needs very few *natives* to upset the well-being of a new and insecure community. The one community's progress is measured by the other's decline. The power of the one community is increased by the feebleness of the other; or better still, the complete absence of an indigenous community — as the Mustles, my own ancestors the Coolman twins, and my own grandfather Ernest Solomon Scat have been so keen, in their various ways, to prove.

I would like you to consider the initiative we see demonstrated here, in these letters of the forefathers; the pioneering, entrepreneurial and opportunistic spirit which soars when there is money to be gained. The initial lease cost them nothing, and the purchase and exchange of rations provides a necessary stimulant to the economy they are creating. Their friend, Mr Starr, advises the department that he could be of assistance because, as the Travelling Inspector has indicated, it is not quite ethical of the pastoralists to provide rations as payment for labour; especially when the number of black labourers does not accord with the quantity of rations being supplied.

But, I digress. This is a simple family history, not a treatise on the economy.

Next mail day Constable Hall insisted that the public queue at the verandah's edge. The window flew open, mail spewed out, the window quickly slammed shut. Sandy Two read out the address of each letter and parcel, and passed it to Constable Hall who then handed it to its rightful owner.

There was almost another Indignation Meeting right there on the spot.

'So, the boy can read? Where'd he learn that?'

'Constable Hall! I haven't got all day to stand here!'

'Some of us need to get replies written to go back with the coach.' (This last, surely, just to brag about the speed with which the speaker could write, and to show that upstart little *darky*.)

A woman became very heated. She didn't want that boy touching her mail!

'Yeah.' Heads nodded at one another in agreement. 'Hear hear.'

'Surely there's better things for you to be doing, Constable.'

Sandy Two looked up. He saw his father ambling up the street behind his donkeys. The dray's load towered above the little man, and there at the very top, peeping over and meeting his gaze, was Fanny. His mother was so high, so very high above the ground. Sandy Two dropped all the letters back into the sack and tipped his head at Constable Hall by way of goodbye.

headache

They had brought another load of forage for the police horses. Fanny stayed on the wagon, and looked down upon the constable, her man and her son.

It was Sandy Two who told the constable they would be around Gebalup for a couple of days, waiting to load up with ore to take back to the coast.

'Let me know if you need a hand with anything,' he said to Constable Hall, waving over his shoulder and grinning as he swaggered back to the wagon where his father waited.

Constable Hall walked around to the back of the timber yard next to the police office.

Daniel Coolman had taken over his twin brother's property. Pat Coolman had not been seen for, what? A year? More? The twins had taken up with Sandy One Mason's daughters, apparently. Daniel Coolman had married one of them — Harriette — a few years ago at

Kylie Bay. The other daughter, Dinah, had been last seen with Pat Coolman. Sandy One said they were still together, roo-shooting somewhere.

There were five adults in the shade of a lean-to. Plus two, three, children. Constable Hall was struck by the sight of it; white men and *gins*, *niggers* right next-door.

The men were drinking.

'We're already married here,' said Sandy One, anticipating the policeman's opening words, 'so you don't need to bother us on that score. The women don't even sip this stuff,' he added, his consonants hissing and clicking. 'This is my son-in-law,' the little man said, flinging an arm around the burly red man.

Once again the constable found himself thinking, it showed what the *blacks* could be. Might be able to do. It depends, he'd wait and see. Careful breeding might … but they could still regress. These women, the children. Perhaps it was true, he thought, that British blood was enough — even from men such as these.

The constable was asking for help again. But of course, he was neither humble nor contrite. After all, he represented justice, and a good influence on the boy. The thing was, he'd lost another tracker. They were useless, he explained. There was no accounting for it, and they were as unreliable as, as … He couldn't finish the comparison.

'There's some grog's been stolen. It's been happening lately. Reckon if I could borrow the boy, I can sort it today …'

'I dunno …' said Sandy One. He offered Constable Hall a drink, and moved the conversation to other things. Like when was the constable going to get a decent office and cell built? What pressures the constable must be under, what difficulties he must face in the pursuit of duty, how he must be looking forward to his family joining him …

'Yeah, I need a miner's homestead lease,' said Sandy One Mason, apparently meandering through small talk. 'It's not a camp. I'm prospecting, I've found good stuff here. There's even a bit of water.'

'What,' Constable Hall asked, 'in among the dunes there? It's just sand.'

Sandy said he knew it was unusual, but there you are. It's luck, everybody knew that. Some people found gold when their horse kicked a nugget.

'It's not good for my family. I've gotta support them, show them a future. I still cart when I can, but it's Daniel who lines up the work these days. But, anyway, sure,' continued Sandy One, laughing. 'Young Sandy will help you out. Give him a call when you're right. Like I said, we're here for a couple of days and he doesn't want any of our grog, anyways.'

Daniel wished his own brother was here. It hurt that his wife's brother could do this work, this black-tracking. His clumsy lips made 'back-tracking' of the expression.

'Don't worry,' Sandy One said to his son-in-law. 'They need a good tracker, simple as that.'

It seemed that the offenders had kept on the move. All day long Constable Hall followed Sandy Two on a meandering path. Every now and then he was shown a small piece of glass, a bottle top, some broken twigs, a collection of footprints until, finally, they were approaching the town from the opposite boundary to where they'd started. They found the remains of a small fire in a dry gully surrounded by scraggly mallee. There were a few bottles and some broken glass scattered about.

'Looks like that's it.'

After a day spent walking in a great circle around the town, they had arrived at a pile of warm ash.

'They're cunning, eh?' offered Sandy Two.

The constable asked Sandy Two if he could tell the identity of those involved by their footprints. Sandy said that he couldn't, but would Constable Hall be interested in hiring another fellow as tracker? Sandy Two knew one — didn't know him well or anything — but he lived about here, this fella. He'd have a better idea. He was much better at it.

So Harry Cuddles got the job.

Starr, the shopkeeper, was trying to knock on the tent flap early the next morning. His ineffectiveness and foolishness made him even angrier, and he shouted and stamped his foot. He called out Constable Hall's name repeatedly, turning around and around on his heel as he did so and Hall had to yell out to him from where he sat.

'I'm on the bloody dunny, don't lose your shirt.' He with no pants on himself.

Starr was an impatient man, a growing man in the town, a member of various clubs and the Chamber of Commerce, the Roads Board and who knows what else. He was yelling across the (aromatic) space which separated him from the policeman long before Hall, tucking in his shirt, came walking across it.

Mr Starr had found his bicycle at least a hundred yards down the street from his house, and what's more it was damaged.

Also, his wife's purse was missing, with a considerable number of coins in it. Two *natives* had been seen in the vicinity late last night. They really should be kept out of town.

'Who?'

'Sandy Two Mason and Harry Cuddles. Your men, aren't they, constable?'

Writing it up in his Occurrence Book later that evening, Constable Hall shook his head. At noon he had arrested and locked up the Aboriginal *native* Harry Cuddles, Police Tracker, and charged him with having, on the night of the seventh instant, been in possession of one bicycle, the property of A Starr.

Constable Hall had obtained information from Mr Starr, and from a very contrite Sandy Two who told him that he just hadn't thought, you know. He'd met Harry walking the bike, and of course he wondered where he got it from, but he didn't really stop to think about it. He liked bikes, and he was excited to see Harry with one. He rode it around the recreation ground, showing off really, and he told Harry to ride it. Harry tried but he fell off. That's how it got damaged, see. And then they run off, because Harry told Sandy where he got the bike from; just outside of Starr's place.

They were worried, because of their respect for Constable Hall, you know. How he'd treated them and all, and seeing as how he'd given Harry the job. Even now, said Sandy Two, he had a headache and felt sick just from letting Constable Hall down.

Mr Starr came in to see Constable Hall. He was pleased to note that there was some justice being achieved. Oh, and the purse? His wife had found it. It'd merely been misplaced.

Starr glared at Sandy Two and told Constable Hall that

he was being fooled. 'Don't trust him,' he said. 'His father's a *native* and his mother's a bush *gin*. Think about it. He's not like you and I.'

At the hotel a few nights later, Constable Hall could not help but complain. He was drinking, a man was driven to it. Well, what could you do? A big bunch of *darkies* in from the goldfields, again. He'd chased them out of town. He'd had to arrest some. 'I do believe they were ready to fight me,' he said.

The bar took it up like a chorus, and they knew all the words:

> *They were drinking, men and women both,*
> *the women were prostituting themselves …*

(the chorus licked its lips, shifted its gaze, adjusted its trousers)

> *It was a serious and growing evil.*
> *Many of these native women …*

(to the sombre tones of the Chamber of Commerce)

> *are suffering from syphilis.*
> *A serious and growing evil.*

They were beggars, were shameless, and bothered white people, white women, trying to get them to buy clothes line props, chopped firewood, possum skins …

'I gave them a taste of the whip,' intoned the constable, contentedly, before lapsing into his official style. 'It seemed most expeditious.' And then there was that trouble his trackers had got themselves involved in earlier in the week ...

'They need to be protected,' someone said.

'They make a nuisance of themselves.'

'It's not their fault,' said a scrupulous man. 'It's unscrupulous whites that have taught them to drink. You get them, like this week, coming in from somewhere else — they're not from around here, you know — they hang around town in groups, begging, and trying anything they can to get a drink.'

'Yes. Yes.' There was consensus.

The drinkers in the bar were prepared to act as Hall's advisors. They knew there was sometimes stuff in the papers about the trouble in the north or, rather, parliamentarians talking about troubles, but really what else could you do? They seemed to be handling things all right up there. It had been the same down here, you had to be firm with the *blacks*. Whereas nowadays, these bastards down here, most of them, well ... And now there was another Royal Commission on in the city. Well, that Roth better come up with something useful. More money wasted.

'It's useless. They're useless. They're dying out.'

They shared their complaints, and the mail passed to and from the relevant authorities.

Even by the campfire, and camped among the dunes, Uncle Will wanted to explain the 1905 Aborigines Act to me. My back was cold, my cheeks hot, and I was the smell of campfire smoke, of banksia and seaweed, of the fish we'd eaten.

'It made such a difference,' he said, 'that legislation.'

But I was bored by talk of legislation back then.

'There was people learning to live in two cultures.'

'Except that one was being eradicated. All that death. And anyway,' said Uncle Jack. 'You could still try, keep trying. We could.'

I could see that Ern was listening to them. Something in the set of his jaw, and his dry eyes. He knew about legislation. Though, of course, I'd hardly seen mention of it in any of his papers. A different focus, I suppose.

'You could be moved anywhere, told who to marry, where to live, had to get a permit to work, not allowed to drink or vote ...' Uncle Will was on a roll. 'It separated us all.'

Uncle Jack let him talk, and then said, 'Yeah, well. You're probably right. I remember Uncle Sandy, even though you knew him years later after he'd been in the war. He was his own man, even then, and knew he was as good as anyone. But I reckon he must've thought he was too good for everyone; Nyoongars, wadjelas, the lot.'

Uncle Jack paused, and sat up very straight. 'But I reckon no one ever told him about the killing around here, that his brothers-in-law teamed up with the killers. Not until he met up with that fellow on the run. Cuddles, was it?'

There are so many things it is difficult to speak of, adequately.

'No,' Uncle Will said, very sadly. Thinking of his father, and himself, I suppose. 'No one ever told me that, either, about all the killing. Until you, Jack. Harley. It's not easy to listen to that.'

stormy birth

My ancestors — Fanny, with Sandies One and Two — had followed a rocky ridge, and when they could see it continue into the sea and gradually became little more than a tumble of rocks and bubbles they turned away, and descended to the shallow bay its persistence had made possible.

There were massive cloudbanks on the horizon, and when my family looked back around the coast to where they had begun they saw the tiny and isolated islands of home huddled close to the mainland, seemingly less substantial than the clouds.

The setting sun had coloured the sky and tinted the sandy crests of the old dunes but — even as the sky rapidly darkened — the ocean shimmered with the blue light of day held within it. And gliding toward them across that strangely lit surface was a low, white-tipped, violet cloud. No. No, it was not a cloud. Inhaling in surprise, my family realised that a vast fleet of jellyfish, driven by their white sails, was silently invading the bay.

A storm raged for days. Young Sandy Two huddled beneath the small wagon and moaned with the wind as trees writhed and flailed about him. The rain drummed the earth, the shrubs, the wagon above his head. Sandy Two opened his mouth and drank from the runnels hanging from the edge of his shelter.

Once, he undressed and went out into the wind and rain and let it lash and sting him until he was almost numb. Then he dressed beneath the wagon, wrapped himself in canvas and blankets and talked and sang to himself until he was warm again.

He awoke in a pale, thin light, and even though his mouth was stale, and his body aching, the new calm of the air communicated itself to him. He saw his father crawl from the shelter of tarpaulin and saplings and trees, and walk away through the dunes.

The two Sandies walked along the devastated beach. The air was still, and the sea rocked this way and that, and rose and collapsed heavily upon the sand at its edge. It seemed as if birds had lost their wings, sea creatures been spewed from their element. The beach was a ruffled crowd of various birds fastidiously picking their way among the debris. A flock of parrots raked their beaks through a pile of seaweed, and — still further away — two sea-eagles feasted on a dead dolphin.

Colour had been washed from the sky, and the ocean was dirty with torn weed and sediment. Even from the beach father and son could see the ocean striking the island, and vast blossoms of white rose and fell onto its stony back.

It must have been the smell that distracted them, made

them wander — perverse and curious — through the dunes and toward the grove. Despite the relative shelter there, some trees had been ripped from the ground, and others clung tenaciously to their roots by little more than a strip of bark.

It was certainly the smell — well, call it a stench — that brought Sandy Two back to his senses from the drifting daydream state he'd been inhabiting. There was a great mound of bodies, lying in a heap. Skinned kangaroos, obscenely naked. The two men followed small footprints to what was left of a tiny shelter, constructed too close to the carcasses to be comfortable. And in the ruin of that poor shelter lay a woman and baby. The woman and child were certainly not comfortable; not with breathing, not with life.

The mother was Dinah — daughter to one Sandy, sister to the other. The daughter and sister of the two men lay staring up at them. Apparently she did not see them, because they came close enough to discern the reflection in her eyes; of the one kneeling, the other partially obscured and framed by what was left of her shelter, and still she did not react. Dinah could only see — or so her boy would one day speculate — dead and yellow leaves, scabby twigs and, beyond that, torn and thinning clouds racing across the sky.

The baby at her breast was wrinkled and thin, its umbilical cord loosely knotted. Sandy One saw flies at his grandchild's eyes, and could discern its bones. Mother and child lay among blood, shit, the stale mess of birth.

Dinah stared deep into the eyes of Sandy One, the father, and saw herself, the remnants of shelter, the hollowness of him and his promises.

Sandy Two turned away, and there were two shivering

children. The girl was perhaps four years old; the boy a little younger. His nephew and niece. The girl was a quiet one, but not so the boy. Despite his years he could talk, he was happy to talk, and he talked as he warmed in their arms. Their names, his sister's and his, were Kathleen (my sister) and Jack, Jack Chatalong. Chatalong you see, because of talking so much. I talk a lot. I don't know why.

The girl was quite fair. A surprising fairness. How the white skin wins.

They had been kangaroo shooting, it was three men, and his mother helped; she cooked for them but then she began having that baby, and the men left. His mother, the boy said, trying to explain, looked after the kangaroo shooters. Oh, they pulled sandalwood too. She cooked for them. But she got sick, it was the baby, and there was a storm and the men got blown away. He smiled. This seemed satisfactory. He kept talking.

They had been lifted into the sky ...

Sandy Two saw his father nodding, and two blood-spattered men were lifted into the stormy sky. The men were laughing and, having waved a little goodbye, randomly fired into the sea, and into the birds and kangaroo hides dancing around them in an ever upward spiral. It was the ending of a spree. The men's crotches bulged, thinking of the mother.

Sandy One continued to hold his daughter's blank stare. His son picked up the boy, pulled the girl close to him. Flies buzzed and covered the mound of carcasses with a black and living skin.

Unbidden, unwanted, the memories of earlier sprees must have returned to the two men.

These are not things handed down to me by Uncle Jack or Uncle Will yarning around a campfire; they are things you might prefer not to say, not directly, to any younger person in your family.

Sandy One and Fanny had learned that it was best for women and children to keep away from the homestead, from any homestead. If there was a white woman it was sometimes easier, but it was never safe.

Especially when there was a spree. When there was a spree, stay clear away. It was not safe.

It was that combination of things called Christmas. It was a spree. A party.

Fanny must've been reminded of the hanging tree, and occasionally she heard shots from the direction of the homestead. The buzzing of flies replayed in her head. The girls were still upset.

That buzzing. She had found a sister, uncovered and dead on the ground. The stench, the buzzing of flies had led her there. She made a mound of earth, left some things ...

Sandy One came back drunk and stupid and snarling at her, through a fug of vomit and alcohol. 'It was three bullets, they put three in her.' Someone. She was rotten with the pox, the bitch, and a hazard to everyone. He spat, was sobbing, lay down snoring.

The boy was fine, was still back there, somewhere.

Sandy Two had gone with his father, so that he might help him home again.

He remembered white light flashing, popping, and music. Everyone laughing yelling looking at him.

There was a house, of mud and stone with extra rooms of thin timber, hessian, iron. Sometimes they put a sign up above the door, especially for the parties.

Men came from other stations and from the 'fields, days away. There was a big tank of grog on the back of a wagon. A spree, they whooped. A spree, a spree.

Sandy Two stepped from among the women and children at the woodheap and followed the red-haired Coolman twins beneath the sign — *Tavern* — and into the homestead.

Christmas. Oh, there was a crowd of white men. Sandy Two trailed the twins, miming them, so that he was the very essence of their back-slapping, winking selves as they swaggered into the noisy crowd. Laughing faces turned to the three of them.

Sandy Two performed as if he was with his mother and the others in the camp, but the laughter and shouting under this low roof was so much louder and uplifting. The twins were unaware of him and — warming to the crowd's response — they enthusiastically shook hands with everyone, and their gestures became all the more extravagant as if it was they, now, who were miming the boy. Men held out their hands a second time, and repeatedly winked at each of the twins, and gave them yet another drink to pour into their upturned mouths until, eventually, the twins had nowhere else to move. It was a small room after all. It was not really such a crowd. They turned to one another, turned back to the ruddy, laughing faces and realised all eyes were upon a space just behind them.

It was as if they had rehearsed. Each moved his gaze to the other's face, and then, perfectly synchronised, Daniel and Patrick slowly and, yes — sheepishly — turned around.

The boy. In a pose which echoed their own. The room

of men roared, and cheered; they laughed as the boy was knocked down.

The homestead was dark, and the roof low. Music bounced within the close walls like a vicious wind.

Sandy Two thought he could smell each and every person, and the rum most of all, disguising the stale air of the room.

A group of men sat tightly together, their charcoaled faces grinning starkly, with a sign — *Black and White Minstrels* — at their feet. His father was dressed in women's clothes and had pumpkins stuffed down the front of his shirt.

There was a photographer. You had to stay still, and not grin. Sandy One sat on Patrick Coolman's knee, and they embraced like man and wife. Sandy swung his leg, and kept dropping his gaze, giggling.

They sat in chairs arranged in a half-circle in front of the sign, *Tavern*, and the men had dressed in dinner suits. Charcoal-blackened faces showed their teeth, and rolled their eyes.

Someone grabbed Sandy Two.

'The kid. Sandy's kid.'

'Here, you.'

'Give him a drink.'

'C'mon, let's whiten him up, eh.'

Dressed in a man's shoes and coat, ridiculously large on him, Sandy Two bent his shadow-thin legs akimbo, and — nestling the violin in beside his big grin — imitated the two violinists.

'Crikey, keep the women out of the bloody photo but. Who let them in?'

'No. Not youse, not now. Get out of it.'

Someone snarled, and took a half-hearted swing at two women who had come into the circle.

There was a piano accordion, and two, three violins. Sandy One, flaunting his huge breasts and lifting his skirts, danced. His son copied the gestures and postures of the two actual violinists so well they almost thought he played, too.

Everyone is laughing, and the women at the doorway shriek and bend wildly at the waist.

Sandy Two sounds the strings with his bow.

Stark grins in blackened faces.

The photographer hides beneath his black cloth. Five legs, one eye. Everyone is still, and the world whirls around Sandy Two; voices, laughter, music rushing away in a vast circle as the centre of silence grows and grows.

A blinding flash, and they are set in motion once more.

Over the next few days they did scenes for the camera again and again.

The boss, with a holstered revolver at his hip, leans on a reclining camel and looks into the distance. He wears jodhpurs, and a pith helmet. Sandy Two, in loincloth, stands at the camel's head, holding its reins.

The men wanted photographs of themselves being attacked by the *blacks*, but the only possible male attackers on the station were very old and it was difficult to get them to participate, let alone look ferocious enough.

A boss bathing in one of the granite pools. On the rock towering above him stands Sandy Two, and, at the very top, out of focus, his naked and charcoaled father, holding a spear, and with one foot reluctantly resting on the arch of the other.

The homestead, what was it? Low, flat, stone and iron. There exists a surprising photo of the yard; timber stacked neatly, a stone wall in the background, three horses and a camel hitched to a flat wagon, upon which sits a dark boy. My Uncle Sandy Two.

What makes the photo unusual for one of the era is that the figures in it seem caught unawares, and have not had time to strike a pose. Two women by the front wheel are laughing at one another. The boy has swivelled on his seat, and stares down the lens. Two definitely white men in the foreground, very shabby and dirty, glare angrily at the camera, and one of them steps toward us.

And so it was with little Jack Chatalong, who was forever stepping forward, stepping up to have his say. He talked and talked, as he also did much later in his long life when he sat by campfires in those dunes, and came to say even the hardest of things, put them into words — his words. But we have met him as a tiny boy, and already explaining things ...

Patrick? Patrick Coolman? The man had gone, left his wife, in-laws, his twin brother as well.

And Dinah would not let go of the dead baby.

Sandy Two stayed with Fanny and the children at their camp, and the old man took the woman and dead child into Wirlup Haven. The medical officer sent them on to Gebalup.

They had to lay her in the shade of a tree in the hospital grounds. Someone took the baby away. The Resident Medical Officer sent a woman to them with a tent.

'It's his own,' she told Sandy. 'He's not supposed to treat people in a tent, but she can't go into the hospital. It affects the other patients.'

Sandy One erected the tent.

'She's not well, is she?' said the woman. 'I'll look after her, and keep the doctor informed. Off you go.'

Sandy One met his family before he got to the camp. They came together, under the telegraph wire, and Jack Chatalong was suddenly quiet. They were already so accustomed to his voice, his constant voice, that the absence of it was a shock, and a pleasure. In the new silence they heard the trees, and the telegraph wire whining in the wind.

'We knew,' said Jack, as we sat around a campfire so long after that event, but touching it because we shared the place again. 'We thought she would die. Pop — Sandy — he complained to the Health Board, and we ended up making trouble that way. They wouldn't let Fanny see her, even, and Harriette got there once, but Daniel stopped that, and well ... Dinah, my mother, she disappeared and I didn't see her again until Mogumber.'

to the chief protector of aborigines

Sir,

I think it would be advisable for me to inform you of the exact facts in the case of the half-caste woman, Dinah.

When she arrived here I made efforts to obtain someone to look after her; she was in such pain that she could not go further than the site of the camp and it was not appropriate to take her to the police station. No one would undertake the nursing of her, save her mother, and the community here does not take kindly to that woman walking the streets by day. However a midwife here was good enough to say that she would supervise the mother's ministrations, and ensure she did not loiter too long.

There was really no one but myself took the least interest in her until it occurred to a man in the town that the hospital buildings could be utilised, and an outburst of vicarious charity was the result. I gave the woman my *own tent. I gave her also a stretcher; the department has supplied her with a good mattress and sheets.*

When the matter was suddenly broached before the Gebalup Medical Board meeting at which I was accused I was annoyed to find the suggestion implied that the woman was not properly attended to, but I welcome a suggestion of someone appropriate properly nursing her (full-time); and I was most indignant when the members of the Health Board met and considered the matter. I would remind you that the treatment of Aborigines in tents was a definite instruction from you that doubtless you will remember I was not in love with. The complaints of the Medical Board, and the man Mason, I consider absolutely uncalled for.

The procedure was improper.

The woman absconded from the hospital grounds and has not been heard of since.

Sir, I am your obedient servant.

Walter Wigglesworth
Medical Officer
Gebalup.

A note pencilled at the bottom of this document:

We have her receiving rations at Kylie Bay.

Cuddles

Constable Hall received a telegram from Frederickstown:

Jock Mustle's store Yarramoup robbed Barney Cuddles suspected heading East keep watch stop.

There was a comprehensive list of what had been taken:

one twelve-shot winchester
knife
milk
tobacco
shirt
rug
one pair of spectacles
moleskin pants
under flannels
salt herring.

An expensive telegram, thought Hall.

Constable Hall went out to the camps, and to the mines. He noted that there were no *natives* camped. So far so good. He visited the homesteads, gathering information. Barney Cuddles had been born at one of the Mustles' stations. He was trouble. Everyone knew that, said the Mustles.

Sandy One passed on to Constable Hall the rumour that Cuddles had cleared out westward, along the coast. Constable Hall thought he had heard the same thing elsewhere. He asked for the use of Mason's son, just this one last time. He felt confident it would stand the boy in good stead should he find himself in any sort of trouble, later. They both knew what young fellas were like. Hall could turn a blind eye.

His tracker, that Cuddles, had cleared out on him. Yep, same name as the villain. Blood ties, maybe. He knew Sandy Two could track as good as anyone, and that he was a pretty reliable boy. Hall didn't add that he'd been unable to find anyone else.

And then there was the matter of the two children he'd found (what were their names? Kathleen? Jack?). Constable Hall felt that legally, they should be sent to an institution.

'There is,' he said, and then feigned his own reluctance to enact it, 'you know, this new legislation.'

Sandy One Mason was affected by drink even at this time of day. But he knew what Hall was getting at. 'Yeah, well my Sandy is more than just a boy, you know,' insisted Sandy One. 'But yeah, he can do it. To help you out. But remember,' he added, 'he's not one of your wild trackers.'

Hall agreed, yes, with what Mason said. By Christ, he

knew the young man could track. And he certainly needed someone.

Constable Hall and Sandy Two met Jock Mustle before they reached his homestead. Mustle was a heavy man, with a dark beard sprouting from his ruddy cheeks and neck. He sat securely in the saddle, a rifle along his thigh. 'Constable Stewart,' said Mustle as he led them back to the station, 'is waiting for you.' He told them Stewart had set out from Frederickstown with a tracker, but the man had disappeared on the way. 'It's the way of these people,' Mustle said, barely glancing at Sandy Two who had been forced behind the two men as they proceeded along the track.

Jock said he'd known this Cuddles' mother and, what's more, he reckoned he'd known the father, some wastrel he'd once employed as a shepherd. 'The worst sort of white man,' he said, 'a terrible drunkard; it's the only kind who'll live with these women. He lived with the mother for a couple of years. This Cuddles, he fancies himself. A bit of an education, from his father, and some ideas that he's as good as, if not better than, anyone else.'

Cuddles had tried to kidnap a girl from the homestead a couple of days ago. 'One of the house girls. Of course she was screaming, she didn't want to go with him. Luckily I was only as far away as the shed. I scared him off. But, I tell you, it's no secret, he's dangerous.' Jock muttered, 'He's a mad, uppity bastard. I'll shoot him if I come across him.'

'Let's hope he's alone,' said Constable Stewart, as the two lawmen settled for sleep in the big house, 'and that we see him first.'

Jock Mustle had refused to let Sandy Two into the homestead.

'Let him go down to the *blacks'* camp. Or, what about the verandah? You won't be held up in the morning then.'

They would leave tomorrow, and hunt the man down.

Over the next days Sandy led Hall and Stewart to various *native camps*. The two policemen lay on their bellies in the bush, watching, while Sandy Two cautiously circumnavigated the site. When the two policemen were sure Cuddles was not there, and that nothing was untoward, they went on their way.

Once or twice, acting upon the advice of pastoralists, and sensing the value of surprise, they sprang upon camps in the dark of early morning, shooting into the air and shouting. Later, the constables laughed at the consternation they'd caused, and the cowardice they'd witnessed. It almost made up for the discomfort of having to get up so early. It was quite amusing, really.

They found a sheep with its throat cut. Only the brisket had been taken. The men shook their heads over the carcass.

Bah! Such waste. As was that Cuddles himself.

The constables rode side by side, and their tracker behind. They were becoming great friends, and included Sandy Two in their games.

'He's a quiet one, isn't he?' said Stewart to Hall, as they watched Sandy pick up his saddle and self from where he'd fallen. Always the practical joker, Stewart had loosened the cinch.

Sandy Two scouted ahead, looking for tracks. Sometimes he was away for half a day at a time.

Flour, bacon, sugar, rum and ammunition had been stolen from a shepherd. There was the remains of a camp nearby; a cold fire, an empty bottle, and a pair of Jock's trousers.

At the occasional homesteads, heading west, people were very helpful. The country grew greener, the shrubs a little more above the earth. They reached yet another bay, where there was a telegraph station, and a ragged, windswept settlement. Cuddles had reportedly been sighted, and a horse stolen.

'A Chinaman?' the constables repeated, almost in unison. If not for the perpetrator they would not have concerned themselves. The victim had been camped with two Aboriginal women, and whisky, some gold cufflinks, a razor, and the belt from his trousers were taken.

Cuddles had apparently yelled, 'Ah Ling, I shoot you,' and deliberately missed.

Well, the constables agreed, the silly bastard had probably welcomed Cuddles in to help with the women. Serves him right. The policemen arrested him for being idle.

'... and without visible means of support?' suggested Sandy Two, smiling.

'Yes,' said the constables, nodding seriously at Sandy Two, as if noticing him anew. 'Good man.'

The policemen felt it would have been wrong to deny the women their primitive, but nonetheless gratifying, expressions of gratitude.

The telegraph operator emerged from his tiny hut — which seemed to anchor the row of posts and wire which stretched away as far as they could see — and handed them a telegram. They were to return to their stations.

233

Although the two men were relieved, they could not help cursing their inability to bring justice to bear upon this Cuddles blackguard. They consoled themselves as best they could before parting.

'It should never have got this far in the first place.'

'We need better laws to deal with these people.'

'The trouble is too many do-gooders expecting too much too soon.'

Sandy Two wanted to build a big and blazing campfire that night, but the constables prevented him.

On the way back to Gebalup Constable Hall called into stations. It gave him some relief from the monotony of the trip, and he was still seeking information on Cuddles' whereabouts. He shot a number of dogs at the camps, and felt rather coy with all those eyes upon him. Even where the pastoralists did not mention it, he enquired as to problems with dogs. It satisfied him, somehow, this punctuating of his return with dutiful bullets.

Sandy Two left Hall at sunset, and an hour or two later the constable rode onto the potted and dusty street of Gebalup. He'd been almost two weeks camping in the bush, living like a *savage*, and now he wanted to bathe and shave. The previous night he had dreamt of a fresh-faced Cuddles, in coloured moleskins and glittering cufflinks, waving and grinning at him. It had been particularly unpleasant to wake up to Sandy Two's sullen face across the ashes of a cold campfire.

When he saw his tent collapsed in a heap, the sentimental would-be-writer Hall thought, my nest, my solitary little nest. He felt more let-down than the tent — not having appreciated how much he had longed for the familiarity of those canvas walls.

He thought it must have been the wind, but the morning light revealed a small hole in the canvas, and confirmed that a revolver and some ammunition were missing.

Having been deflated, Constable Hall now began to swell with righteous anger, and indignation. Cuddles had obviously been here while they were chasing an old trail through the sand, a couple of days away. Constable Hall felt quite violated and, although he couldn't say it, not even to himself, he was hurt that no one had bothered to straighten things up for him. When he asked around, they all said they hadn't noticed anything amiss. The tent had been up yesterday all right.

And so when the telegram reached him: *Cuddles seen Wirlup Haven stop*; he did not stop at all but got both the horses and cleared out. Sandy One Mason was unloading his dray at the store, but he'd not seen his son yet, and so there was no help there. Hall turned to the son-in-law, Daniel Coolman.

'Nah, haven't seen the bugger.'

It gave Constable Hall a little start to see Daniel Coolman's woman (wife? Harriette?) brazenly glaring at him over a child's shoulder. She was remarkably attractive, for a *black*. Her features unusually fine. The Chinaman's women and the camps crossed his mind, briefly.

As he was about to head out of town again the constable asked Sandy One about the whereabouts of the little children, the ones he claimed as grandchildren.

'With an aunty. Their aunty's looking after them.'

Constable Hall told himself that he'd get back to that matter very soon. They couldn't do that, just move their children wherever they liked. Legally they were wards of the state, and deserved every opportunity.

Constable Hall collected one of the Mustle boys, and a Done, from the hotel. They were happy to offer assistance. The fellow was armed, after all. 'You were lucky to catch us, Constable.' They both thought there'd been a stop put to the likes of Cuddles and this sort of trouble years ago. It was no good just sending them to prison.

The three of them reached the coast in just a few hours, and the horses looked just about knocked up as the men slid from their saddles and into the telegraph office.

It was the *half-caste*, Sandy Two, who had apparently seen Cuddles. No one knew where the boy was now, but he had left directions as to where he'd made the sighting.

At around noon the next day the three men found an old campsite. It was Cuddles' sure enough. The remains of a fire, some sheep bones, a flour bag and, arranged beside the fire, a set of what appeared to be Jock Mustle's clothes. They were laid out neatly, as if the body had been slipped from within. Jock's spectacles, with the lenses smashed, were neatly folded above the collar of a flannel shirt, and those were definitely his patched moleskins tucked into a pair of old boots. The men blinked. Poking through the buttons of the trouser fly was a fish head. They could not help but peer closer. The fish's tail was jammed into the ground, and its clean ribs and spine curved up out of the clothing. Ants filled the eye sockets with busy life, and the dead fish's mouth seemed formed into a grin.

When they got back to Wirlup Haven the postmaster handed them yet another telegraph:

Cuddles seen Gebalup with horse and half-caste woman stop.

No, there was no stopping them now. The three of them surprised the *native* camp before sunrise the next morning, and those they awoke were whimpering, apologising, grumbling and shouting; all at once. Constable Hall was shocked to see Sandy Two there, and told him as much. The boy claimed that he was trying to gather information about that bloody Cuddles.

'You lying bastard.'

As soon as Sandy Two was given a moment he dressed himself, and stood on his own in the early light of day.

The three white men dispersed the group, and sat on their horses with spines erect and flies busy about their heads.

'He didn't even have shoes on,' said one of them.

A couple of days later there was another telegraph from Old Jock. He'd had a horse, saddle and bridle stolen. And the house girl was missing. He'd known it was Cuddles, Constable Hall found out later, because Jock's stolen underwear had been returned. Soiled, of course, but what would you expect from a *black*?

The Dones and Mustles were helpful. Old Jock Mustle, well, he was family, wasn't he? They were old families, and they knew about the *blacks*. They kept telling Constable Hall this.

'Oh, and Mason; well, he's harmless enough, but ... Well, he hasn't made much of a life for himself has he? I mean, he married her. It's about standards, really. And what sort of country we want this to be.' They were sincere. They had a vision, of how other places were. One of them had been born overseas, the others planned to make a trip to the mother country one day.

'Sandy Two? The son? He spends all his spare time at the camps, the women, you know. They regress, the black blood takes over, whatever some people might hope for.'

Kevin Mustle invited Constable Hall home for dinner. The Justice of the Peace from Kylie Bay would be there.

to the chief protector of aborigines

Dear Sir,

In response to your enquiries and pertinent to the new legislation I beg to report as follows:

There are a number of natives at Mustles' outer stations closer to Kylie Bay and Yarramoup, and I have removed all from the ration list for one month September 25 to October 25 during shearing season as per our correspondence, excepting Teapot — very old and infirm.

I don't feel satisfied to continue certifying these without seeing them although I get the best reports I can from PC Hall and Mr Mustle himself.

As everywhere it seems, some of the teamsters have taken native women and it will take some time to inform them of the new legislation making it an offence to cohabit. They are, of course, very mobile and independent of spirit.

At Gebalup itself there are very few natives. There is an older man here who has married a native woman.

What is the ruling regarding their progeny, and so on? They have one son, who Constable Hall informs me has been of some help to him but who has reportedly taken to spending a lot of time with natives even though he does not see himself as fitting that category. He is half-caste. There are another two children living with the same family, both half-caste or possibly quadroon. It is hard to tell. How does the legislation apply in instances such as these?

I am informed that last year the question was mooted of making a native reserve and bringing down goldfields natives. It would be quite impossible to keep them on it. But I was informed that there are islands between Wirlup Haven and Dubitj Creek which have very good soil and although some have been grazed they are all now abandoned. If your department will pay my out-of-pocket-expenses (chiefly steamer fare, or hire of Mustle's cutter?) I would go down on a trip to the islands and identify those suitable, and also, if time permitted, the natives and stations on the coast further around from here.

Many of the islands are apparently well wooded and abound with Tammin, Cape Barren Geese, Muttonbirds etc. On some I am told many rabbits. I cannot help thinking that if any honest old couple of sober habits (or for a small wage the man living hereabouts and who I mentioned as married to a native woman might be interested in such a position) who may now be on the relief list were placed in charge of these islands the natives could be induced to till sufficient garden land to keep them in vegetables and a few goats and sheep would stock the land to keep down weed, and to provide meat to supplement the natural game.

These southern blacks would then have no claim to stations, and the squatters themselves would soon weed out the useless mischievous ones as they did in the old days when Mustle informs me they used isolation on the islands as punishment.

I have spoken to Constable Hall and all he has to say is that the islands are too good for the blacks. Some of these outlying islands ought also to be used as native gaols once again. As is they return sleek and well fed from Frederickstown and bragging to their cohorts of their adventures.

Yours ...

whispering stories

Once more the three old men and I camped among dunes and small trees, and were sheltered from the wind; as Sandy One, Two, and Fanny had been. It was not so far from where they'd found Chatalong and Kathleen, and a beach walk west led to the town of Wirlup Haven where a jetty was being built. Such was the angle of the coast that it seemed possible the jetty might eventually reach all the way to the island.

Sandy Two came from the paperbarks of the soak, through the dunes, to the tossing sea. He carried his new little brother on his back, and his mother walked beside him. Jack Chatalong was riding high, looking around, enjoying the wind blowing from the sea, from out past those islands which they could not make him see. Out there, they pointed, out there! There! as if they were apparitions in the glare and salt haze.

Jack liked it but. Look at him.

The boy's nose was up; sniffing the wind, he was remarkably quiet. The wind blew his hair back, showing the extent of his forehead, and how vulnerable he was. He grinned, put his tongue out and, tasting the wind, let it whip his words away before they had even formed.

The light raced along the face of the tiniest waves as they curved and crashed onto the sand. It was dark blue out there but so clear here where tiny bubbles of ephemeral white froth floated in the water.

They walked around the beach, just to renew footprints, to skirt the edge of the reaching, receding sea. It was curiosity that made Sandy Two go that little further around the bend, to see what was stranded there.

Fanny hung back, but Sandy Two kept on, with the boy on his back until they looked down upon the body. Sandy Two thought of his mother, and what she had told him of some ancestral hero, and of how she came to be with his father.

This man had been dead for a long time. Sandy picked up a small axe which lay beside the body, and its rusty outline remained on the crushed billycan it had rested on.

The man had been tall. His clothes, although somewhat deflated, still held the shape of what the body had been. The rim of a hat remained, circling the skull. There was very little smell. Sandy noticed that the body wore two pairs of socks, and that the too-big boots had been fastidiously placed more than an arm's length away. Then the man must have stretched out, belly up, and gazed at the sky. Still beside him was the faint remains of a fire, and one hand rested upon a small Bible.

Sandy Two was fascinated — although he could not have said quite why — that the man should choose to read so close to death, that he had stayed away from his home, that he wore the clothes of Sandy's brother-in-law, Pat Coolman.

Pat's name was in the Bible.

The body was surrounded by the tracks of lizards, birds, crabs. Bits of the dark vest and moleskins had been picked away, but the cloth had proved too heavy and thick.

Sandy Two ceased his inspection to shoo little Chatalong and his incessant chatter away from the body. The boy tottered in the discarded boots. Sandy Two took them from him. They were pretty good boots; lace up ones.

'Not gunna do him no good, eh little brother? He just another dead man.'

They were stiff, but otherwise a perfect fit. Sandy took some trouble with the laces.

Sandy Two told his father all about it that evening, discreetly, so as not to disturb the children, Kathleen particularly. It was his contribution to the evening's talk.

The things they used to talk about of an evening. It was the old man mostly, with Fanny filling the gaps, adding body to the yarns. She talked in the day though, when it was quiet and you were close; when you were not really listening, or didn't want to be, sometimes. She seemed to be talking to herself, and it was not that she was sad, because she laughed so much so often, and used to say that she was home, this was her home. But it was like she was lonely. Well, what could you do?

Around the fire everyone is shadow and firelight. If you hold your hands before you in that light you see all the lines and pores. The light flickers, dies, comes back again.

The talkative — and yet always ready to listen — Jack Chatalong would fall asleep, and then there was space for others to speak.

Sandy Two, his body still learning the way of a little rum and a day's work, would be drifting up and down; asleep, awake, asleep.

The fire crackled, flared for a moment, making their skin look old, like parchment. Unlike my grandfather and myself they had no words written in their skin, but there were lines, and small markings, and it is this you have to read on such fibre. You have to read the very weave of the stuff itself, even your own. There is so little else.

Fanny led the sleepy but excited Chatalong away. As he lay prone in the dark, stars fell into his eyes, words leaked from his ears.

Sandy One boasted that he told all. Of when he first came here. Of when they lived in Frederickstown, and his children were registered and went to a mission school for a few years, and he worked the boats again. How he and Fanny and the children were reunited, and came back this way, further east, went from the coast to the goldfields and back, worked on the stations. You remember, he said to Fanny, how I saved you. Saved us all.

In the firelight, the movement of eyes, seeking reassurance.

Fanny embellished, linked, led him on. Later in the night, Fanny and the fire spoke to all the sleeping, slumped bodies. She mumbled, and sang softly to herself, often with words that they might not know. Sometimes of children she had lost, the father mother that were taken. Her brothers, sisters.

Wondering, always, how to say it softly enough so that they might remember.

At the stations, Fanny used to go to the camps to find who remained, and where she could place herself among the living. Those who had been closest to her were gone. She felt surrounded, almost, by the dead. They circled her, and there were more and more of them.

At times she still wondered if it were true, that the white ones were the dead returned; brains askew, memories warped, their very spirit set adrift. But this one, her own man, was growing stronger.

And she had recognised her children. That was the connection between the past and now.

At one station, the one at the bay shaped like a boomerang, Fanny was sitting on a wagon, looking down upon the upturned face of a sister who worked in the house, when she heard a sound, a bell, a sweet sound something like water in rocks. The expression it caused upon the face before her. It was as if that sweet sound was a frightening command, and her sister was gone. Fanny watched her disappear into the dark and solid house.

In the house — Sandy One told her — there were coloured ribbons hanging. Each rang a different bell, and each was a command to a different person to come running.

An uncle slept on a verandah. The woman of the house used to wake him in the night, give him cakes, and have him hurry hurry himself to the hut on the bay and fetch small packages of paper from the ship. Sometimes, the old man said, it was in the deep of night. The light in the window there, the post office window, told the missus to send him. It was words from her family.

Fanny saw the old man again at a later time, through the doorway. He sat beside a fire, wrapped in shadow and the smoke of very green wood. He coughed his way out to see her, and she could smell the staleness and the smoke on him.

He sat by the fire all day; it was a warm but gloomy place to be. He blew to keep the flames alive. He thought there was nothing left for him, nothing but the sound of the flame, the word for which was his name. He was the sound of flame burning low, burning backwards along a piece of wood.

A third time she called and he had gone. It was a sickness that had come with the white people. The smell of them. There were still people dying from it now; and the very boldest ones, those wanting to escape the savage fire inside them, they ran into the sea and were quenched.

The old man had stumbled, shuffled away from the verandah. Someone jeered, said look at him look. The white woman called him back, said there was a message. She shouted at him as he threw off his clothes. See them, the clothes, his erratic footprints? He was out of balance, his weight was shifting about. He walked into the sea and it swallowed him.

Sometimes, Uncle Jack Chatalong brought guests to our campfire as we moved along the coast in those years after I had first attempted reading and rewriting, and then burnt my grandfather's work. The survivors. Only a few, because not only was there the passing awkwardness of my fair skin, the searching for family names, but there was also the fact that I usually hovered in the air just above everyone's head. It was laughable, it was frightening.

'What is he?' I heard them say.

a writer

Constable Hall was a writer.

Sandy Two was a reader, and in the newspaper he read:

> *Your character, as told from your handwriting, is the truest index of your future. The tail of your J may betray meanness, whilst the forming of a T may show generosity.*
>
> *Professor Banks delineations are pretty correct. If you dislike plain speaking do not reply. Send sample of your handwriting and postal note for one shilling sixpence or twenty four penny stamps and self addressed envelope to:*
>> *Professor J J Banks,*
>> *care of post office,*
>> *Perth, WA*

Sandy Two showed the advertisement to Constable Hall several weeks later and told him he'd taken the liberty of sending some scraps of the constable's handwriting to the good professor. It was a mail day, and Sandy Two — indicating an envelope on Hall's desk — said, 'You've got your reply, by the look of it.'

Constable Hall was ever alert. It was his training, see.

'Oh yeah, I got my own results back,' said Sandy. '"Creative, and confident",' he quoted at Hall, grinning, '"Destined for great things".'

'Oh yeah?' said Hall. 'You heading out of town yet?'

The constable waited until he was sure Sandy had gone. He didn't want to snatch at the envelope too soon, because Sandy was likely to put his head back around the corner and laugh as soon as he did so. The letter was sealed, but the postmark faint. Still, it seemed genuine enough, no point accusing the bastard without good proof.

He opened it quietly.

He swore he could hear Sandy Two's laughter as he read the letter. He went out into the street. There was no one about. The air felt particularly cool on his cheeks, and he hoped he was not blushing.

jetty

Chatalong and Kathleen. The boy was not a quiet one, whereas she was. She was very reserved, as if frightened. Kathleen would knot her hands together, slowly twisting the fingers in so many ways. Perhaps she knew she could do little but listen, because Chatalong talked and talked. He liked to hear sounds emerging from himself. He farted, hummed, sang, and — when he talked — obviously shaped his words at the very last moment. It gave him an engaging charm; it made him honest, even though so much of what he said was full of contradictions. Most of it, they were sure, was true. They were equally sure he never intended to lie. It was just that he spoke as quickly as he thought and, having picked up so many strange bits and pieces of stories in his short life, understood that the only way they could be connected was by his utterances. Sometimes he presented little recitations. Chatalong was the entertainment of the camp, and Sandy Two encouraged him, thinking of his own boy self.

Fanny said, 'They're our people. We'll look after 'em.' She was thinking, I hope, of all her grandchildren, and beyond. Us and ours.

'Look, the two of them seem so pale sometimes.'

The girl's head came up, as if challenged, but Chatalong took up the words. 'I'm like a ghost,' he said.

Then whose ghost might he be? There were so many wandering about here.

Sandy One welcomed the boy. It was true, you could see it, the likes of himself, they would always be here. He said it to Daniel, and didn't bother to curse the other son-in-law. Sandy One had these moments when he wanted to sing, but he had no song left; just plans, and faith. He might have prayed, but worried that there was only himself. And her, this land, their children.

He thought of the clubs that didn't want him, and would not take his son. The Australian Natives Association, the Oddfellows ... Against all that and theirs, he had his own, admittedly frail, exultation of which he wanted to bray and boast.

He had passion aplenty, but not the words for it. Now his words left him faster than he had ever acquired them. There was the trouble with his tongue, at the tip. It was wooden and dead, the skin turning black and flaking all the time. He sighed, quickly rose up on his toes and down again, adjusting himself.

Sandy One took Chatalong with him when he carted water to Daniel's yard, and carried between the stations, and between the port and Gebalup. The boy heard things, snippets, bits of this and that, and the old man tried to explain and fit it all into a pattern for him.

Occasionally they had cause to follow a trail Fanny had

led him along years and years before. Inevitably, it merged with that of others, from soak to soak, becoming a road.

Kathleen and Fanny walked along the beach and rocks. Fanny gathered very little food from the bush. There was the sea; shellfish, fish from the rocks. Salmon came each year, herring ...

Sandy One returned with the boy asleep on the dray. Fanny was relieved just to see him again. The two children, for the ones she had lost; kept losing. She would smile even as she checked their breathing.

Sandy One, Two, the chatty little boy with them; they went into Gebalup. The townspeople looked at them. They saw a small, tanned man with a long and sandy-grey beard. Sometimes he wore kangaroo skin shoes, or worse, stood in his bare feet.

The older boy — Sandy Two? — in contrast, dressed as well as any teamster or horseman could. The fact was, he dressed presumptously. A good-looking boy — for a *native*, of course — he was very thin, and taller than his father. The little boy — Jack — was obviously indulged. It was uncomfortable to see them, it was confusing.

You could say that the old man was the blackest of all of them. It must be the influence of that woman.

Generally, when someone spoke to Sandy One, to give him instructions, say, he would raise his chin and glare at you. He would put his hands on his hips and stare. And the two boys, as likely as not, would do the same.

Still, old Sandy One, he was an original. He was old, harmless enough for the good people, in their prospective prosperity, to forgive. An enigma. An eccentric. A tough old nut. A pioneer, of sorts.

There were posters in the street and it was written up in the newspaper. Wirlup Haven was to hold a week of festivities over Christmas and New Year. Euchre Evenings, the Grand Carnival Ball, the Evening Concert and Dance; Sandy Two understood by now that such things might not be for him, and didn't entertain the idea of being involved. Not interested. He did, however, have hopes of entering the rifle match, but Constable Hall said he couldn't be allowed a firearm.

'You need a license — and if you already got one,' Constable Hall said, quickly, 'I'll revoke it.'

Sandy Two thought he might enter the bicycle race, but there were problems with that, too. The race left from Gebalup, see, and Constable Hall had warned Sandy Two away from there. Sandy Two couldn't even drive a team into the town now. He asked his father for help, but his father said no. After all, he only had the Dones' animals and wagon, and they wouldn't ...

The teamsters kept a close watch on one another in the weeks leading up to the games. They didn't want to see any of their rivals in special training, and any horse that had been out of harness and not working was disallowed an entry.

Despite their intentions to keep their horses rested, the carts and wagons and drays rolled out to Mount Barren at a frisky pace. The drivers excited their passengers, who laughed and sang; the telegraph operators, the jetty workers, the mariners, the storekeeper, the family from the pub, the workers from the mine. And none of them liked being passed by the pastoralists in their sulkies and two-in-hands, although everyone waved, friendly enough.

Wagons and drays rolled along, slewing here and there in the sand. The children and some of the adults leapt off and walked when the track began to rise. They went only a little way up, to where there was a small, grassy plain among trees. It was — oh, it was just like an English Parkland, people said. Again. Fanny looked around at the dry grass, the tight and tangled growth beneath the trees. It had not been burnt for years.

There were people everywhere, and with all the newly scented cloth and colours it was like flowers about to spread their seed. They were scattered, too, by wind and sun into small clumps, and gathered around blankets spread with food. Those who could not find shade sat beneath umbrellas, or tarpaulins spread between wagons.

Fanny, Sandy Two, Jack Chatalong and Kathleen Coolman kept together. They were among the other teamsters and their women, among farm labourers and shepherds. It was a group comprised mostly of surviving Nyoongars, and Wongis forced here from other areas to work on stations.

Sandy One returned, already grinning with the grog, and took Chatalong and Kathleen firmly by the hand. The three of them walked over to where Chatalong's Sunday school teacher sat on a blanket by the Mustles' sulky. Children were playing around her.

The two children ran with the others. One or two parents grabbed their children by the hand and walked them away. They who were thought so pale, must have suddenly appeared so dark.

Jack's view was divided into segments by the spokes of a wagon wheel.

There were races between children with their legs in

sacks, between couples with their legs tied; there were runners balancing eggs on spoons, or hindered by unlikely combinations of cigar and umbrella. Children and women danced around a tall pole.

Kathleen played with Will and other small children. Daniel had brought his son, but left Harriette and the girls at home.

Someone beside Fanny muttered, 'She too black for him? Frightened she might catch something from us, eh?'

Fanny smiled, shook her head.

The men went in a foot race, but the cheering seemed somehow thin, and you could hear Fanny's voice, particularly, singing with that of her grandchildren as Sandy Two threw his grin and arched chest across the line. They saw him raise a finger at Kevin Mustle. Breathless faces gathered around Sandy, and Daniel slapped him hard on the back.

A voice came past them, soft in the wind.

'He shouldn't be racing with the others.'

It died, or continued on to elsewhere or some other time. There was just too much laughter, the men so red-faced and loud, and people distracting one another all the time.

Old man Mustle was on his feet, and his voice reached as far as to where Sandy had gone, to where Chatalong sat. The old man was swinging his arms about.

'Treacle-buns, the treacle-buns,' the voices called.

Bread buns, dipped in treacle, hung from a line strung up between two trees. People were gathered parallel to the line of buns. One of the Done sons nudged young Sandy in the ribs, saying go on have a go, and then had him by the elbow and what could he do but grin, and go along? Jack went to go too, but someone pushed him back. 'Not yet, little fella, wait till you're a bit older.'

'Look at 'em, the *darkies*.' A woman's voice this time, rising, blooming above those others which rose and fell and faded everywhere about them.

The young men's hands were tied behind their backs, and each had a sticky, treacle-coated bun dangling just before his head.

'Go.'

And the people in the crowd were all laughing, up on their feet, the women craning to see, the small children being lifted, all wanting to see this sight. Telling themselves of the simple obvious greed of these *natives*! Shouting their delight at seeing dark heads jabbing, bobbing and twisting. And all lips, all tongues were so alive and so pink, albeit engaged in such different ways. And there, there, everywhere; everybody showing their teeth.

Everyone laughing.

Faces smeared with treacle.

Everyone having such a good time.

Or nearly everyone. Sandy Two had hardly moved. He glanced along the row either side of him. Saw the intense faces which surrounded them.

'Get into it, Sandy.' But now Sandy was also laughing. He laughed at those pecking at the swinging, sticky buns. He stepped back, and he laughed at the spectators.

Daniel, his brother-in-law, ran along the row tossing flour into the sticky faces. It clung thickly. The faces were suddenly white, shocking. One of the Mustle boys ran from the other side. He grabbed Sandy and pushed him back with the others. Sandy staggered, struggling to keep his balance because his hands were still tied behind his back, and one of the Mustles was smearing treacle into his face. Sandy felt their hands leave him, and he tried to stand as tall and proud as he could. Even with treacle smearing his vision he saw Daniel Coolman running at him, and that he didn't hesitate before tossing the flour.

Laughter rose and broke over Sandy like waves, rose and roared like the air through the blowholes along this granite coast. He held himself still, like granite, remembering black and white minstrels, and various other shameful entertainments.

As soon as he was free he splashed water on his face, and rubbed at the sweet shit, the caking flour there.

There was a corroboree at the end of the day, for the white folk. Some very old men from Mustle's most distant station arrived in the back of a dray, dressed in old underpants and pieces of cloth. A couple of farmhands joined them. Sandy would not dance. 'What do I know about that stuff?' He stood away from his mother, asking this of anyone who would listen. He stood over amongst the paperbarks, sneering, crying inside.

He felt a hand run down his back and squeeze his upper arm. He snorted, and turned to his mother with his chin raised.

The dancers went through the motions, and young Sandy heard children crying, the harsh words between the mothers and fathers; saw his father helping his drunken brother-in-law to the cart, and a little boy behind them.

Constable Hall and Kevin Mustle left him with four donkeys and an old cart to carry the dancers back to the camp.

Wirlup Haven had a school, and barely enough students to keep it open. In the one room were the children of the telegraph operator, the postmaster, various harbourside officials, the storekeeper, and a station manager. Gebalup's school was larger because of the company mines, and a few farmers lived close enough to the town boundary to make the trek to school worthwhile for their children. Occasionally, a family — hesitating before leaving the port town — found their children had already been enrolled at the Wirlup Haven school.

Sandy One, Fanny, their boy, and the two small children had a permanent camp in a small grove of peppermint trees, a couple of miles west of Wirlup Haven and the most easterly examples of such trees along the whole south-west coast. You could step out from among the dunes, onto the beach, and then around the sand into the town; a store, a pub, a telegraph office and a clutch of shabby storage sheds. The schoolroom leaned against the back of the telegraph office.

Sandy One walked Chatalong and Kathleen to school for their first day. He swaggered into the schoolyard, calling out greetings to anyone in earshot. Chatalong jogged at his side, Kathleen close behind. The teacher seemed surprised but warmed to Sandy One's friendliness. After all, the school needed to keep its numbers up to retain its funding. Here were two pupils. They were likely to stay. She liked the job, and was courting one of the Mustle boys.

She swept little Chatalong and Kathleen into the classroom with one arm and closed the door with the other. The boy turned as she did so, glimpsing the old man's back as the door closed and he stepped from the tiny verandah.

Kathleen scanned the class quickly, saw the faces turned to her, the teacher's desk, and the dark surface behind it all marked with loops and lines and squiggles of white.

So they were welcomed in, this brown-skinned boy and his fairer sister; this talkative boy and the girl who stared and listened. The first thing Chatalong needed — it very soon became obvious to his teacher — was to learn to listen. Like his sister. It was not easy, Chatalong seemed to talk as he breathed, and so the teacher simply had to tie a handkerchief about his mouth to accustom him to the absence of his own voice, and to help him realise that daylight and his own silence could coexist. Kathleen sat with him, reading his eyes and small movements, fearing that otherwise she would lose touch with him completely. He would not stand that isolation. He needed words moving in and out as he breathed.

But the boy took to his books with an appetite, and readily wandered into the stories the teacher read to them in the afternoon. Learning silence, he played the voices inside his head, and brought them out for his sister to accompany in their intimacy as they stepped the white strip of sand in the afternoons.

Chatalong, particularly, was elated when he saw only his own footprints on the morning's sand. He liked to judge just how far the tide and waves would come during the day, and then see, in the afternoon, the evidence of where he must've flown for a while before the marks in the sand resumed. Kathleen walked higher, taking the soft sand, and preserving her trail. In the afternoon she walked the same path so carefully that each footprint was surrounded, before and after, by its companions going the opposite way. Chatalong experimented, walking backwards in exactly the same prints, and concentrating on getting his weight right so that the marks would still read of forward movement. He never achieved this, as Fanny proved to him.

He dreamt of chalk moving across the black space of board, and how it left small trails of powder. He liked the curving letters best. Some of the others were like weapons, he thought. Spearheads, axes and shovels. Kathleen took pleasure in the regularity, the patterns of their writing exercises, and cared less what these things said.

Fanny left them in the mornings at the spot where the beach curved to show the little town, and each afternoon as the children rounded the same curve they saw her waiting at the edge of the dunes.

Late in the year Chatalong began to linger on the beach where the boats unloaded. Kathleen continued on, and the boy would see her and Fanny as he rounded the curve of the beach, the two of them talking softly and drawing in the sand as they waited for him.

They had begun building a jetty. Jack read the numbers, 1906, cut into a pier, and when he got around the curve of beach to where Fanny and Kathleen waited in the shade of some rocks he told them of the numbers, and drew them in the sand. He drew other letters, and read the words.

Sometimes Sandy One would be there also, and he laughed at Fanny and read the words and numbers with the boy and girl. They counted together on their fingers and taught her something of what they knew.

'Yeah,' Uncle Will said, in one of those long spaces between memories. 'I went to school in Gebalup. Me and some of my sisters. They were fostered out.'

The smoke caught me, lifted me with it. I looked down upon scalps, and an occasionally upturned face.

In the afternoons Chatalong counted the jetty piers. They stepped further and further from the shore. He thought of them as like steps, like places where some athlete in giant's boots could leap, from one to the other. But then what? Wave his arms about, this pretender in giant's boots? Wave his arms about and fall into the sea.

'Sometimes,' Uncle Will or Uncle Jack told me, 'Fanny talked about those islands. They used to take our people out there.' So it must've been Uncle Jack talking, because Uncle Will never talked that way. 'They took people out to the islands and left them. They were places of the dead. Some of our spirit is out there now.'

The jetty stepped toward those islands which often looked like blue haze or heavy clouds on the horizon. Other days, you could see the detail of them, the furry vegetation, and the grey-bone parts of them where the sea smashed. Between the island and a distant headland, the horizon shifted and rippled.

Jack Chatalong used to watch the lines of the horizon moving right to left, disturbingly contrary to the way his eye learned to follow the words on a page, until they gathered themselves together, and the world split, and that white flower forced its way through. It blossomed, died, presumably sent its seed away. Each different, each the same.

Sometimes, from their camp, you saw the sun appear at that intersection of sea, sky, and land.

The jetty stepped toward those islands. Stepped toward

the ships which came from out there, as if squeezed from that regular, rippling rent where sea met sky.

Chatalong waved to Sandy Two, who leapt from one of the teamsters' wagons and came over to Kathleen and him.

Chatalong leaned against the young man's leg, and wrapped an arm around it as if it were a sapling. This was their home. They watched the ships rock on the windswept sea, their bare masts swaying like skeletons. The boy and Kathleen held Uncle Sandy's hands. The ocean was rows of white-haired heads moving toward them, with that quick moment of darkness between each one. The sea outside the reef was covered with them and inside the crashing foam, after a little peace, they formed again — smaller, weaker, fewer — in the blue and green around the moored ships.

Tiny men swayed on cobweb ladders and clambered over the sides of the ships into rowboats. Each tested his balance for a moment on the thin wood between himself and the sea's surface before falling to his knees, or into the arms of his fellows. They folded themselves among one another and the boxes and bags of supplies.

Sandy Two told the children of when he was a boy — but it was at Kylie Bay, not here — and had seen hundreds of white men running along a beach after one of their own, who was dressed like a woman and howling like a mad thing. His tongue had lolled from his mouth and trailed in his slipstream. The police stood befuddled, but then — working like sheepdogs — they caught the madman. He protested, laughed that he was just pretending, was just bored with drinking and waiting for his miner's license.

The jostling, jeering crowd of men turned their

attention to the bellowing cattle swimming ashore. A cow fell as it came into the shallows, its eyes rolling in its skull, and its blood flowed with the turquoise water.

'Shark! Shark!' Sandy had seen the man carrying a woman in the shallows, and the man had jumped and lifted his feet as quick as he could when he heard the shouts. He didn't drop the woman or, if he did, she walked on water. The woman was a Mustle, a new Mrs Mustle.

'And that's how Mrs Mustle got here,' said Sandy Two. 'My dad brought her across and your mother was already here, and Uncle Daniel and Aunty Harriette. All of us were here already.'

Now the three of them watched cattle tossed overboard, and saw how their eyes once again rolled as they staggered from the water suddenly burdened by the return of their own weight.

Like cattle themselves, men had for some years milled about on this shore; circling, trying to centre and make themselves steady. Some slung their swags onto a wagon, and followed it to the goldfields. Wagons were loaded with axes and shovels, with iron and cloth, with timber, with foodstuffs and finery, and then rolled away, groaning, from water to water.

Fanny and the two children, as her other children had done, climbed to the top of the load. It was as high above the ground, swore Chatalong, as the tips of the masts were above the ships' decks. They peered over, down, grinning.

Men looked up, and saw the faces of that black woman and the children gazing down.

There was a trail of things discarded; coats, collars, ties … Hooves and wheels compacted, crushed, cut the earth, marking strong lines through the piles of bullock camel donkey horse shit. Coming up past their very own mine a half a day from the ships, Jack saw the sea a last time, and that white line beside the islands where the swell broke.

And now it was his, Chatalong's, turn as a little boy, said Sandy Two. And soon there'll be this jetty for the boats to tie up to, and those ones will walk down onto the jetty, and across the water and onto this beach right here.

Sandy Two sat in the soft, white sand and held the boy within the curve of his own body. Kathleen huddled in front of Chatalong and between Sandy Two's outstretched legs. It was early morning and there was a chill land breeze. They watched a huge boiler being rolled off a ship, and heard it resounding like a vast drum to each tap and knock as it was rolled and jostled into position. The boat tilted alarmingly — it seemed it must capsize — and then the boiler was released. It rose again with a great flower of water, and they could see it, each time, like a vast hollow seed as it bobbed, bobbed, bobbed; it and the boat both.

In the little classroom the school children heard the teamsters cursing the donkeys, horses, and bullocks, as the animals leaned into their creaking harnesses and toiled up the slope of the beach to bring the great tanks ashore. The resonating cylinders rolled inland, to the 'fields, with long lines of beasts straining before them.

At the top of the hill leading away from the beach Constable Hall rode alongside Sandy One and two other men as they trudged through the soft sand.

'You got a permit to employ these men?' asked Hall of the teamster, who was congratulating the long line of animals for having reached the crest of the long sandy slope. Constable Hall repeated his question, 'These two, Sandy

Mason and Harry Cuddles, you got a permit for them?'

Sandy Two called across to the policeman. 'I'm helping my father. You know that. I just come over to lend these fellas a hand, all this sand.'

The policeman turned his back on Sandy Two.

'Don't be bloody ridiculous,' said Sandy One. 'Don't you know your own laws?'

'The law's changed,' said the constable. 'Whoever employs him needs a permit.' He continued, 'No drinking.'

'He's not of age.'

'Well, even when he is. If he looks under sixteen, then he's an Aborigine. He looks it to me. You want to keep him away from the camp if he's not, Sandy. He's got a woman there, I hear, better be careful — associating with them, you know. Might pick up something. Course, if he's white then it's an offence to cohabit.'

'Trouble for being there, trouble for not being there! Well, me and Fanny, we're married. Got the paper to prove it. And the boy's birth certificate too, so that'll prove his age.'

'I'm not talking about your wife. I'm talking about that boy of yours, he's caused me trouble, you both know it. I can put him on a reserve, I can send him away. If you don't. And I'm keeping an eye on those younger ones of yours too.'

'We've all got rights. They been all brought up as good as anyone. They're not *savages*, they're my kids. They're people.'

'Yeah, well, you don't want them associating with *darkies* then, and you want to tell your missus that too. Tell her to keep her visitors away.'

a rich lode, or

Sandy One and his family were a little way inland, living on Mustle's property. It was winter and the storms lashing the coast had swept into their little grove. Sandy One was not as young or healthy as he once was. The Mustles let him erect a humpy on their land. After all, he was still useful enough around the sheds, and they felt a certain obligation to him and his family.

A Sunday. Sandy One wandered away, going nowhere really, although he hoped the rifle he carried signalled some firm intention, such as hunting. Unknown to the old man, Chatalong followed him and — even secreting himself along like this — continued to whisper some sort of commentary.

They moved off into a fine, drizzling rain; the old man, and the whispering boy following a little after him, as if they were part of a series, or a variation upon a constant pattern. By the time they had, as it were, merged, and a tiring Chatalong was beside the dreaming old man, they had already walked a long way, had moved through the series of hills and gullies that ran between the coast, several miles away, and a chain of salt lakes to the north. The narrow-leafed poison bush (so called because it is poisonous to stock, although indigenous creatures eat it with no ill-effect) was rampant in a thin strip of land here, and had provided the apparent reason for the Dones to erect a fence around it some time before they relinquished the lease.

When it rained heavily, the water rushed through this land via a gully and into a soak near where the Dones' first homestead had been, and from where they had moved a little over a decade ago, stripping the place of what they could and leaving behind them only dry and already crumbling stone walls.

Sandy One and Chatalong came across a mob of kangaroos in a small plain of waving grass and Sandy, for some reason, shot at a big buck which would have been too tough for eating. Perhaps he targeted it because of the way it glanced over its shoulder at them, or because it would provide more sport for the dogs, or ... Jack Chatalong could see no apparent reason. But Sandy One only wounded the animal. They followed its blood-spattered trail, and heard the dogs at it, then one of them yelping in pain. The sound sent a thrill through the boy.

They found the dog whimpering and with its guts hanging out. The roo had sliced it open. The other dogs were tearing at the writhing kangaroo and blood spattered their eyes, ears, snarling snouts.

Old Sandy shot the injured dog and, as he turned, he saw Chatalong with something in his hands. The boy's hair was damp from the drizzle; the water in drops and web-like strands, and through the fog of years, of the rum and disease eating him, Sandy One once again saw a piddling little creek, the small sheet of granite and its boulders. Almost all the trees had gone.

Chatalong stood on a piece of granite which stuck out from the slope in the way bone, broken from its skeleton, emerges from split flesh.

'Look.'

Floodwaters had torn at the last tree, an old one bent by winter gales, and toppled it. Small gullies had been cut into the soil, and now there were collections of bones, mixed with sticks and small boulders where they had been caught and dumped by the rushing water. Brittle lines of white, of yellow, stabbed from the flat spaces of clay and sucked at what light there was on this day.

'There's more,' called Chatalong, faltering. It was a skull he held in his hands.

Sandy One called him away. 'Leave it be. Don't muck about with them, Chat.'

Hard hooves galloped in his chest as Sandy One called the little boy to him, noticing (in a strange parenthesis as he did so) how pale he seemed. The day cleared momentarily, and Sandy saw a single expanse of grey-black sky and sea over the boy's shoulder, and a white line appear in it, way out there, about where the horizon would be.

Then saw gold at his feet. Perhaps a reef of it …

As you know, Uncle Jack, Uncle Will, with me carrying my grandfather — we went to that sorry place.

'We had the mine just a little way over there,' said Uncle Jack.

We were quiet. Where were the words for what we felt?

The boy Chatalong had to speak, always, as if something spoke through him.

Once again, Fanny came singing, Sandy One trailing behind her …

Collect them, all, and stack them, place them rest them together. Bones, white like the skin of the young ones will be, the children flowing on, becoming paler and paler and just as dead.

Well, Fanny sang. Something.

We had hidden them away in a crevice, those silent bones. Why? Well, what could we do?

mine mind awaking

Daniel Coolman slapped himself on the back. Of course I do not mean this literally, because already he was a bulky, inflexible and stiff-limbed man. He shook hands with himself — if you know what I mean — because old Sandy One had made a find and had come to him for help. They had thought it was reef gold, and they could just pick it off the surface. Trouble was, it shifted about.

They shafted the earth, but still couldn't hit the gold spot.

Daniel had a haulage contract with the Dones, so the mine provided a further connection to the pastoral family, which was good for business.

Sandy One worked for the Mustles, the Dones, and for his own son-in-law. He kept thinking, strike it rich, be a boss man in this way, his son-in-law's way. Do that for Fanny, show Harriette, the little ones, that this is the way. Daniel was a man in the town; he kept his wife to the house, their kids at the Gebalup school.

Sandy One wanted that gold to prove he was someone. He was wishing, hoping it could be so; if only it was not at this place. He told Fanny as much, scraping his sore and stinging tongue through his teeth all the time. Of course, he would rather not dig there, but ...

And if Daniel didn't want young Sandy working with them, well what could he do about it?

Daniel hired some men and they put down a shaft. There was always just enough to encourage them. To begin with, Daniel made just enough to buy materials to begin a shaft, to begin to dig. They found just enough to encourage them to continue down, down, down. Like rabbits, said Chatalong, on one of his weekend visits, those rabbits which had followed the Coolman twins across the continent.

They found just enough to encourage them to cart ore to the railway which ran to one of the big company's batteries for crushing, then back to the port. This was all the railway they had, despite the persistent protests of the Chamber of Commerce, for whom the isolation from the vast and spreading lines of steel to the north and west was a continual source of anxiety.

The train grumbled and snorted, rolled to and fro on its strips of steel, ignorant of its isolation, impatient for connection.

'The end of an era,' the teamsters muttered to themselves.

The trip from Wirlup Haven to Gebalup had been Sandy's livelihood, necessary to his independence and self-respect in the town. Now he depended on his son-in-law and the likes of the Dones, the Mustles and more, simply for cash. He carried goods from the harbour to Mustles' station, and even more occasionally from

271

Gebalup to other stations. Whenever he could he went to his — their — mine.

Sometimes, coming up from the darkness into the sun, he felt a cold and numbing fear. He felt them there like a whisper, like the memory of a whisper; so how must Fanny feel, she being so much stronger than he? Such loss.

He crossed land which, neglected, was opened to the sun; was grazed, razed, shaved, plucked. Now the crevices and dimples which still held moisture and where a few trees remained were lavished with visits, had paths worn to and away from them.

But what made him think a land could be lonely? As if it felt, or thought, or dreamed. Where did such a thought come from?

So the mine made just enough to keep Sandy One working. And just enough for Sandy One to dream a dream this late stage of his life, because he knew he was dying. His words, his stories were going; now it was his tongue.

Sandy One erected a hut, a most firm and rigid humpy, around the corner of the beach in what had become their little grove. But, there were laws about camping now. There were reserves, too, for *blacks*. Even those teamsters still in work had sites where they could and could not camp.

Chatalong and Kathleen were at the school. *Blacks*, said the adults. Those pale and tanned black ones. Chalkybones, said the children. The adults kept an anxious eye on the fluctuating enrolment numbers.

It seemed the mine was nothing but dirt. And there was less and less work for a teamster. There was less and less work for an old sailor, an old shepherd, even if he could read and write. And if there was something about him that made people uncomfortable, this teamster with a *gin* wife and a bunch of mongrel kids.

He used to keep a roo carcass hanging in a tree. Constable Hall came to see him about health requirements, noted the roo and the rough toilet, sniffed about the camp.

'Breathe in deep, constable.' It was a whisper.

'What?' He spun on his heel.

Sandy and Fanny, those two children. It was now not so much that they kept themselves apart, but that they were kept apart.

Young as he was, Chatalong helped the tongue-clicking old man. When they set the explosions underground and mouthed the numbers up in the bright light, Chatalong would watch Sandy One's tongue, its tip scarred and hard like a parrot's, and shiver as the earth trembled under his feet.

The horses carted ore to the railway in tipping wagons.

From her vantage point on a ramp beside the railway, Kathleen watched the old man approach. His hair was as white as beach sand, and yet bounced like the tip of a wind-wave. Chatalong walked behind him like a small and solid shadow, and then came two teams of horses, each pulling wagons. Sandy walked up the earthen ramp, and Chatalong joined him. The horses paused while the ore was tipped into the railway car below, then returned to the mine without needing a command.

Sandy and Kathleen rode the second cart back to the mine and Chatalong stayed at the railway for a rest, and waited for the next load. He listened to batteries hammering in the close distance, crushing the ore, pounding. He, the raw earth; together they trembled and shivered.

Chatalong sat up, wondering at himself, this sudden dragging from sleep into consciousness. Sandy One was lighting a lamp, and the hessian walls leaned into its glow.

The batteries still pounding in the distance; his own nervous heartbeats.

The old man's footsteps faded away and Chatalong was left in darkness, imagining underground. If only the air could stay as sweet and fresh, he could stay underground for ever. He liked the closeness, the way the space around him closed and forced him inward, and how the boundary between inside and out seemed to move, to go away.

Once he had entered another mine, and they had walked along dark tunnels until his legs were numb and the soles of his feet ached.

He thought these secret tunnels under the earth might, someday, connect. People walking above need never know those hidden beneath them.

Fanny would not visit the mine let alone go underground. She refused to come, refused to descend. But Chatalong loved it underground, the way you fell from the light and rumbled deep into the earth. Down there he was hidden, was a secret, and yet might return at any time with riches. Coming up to the light he felt like a hero, must have been, the way Fanny embraced him upon each return.

Chatalong dreamt, underground. In his confused waking he was gummy-eyed and gaping. The brittle sunlight, the air, the sharp noises upset him somehow.

He listened to his own footsteps approaching the mine. Several people were gathered around the shaft. The construction leaning awkwardly above them — its erect geometry ruined — looked particularly feeble. One of the men put an arm around Chatalong's thin shoulders.

It seemed such a long trip back to Wirlup Haven, days weeks years and years. Sandy One should have died. Instead, he was a silent shape huddled on the floor of the wagon, a face lined with suffering.

Fanny saw strangers arriving with her boy. And they, in turn, saw the challenge in her face. Chatalong, perhaps for the first time, saw that she was a Nyoongar. She was standing before the humpy, and yet moving toward him and growing larger like a plant blossoming. Kathleen seemed sliced by sunlight into shade, light, shade; and the three pieces of her, neatly stacked, leant in the doorframe.

The earth had closed in around this father-man and left them a remnant. The faces around him told Chatalong this.

The town rallied. First, the Dones and Constable Hall had a good talk with Daniel Coolman. Wise heads offered advice.

That poor family. The man of that family was as good as dead. Their breadwinner. Their saviour. They would not be able to fend for themselves, they would need help …

Others might come, their kind.

Why, there'd be a *natives' camp* right in town before you knew it.

See! That Sandy Two was back already, as if he knew this was going to happen. And that meant a Cuddles would not be far away.

They were family, together. They placed the husband the father into the wagon, and bundled blankets and cushions around him. Fanny and Kathleen went one way with him, their cargo, and Sandy Two and Chatalong went another. They were family, together.

Once around the foot of the ranges, Fanny, Kathleen and cargo camped at a waterhole. Kathleen leaned toward the water, and saw that the paperbarks behind her did the same.

The dogs barked a warning. She and her reflection spun away from each other, leaving only trees, clouds, sky in the pool. And now, from between the trees, came oh so many people. There were kids, men, women; there were horses and a couple of carts. (One of which, Kathleen saw, was held together with wire and rope and continued to sway even after the horse had stopped.)

Sandy Two waved to her from a cart which was laden high with possum skins.

And there, standing precariously at the very top of the load, so dark against the sky and holding his arms out as if he were about to fly away into it, was Chatalong. Chatalong — where's he been? Doing what? He was grinning, laughing, letting words fall fast and almost incomprehensible from his lips.

What parson tellin' you,
Ole Mister Dodd,
Tell you in Sunday School?
Big pfeller God!

He slid down the skins, and came to a sudden stop right between Fanny and Kathleen. The two women stepped back, and Sandy One, who they had carried and propped protectively at their feet, keeled over. Now they bent to him, and their patting, plucking hands reassured him and one another.

Chatalong explained as best he could. 'You know 'em,' he said to Fanny. 'They know you.'

Fanny thought of a young dog running to and fro, excited, not sure which master to stay with.

Kathleen climbed the stack of soft possum hides and looked down upon Sandy One, the father, who once again had fallen, and lay stiff and pale amongst animated limbs, mouths, voices. He seemed another being. Suffering.

Kathleen had seen a dark-bearded man on a cross, in the schoolroom and church.

She might also be one apart. Like Chatalong, who — because of all that talking — also was. And yet was not. Because of all that talking.

The other children, having looked at Sandy (what's this, a tree? Oh, this is old Sandy) now dispersed in the way water rushing down a gully might pause and divert its flow at a heap of earth before spreading across flat ground.

It was sandy ground they camped on, shaded and dry. At its centre there was a spring.

The elders circled this one who had called himself the father.

They were moving again; there were buggies, carts, horses, but mostly it was walking. Some would stop, dig in the earth, collect food.

Sandy One lay, pale and paralysed, in the wagon. His gaze moved about the sky, focused on the edge of the blanket they'd rigged up to shade him, returned to the distance. He looked impassively at faces that happened into his vision; his family's, or those many impelled by curiosity and who spoke his name.

Sandy Two and Fanny would lift the old man down, and drape a blanket from the wagon for Fanny to bathe him.

Chatalong came to Kathleen with some kind of fruit. From that plant with the blue flower. It dries you up.

Its bitter seeds took the moisture from her mouth.

Fanny would wander away during the day, as she used to do when she was young, and in the years her children were at the mission. Once again, she was not alone.

They came back with vegetables from the bush. Usually, there was kangaroo, rabbit, possum. So much more here than at the goldfields or the drier land to the east. But not quite like home.

Late in the day, when they stopped, shelter quickly grew. Some places it was something draped over a buggy to block the wind while the buggy kept off any rain. Or it might be a tent, or a wall of bushes. There were rushes or bark woven through sticks jammed upright in the earth, and small bush shelters leaning each side of a tent, with a leafy roof reaching out to the fire.

These were uncles, aunts, cousins camped around them. And although Sandy Two surprised his little brother by saying that there were lots who had gone and were dead, still there were many people, and in some places they stopped it seemed that there were fires going all about them as if they were only one among stars in the sky.

They camped close, families in their own places, several steps away from one another. There was rabbit stew, or roo onion potato, maybe possum baked on the coals.

They propped Sandy One among them, and Fanny fed him.

A great fire, a party crowd. This wasn't just corroboree stuff, Sandy Two told his little brother. You got all sorts of Entertainments here. There were people here who could play a piano. Plenty could paint in watercolours and oils. Some read and recited poetry.

The strange wheezing of a piano accordion drew Chatalong into the circle of firelight. The flames and music leapt away from him, up. Pieces of wood tapped, but they were dancing a waltz. A woman grabbed him, 'I'll show you.'

'But,' he boasted, 'I already know.'

The woman's face in his; together they looked at their feet sliding across the earth, looked back into the other's grinning face.

Sandy One came gliding past.

A woman held him in her arms, and was skipping, was dancing on the waves of the accordion. Chatalong could see old Sandy's toes trailing on the ground. The woman's laughter was unceasing, rolling with the music. Fanny pushed through, saying no no, but her hands slid down the back of the dancer and she was laughing too, unable to stop herself. People bent double, slapped their thighs, and all the time Sandy One's expressionless face, its chin contentedly resting on the woman's shoulder and its watery eyes blinking, seemed to float through space.

Kathleen was laughing with the rest of them.

Fanny kissed her husband on the cheek. People chuckled still, even as the music and the dancing finished.

Chatalong sat at the edge of the circle, behind the shifting accordionist. His back was cold in the darkness, his face hot from the smouldering inside him.

Chatalong shivered. He went to the fire and joined the kids already there. They built and stoked the fire until it was crackling and throwing tongues up at the icy sky, out to the random geometries of bush shelters and tents. The shadows played, caressing the ground, only settling, only drawing the night back in from between and beyond the trees once the children had fallen asleep.

Chatalong wanted to creep to Fanny and Sandy One, mother and father, and sleep with them. He found Fanny curled around the old man, whose face held a thin moon and sharp stars.

So he huddled with the others, fire warming them all.

Mostly they burned off timber which had been cut and stacked the previous year. Some of the men knew the older farmers. They spoke of how there were so many new farmers, spreading out from the snaking spine of the railway Chatalong had still not seen. There were new fences, too.

Sandy Two went with some of the old men, and they organised work. If the farmer knew the police, or had a general permit, they also organised the money among themselves.

Occasionally a woman did laundry for the farmer's wife. They never went into anything like a town. 'Wait until closer to home,' said Sandy Two to Chatalong, 'you can stay with us. Uncle Harry has a block there. You're not too old for school, never too late to catch up.'

The farmer who came down to their camp on horseback had a rifle. 'You're not camping here.'

But they always had. And he owed them money.

'Only for a job well done. Look, this is my land. I've sweated for it. You're fouling my water, the dogs will have my sheep.'

He fired the rifle into the ground in front of them, and left no way to argue.

They used the axes, and rolled small timber onto tree stumps, felt the wind; a good wind meant a clean burn. They lit fires early in the day to burn the roots out of the ground, then went out for meat. After dark they walked back among the fires, stoking and rolling red orange yellow hearts back over where the claws of stumps still gripped the dark earth.

Back closer to home, Harry Cuddles, who had hunted possum with Sandy Two, held a small property the white men's way. With him lived his mother — a cousin of Fanny's — and a wife and several children. He and Sandy Two had been earning a good living from possums for years now. Like Sandy, Harry had a wagon and horses, and had money to build a shed, put in a well. He would need to make improvements to keep the lease.

'No woman good enough for me,' Sandy Two would say, often, grinning.

Chatalong and Sandy Two built a little bush shelter beside the tent for old Sandy to sit under during the day. The old man was improving. He could move his head and right arm. He could read — if they held a page before him — and signal with a gesture of his head, and speak just a little. At least, he made noises and Fanny interpreted for him. Chatalong liked to sit with him. He would take out the old fellow's pocket watch, show it to him, and put it back. He began to find it easy to be silent.

The old man's eyes often welled with tears, which ran down his face and onto his chest. If they propped him up he could remain in a sitting position, although he had to be shifted regularly because of his sores. He would close his eyes, and still the tears ran. Chatalong wondered at this desire for blackness before your eyes, at what went through the old man's mind.

At least now, Sandy One was remembering. He must have seen it clear; such things as corpses shifting with the wind or ocean water, scattered bones, ears and other purses of flesh strung over a mantelpiece, and pools of water showing his own face against a blood-red sky. Yes, like an island in some bloody fluid. And he had memories even — although not strictly his own — of his own absence. And the island sinking in the rising aftermath of violence.

Harriette came to see them, with all her children. Daniel was ill, she said. He's in the hospital for a few days.

It was the first time she had visited, a long time since they had spoken.

They sat around a blazing fire. The night bright with a moon; calm, cold. If you let your eyes adjust you could look into the dark and see shadows, and each leaf seemed cupped to take water from the air.

A bird called hauntingly. A curlew.

The dusty roads gleamed in the moonlight, and

curlews walked along them, uttering their weird, mournful cries. They held their heads high, and lifted and replaced their feet so proud and fastidious.

Harriette said to her child, 'Listen? Hear that?'

Listen.

'What? Someone been dragging their toes in the ground. Not lifting their feet proper, not putting them straight in front.'

'Not me, Mum,' said Will.

'Well, they're crying. They're crying for some silly people not walking properly; not walking proud. They feel sorry for them — they always walk so nice and proud themselves.'

Harriette looked across at her mother. Was she thinking the same thing, of a young girl barely out of the mission being lifted from the wagon by a group of strange men? The mother did all she could; she threw a blanket over the other children so they would not see.

'Constable Hall is no more. He's gone; to war,' said Sandy Two. He was fairly beaming. Bobbing and ducking to keep his image in the tiny mirror hanging on the tree before him, Sandy Two shaved, slicked his hair with water, and when they came back from town he and Harry had new clothes and shoes for all the kids.

Sandy had seen the constable. It was true, there was a new one. The constable said that the kids had to go to school.

'And me,' said Sandy Two, 'I'm joining the army, the horses.'

Now, as both Uncle Will and Uncle Jack liked to point out to me, the roads in the old days were quite different to those of today, even if we disregard the bitumen ones.

All that talk of roads on which they'd worked. Of corners where the gradient wasn't right, or where the surface had become holed and pitted. Maybe it was because they'd worked on the Main Roads Department gangs, or because we so often spent our days on bitumen. Sometimes we drove with the windows open, slowly enough that the wind did not roar or whip at us too much. I felt like I rode its back, or within it, quite still at its centre, yet rushing along. You could taste the air, even amongst the desolation of cleared and fenced land. Yet, because Grandad or Uncle Will often had some sniffle or cough, we usually drove with the windows up, and drove faster because of it. Then the air was stale, and country and western music or weary voices came from the radio; too loud and too thin. I used to lean my head against the glass and see my reflection superimposed upon the landscape behind it; monotonous, flat paddocks stretching away from the fence line either side of this black strip we sped along.

'The roads then ...'

They used to talk like this sometimes as we sat around a fire of the evening and they sipped at their cheap, sweet wine, even holding a glass of it to Grandad's lips at regular intervals. The roads then were mainly tracks on the natural surface. Sometimes limestone, or gravel over the boggier parts. Powder would form from the earth being ground by the steel wheels of loaded wagons and the tramp of heavy draught horses. The surface of the road was powder, and was not at all corrugated like today.

Such smooth dusty roads made a wonderful surface for reading imprints of man, beast or bird.

Slow speeds are good for thinking.

Sandy Two left for Frederickstown, thinking of the people Hall had chased away. Unlike them, he chose to go. Hall had gone first. It was almost as if Sandy Two felt he had chased him away, and meant to chase him still. Now Sandy Two, a citizen (he believed) and a taxpayer, was going to fight for his country.

He left in a sulky drawn by a big grey gelding.

Sandy left. Harry Cuddles had children, a wife. 'It's not my war,' he had said. 'Not that one.'

Sandy was alone. The clouds in the sky.

He felt it was almost like sailing. He sailed on a breath of trust toward new country. But the land was not like the sea in that it slowed you, dragged you down to it. It was slow moving.

He read the road. Hooves, wheels, snake.

The gentle jingle jangle of draw bars in their steel rings, clinking of chains, creaking of wagon timbers; the murmuring of iron tyres along a sandy track.

A horse can follow the way and it swings along easily.

Clouds. Sand. Disturbed stones.

It is hard to stay awake.

The footprint of a bird.

When he woke in the night and heard the call of the curlew, it occurred to Sandy that their steps were not so much careful as tentative. Stepping out on the moonlit road, they held themselves proudly, and yet were careful, were cautious. You had to be.

What with Hall, Done, Starr, Mustle ... What was expected of him?

He was as good as any man. As good as any white man. Better.

He must believe that.

a coolman and school

'Nah Will, it wasn't your fault. Leave that one out.'

Well, Uncle Jack saying that just fired me up. Any suspicion of the two old men censoring a story, especially on the grounds that it might prove awkward or embarrass any of us, and I became fervent, mad, desperate to hear it. Straightaway.

I knew Uncle Will wanted to tell, really. He was brave enough to recount memories which hurt him, and while I have none of his courage, we did share a certain masochism when it came to words. But my desires had developed more strongly in other directions. It used to please me, when my grandfather and I lived in a crumbling house, to carve words into his skin. My blade drew letters with a fine white line, but in an instant all precision would be lost in gushing blood. I bandaged his wounds to conceal what I wrote and, bathing them, considered how they grew, how they altered and elaborated on what I had intended. Anger was all that was available to me, back then. I burnt with it, was cold and sneering with it, and wanted to scar and shape him with my words because his had so disfigured me.

I was a success.

And Will had his way after all, and he and Uncle Jack gave us a speech, a newspaper article, and something else they had learnt at school.

The new constable at Gebalup was prepared to go against the wishes of the local community to see the letter of the law upheld. He visited the Cuddles property and told them the children must attend school.

It was a long trip to school for Kathleen, Chatalong, the Cuddles kids, and they were lucky to have one old horse to share between them.

The date on the blackboard at the other end of the room was refined each morning, and each morning Chatalong did the subtraction: he was eleven years old. The oldest of his family there.

So Gebalup School had seven new pupils. Five — the Cuddles kids — had never been to school before. They had been kept away, one way or another, from towns.

It was a crowded classroom, and organised according to age; with the exception of the new kids, who were all put together. Will — even though he was not the eldest — was stationed among them as a sort of apprentice teacher. The teacher ordered him to hand out materials to his cousins, and called across the room that he'd have to help them.

The name calling began on the very first day.

Nigger.

One of the older students — Mark Mustle it may have been, someone anyway — used to turn around when the teacher had turned her back. Sneering and smirking, he would hold his nose, *Pooh*. Whenever he could he grabbed the skin on one of the little kid's forearms and twisted it. 'See,' he liked to say, doing it more gently on his own arm, 'mine goes white and then red when I do it.'

Kathleen and Chatalong were jogging to catch the others. They'd been detained, and asked about their previous schooling. 'Oh, I see,' said the teacher. And then told them that Wirlup Haven school was closing down. 'Were there any other Aboriginal children there? No? Good.'

Now some of the boys from their class converged into a group, trailed behind the hurrying brother and sister. *Pooh, pooh*, they cried, and they held their noses up in the air. *What a smell, what a stink, such perfume.*

Nigger nigger pull the trigger bang bang bang.

Chatalong bravely ran toward the bigger boys, and they fled, just a bit, before regrouping like seagulls.

The next time he ran at them they fanned out and made a circle around him, then closed it and, jabbing and poking, pinned him to the ground. One of them chased after Kathleen and brought her kicking and struggling back to the group. They were town boys, that shopkeeper's son among them.

They held Kathleen down, and one sat on her chest with his knees on her arms.

'Now, look, you're a pretty white *nigger*, ain't you? You could play with us, if you wanted.'

'Nearly as white as Will. He's your cousin, isn't he?'

Just how white was she, anyway?

They pulled her pants down to look for the paleness.

'Well, look at that,' said that one, Mark. 'You should

stay out of the sun, anyrate.' Turning his back to where his friends held Chatalong and Kathleen, he pulled his trousers down and bent over. 'I'm a bit dark myself, if you look closely,' he said, and wriggled his bum.

'My dark ring.'

'C'mon.'

The boys released them. They made a show of wiping their hands as if trying to rid themselves of some stubborn stain.

Will held a hand over his mouth and thrust the other into the air.

'Please, Miss, I feel sick.'

He rushed out retching, and sat on the steps just out of view of the classroom. The magpies warbled, sunshine streamed into the dusty schoolyard, the teacher mumbled. Strips of bark hung from a tree; one of them unpeeled a little further. Will felt at peace, he could relax when he was alone. He could not understand how the arrival of his cousins had made him such a different person in the eyes of everyone else at school.

A boy came out of the room and, smirking at Will, rang the bell vigorously. Its notes drowned the magpies' warbling, and the voices of the children — the children themselves — came spilling down the steps, tumbling over him.

Harriette went with Fanny and Harry Cuddles to the hall where an Extraordinary Parents and Citizens Association Meeting was being held that evening. They stood at the back of the room. Listened.

It was not easy to keep listening.

Rather than call out from where she stood Harriette

strode to the front of the room. Her voice was soft, yet it carried to those furthest away.

'We' — she said we — 'We have as much right as anyone to give our children an education. More right.' She said she had been brought up and educated pretty much the same as any of them. Better than some. Her ideals of life were not so different from those of white people. She thought it was possible for her children to have the best of both worlds, the white as well as the black. To be proud of themselves.

'There's only one world,' someone called out. A few laughs. 'Hear, hear.'

'There's plenty of you here know me, know my father. He's dying, but he stood by us enough to make sure we got a chance in the world. There's men here who've not done that, who leave kids everywhere, or send them away.

'Some of you say you want a civilised and kind nation.' Harriette paused, seemed to be trying to adjust herself to the tension and hostility in the room, but when she continued her voice was a little more strained. 'So why you acting like this?'

'Go back to where you came from.'

Harriette had had enough of pausing.

'I come from here. There were a lot more of us at one time. I'm married to a white man.'

'You should be with him now.'

Harriette ignored the call, and continued.

'Some Aborigines they might need some help. We don't. Just the same chance as you others. Why you trying to keep us back? Is it to make yourselves feel big? Give all children the same chance as your own, and they will do just the same; some good, and some not so good probably.

I tell you, we're no dirtier, or lazier, or stupider, or badder than you. You want to throw all the blame for our troubles — and your own troubles — onto us. You try to keep us out of town, out of the hotels — even some of us who been paying taxes and working as hard as anyone, and you want to keep our children out of schools. How would any of you stand up to that sort of treatment?'

'Someone go and haul Daniel Coolman out of his sick-bed, will they? His missus needs it.'

Bursts of laughter scattered around the room like small fires wanting to join, blaze, destroy. The circles of light around the lanterns reached out to one another.

Harriette's breathing was light and rapid. The nerves and anger could be heard in her voice.

'Daniel, my husband, horsewhipped a priest just for telling him — screaming at him — that he'd married a *savage*, a heathen. If he was well enough, he'd stand by me now. He always stood by me and our children. Maybe you men here tonight are more like my brother-in-law was. Some of you remember Patrick Coolman, don't you? The sort of man who won't stand by his kids, who abuses women, who'll run and leave a woman and children to themselves.'

The principal of the school tried to restore the tone of the meeting. He said that personally, he had no problem with the Aboriginal children. They were no less clean than many of the white children.

But Harriette, Harry, and Fanny were no longer there, anyway, because because because … It was like the sort of hunting that starts off quiet, but then the dogs start howling and there is no calling them back. It was that sort of meeting. At their backs they heard the muttering.

'Any other town around here, they wouldn't be in town this time of day.'

'Any day.'

Chatalong had a newspaper, and he propped old Sandy One up and, looking to the old man's face for signs that he was ready, he turned the pages. Chatalong had learned to read the flickering of eyelids, and the movement of eyes. Sandy One would squeeze the boy's arm, and tilt his head for yes or no.

Fanny came over and sat with them. She put her ear to her husband's lips now and then, and seemed to understand the clatter of his consonants, the hissing and buzzing of his cancerous tongue.

The three of them huddled together, their hands trapping the fluttering pages.

Aboriginals in and about Town

Saturday's public meeting to discuss the undesirable association of black and white in our school was enthusiastically attended and all agreed it an unqualified success.

About one hundred and fifty people were present and the meeting voted as one on the issue. It was resolved that unless a reply is received from the Minister of Education by the thirtieth of this month all white parents will cease sending their children to the school until the blacks are otherwise provided for.

It must be stressed again that unkindliness of feeling towards the blacks is not a factor in this matter of black and white in our school and, indeed, in our town. On the contrary, if the townspeople were not so indiscriminately kind to them, the present trouble would not exist. As it is the place is getting far too good a name among the aboriginals, for every week heralds some fresh arrival. The number of the local tribe is extremely small. It is the threat of the coming of all and sundry that is the disquieting factor.

The teacher's mouth was tight, her eyes narrow.

'Mark,' she hissed. 'Move away, now. Move to the back of the class. There.'

Admonished, but pleased at the attention, the boy moved to the corner not occupied by Will and the others. He faced the corner. He glanced across at them a few times before putting his hand up for the teacher's attention.

'Yes, Mark.'

'Please, Miss. It stinks down here near the *blacks*.'

'You're there because of your behaviour, Mark.'

'But Miss, I feel all sick. We shouldn't have to be with them, anyway.'

'I will tell you when you can return to your seat.'

Mark was mouthing the word '*Nigger*'. *Nigger* Will could see him. The teacher couldn't.

Mark knew they shouldn't be going to the same school together. They were like monkeys they were, and filthy. His dad talked of a *White Australia*, about the dangers of contamination and infection. It made him passionate, even in this dull schoolroom.

The boy suddenly fell to the ground. When the teacher got to him he sat up, then fell back into her arms, rolling his eyes.

'It's the smell, Miss. I ... I must've fainted.'

Uncle Jack and Uncle Will kept shaking their heads. The

two of them were often unsure of their footing on these evenings around the campfire, but on this particular night we'd drank a little more than usual. The two uncles were garrulous; one moment weeping, the next laughing, the next shouting into the darkness which surrounded us. At regular intervals one of them would totter into the darkness for a piss, only to reappear in the firelight like some befuddled ghost.

I floated in the warm smoke a few metres above the fire, watching the transformations in the flame and embers below. My grandfather sat motionless, as Sandy One — my ancestor before him — had also done. Then he suddenly fell over. I think by now it had become a habit. Sometimes he did it to gain our attention, or as a ruse to distract us.

Will, as I said, was particularly pissed.

'I hate myself,' he said. 'I turned my back. I was the only one who could get away with it.'

'Nah, Will, don't worry about it,' Uncle Jack tried to reassure him. 'We were all like that, I reckon. Had to be. I would've done the same. You're a bit fair. It was different. Don't worry about it.'

Next week Will Coolman and his seven newly enrolled cousins were the only students at school. The town had withdrawn its children until the issue of the Aboriginal students was resolved.

The eight students sat together at the back of the class. It was very quiet.

The principal gave them instructions on what tasks were to be completed for the day. They coloured things in, looked through books.

The boy Will was ashamed. The whole school had left because of, because of ... What? His cousins? Him? When he spoke his muffled voice sounded strange to him, and although it matched the motion of his jaws and tongue it seemed to be someone else's voice. He hated to speak in class at any time, but today he feared what words might come out if he were to open his mouth.

As bad as it usually was, it felt worse this day, with all the white kids and their usual teacher away. The school seemed so quiet, so impatient and angry.

To make his misery all the greater, Will was hurting, almost bursting with a great ballooning bladder. He sat trying to resist the increasing pressure, making tiny cautious movements in an attempt to ease himself. He crossed his legs once, tried to cross them a second time and somehow knot them together.

He had to go. Now. He saw the principal's head turning as the door swung closed.

He was pissing as he entered the toilets. It was a great hose he held, and he was a firefighter, had tapped some great reservoir, and it flowed through him and flung him about with its force. He tried to keep his feet and direct this yellow fountain.

He'd have to wait for his pants to dry, couldn't go back and face the principal and his cousins with wet pants.

Will slipped around the back of the toilet, and sat in the sun with his legs stretched out.

The shade moved up his legs.

As if in a dream he heard the others being dismissed from school. He peeked around the corner of the building and saw the principal at the steps, and his cousins already in the distance. Their voices were soft, and retreating further yet the sun was still too high, the day too warm for school to be finished.

He was still sleepy from the sun and thought it must've been some remnant of sleep which altered his perception, which gave him this sense that he was watching himself, Will, who was in turn watching Jack and Kathleen and all the Cuddles kids as they walked away from him.

It was dreadfully quiet. The day ticking, rustling and shifting its restraint.

Will moved out of hiding. The school principal was walking to the gate; and waiting for him were Harry Cuddles and Fanny. The children had climbed onto the wagon behind them. Chatalong was struggling to open the gate so that the wagon could come through. Harry and Fanny were smiling at the principal.

Five or six of the townspeople had gathered a stone's throw behind.

Uncle Harry called out, cheerfully, 'These children of mine, they're being cheeky. They told me, they reckoned you let them go home, and I said no, they must've got it wrong. No teacher said that. They're telling me there's no school today.'

He laughed again. 'I'm telling them they can't fool me.'

Fanny interrupted. 'You must be making them work good and hard. That's good, make them learn. Maybe you want us to round up some other kids for your school as well.'

Her eyes; Will could see them twinkling even from where he was.

'I did send the children home. We can't go on like this,' said the principal. 'It scarcely seems worthwhile for so few children.'

'How many would that be then?'

'Seven. Not counting Will Coolman, who took himself off earlier for some reason not known to me.'

'But there he is!' Jack Chatalong was pointing, and the principal turned to look at the runaway. Will felt all their eyes drilling into him.

The principal turned on his heel. 'Bring them in,' he said. 'I'm teaching them myself. I've sent the other teachers home to prepare.'

Will saw the waiting, watching townspeople mill about like cattle or sheep, then move fitfully away, stopping now and then to chew their ill-feeling.

His father, Daniel Coolman, was riding toward him on a great Clydesdale.

'Vill!' he said, 'Vill.' His voice was muffled and soft, yet it carried across the distance and was easily understood. He rode past Harry, Fanny, the children without acknowledging them. 'Et on.' And he indicated the space behind him. Bandages covered much of the lower part of his face and only his lower lip and chin were revealed. His beard had been shaved.

Will stared into the weave of his father's jacket as the horse turned and they went back past his cousins, his grandmother, his uncle.

'Harry's not even your uncle, not really,' Will's father told him as they entered their yard.

Once he had set the children working again, the principal returned to where Harry and Fanny waited outside the room. The children watched the thin shadows at the window, and thought of the inkstains on his pale fingers, and of his watery eyes.

The principal glanced around the schoolyard as he spoke with Harry and Fanny, his attention alighting on this or that with as much apparent purpose as if his eyes followed a butterfly, and told them that he didn't know what would happen, but if the experience at some other places was any indication the problem would not go away.

'So, then, you think we should?'

'Well, if I might say so,' said the headmaster. 'You need a school of your own. I can't control what children say in the grounds. It's not that I agree with it, of course, but they are obviously not welcome here. That can't be doing them any good, not at all. And the feeling in the community, well … We expect word from the minister, and then the police.'

white, right?

It had been a quiet school for some weeks now, and not because of holidays. It had been quiet, and you could hear chalk and teacups in the voices of the teachers. Something acrid, something bitter, the hint of a screech.

Those students stubbornly continuing to attend school said as little as possible. It was their right to be as good as anyone. Will Coolman was taken ill.

That fucking Harry Cuddles. Remember the other one, caused all that trouble? And there's that crazy cripple, Sandy Mason — remember him? — living at the camp. That's not right.

The school expanded around those students who remained; the walls, the fences moved further away — or perhaps it was that the students moved closer together. Even at recess times, they never moved further apart than the distance a ball could cross.

Fifty-three students had been absent for two weeks. The local member of parliament and the members of various civic bodies were very busy. Doing their duty.

And then, a next day and things were back to normal. Busy. Children studying, playing; exuberant and innocent. Free from moral and physical contamination, understanding that it was best for the races not to mix, comfortable at the pinnacle of creation.

There was a smug silence most of the day, punctuated with sharply triumphant whoops and the surge of children's voices. The absence of seven or so young ones was a great victory.

Within a few days Will Coolman was also back at the school.

Harry Cuddles took Chatalong away with him, and the two of them worked for next to nothing. There was no longer a market for possums; the government had banned the hunting of them. Now it was illegal for them to work, and anyway, they were told, they were undercutting the cost of labour. A betrayal of the working man, said some.

It was no betrayal.

There is a far greater betrayal.

They were being squeezed further away to find work. Anything inside of a day's ride from Gebalup was marginal land at best, and still too far from the railway. But even that land would be cleared soon enough, and in a few decades they would say; *What the hell, you can start again, somewhere else, work it for twenty years and when it's fucked you move on. Our goal is to clear a million acres a year.*

Course, Harry Cuddles had his own land, same way as any white man, but there was little enough money to develop it. They'd take it off him, probably, unless he could improve it, get some fences up, build a house, a shed. The banks would not help him. In the towns he visited, he saw how people were kept in reserves, usually close to the rubbish tip. At Kylie Bay the reserve was downwind of the shit dump. They were breathing it in, deep, all that shit from the town, and you could hardly move, not once you got there like that. Squeezed between spreading refuse, it didn't matter whether it was a land or sea breeze blowing. The sun rose each day from domestic rubbish; carcasses cans wrappings, and it sank into a growing mound of shit.

The hessian bags in Harry Cuddles' buggy moved about and squawked. The fellow he'd got them from had shared a drink with him. A good man. You know, him and Harry could both get arrested for that.

Harry was going in for poultry farming.

Those same chickens were scratching about, clucking to themselves, and every now and then coming up straight and staring as if remembering something. Suddenly they were all squawking, and running about flapping their wings, and the dogs were barking.

The policeman appeared from between the trees, on horseback.

'Hello, Constable.'

The new constable's face was flushed, and his small round eyes moved quickly about the camp. Their home. He would have seen the two horses with their buggies; the hut, the tent with its little bush shelter next to it, the boughshed for meals.

The new constable was learning fast. He didn't get down from his horse.

'If you want to be treated like a white man, Harry, you know, you can't mix with other *natives*. Who's this?' He gestured at Chatalong.

'My nephew.'

'No matter. You'll still need to get a permit to employ him, just like anyone else, if you're contracting. You can get on, that doesn't mean all your family follows you. Not all your bloody relations.

'Where's this fellow, Sandy Mason?'

'He's away, gone to war.'

The policeman saw old Sandy One sitting erect and pale in the shady mouth of his bush shelter.

There was silence between the people standing in that little clearing with its track thinly snaking away among the trees. A solitary crow called from somewhere in a tree above them.

'Who's that?'

'Oh, *that* Sandy Mason. I thought you meant the other one, his son.'

The policeman dismounted. He went across to Sandy One, bent over, and looked into his face for a long time before looking away, and the others saw Sandy One's gaze drop for a moment, as if resting. But when the policeman looked back Sandy One's eyes were staring into his own, same as before. The policeman waved his hands in front of Sandy One's face and the eyes followed the hand. He raised one of the old man's arms and let it fall. Sandy One had raised his right hand at the wrist as if attempting to offer it for shaking.

Fanny used her finger to wipe some saliva from the corner of the old man's mouth. She spoke to the policeman as she did so, wanting to explain. She didn't take her eyes from Sandy One.

'My husband. The other one you said is my son.' She had the marriage certificate ready to show him, she said.

'Hey, where are you from? Where were you before you came here?' The constable looked at Harry, gesturing at Sandy One as he did so. 'He'll have to go to an institution. You can't look after him.'

His gaze shifted to the others, to the children, and to Fanny. 'And you will too. Have to go, I mean. There's a law.'

The solitary crow flew away, and Chatalong saw that there were little corellas also, scattered through the canopy on the far side of the clearing. Each one's plumage seemed grubby and blood-spattered. They have small blue marks at their eyes. Once, he had found a nest. There were just two dirty white eggs among a nest of decaying debris. The birds had squawked, and harangued him.

The policeman returned to his horse and Chatalong noticed his short, bandy legs, and that he rocked from side to side with each short stride. The policeman took a track which entered among the trees. He turned, spat something from between his teeth, lifted his arms and was gone.

Another inspection was over.

The birds had also moved away. But not too far. Jack Chatalong listened to them squawking away among the trees somewhere.

I feel obliged to say that in my youth I particularly enjoyed the story that is to follow, of how Sandy One — paralysed, and probably imbecilic — wrote Fanny's letters for her, for all of them. It reminded me of my own actions, with Sandy One in my grandfather's place, and

Jack Chatalong in mine. But there was nothing noble or dignified in what I wrote, in my grandfather's hand, as it were. I squeezed Ern's useless hand around the pen I had placed within it, and formed various words.

Ern Solomon Scat:
>>> *has failed*
>>> *fucks chooks*
>>> *fucks his children*
>>> *fucked all our family before him.*

I looked into his face for a reaction to what I — we — wrote. It amused me at the time, gave me a bitter pleasure.

I listened to the story Uncle Jack told many times over, around the campfires and — later — the kitchen tables of people to whom he was slowly introducing me.

Fanny had thought a lot about the schooling of Chatalong and Kathleen, and of Harry's children. They needed letters demanding justice, and — if possible — a white *citizen* writing them. She thought they needed the urgency of telegraphs, the humming of wires, the business of *getting it in writing*. Justices of the Peace promoting them.

It took many drafts to get the writing not only legible, but neat. The letters sloped evenly, as if blown by the same strong wind.

Fanny placed her arms around her husband, and kept the small man steady in her embrace. Chatalong's right hand kept Sandy One's wrapped around the pen, and together they formed the words. Chatalong's left hand held the old man's right upper arm, and he could feel the old man's tendons, the thin cord and wad of muscle still there.

Fanny spoke, and Sandy One muttered and made his noises; Chatalong heard each buzz, squeak and explosion for the word it must be. The words of the two of them flowed through him, ran like sap through the capillary of the pen, flowed to its very point. But they were not easy to form once there. It was clumsy, the two hands unable to quite move together.

In one draft — perhaps it was the third — the old man's feeble left hand somehow came across the wet ink. Irritated at the mess, Chatalong flicked at the hand and it slid away like a dead thing.

By way of apology, Chatalong squeezed the almost lifeless hand and once again inclined his head to the work.

It was a new pen, new ink, and the new, expensive white paper was thin and crinkled like a ghost's sloughed skin.

Dear Sir,

I am writing to you on behalf of my son, his cousins, and our future children.

These children, all of whom are at least half British, should be allowed to go to the State School. I wish to know what reasonable objections there can be to this.

I myself am crippled now, but I have worked all my life to make a better life for my children and now my grandchildren are the only ones left to me and I want them to finish their schooling.

My boy (and his cousins) are as deserving as any other persons of being allowed to continue their good education which they had already begun before my accident.

I don't want to see my offspring degraded which seems

to be what the law wants for them just because of the colour of their skin.

The signature was difficult. Chatalong practised for much of the afternoon before he was able to run it, slowly and fluently, across the bottom of the page.

Did that letter go by sea, around and slow? Or did it go by railway line, cutting across to the capital, reaching out from the heart of Fanny's known world? Telegraph lines hummed with the passage of brief words.

Harry Cuddles also wrote, and he and Fanny took it further. They rode through the main street, collecting signatures on a petition. Several people signed, including the schoolteacher. However ...

Chatalong had a stub of chalk, and a board fashioned from the blackened base of a water tank. With the stub of white chalk he wrote the word 'black' on the board. It looked like nothing, and a lie. The word said black, it was written in white. He rubbed it with his hand, making a white smear, and then wiped his hand clean of it.

He was under a tree, in the dappled light. Sandy One, sitting in the little bush humpy beside the tent, looked like something carved from cuttlefish shell.

Fanny was hanging out washing. She moved, solid and secure, and although the pale clothing swayed and danced around her, she stayed in her place.

Chatalong rubbed at the letters until they were completely gone.

who is exempt?

'Well, what could I do?' said Will, although no one had accused him of anything. 'Yeah, I went back to the school. Dad was thinking of the best for me, and for Mum.' Will believed there was no place left for him in this story, and that it was Chatalong who must continue. Will said he didn't know this stuff, it wasn't for him to say. He had just ignored whatever people said, held his head up, walked carefully, gone to school, kept on. Most of the time he lived just like anyone else in the town, really. He kept to himself, he said. They kept to themselves, just the family. They knew who they were. A little family.

'Nah, I can't. It's the law. I can't employ any Aborigine under sixteen years old.'

Why, you know, that could be years into a man's working life.

'And, even if he was old enough, I'd need a permit. It means more trouble. More money.'

School had left Chatalong, and that meant he must find something to do that somebody else wanted done. That was the way of things.

But what? There wasn't much; not clearing not anything, not even for anyone thinking he was a white man so what chance a boy, a dark boy.

At least with the rabbits — more and more of them all the time too, and moving beyond the fence put there to stop them — there was extra food. The rabbits and the new people, moving toward one another.

'Tell you what, Harry,' offered the senior Starr, a storekeeper branching into farming considerably east of Gebalup, where he hoped to become one among a pioneering community. 'Tell you what, I want you to get work as much as anyone. Why, I remember when you were just a boy. And, of course, I want you to pay back what you owe me at the store. Business is business. I could hire you, but if you agree to have the others here' — his hand swept around to Harry's family, extended to old Sandy One, Fanny, Chatalong, Kathleen — 'working with you; then we could do a deal. I'll pay you generously, of course. You know that. But, of course, apart from yourself and ... Well, you're the only one I can expect a man's work from. I want to help you, see. And him.'

Mr Starr waved his hand in Sandy One's direction, shook his head ruefully. 'I remember better days.'

They camped on Mr Starr's property. It was the only way to try to raise some money so Harry could develop and improve his own land in the way he had to, when he could get back to it. Since there was no school even the children could help.

Propped in the shade somewhere — against a tree or under the rickety wagon — Sandy One oversaw it all.

They picked wool from dead sheep. Or plucked the stones and sticks from the soft soil, their legs aching from the effort to lift their feet from its clutches. They wore leather aprons with a pouch, which they repeatedly filled and then emptied at a growing mound of stones. Chatalong thought they might be building their own memorial.

His back ached from the bending the bowing the carrying the weight, and after a few hours it was silent work, even for him. Words dried up, windswept sand stung their eyes, dust coated their lips, and the skin wore from their fingers which, in the evening, they soaked in the methylated spirits Mr Starr supplied. 'It'll toughen them,' he said.

It was clear Chatalong shared his Uncle Sandy's gift with horses.

The horses snorted like trains, and their heavy muscles rippled. Some mornings there was frost on the chains, and Chatalong had to resist the links fusing with his fingers.

He followed the horses back and forth across rectangular paddocks, cutting the earth. His heavy feet appeared misshapen and roughly hewn, as if they were no longer toes or bones but were torn from the earth itself, and he was some weak sapling growing from them.

He leaned with the horses and they pulled old stumps and vast networks of mallee roots from the soil.

Starr offered Kathleen a place working in the house, but she wanted to stay with the rest of her family. So, well; there were plenty of others more than ready to do the work.

They tried hunting possum again, staying east of the Great Southern Railway Line. It was good country there. They pegged the skins out on the ground and scraped them with the glass of broken bottles. Sometimes, the children scraped and scraped until, suddenly, there was the ground coming through the animal's hide and into their daydreaming.

The scraping, and then the sun, cleaned the skins sufficiently for them to be sold to a man with the piece of paper, the license required to deal in possum skins.

They piled the wagon high with skins. Harry had worked like this before, made money enough to help get that block of land, but the money was not there now, not with no license.

Fanny and Harry dressed up for town and the annual agricultural show. All the kids, too.

But that policemen, and a partner, visited again.

'You need licenses for possums, if you're selling. Oh, kill as many as you want for food, for yourself. It used to be your country.'

The police took away pieces of wire and rope which might be used for snares.

Smiling, they took Harry's gun. 'It's the law.'

They shot the dogs.

'This is private property,' tried Harry.

'So's that of your neighbours, their land's private too, and your dogs are trouble to them.'

'You get two pounds a scalp for them dogs. Who gets that money?'

'You can't be too hurt, if you're talking about money. Anyway, we're the police. The law's the law. These dogs, they been killing sheep.'

The second policeman came and stood very close, chest to chest with Harry. He grinned.

'Yeah, we're your protectors. Just helping you.'

'They got wheat, now, my neighbours,' said Harry. 'How dogs worry them?'

'They have valuable sheep. Poultry. And the white ladies, they don't need to be upset by the likes of you. They don't want to see you.'

Harry had once organised whole teams of people to work for him; clearing, picking sticks and stones, even cutting wood. They might have tried stripping the bark from trees, as once they had. Sometimes the farmer would go halves in the money you made; others might let you collect it all. You stacked the bark and ignored the startlingly naked trees at your back.

But suddenly, no one wanted bark any more. The whole of a tree was going, all of it. All of them. So there was nothing. And now acres of wheat rippled closer and closer toward them.

Starr reminded Harry that he still had a problem with credit at the store. Harry owed Starr money.

What could Harry Cuddles do? There were more and more farms all the time, more and more people, and those farmers worked on one another's property, and Nyoongars had to work for next to nothing — for shelter, and a bit of food.

These new people, they were growing a community like they grew their crops. They focused on money and time, on cause and effect, and knew they would have to modify what was around them if they were to grow as they wished. They were not of this country but, looking outward, believed they understood its potential. It was necessary to believe that the land's people and ways were inferior, and to ensure that there was proof of that.

Starr's customers certainly believed they knew all about those others, those dark ones camped on the fringes of towns, edging closer and having to be chased away; away from the school shops and oval, off the footpath, off the fence, away from the water trough, away to the tips.

Starr's customers had words; *darkness, shadow, savage* ... and they made sharper ones, harmless to their own ears. *Boong. Coon. Nigger.* Just the launching of them gave satisfaction, inflicted pain. And if they curled their lips, maybe laughed and sneered, believed what they said then their very sincerity itself could cause pain.

Once you shared this tongue, you could taste it. Evolution. Light out of darkness. Pyramids and pinnacles. With such a language, it is hard not to accept such concepts.

Harry couldn't get a loan from the bank. It was the law. His property wasn't securely his. 'What if you should die,' smiled the bank manager. 'It's nothing personal,' he added, after a pause. 'It's the law, it's the colour of your skin, Harry. Who your mother was, and your father too.'

Mr Starr called again to see him. It was about that debt at his store in town, and, well, really. Something'd have to be done.

Harry looked to Chatalong and Kathleen. Could they work for him, work off the debt?

'No,' said Starr. But he looked at the girl for a long

time. 'No. Too long, too big a debt, too difficult with their age, and the law and all.'

'The law? The law? How long's there been this law? That says I'm a lesser man than any of you?'

Mr Starr never got angry, not any more. 'Oh, ages Harry. Nearly ten years now. The 1905 Aboriginal Protection Act. A new amendment, just a few years ago.'

'Protection Act? I don't need it, I don't need that. Just fair treatment same as anyone. That's what I want from a law, any law, new one or old one just the same.'

'I know, I know. Anyway, why worry, we know *you're* all right. You got an exemption, haven't you? But you don't want to let the others drag you down, Harry. You don't want that. Look, I tell you what I can do.'

And Mr Starr said Harry could mortgage his property to his store. 'It's like a loan. It is one. As a reserve sort of thing, in case you can't clear this debt. Plenty of time, say a couple of years. Just till things got sorted out.'

Mortgage it for what was owed.

The policeman came demanding payment, or Mr Starr would be forced to put the land on the market.

'You his boy, are you?' said Harry.

On the allocated Natives Shopping Day at a nearby town Harry, Sandy One and Fanny went to a solicitor to arrange for the land to be transferred to Sandy One. They held their token white man between them. Could Sandy, as they understood, take out a mortgage with the bank to pay out their debt at the store.

Possibly. It would take some days to arrange.

The bank manager was puzzled. 'Will he be able to sign? Is he fit … ?'

Fanny fingered the vertebrae of Sandy's back, and the old man nodded his firm assent and understanding.

The police came, and gave them fourteen days to move.

Starr had sold the land to one of his sons.

The local magistrate, when a reluctant but Harry-harassed Aborigines Department made its enquiries, agreed that it was not justice. The Starrs had got the land at well below market price by using family as dummy buyers. But it was legal. And he didn't think Harry would cut much of a figure in court.

'Stay here,' Harry told Chatalong as he pulled up outside the pub.

Harry scanned the bar. Faces turned to him, then away. No words.

Mr Starr sat around the elbow of the bar, facing the door. His face registered a little surprise, and then he nodded — once, sharply — at Harry Cuddles.

The barmaid would not serve Harry.

'It's the law.'

'I got an exemption.' Dog tag, he thought. Dawg.

There was a pause.

'Oh,' a man said from within his glass. He drained it, then placed it before him like a tiny column. 'Listen mate, you might have some bit of paper but we know what you are. You don't belong here. Not with us.'

Harry glanced around the room. Most eyes were on him. Starr was looking into his glass.

'I don't think we've met,' said Harry to the first man. 'You don't know me.' He held out his hand. 'Harry Cuddles.'

Harry saw his own hand trembling in the unfilled space between them.

And then he was striking the man's face, throat. The man was down. A roaring, there was thunder in his ears, and voices from all around, leaping back from the walls and ceiling.

His arms were held, and bodies were all about and close. Boots, fists.

A screech. The blows stopped. A man held each of Harry's arms.

A policeman's uniform stood in the small space before him. The policeman nodded his head and the men let their hands drop from Harry's arms.

The policeman spoke into a new silence.

'You'd be best to leave. I'll turn a blind eye.'

'Why? I got an exemption.' Harry's voice was husky, and shifting so that even he could not trust it. He didn't want to whine.

'Not anymore. Inciting trouble. Associating with *natives*.'

The policeman gestured at Chatalong, who bent forward on the wagon the better to see through the doorway.

'You want to lose your kids as well?'

The room waited.

'We don't need police to sort this out,' said the man Harry had struck.

'You're under arrest,' said the policeman.

Uncle Harry let himself be led from the door by the bandy-legged, uniformed one. As they passed before the wagon, he pushed his captor aside and ran into the middle of the street. It was recently paved and the town was proud of it. Harry swung around to face them.

The policeman dusted himself off as he got to his feet. A few men were shoving one another to get through the door. Starr finished his beer, remained seated. He saw only the backs of men mostly too old, weak or disabled to go to war.

Harry threw off his coat, stamped his feet, and put his fists up in front of him, sparring. He forced his feet to move like those of a boxer, rather than in the frustrated dance of a child's tantrum. His pulse throbbed.

Sometimes the world moved so slowly; nothing changed.

'I can go where I like. I can go where I like. Wadjela. You wadjela. You think I'm a dog (a dawg), or what?'

The policeman scurried at him, and Harry hit him quick and hard, just the once. Harry picked up some stone, some piece of the reformed earth, and dared the others to come get him. They smiled at him from the door.

The cop was up again, shaking his head as if reluctant in his duty, as if disappointed. As if superior.

It was Starr who moved forward.

'Harry, this is no good. There's nothing can be done.'

He put his pale hands on Uncle Harry's shoulders. Harry looked over the storekeeper's shoulder, and taunted the red-faced policeman.

'You fight for yourself? Like a person, like a man?'

The veins in Harry's neck were like ropes and his eyes were moist. But he was quietening. He looked into Starr's face, flicked the storekeeper's bloodied hands away, and turned and walked. The little policeman trotted after him.

Some of the townspeople spoke up for him in court, including Starr. Uncle Harry smiled wryly almost the whole time, as if to himself only.

He said nothing. His family were not allowed in court. He said nothing. He looked at the floor somewhere in the centre of the room, sometimes at a dark jarrah chair with red upholstery, occasionally out the window. He seemed calm, or bored.

He said nothing.

Harry Cuddles wore a three-piece suit with wide and expansive lapels. Its stripes were bold and straight. He wore spats and held his smart town hat in his hands before him, and looked down, around; into a different space.

Six months disorderly conduct.

Three months resisting arrest.

Six months assaulting a police officer.

He said nothing.

Fanny and Chatalong loaded up the wagon. They wanted to take everything, but were given so little time that they couldn't dismantle the huts and Fanny suddenly found herself grateful to be able to take even the tent frames. They had hidden Sandy One among the luggage, and hoped that no one would ask after him.

Chatalong mouthed the policemen's clipped instructions, mocking them, and Kathleen and he grinned at one another. They left in silence, with the police riding behind, and when they were approaching the edge of the next town, obeyed the policeman's instructions and turned down a small track just before the railway crossing.

Mt Dempster's reserve was between the rubbish dump and the sanitation depot. Whatever the time of day you breathed the town's shit.

There were tiny huts, shabby tents, shelters made of packing cases, of flattened kerosene-tins, of hessian-cloth-

boughs-bush. They were scattered as if they'd been thrown, or had fallen from the trees which shaded them. There were a couple of hessian-covered pit toilets at one end of the reserve, and Fanny, Sandy, and Kathleen and Chatalong were obliged to camp close to these. The Cuddles family had to find room at the other edge of the reserve.

Like some of the white people said — not all meaning quite the same thing — there were too many people at the reserve already.

The old people were apart. Their grandchildren — with no school to go to — ran within the reserve and even into some of the bush surrounding it, and thought that they were free.

There was a lack of space. Fanny managed to keep her small brood together, and they all slept in one small shelter.

There was no water on the reserve, and so they braved the dogs and pilfered from the rainwater tanks of the houses closest to the reserve. There were horse troughs in town, but it was a long walk back with an improvised bucket banging your leg, or carrying a sloshing pair on a pole across your shoulder.

'Who is that old fellow, paralysed one. The white man?' someone in the reserve asked of their campfire partner.

'Dunno. Where is he?'

'Dunno. Can't be far.'

But despite the knowing laughter, Sandy One was quite some distance away, and bouncing around in the back of a cart, his limbs flopping loosely with each jolt. Fanny held his head on her lap and had stacked hessian bags beneath him. Chatalong was at the reins, and they followed a trail north and around the ranges. Going home.

They had kissed Kathleen goodbye and left her in the care of the Cuddles family. They would be back for her. With old Sandy as he was, and only the small cart to put him in, there was just no room.

Fanny needed to get closer to home and to see Harriette. As bad as it was it was still home, and if they broke their ties there, what good could ever come of it again? It was home. She held her husband's head on her lap. He was alive; she regarded him almost as a hostage. There was a law and this man meant that they might escape it. Their almost-a-white-man.

The old man's eyes showed the sky, and the bumpy ride kept his limbs in constant motion, as if he were restless and fitful. Chatalong told him again and again that he understood. How could he possibly be still? He understood.

'But not yet,' Fanny said to Chatalong. Not yet, they could not go into the town yet. Not even for a daughter who would help her. They turned the horse for the coast, running south-east of the ranges.

Next morning, when they stopped, it was in that bay where the land ran out and dissolved into the sea. Chatalong thought of his mother, the kangaroo shooters, the rifles and the rum. He realised how the men had treated him, how they had disregarded him.

Fanny lifted a small thin shard of rock from where it rested at the base of a wide, flat depression in the granite. She drew water from the waterhole beneath it, and replaced the lid-like rock.

She held the cool water to her husband's lips. 'Not far. Remember?'

Water welled in his mouth, ran into his sandy-grey beard. People died not so far from here.

Sandy One coughed; he made little eruptions. Snot bubbled and ran from his nose. His limbs jerked as they had in the wagon.

They were miles away — had passed their old mine, and were almost at Gebalup — when the cart bucked. It balanced upon one wheel, and Fanny threw her weight — you would have to say the wrong way — and then over it went.

A wheel continued spinning, but the one beneath the wagon was broken, and the wagon itself had split and collapsed at one corner. It wasn't a wagon anymore. The horse was already small in the distance, and the traces trailing it could no longer be distinguished. The sound of the horse's pounding hooves became the rumble of the one wheel and that sound continued to diminish until, eventually, even it stopped.

They propped Sandy One against the wreckage and, after considering the cart's shafts and planking, cut two strong limbs from a tree. Fanny wove bark and twine between the poles to support Sandy, then they each took two ends and set off along the thin track.

The trailing end of the poles bounced across rocks and indentations, but they flexed enough to allow the old man a reasonably comfortable ride, and Fanny had pulled his hat over his face to shelter him from the sun.

Chatalong looked back at the parallel lines the two poles had scratched in the earth. He was reminded of the railway, and these lines led back to a heap of junk with one motionless wheel at the top.

Harriette stayed in the house, and Chatalong led Daniel out of town to where Fanny and Sandy One were concealed among the scrub. There was no moon, and on such a cold, clear night the stars were insistent. Sandy One would have been watching them for hours, perhaps feeling the night condensing upon his cheeks and lashes. Licking his lips.

Fanny and Harriette embraced silently in the house, even as they felt that space closing in about them. Daniel watched them with his lips pressed tight, and Chatalong had long ago learnt that when Daniel said shut up then …

Well, he hoped they would be needing him now.

steel fences

Grandfather, Uncle Will, Uncle Jack and me; with each trip we edged a little further east from Wirlup Haven. We made that early trip to the death place and, having traversed that, we went a little further each time. We moved along the coast, mostly, and further and further from the railway that first fenced off the corner of this continent.

Ah, the railway. Once it was shining and new, and so was the Chief Protector, Mr Neville when he first travelled it. By the time my own grandfather and the Travelling Inspector of Aborigines skimmed its parallel lines, some ten or fifteen years later, its shiny metal had dulled except where the wheels rolled.

The railway shunted a new generation of pioneers to the smoky frontier, and allowed the Chief Protector to make his inspection in much greater comfort than the first Travelling Inspector, who had only the assistance of camel, cart, and *native boy*.

I found the notes of all these various inspectors among Grandad's research files. I fairly made them rustle about my ankles as I hovered in that room, kicking my legs amongst them to disrupt their neat order. Perhaps it was unfair, even petty of me.

When I write like this — of railways, and fences, and of extensive pages of notes — I give a nod to my grandfather; to his lines and his discipline, to his schemes and his rigour. And I further acknowledge, and nod to, the demands of Historical Fiction. And I nod with the resentment which those I will call my people felt, still feel. Nod nod nod.

I hope you are not falling asleep.

Sometimes, my grandfather's chin used to drop to his chest even as I spoke to him. He snored, and I recited in the brief and relative silences of each inhalation. Such a strange rhythm it gave my prose.

My grandfather's mentor (*snore*), the Chief Protector (*snore*), on accepting his new position (*snore*) — for it was about this time (*snore*) that he seriously took over an inefficient Aborigines Department and proceeded (*snore*), in his rigorous and zealous manner, to whip beat cut the whole thing into shape (*snore*) — took an inspection tour.

I hovered in the firelight and smoke of our campfire, sometimes even in the thin torchlight beside a gas barbeque, and recited to the old men of my family. I mimed the great blind beast of a train, even attempted to mime the cut and slash — and simultaneously, the detached observation and control — of *rigorous, scientific* activity. In short, I performed many graceless and blundering acts.

Making my contribution, I hoped. I hope.

Once upon a time Grandad rattled and snorted along the Great Southern Railway. How crucial this railway was in facilitating the development of the wheatbelt, this lucky land's prosperity, and the alienation of so many of us.

Nod, nod.

And how strangely fortunate we very few were — only my grandfather would disagree — that the railway at Gebalup went only to the coast, and never connected with the rest of the lines reaching out from the capital city. Thus it remained as ineffectual as the rabbit-proof fences either side of us. We slipped away, made some sort of escape as the line from Gebalup to Wirlup Haven shrivelled and floated on the surface of the earth.

In other places, Chief Protector Neville would stand impatiently at the carriage door as the train slowed, and disembark before the train had stopped. He would run a few steps, then slow to a brisk walk and begin this specific inspection with scarcely a loss of momentum.

He asked the police — who were, after all, his employees — to take him to all *native* camps within the vicinity. Squawking, they flew to announce his arrival, and perched sullenly above us.

Chief Protector Neville made notes. He spoke to various authorities, to all those white men with knowledge and experience of The Native Problem.

He had ideas, this man. Ambition. He wanted to establish settlements for the *natives*. The result? *Considerable savings in the cost of the maintenance of natives in the Great Southern and South West districts ... children that are growing up can be turned into useful workers instead of becoming a nuisance to the inhabitants of every town in which they are settled ... concentration of the natives at Carrolup will be a great relief to the residents of those towns near which they are presently camped, and will be to the ultimate advantage of the natives themselves.*

In the various camps he visited there were *numbers of half-caste children, some of whom, he wrote, are as white as any of our own children, and should be under proper care and supervision*

Of course, it was *within the power of the Minister under the Act to place natives within a reserve,* but Mr Neville — having taken on the position so recently — insisted that he would rather the *natives* went to his settlement of their own free will. It was very early in his career.

Regrettably, as he explained to various small meetings of concerned citizens, *there are ... families that will have to be moved ... they are a burden on the department, and the children are not being properly looked after ... mostly in the case of women who have lost their husbands.*

In one or two places the *natives* were particularly *intractable*, and would consider no other proposition than that of sending their children to the local school. Mr Neville did not want a repeat of difficulties associated with the so very recent troubles at Gebalup and a host of other schools.

Mr Neville did, in fact, use the Gebalup example to explain to the Minister that there was *no chance of their children receiving an education* in their local schools. It must be at a *native* settlement. *The difficulty,* our Chief Protector confided to his minister — adding that he was sure that the Honourable Minister would recall that this, to a lesser degree, was also the case at Gebalup — *is that two or three of the natives with big families are in possession of town lots, whereon they have erected huts in which they are living, and they naturally do not wish to shift. These townsite lots overlook the town and are splendidly situated.*

My grandfather was so taken with our Chief Protector, not only because of his vast reservoir of civilisation, his rigorous and scientific mind, his energy and organisational drive, but also because he was a man of letters.

About the time of this railway tour and about the time a few of my family were so kindly offered the sanction of a town's designated reserve, our Chief Protector wrote to the superintendent at Carrolup and enquired whether it might *be possible to take charge of any orphan half-caste children ... should the department desire to send one or two to the settlement?*

Just the one or two.

Mr Tryer, the superintendent of the Carrolup Native Settlement, had no problem with this. In fact, as he wrote in his letters, it was a trivial matter against the worry and anxiety engendered by planning for quarters for his wife and himself. He enclosed several pages of drawings, and detailed specifications and quotes. He would have to engage a carpenter to assist him.

How valuable Mr Tryer would have found it to have had my grandfather there. If only my grandfather had arrived in this country at this time and offered his assistance to Messrs Neville and Tryer. He could have begun making his contribution so much earlier.

My very literate Neville continues to write. He enthusiastically scribbles to his minister in government — recommending the purchase of an oven, boilers, a sewing machine, a regulation pattern dress or suit for the inmates

— and then communicates his high hopes in a letter to Mr Tryer.

But his recommendation is refused. He is asked to remember that the department has only five thousand pounds per year available to it. And this request is for such a small part of the state. It is settled. The *natives* are dying out.

Not quite twelve months later our Chief Protector records his satisfaction that Mr Tryer is so well pleased with his own quarters and, in a personal touch quite rare in his correspondence, he congratulates Mr Tryer and his wife on the birth of their child.

He encloses a small square of hessian stapled to one of the pages of his letter as a sample of what he recommends Mr Tryer use to wall the remainder of the buildings.

Mr Tryer writes that there are ninety inmates at the settlement. He eventually used a cheaper hessian for the girls' and boys' dormitories. The twelve-inch gap at the top of each wall does indeed assist ventilation, but in future he will extend the roof overhang further to prevent rain being swept in. He reminds Mr Neville that it was just as well they decided on tiers of hammock-like bedding because there would otherwise be even more of a problem with overcrowding.

Difficult children are confined to smaller shelters.

There have been a number of deaths.

He recounts an anecdote concerning one of the *native* boys who, sick and tormented as he lay in bed, swore that after he died he would ask God to come down and burn them all up. Fortunately, notes Mr Tryer, this did not occur, although we could certainly do with divine assistance. I hear Tryer's humour, his chuckle among these rustling pages. A rueful chuckle because in actuality, Mr Tryer is quite concerned.

> There are a lot of natives here ... It is impossible to get everything done. We are giving meals to single men at the compound to try and get improvements done ... We don't do these things to please ourselves.

The cooking. The mending, ironing, washing. The supervising of the dormitories.

> You cannot leave the girls to do things themselves. They must have someone with them to get on with the work.
> They are like children, and respond best to being treated as such.
> There are a lot of natives here. And Mrs Tryer has the baby which takes up a lot of time.

It is such places that my family has largely avoided. But into this place, briefly, came Kathleen and the others from the reserve at Mt Dempster.

kathleen returns

Kathleen had kissed them all goodbye a good distance from Mt Dempster's reserve, and Fanny said they'd be back to get her. Sandy One being like he was, there was only so much room, see.

Returning to the reserve Kathleen saw, through and among the trees, some men from the town; a policeman with them, two ...

It was like dogs surrounding kangaroos for the kill. The old people were already huddling on wagons. Others stood around in a tight group. People had bundles of clothes, a bowl, a cup; Kathleen saw a broken clock tucked under someone's arm.

A young man — a boy — turned from the edge of the group and ran several steps clear. He fronted up as best he could to the policeman on a horse, tilting his face up to him. The policeman shook his head, turned, said something to one of his colleagues.

Quickly.

The boy was outside the circle of police and townspeople. Running. The shouts Kathleen heard seemed small across such a distance.

Kathleen called silently to the escapee, wanting willing him away. To her? No, the only way would be up, up into above the trees. Away, away. She watched him turn. He pranced, was up on his toes; swung his thin arms. Kathleen made little noises in her throat as the men walked through his fists. They kicked him, tied him, threw him on a wagon.

She walked to keep ahead of the man she sensed behind her. A hand held her arm, its grip loose but inescapable.

When she finally dared to turn the man smiled down at her, his Adam's apple bobbing above the white collar.

They were well away from the reserve when Kathleen smelled the smoke and turned to see the narrow shifting stem of it joining the cloudy sky. She let her head fall against the soft and forgiving flesh of the woman whose arm surrounded her.

When the little troupe stopped it was all but dark. A circus, someone said, laughing. A zoo. A bloody freak show. There were a few rough shelters, and a small house and stable.

In the darkness, among the stuff thrown from the wagon, something struggled and made noises. It was the boy she'd seen trying to escape. His eyes rolled above the gag at his mouth as he was pushed into a large hessian bag. He continued to struggle; Kathleen saw the bag swinging on the rope which suspended it from a tree.

In the morning a rectangle of flapping canvas showed where some of the girls had escaped.

Somewhere around the middle of the day they shuffled back through the gate, followed by trackers on horseback.

Kathleen watched from the canvas kitchen. Dinah called her over, sat her before the fire, and had her knead the dough.

Outside, someone chopped wood. Kathleen sat on the step and saw the symmetry of the growing stack he made, and how the wood parted before his blows. The axe rose and fell, rose and fell, and only its rhythm held her day together.

Shaven haired women, dressed in hessian and flour bags, stepped from the kitchen with food slops.

An old man felt his way along the wall toward her. Kathleen did not move, she held her breath, and the old man's hands found the doorframe. He detoured in a little half-circle around where she sat. The old man's eyes were sealed, and he moved slowly, perhaps one or two steps to each blow of the axe.

Kathleen felt herself at the centre of a most orderly destruction. The wood split, was stacked. The axe man winked and smiled at her.

Once he was past her, the blind one resumed feeling his way along the wall. He coughed, and seemed to tremble with each axe stroke. Kathleen watched him draw himself up and, in a show of bravado, stride across the open space to the stable. Then he followed his hands along its wall of stone until, finding a doorway, he turned and disappeared.

Mrs Tryer carried her baby into the kitchen, and handed it to Dinah, the woman who took responsibility for the food preparation and who Kathleen had been told to assist. Dinah handed the child to Kathleen while she continued to receive orders from Mrs Tryer.

The baby held its head back, and looked into Kathleen's face. Kathleen tickled the infant, and it chuckled and clutched at her.

Kathleen realised Mrs Tryer had stopped speaking. She turned reluctantly because surely there would be a rebuke but the pale, furrow-browed woman only smiled at her.

'Dinah, how old is this girl?'

'Oh, about ten years, Miss.'

Dinah spoke without hesitation, as if she knew.

A small boy sat on the steps one afternoon. He was thin, his bones but a frame for the rags he wore, and his head seemed too heavy for his neck. He rested his chin on his knees, and turned his head to Kathleen when she sat beside him, then turned away again. His eyes were open, soft and unseeing.

Light thickened. Kathleen was in a wash of purple, and the raw wood, stacked and rigidly patterned, bled into the air. The flickering yellow light of a fire was at her back. The rhythmic cracking and splitting of an axe.

Kathleen put an old jam tin of tea and a piece of bread at the boy's side. The axeman shook his head and would not stop. The boy dipped his bread into the tea, pushed the soggy pap to his mouth, but hardly chewed.

Mr Tryer appeared from the darkness, and put his hand on the axeman's shoulder. He took the axe from him (you have done well) and pushed him away.

Shivering in the pale morning, Kathleen stood at the woodheap. There was yesterday's symmetrical stack of wood and two cylindrical bundles of canvas, one larger than the other. One held the body of the old blind man; and from the smaller bundle a small hand protruded, as if frozen in a secret wave of departure.

Kathleen helped clean the fireplace. She rubbed the ash into her hands, and made the fire blaze and crackle.

In the kitchen, white flour in the skin of her fingers.

Sometimes there was a teacher and Kathleen sat at the front of the class. Sat still. Did not speak. Learned to empty words into her head and spill them out onto a blank page.

She wondered what it was like in the wood-box when the lid came down, and the silent class listened to your snivelling. And she was glad she was not the one roped beneath the faraway desk at the back of the room.

When she spoke she wondered why her voice did not spring from her as other people's seemed to. She thought of her brother, Chatalong, and how it must be to see people smiling back at you when you spoke.

Her voice did not carry, only some of her words left her. She felt them all, trapped, vibrating the bones of her face. It was easier to keep your face averted, to remain intent upon a page, or weaving, sewing.

She liked to be among others in the kitchen; the warmth and sound of fire, the smell of dough, the soups they made in the vast pot. And the kitchen had Dinah who immediately reclaimed the place taken by Fanny.

post marked kathleen

Dear Mr Tryer,

I would be glad if you will inform me whether the young Benang girl is in fact Kathleen Mason.

Sergeant Hall, of the Police Department, Perth, believes we have a girl of the above name and is desirous of obtaining her to assist his wife in domestic service.

Yours sincerely,

Chief Protector Neville

Dear Mr Neville,

I have the honour to inform you that the girl's mother does not wish her girl to go to Perth. She thinks it is too far for her to be away. The mother thinks she may get sick at any time and would not be able to see her daughter.

Yours sincerely,

Mr Tryer

Memo:

Mr Dean. Inform Mr Tryer I shall be glad if he will give his own views when replying to our questions as well as consulting the wishes of the natives. Furthermore, inform him that we very much doubt that the girl's mother is at the settlement.

A O Neville

Mr Neville,

Regarding your correspondence of ... and the matter of the girl referred to as Kathleen Benang. In fact her actual name is Kathleen Mason. She is a very quiet child, but it appears that the girl is not in fact Dinah Benang's daughter but was only adopted as such by Dinah once she arrived here. Such is the attraction between the two however that Dinah is now claiming to have changed her own name from Mason back to Benang, her own mother's tribal name and has concocted a remarkable story to support her claim.

Kathleen is a most capable girl, although perhaps a little young for such duties. It is believed that she is about ten years old.

Yours sincerely,
Mr Tryer

Mr Tryer,

Please arrange for the girl Kathleen Mason to come to Perth by train and inform me of expected arrival time. I will arrange to have her delivered to Sergeant Hall.

Yours sincerely,

Chief Protector Neville

almost a grave orgasm

'Well, the train had a lot to do with it,' said Uncle Will.
'What happened to our family. Yeah. And the law, like I
told you. The train took over for a lot of the teamster's
work. Grandad — you're calling him Sandy One — he got
by for a while because he worked for the Dones, and he
got that mine. My dad, Daniel, he became a businessman.
What could he do? He had to look out for us, his children.
I was a grown boy now. I was his only boy, the rest all
daughters.' Will paused, and I suppose he was thinking
about his sisters, and himself. Their pride and their
shame.

'Yeah, the girls all married white men. Dad wanted
that, it was an escape, see? And Hall, the policeman, he
thought that was the way to go. No, he wouldn't've let
'em marry Nyoongars, he wouldn't even let any get close.
And the law said that, you had to get his okay.'

Uncle Jack wanted to have his say. 'It's another sort of
murdering. What the law was doing. And helping people

do. Killing Nyoongars really, making 'em white, making 'em hate 'emselves and pretend they're something else, keeping 'em apart.'

Uncle Will was not comfortable with such an explanation. He liked to speak in the way of the local histories he had read; of individual struggle, of alignments of technology and progress. 'And the train, to the west, brung a lot of people close to here, but not quite this far, most of 'em.'

Yeah, one train wheezed along the railway stitched from Mustle Haven to Gebalup.

There was a big show; speeches and clapping and all that stuff when the train made its first little trip. Almost the whole town was there. They cheered, and the train showered them with what it coughed and spat.

Daniel Coolman, wanting to make a mark, to be a pioneering man of the town, had diversified. He took Will with him whenever possible, and they — Coolman and Son — carted water to households, and various stuff from farms and mines to the railway. The train showered them in black shit and rain and deafened them with its puffing and screeching.

There was still a living to be made with horses; at the mines for instance, and clearing, and carting.

The government built dams and there was less need to cart water.

Daniel Coolman's body began to swell, and he could dress himself only with Harriette's help. She draped a coat on his shoulders, and tied shoelaces across the increasing space between button and buttonhole.

He had lost his upper lip through cancer, and so grew his moustache long, combing it down over his mouth and parting it when he ate. His food disappeared, as it were, in encores of exits, entering his mouth as if between curtains.

'Youse vould ve starving if not for ve,' he yelled at Harriette, in his frustration, 'vere vould you ve if I vasn't here?'

Once Constable, now *Sergeant*, Hall returned to Gebalup with his wife and new servant, Kathleen Mason. He noted that Fanny and Harriette were working as domestic servants in the town. It was a very good thing, a very suitable position for them, he said.

And it was also just as well, said Sergeant Hall, resuming a twenty-year long habit of social visits, that Daniel had been such a well-known man of the town, regarded as a pioneer in fact, else ... Well, people would have talked.

Had been? Daniel worried at Hall's use of the past tense. But what about Hall's use of the conditional? *Would have* talked?

Of course people talked. They yakked and yarned.

Look at him, sending his two *gins* out to work and staying at home. Always was canny, and shrewd. You know he helped kill them, all his wife's people? You know?

And see how fat he's got? Yes, there's two men there, you know. Being kept. Living off the earnings of ...

Well, of course.

You reckon?

Sergeant Hall had known Daniel long enough to talk straight to him. 'Your wife, well, she's ...' His voice trailed off, and he began again. 'You married her, so she's exempt. And your mother-in-law is too, while Old Sandy's still alive and she's with you. While you can support them, Daniel. You're fortunate you've only the one left at home, and that I keep the *blackfellas* away. And lucky you got your daughters into good white marriages, it was worth marrying them all so young.'

What could Daniel say?

'There's Will — he's yours — and Chatalong ... Well, I can turn a blind eye. He looks all right, could be *quarter-caste*. But really, legally, he's a ward of the state.'

But Chatalong was working, and he and Will were bringing in money.

Sometimes, during the long days, Daniel wheezed and shuffled to where they'd propped Sandy One so that he might see the sky through a window. Sandy was a sailor once, you know. He liked to watch the clouds sailing across blue sky.

No one came to see them. Daniel and Pat had thought themselves such wild men, once. Daniel wondered where Pat was now. What made him just off and leave Dinah like that? Now their sons were working together to help support the family. It was funny how things worked out.

Old Sandy One had shrivelled. He had never been a big man, and now he seemed just a pile of clothes with a head on top. His eyes rolled, tears welled and rolled down his cheeks, and his jaw worked almost all the time, and he made strange clicking sounds.

Daniel eased himself to the floor beside the little old one, and tried to see what was worth such attempts at singing, for this was what he supposed old Sandy was trying to do.

It was sometimes a cloud, sailing. A bird. Probably the light changing over the course of a day. Oh yes, old Sandy One sang, after a fashion. It sounded very much like a moan, and he clicked his tongue. Remembering.

At Dubitj Creek Station, and not long after that last spree, he'd been going to shoot Patrick Coolman. Daniel had stopped him.

He could have shot them both.

Of course, he could understand what Patrick had done; he knew plenty who'd done the same thing. But, for it to happen to both his daughters? Harriette's was the usual brutality, and he'd not been there. But he'd introduced Patrick and Dinah.

Sandy One went over it all again, in his mind.

It was the southern coast, a long way between two capital cities. It was the edge of the desert, but there was grass for stock, and some water. There were a number of little bays which made good harbours, sheltered as they were from the south-westerly wind and swell; from Wirlup Haven, you headed east and it was Kylie Bay, Dubitj Creek and then Point Zion. With the right eyes it was easy to find water, and grass for stock. From Point Zion you went north-west to Badjura, and then Norseton, and waterholes led you across to the goldfields, or back down to Kylie Bay.

There were pastoral leases in the name of ex-convicts, of men who'd worked on stations further west, of men who'd jumped ship, of their cousins, their nephews. They were all hoping to get in on the action.

There was a new workforce being built. The children, paler with each generation, gathered at the woodheap. A new skin.

The women, many of them the men's own daughters, were in great demand.

Gold attracted more and more men. Someone nailed a sign to one of the flimsy walls surrounding a big tub of grog, and thus began a tavern.

With so much activity at the goldfields, and with no railway yet built from the capital city on the west coast, there was more than enough work carting goods from the south coast up to the fields. Someone like Sandy One Mason, for instance, knew the coast from years of sea-faring, from working on the telegraph line, from carting for the stations and homesteads; and from some deeper knowledge, some more intimate acquaintance. People said it was his missus.

Teamsters waited for the boats close to Point Zion. The telegraph line touched Dubitj Creek, kept going. Very soon it was neglected, and disappeared, but here it passed between the teamsters' camp on the coast and a range of hills. Granite peaks rose to the sky and helped keep the westerly winds from the bay. In the mornings, those rocky slopes, long polished by blowing sand, glowed with the colours of sunrise, and at their base old dunes rolled away toward the white beaches and the sea. Midway, there was a grassy plain and a soak for the animals.

Close to the ocean the crest of each white dune was as crisply edged as folded paper. The white sand was soft and deeply scored where the teamsters had cleared a way to the beach, and rocks and timber had been placed there to stop the carts from bogging. Either side of the trail lay rubbish; a horseshoe, a bottle, an old boot, piece of rope, sheet of iron a strap a broken box. It seemed, among these slow and reforming mounds, that there floated the remains of some strange wreck. People had disappeared beneath the surface, the earth had closed over their passage, and only this flotsam remained.

There were campfires in the soft gulleys. White and ruddy men, dark men and women.

'They're my daughters,' Sandy told two tall twins who arrived in rain and stood at the end of tracks you could follow eastwards back across a red-earthed continent. Twin ruts which remained in the mud, and where vegetation never again grew, and which were later sealed with bitumen and crushed stone.

Sandy One welcomed them to his campfire. He advised them.

'My daughters,' he said. 'They are educated, they can read and write.'

The twins spoke of their horses, sired by a stallion brought across the sea. Like ourselves, they thought, looking at one another and fingering their moustaches. The three men stroked the horses, looked at their teeth, lifted the tails, stood back and admired them. Well-bred, and strong. Intelligent.

The twins helped Sandy mend his wagon. The men held the metal in a fire until it glowed red, then hammered and reshaped it. The next day when they attached it to the wagon they thought it was like new.

One of the twins tousled the young Sandy Two's hair. He had watched them the whole time. 'Good on a horse, is he?'

'My daughters,' said Sandy One. 'I registered their births. I will marry their mother. She's everything you want a woman to be ...'

Mother and daughters were with the other women at

another fire further back among the low and twisted trees.

'A good partner, knows this country, keeps out of the way. Food everywhere. A best partner.'

The twins thought of how it was with the women. They were lonely, those twins, scared even in their togetherness. The daughters were quite fair, really.

'She's been good to me,' said Sandy, whose words were thick and sticky, whose tongue was black from rum and tobacco. 'If it wasn't for her ...'

Those red-haired twins, Daniel and Patrick Coolman, went to the goldfields and were back within a matter of weeks. Pragmatic opportunists, they could see a better plan than the dust and foolishness of that place.

They had good skills. Each of them could do a blacksmith's work, could build wheels, fix carts. They had their own wagons and horses, and Sandy One — continually journeying from Dubitj Creek to Point Zion, Badjura, Norseton, Kylie Bay, sometimes westward along the coast then back to Dubitj Creek again — was there to help them out. The men had not much else to do but tend their animals and help load and unload. Fanny and her children navigated. Her children.

'Um, those girls of yours, Sandy.'

Sandy One was vigilant, adaptable, flexible; but for all that it is as well that we have more than him and his memory to rely on. He was a little man, and with his olive complexion and fair, almost blond, hair he looked quite exotic, reminding travellers of some people in the south of Europe. The sun left its mark on him as he aged so that you could date him, almost, by the lines where his hair had gradually receded.

Sandy One was a man with a long past, an insecure present, and a particularly uncertain future. Consider, for instance, myself as his future, and you will appreciate the uncertainty of it.

He thought he knew the pattern of things, of new relationships being forged in the land. And so, when Dinah came limping and snuffling back after being caught at a spree, Sandy was about to go for his gun. Then the very Reverend Harton visited.

It was an afternoon, the granite peaks hardening against the sky, when Fanny looked up from the campfire and grabbed Sandy One's arm as he was about to go for the gun.

Was it a man? Cresting the hill, rushing down the slope at great speed. Crazy wings flapped about him — but yes, it was a man — and he moved between two thin wheels, his feet just above the ground and making small circles.

Then he was among them, was there, and Fanny was embarrassed for her laughter. He spoke first, might have said something like, 'You lucky sinners. Here I am, vestments and all.'

Then he spoke about his bicycle, and how far he had come.

He moved among the men, wanting to talk — very softly — of sin. Most listened to him, but there was more respect for his technology, and for the fact that he'd taken the trouble to reach them, than there was for his talk of prayer and God. Men moved away, but one — Patrick Coolman — returning to the campsite, joined the little group around the good reverend. Sandy One went quickly to his side, shoulder to shoulder, and immediately felt very small.

'It was the camel pads,' said the reverend, 'and God's wind at my back.'

The men listened, their various brows creased. The talk was of sin, and what is sacred. Of a life after this one. Of love.

You could hear the sea just beyond the dunes. You could smell it. You could smell the grasses, too. The thin blond-headed man, the tall red twins. Fanny willed that they feel the light feet running all about them, and the nervous hearts' beating.

After he had talked with Sandy and the twins the reverend said, 'Come and see me, then, when you are at the town, and I will marry you.' Sandy thought this might be the way to do things, the way of surviving.

Sandy One had tried to arrange that they all get married together, the white man's way. Sandy Mason and Fanny, Daniel Coolman and Harriette Mason, Patrick Coolman and Dinah Mason. Father, mother, daughters and sons-in-law, all on the one day.

They went as a group, the new sons following the wheel ruts. Sandy at least was proud. So many children had been lost, but now their daughters should be safe.

Fanny was thinking of lost children too, of lost family.

After the wedding ... Well, there was no party. No *reception*. No guests, no bits of torn paper fluttering over them. Rather, there was an absence of paper, because the red-twin-Pat and daughter Dinah had got waylaid somewhere somehow. Pat had met some friends, gone on a bender. He missed a wedding and its certificate. 'But let us celebrate,' Sandy said.

Just the two certificates which, almost a century later, I

studied so carefully, again and again, before letting them fall to where so many other leaves lay. I sank into all that paper, and it rustled like snake skins, like cicada shells, like the feathers and parchment wings of long dead things. I thought of all those the papers named, and of how little the ink could tell.

The two couples and the boy camped just out of the town of Kylie Bay, made a fire blaze, drank rum. Sandy played the piano accordion, and the lone red twin (Daniel), his nervousness drowned in grog, danced with his woman and his mother-in-law. They laughed about who was who, who married who — for they were all thinking of when Patrick and Dinah would do the same. Sandy Two staggered about, his blood roaring with drunkenness, and the many shadows, the many shadows flickering and shifting in the firelight danced with him until he fell asleep.

Sandy Two once staggered, and I now hover, but the ageing Daniel Coolman could only shuffle as he went from room to room. In fact, he mostly just lay on his back, staring at his puffy hands where they rested on the great mound his chest and stomach had become. He could feel the air move on his teeth, where the lip had been cut away.

With considerable difficulty he took out his pocket watch. He never touched a drop of grog until midday.

Chatalong began working when the war was still on, and with so many men away there was a demand for labour. Chatalong worked at many things; he was useful, fit, strong. It meant Will could be with Daniel. Chatalong could charm anyone, with all that talk and nonsense.

He cut and carted wood for the smelters.

He was good with horses.

Eventually, he settled at the smelter. He worked on the top floor, keeping the furnace stoked. It was not so bad, on the top floor, except for the sulphur fumes.

He often helped men who had collapsed. The breeze was always so very sweet after the sulphur fumes and the heat.

The sulphur made him cough, and slowed his talking.

In the evenings Chatalong sipped some oil. It soothed his throat, and was what men and horses drank after collapsing from the fumes.

It was usually Jack who carried Sandy One to where Fanny and a number of children sat by a small fire hidden among the chaos of timber, corrugated iron and horse stables. The police office was next-door, but they were out of its sight.

Sometimes, before he got too big, even the bloated Daniel joined them. The children were hidden away. Daniel took tiny sips of his grog and held a pipe in his teeth; a grip which was framed by a hirsute lower lip and the startling absence of an upper one. The flickering flames made evil shadows of that hole in his whiskers, and of the long and yellowing teeth. Chatalong coughed and sipped oil, and Sandy One gazed up at the night sky, clicking and moaning his songs while the women mostly talked among themselves. Fanny said something, and her daughter laughed.

I used to read to Grandad, purely for the malicious satisfaction it gave me. I wanted him to see that I was a failure, one way or another. That I was resentful and bitter. I wanted to undermine what he had done to the extent that he could never know where or when it might all collapse and send us plummeting down to … to … Well, certainly not to a place of heat and sulphurous fumes. I have already touched upon such a place with Chatalong in this chapter, and that was tolerable enough.

One at a time, bit by bit, I wrote out Grandad's so carefully collected and meticulously filed documents. One at a time I held each before his eyes, put a match to it, and let it fall when the flame reached my fingers.

Perhaps I could have found something more valuable in them had I kept them. When I later recited to Uncle Jack and Uncle Will I know we sometimes regretted the loss of some of them, but all that was before I began to reproduce much more than words.

Increasingly — reading and reciting my work — I wanted to impress each of my audience; I so wanted to somehow bring Uncle Jack, Uncle Will and myself together. And if Ern could follow, so be it. But I seemed unable to satisfy our diverging needs.

Uncle Jack would say, 'You gotta get back. Work your way through this shit. Find that spirit which is in you. The land is still here. Trust.'

Sandy One had a space in the narrow passageway just inside the front door of Daniel's house. There were no visitors. They propped him in a corner there, and stepped about him as they passed. Until they could decide. To begin with, Fanny slept beside him, right there, and bundled their blankets away each morning.

Sandy One remained in that gloomy space. The window faced south. He watched clouds move across it. Sometimes the branch of a tree, a bird might pass. Flies buzzing. The flyscreen moved in the breeze, changing the way it held the light in the squares within it.

Each time Fanny stepped in the door she forgot, say, the ache in her knees from all day kneeling, or the wrinkled peeling skin of fingers too long in water. She felt the light move away, the cold floor under her feet, and heard the jangle of keys just as she had once, a very long time ago.

Sandy One, his hair now completely silver, may as well have been chained there, and his hazel eyes seemed to beg her not to remember.

Well, of course we spoke of many things. Me and Ern, in the time before Uncle Jack and Uncle Will came back to save me. And then, around the campfire, all of us men. But, they were very old, and I was feeble in my own way. All of us past it, and nostalgic, and they with a terrible sympathy for my plight.

'You're so young. And you had just did it the once with both those girls?' Uncle Jack laughed, 'You just kept at it, again and again, all day long, unna?'

Given my predicament — shall we say my medical condition (you remember, the car accident?) — it is hardly surprising that they were sympathetic, sad, curious.

Oh yes, I had told them. 'I've had women. Well, they were girls, and I but a boy. We all went up in a bang, as they say.' But no matter how much I tried to savour my memories I tasted only bitterness; what has been taken away. I admit to hours spent fondling myself. Hours of futility. Perhaps, astute as you are, you see this narcissism in my prose. Naturally, I would prefer the flaccidity, the limpness, to remain undetectable.

We would end up discussing Fanny and Sandy One. They must have had something special going, unna? Really. All that time alone, following the team, him watching her, and she absorbed as if — I say — as if reading. His awareness was growing, he was becoming intimate with their land, with her. She laughed, showed him the plant with a great many stiff, thorny stems. 'Devil's, devil's …' She tapped his crotch.

It must have been something other than a sort of moral obligation or a sense of guilt that kept him with her all that time. Perhaps it was her relative youth. The firm flesh, the soft and delicious skin. The generosity of her, her softness and scent. The children and he, they revolved around her.

They were a long time together. She must have been not much more than a child when they met, given the date of the last birth.

Those last years, so gloomy and cramped. Sandy One, as I have described him, was not much more than a head balanced upon a wasted body. A clicking and stiff-tipped tongue.

Well. Perhaps there you have it. Her tending him. Wiping, washing, drying. Gently, not rushing. It was a rare time, to be safe and alone together, those last years.

Her gentle hands. Teasing a reaction out of him. He as light as if he was hollow-boned like a bird.

She was bathing him by the fire. Alone, somehow.

The firelight made his skin glow. He was flushed, pink and white, and his eyes glittered as she had not seen them do for, oh, so long. She considered his wasted body, his groin. How long? Well, long enough eh? Even now.

She straddled him. On her knees, making her way up and down his so scrawny body. She was using her memory and imagination. A knee? No, his leg gave way. An elbow? He was talking to her, his tongue clicking, crackling now like fire. She slid his body along the ground to position him, and his tongue was there. So quick, so stiff at the very tip. And her hand, reaching back, her voice helping him.

It was easy to slide him into her after that. She moved for him, and felt the little convulsions, the spurting.

A last time. You would think such a little ecstacy would not be enough to start a life, let alone finish one. Perhaps it was what Sandy One had been saving himself for, waiting in the half-light all that time.

Of course Fanny had to dress him before the others returned. She searched until she found his sea clothes, from when she had first met him. They were musty, and crinkled all the more because of how he had shrunk. She put aside his beanie, set aside the pipe and boots, decided against seating him on Daniel's chair by the fireplace in the house. She could smell the salt water on him, and even though it was midday, she made the fire blaze.

Daniel, wheezing from the wagon, squeezed through the door, stopped. His wheezing continued after a short pause. Harriette peered over his shoulder.

Sandy One stared at them from where he was propped by the fire. He was naked, except for a hairbelt and a kangaroo skin draped over his shoulders, and he stared at Daniel as if defying him. His old resolve seemed back.

Fanny, looking into the fire, wailed and wailed.

Daniel made the coffin himself; it was a question of

352

money. Such was the extent to which the old man had shrunk that it seemed a child's coffin. Daniel's hands — once so cunning and clever — now held and hammered tentatively, could not grip the saw, let the chisel slip. The small coffin seemed too small for the adult-sized grave they'd dug.

Sergeant Hall joined them at the graveside.

The graveside.

I have visited gravesides; my father's, grandfather's (eventually), Uncle Will's, Uncle Jack's ... and so many after that. Each, at the time, seemed a full stop. But I have continued on. I continue them on, in various ways.

Oh, how wonderful it would be to end my life like that of my ancestor, Sandy One. But just as I know this story will not conclude with my death, so I can assure you of this; there will be no final orgasm.

a place for jack

Sandy's death made one less mouth to feed, so much less work for them all. Daniel, however, deteriorated further.

'Ve are naking no infrovents,' he would say. 'Vat vill ve ve avle to leave the voy?' He sat on a rough stool at one of the doorways, taking the sun or shade as he could.

Harriette took the rifle, the old mare and a cart, and came back with meat. A small vegetable garden provided most of the rest of their requirements.

Sometimes Fanny went hunting with her. They killed kangaroo, bush turkey, tamar, wallaby ... An enquiring mind would have thought it strange that they used such a large cart, and untidily left so much on the tray in the way of boxes and blankets and hessian. It was almost as if they were concealing something.

Daniel sat at the house front, and tried to smile at everyone he saw. At least he could resign himself to his melancholy when the women bundled him, bloated and wheezing, on board the wagon. They went off for days at a time, then. To the east, along the coast where the posts of the old telegraph line still ran.

They camped by creeks where there were pools of shallow flowing water, and Qualup Bells standing among the grass. The women found yams on the sandplain; big, pale yellow and juicy. Daniel was alarmed at the number of children they sometimes had with them on these occasions. He was nervous, all the time looking about and keeping watch.

It was Harriette who had taught Will to hunt and shoot.

Will was a little behind his mother, both of them on their bellies, and he had his head level with her feet. She had told him not to lift his head until she signalled, and he kept his eyes on her hand.

Will always remembered the painstaking care and caution of that long crawl to his first kill. A gentle breeze moved into their faces, and the animal was staring into the sun.

Harriette watched the roo the whole time, and the roo seemed to stare straight back at her, but each time it lowered its head to feed, Will and his mother wriggled forward. They froze as it raised its head, and waited while it scratched, swivelled its ears, looked directly at them once again.

Harriette signalled Will forward.

Freeze.

Forward again. She motioned him beside her.

Will took the loaded and cocked gun into his hands and sighted along its length. He thought the kangaroo looked beautiful. It was a grey, and he was close enough to see its liquid eyes shining in the late, low sun.

The rifle hurt Will's shoulder but he was satisfied to see the roo fall dead, and hear his mother praise his marksmanship. He was proud to feed the camp.

Literate Will, just out of school and a keen reader, thought of Hiawatha.

Hiawatha, eh?

His mother helped him carry the kangaroo to the camp. He was almost a man.

Hiawatha, eh? Fanny also asked what he meant.

One time, on the old trails, Sandy One and Fanny had met a man. He wore only his scars, and a hairbelt. His hairline was plucked to show a smooth, high brow. The sight was an anachronism already; and he stayed to the trail, even though the hoofprints and wheel ruts made it hard going. But as there had been no fires for a long time it must've been hard travelling whichever way. What was remarkable was that he did not stay out of sight.

He carried an envelope wedged in the fork of a stick. Just him, the stick, the message.

He stood, breathing deeply, and studied the wagon, its horses, the dark woman and children, and the fair but familiar man.

Fanny and the man spoke in their age-old language. Sandy, looking back, caught Fanny's eye. He understood much of what they said, waited to be called.

But the man jogged away, following a tangential trail. There are in fact many paths; some only ever marked by feet, some which became wheel worn and linked water to water, others were traced by telegraph lines. All are linked by the very oldest of stories, although many of these have been broken by the laying down of lines of steel, or have been sealed with black tar.

Fanny's eyes went to the wagon, her feet took several steps after the man, but then she stopped. There are many trails.

My grandfather's sources have occasional references to such letters carried by *natives*.

The messages must have seemed important, like sacred things, to put people to so much trouble.

This man kept the message away from himself, knowing well the damage it could do if its words fell into your ear. It is best to keep it away from yourself; at least until you learn to understand it, to have some chance of controlling it.

I think I understand their concern. Sandy One, and the children; Dinah, Harriette, Sandy Two. All had listened to the language held in this forked stick, as did their children, and theirs in turn, and theirs ...

I sometimes feel as if I have been sealed within such an envelope. It makes it hard to stay at ease with yourself, hard to speak out from the heart.

As a child Uncle Will sometimes called himself Hiawatha, which was as good as any book could put it, back then, for him.

And if I had a gun, then, in the days before Uncle Will and Uncle Jack came to me? I might have sighted along its stiff barrel, at my grandfather's liquid eyes. Tried not to think of my father's eyes, draining like whirlpools as he dissolved, disappeared, went away beside me.

Daniel Coolman walked slowly, very slowly, down the

street. Jack Chatalong walked beside him, felt the earth shake with each footfall, and restrained himself from skipping and running in circles around and around the big man. He didn't do cartwheels, didn't stop to sit and rest and then only race to catch up when Daniel — finally — reached the door. No. Jack Chatalong kept to Daniel's very, very slow pace. He had even stopped talking, and kept his tongue between his teeth because Daniel had said shut up.

Mr Starr pushed the till closed and looked up as he heard the door open. A grotesquely swollen man manouevred, with some difficulty, through the door. The man's beard was poorly trimmed yet fastidiously combed. A *half-caste* youth trailed him, stepping from side to side to see what lay ahead. The boy darted out and moved a chair from the monolith's path.

'Okay then, whadoo I owe ya?' Starr smiled at his parrot, and scratched its crest while he waited for the two of them to reach the counter.

Daniel Coolman. Starr had heard he was not well.

It took more time than Starr wished to hear Coolman out. He listened to the laboured breathing as much as to the slow speech, and observed the moustache which moved in and out with Coolman's breath. He noted yellow teeth, absent consonants. It seemed that it was not only the production, but also the conception of words that gave Coolman difficulty. Indeed, it was not until the youth, glancing regularly at the big man, summed up their situation that Starr finally understood completely.

'Okay then.'

Starr inserted a piece of cuttlefish into the bird's beak.

'Yes,' he said. 'But it will have to be at our family property, that's almost at Kylie Bay. We've a wagon going across in a few days. Friday. He can go on that, and I'll send a note with him.'

Mr Starr watched them go. That man had married Sandy One's daughter, hadn't he? She and her mother did a lot of domestic work in the town. It freed up our own women for better things, so his wife said.

It just showed you what people could achieve.

Uncle Jack had to go. The smelters had closed. There was so little work in Gebalup now. The Starrs had all sorts of enterprises; fruit and gardens, licenses for stripping and carting bark. Jack was a fast learner.

I think of his skill with horses and stock, and consider him at work in the orchards, pruning the fruit trees which — in what seemed yet another manifestation of the possibilities of place — grew in such a spot.

and salmon fishing too

To the Chief Protector of Aborigines and Fisheries

Dear Sir,

  you will probably hear by this mail from the Resident Magistrate here of a boy named Jack Chatalong who was given in my charge by his — I believe — uncle, although he may be the boy's brother-in-law. The point is that the man is a small farmer and businessman in Gebalup, and is married to a half-caste native woman, who is a marvelous example of what these people can achieve. Her garden and house would shame that of many white folk.

  The youth has been in my employ for the last 3 months in my orchard at Dalyup and riding about after my stock being useful but some of my neighbours appear to have been misled by a deliberate lie that he was visiting the blacks camp and that the boy should be sent to school this is the complaint and I deny the whole of it.

  In consequence of this I got the police to bring him in to town and an inquiry was made by the Resident

Magistrate Mr Mustle — to which the result you will be made acquainted with. the boy is now held by the police after my clothing him as he was quite bare of clothing when came to me

I am willing to keep him and clothe him and give him some pocket money too when required I hope to hear from you that he is not under your control having a white uncle who is perfectly able to watch his interests.

I might say the boy is just about 15 and quite willing to live on my farm

As he gets older its my intention to give him a wage.

I am sir your respectfully

A Starr

To the Chief Protector of Aborigines and Fisheries

Mr Neville

I would be obliged if you would kindly inform me where I could send a boy supposed to be a half-caste under the following circumstances. He was brought up before the bench and charged as a neglected child. Constant complaints have been received of him frequenting any black camps that are set up before we are able to move them along and that he is becoming a nuisance and an embarrassment. I have put him in the charge of a storekeeper and sent him to school. I think it would be better to send him to some institution if possible, but as he appears only about 1/4 black I do not know whether he would come under your dept.

Yours,

Mr C Mustle

Dear Mr Starr,

The Resident Magistrate, Mr Mustle, has written to inform me that he has arranged to have the youth Jack Chatalong sent to school and placed in charge of a storekeeper, who I presume to be yourself.

As you seem concerned for the boy and his welfare, and as we are an inadequately funded department with many demands upon our resources, and as there must be some allowance for judgement in these matters I am able to say that he need not be under the jurisdiction of this department.

I wonder if you could be so kind as to inform me of the catches of salmon along that coastline at this time of year?

Yours,

A O Neville
Chief Protector of Aborigines and Fisheries

tommy

We very rarely saw any other people as we moved along that coast. We preferred it that way. I was very nervous of company, and perhaps my uncles were wary of the four of us being seen together; a cripple, a freak, and a couple of old Nyoongars.

It is an isolated stretch of coastline. We never took these little trips in the holiday periods. Even when Uncle Jack began taking me to visit relations, we were rarely away for much more than a week at a time.

On the rare occasions when we did encounter others, it was usually Uncle Will who'd talk with them, if we could not ignore them altogether.

We went along small and fragile tracks, with roots rising from the sand. One or the other of the old men drove, so slowly that the car would stall when the track got soft. Then we'd reverse out before getting too badly bogged, and gently try again, inching our way along by compacting the sand a little more each time. Spiky, tough shrubs scratched at our arms if we leaned them out the car windows.

I think it was only once that we came across anyone we knew. There were two women playing cards, sitting in the shade away from their rusty station wagon. They looked up, it seemed resentfully, until Uncle Jack called out to them from the back seat. He went over to them, called us across one by one. We left Ern in the car.

'Harley,' Uncle Jack said, 'this is your Aunty Olive, Aunty Norma.' The women looked at me.

'Yeah, I remember your father, Tommy,' said Olive, after a time. 'He used to come and see us all the time when he was working on the roads out this way.'

'Tomcat,' said Norma, laughing. My father would've been about her age, if he'd lived.

'Yeah, he was a Nyoongar all right,' said Olive. 'A lot of his family thought they were too good for the rest of us.' She glanced at Uncle Will. 'Your people are from here, you know, but Jack would've told you that.' She looked again at Uncle Will, as if expecting he might say something.

'Now your father,' said Uncle Jack, taking the initiative. 'He lived with Harriette when he was little, didn't he?' He was asking me, he was asking Will, he was asking the women to contribute.

Ah yes, my father. The few words it must've taken a lifetime to find, and which he gave me just before ...

You recall the photo sequence, again? The one which we are nonsensically asked to read from left to right — and which shows my father as perhaps the first white man born. But new legislation, referring to the day before his birth, prevented Tommy being our first white man born, and put him in danger of understanding himself in ways that would only deform and oppress him. His grandmother gave him pride, and a sense of his spirit, and then Ern and Aunty Kate conspired to keep him ashamed and on the run.

It was only when he was grown — when he was an adult, with children — that he began to listen again, and to try to put words to how he felt, to who he was.

I have so very few photos of him, and the one above — the family photo — makes nostalgic, secure viewing very difficult. Thus my desire for alteration. After all, what does it matter what my father looked like, save that he was among those who:

> ... are almost white and some of them are so fair that, after a good wash, they would probably pass unnoticed in any band of whites ...

and that he was one of a:

> ... family quite white enough to walk down Hay Street and attract no particular attention.

What does it matter, save that he could pass, that we could be anyone, and from anywhere?

I used to read the large letters on the back of my father's overalls as **MR D**. Does this reveal my own attitude to authority, a conferring of respect? Or merely a propensity to rearrange the alphabet in my own interests?

He worked for the Main Roads Department, as one of what was known as the *Boongs Gang*. Ever ambitious, perhaps needing to prove himself, he got to be Leading

Hand; and as one who could pass unnoticed, it was he — like a *dawg* — who brought the grog back to camp on pay-night. As the boss, it was he who stood up to fight the challengers around the campfire late in the night, and took the curses of the men he roused next day.

And the Main Roads Department took him along what we recognise as familiar paths, similar paths to the Premier Man all those years ago, similar paths to those trodden forever, paths still there and clear. And even though he was breaking up the crust of the ground, and even though he was resealing it so that it might be travelled as quickly as possible, still it taught him. That place, and some of the men he worked with, taught him. The country taught him, even as it diminished under the exhortation that a million acres be cleared each year.

He scratched at old trails while, around him, massive, clunking chains dragged across the earth. There were great explosions, and it rained earth and mallee roots and small dead animals. Animals fled, they scampered in a mostly tiny-footed stampede away from chains, ripping machines, explosions. Smoke and dust spread further than you could see.

Of course, it is never easy to say what you are learning, nor to pass it on to others. I remember him on his knees, having shucked the MRD overalls, and sparring with me.

'You hafta learn to stand up for yourself.'

'You belong here.'

He showed me — what was I? A few years old? — how to hold my hands and fists, and to watch their eyes. And yet it must've been short years later that I heard him saying you can't keep winning, you're not gunna win all your fights, it's best not to fight if you can, but when it happens it is whoever hurts the other most, first, whatever way, who wins.

Not so many words to remember. Not a lot of words to live by.

And then Grandad came to get me, and I went to boarding school, and in the holidays to live with him in the boarding house he owned. My grandfather was perfecting a process. He must've suspected that he'd failed with my father, and that this was a last chance to get it right.

But again, I digress and confuse all of us, one with the other. As if we were not all individuals, as if there was no such thing as progress or development, as if this history were just variations on the one motif.

And, after all, I have a story to tell. This little family history to share with you.

Yes, it is hard for me to write of my father. Hard for me to think like this of my father, of myself. So I must slide away a little, and come at it from some other way to build up momentum.

Ern had a new domestic servant, Topsy, who arrived with the salmon but from the opposite direction and — of course — by land. Ern soon got rid of his old wife, promoted the servant in her place and went to a war; and when he got back he took Topsy and their child away, as the best white men so often did, and they all went to live in the city.

Ah, I summarise it so glibly. Glide across these lines of print.

Tommy went to the local school. Topsy walked him there and back.

Now, really, Topsy had little choice but to be like a white woman; a very humble one because she could not show herself off, or move among them. They would always ensure she knew the difference, and the difference was that she was all the things they were not. They would say they were clean, industrious, thrifty. They were pioneers, even here in the city. She was not such; could not be; it was impossible.

On her own, living in the city, how could she think any other way? How could she think for herself against all that? The only way was to be them, and then more. To be all that, and then more. The *more* was the important part, that would be who she truly was.

She had worked like a man, beside Ern. She could dress like any woman and keep house. And she had to be more. A saint, generous and healing; full of love.

She was happy enough to stay inside. It kept the sun away, and goodness knows she did not need more of that exposure.

There were the children to think of.

In the photographs it is clear that she believes she is too tall. She stoops, inclines her head to one side and holds her hands in front of her waist, one covering the other. Topsy was a very determined woman and so she tried only to exhale, as if by doing this she could expel that part of her that was deemed so unattractive, and perhaps it would keep her nostrils narrow. But then her nose seemed to grow longer, and her face began to remind her of a kangaroo. Her body sometimes curled and twisted as if trying to find new shapes to accommodate that which burnt so ferociously within her.

Topsy made things clean and dainty. There were lace

doilies. She cleaned beneath them each day. And sometimes she cleaned morning and afternoon.

The mop was not good enough. She liked to scrub the floor on her hands and knees. And have flowers.

She wished someone would visit to see how clean the house was, how welcoming, how much like their own.

Sometimes she read. There were all the labels on the food tins. But the sauce bottle, the coffee and tea. All those dark people.

There were those novels of Ern's. Upfield, Idriess and so on, with *savages* in them.

There were newspapers and magazines. It startled her, the way they showed — if at all — those such as herself.

The mirror in the bedroom had patches missing and her face was incomplete. There were areas of blackness, pieces where there was no her.

She lifted the boy, and held him in her arms before the mirror. All four of them wiggle their eyebrows and laugh at one another.

Living in the city, sleepwalking, Tommy stumbled in the dark house and saw his mother, half-prone on the floor, her hands tied to the foot of his father's bed.

Occasionally, Ern brought a child home. 'Your sister,' but it was not the one Tommy remembered, the dead one. The girl would smile, or look away, and was pleasant enough to Tommy. She would spend most of her time with Ern, who took her out to the cinema, to the beach, to town, and left Topsy and Tommy at home.

Living in the city, grimacing in the harsh light, half-blind Tommy walked in upon his father and a sister, curled together somehow, in the living room. The light was cruel to Ern's pink and hairy skin.

They were living in the city. And Topsy, the mother, quite suddenly became ill. Or, perhaps she had been ill for a long time. At first, it was as if she were pregnant. It was a sickness which went away late in the morning. And her abdomen became swollen, too. At last, thought Ern, and he kissed her quickly before closing the door.

There was just her and the boy now, in the house, in the street, in the town. Just her and her hazel-eyed boy. Topsy would walk Tommy to school, and be most polite and restrained in her small conversations with other mothers. Who all seemed so very cold, as if ice still ran in their veins.

Whereas Topsy herself was hot, so very very hot. Tommy put his hand to his mother's face, to where the red glowed deep in the brown cheeks, and felt how she burned. He spat on his fingers and reached again, knowing that his saliva would sizzle bubble bounce as does water on any hot surface.

Tommy followed his mother as she walked through the house. She kept one shoulder to the wall and traced the perimeter of each room. He felt the heat of a burning sun radiating from within her. Yet she shivered all the time as if cold and held herself, stroked her arms, her stomach, her thighs. Tommy, listening closely to her rapid and melodic speech, heard not a single word he knew.

'They keep sending me home from school.' Tommy spoke to his father's back as that silent man paced the house. It was tidy, but stale. Dust in the drawers. Ernest saw that Topsy seemed drained, but he could not help but be pleased at her appearance. A little illness became her, he thought. It made her skin a little lighter. A small price, Ernest decided, for staying out of the sun. For being a little off-colour. He smiled; it was as if his very presence improved not only children, but his wife as well.

In the morning Ernest awoke to the sound of whispering. Topsy, beside him, fell silent as he turned his head. She lay on her back, just the thin sheet over her body, and her knees high and apart. Her dark hands rested, palms down, upon her stomach. In the washed light of early morning her skin shone with a film of sweat.

It was not until he rolled off her that Ern realised she was in fact a very great distance away, perhaps as far as where her eyes were focused. Her breath came fast and shallow. A moment ago that had excited him; now there was a prickle of fear.

He had to help her dress.

'No. I can't allow her in here. It's against the law.'

The doctor's surgery was in the hotel. No one knew Ern, he was just this white bloke with a *gin*, a *darky*, a *boong coon native* with him and they weren't allowed in pubs. Shouldn't even be with a white man like this, at all, anyway, not here.

'There's the hospital. There's a section for *natives*. You'll have to go to Native Welfare.'

Ernest argued. A white woman, the same as. My wife. My.

'We'll let the doctor know. Leave your address, yes I know the house.' The woman was polite, cool. Ice, again, ice in the blood which has not thawed.

Despite all his training, the doctor's nostrils wrinkled at the smell. He saw a grey sheet, a wasted body. Gloom. His eyes flickered over the woman, the creamy-skinned boy. His vision tripped him, and he was looking into hazel eyes. The hazel eyes interested him, and his high thoughts circled and descended to the carcasses left by great men's minds; notions of genetics and of breeding. What he'd read before the war. It was true, you could see it.

The learned man shrugged his shoulders.

'You've done all you can. Some of these people,' and he looked at Ern, turned back to the patient, 'they just give up on life after a time. Have you heard of the bone?'

He recommended alternate hot and cold baths. And the Aborigines Department, sorry, Native Welfare. Surely they should be contacted?

Tommy saw water on the floor, puddles of it in a path leading to the fireplace. His father was on his knees, and reaching into one of the bathtubs set out on the floor.

Tommy saw his mother being boiled, her skin and her bones dissolving. Ern lifted the mother, and wrapped her in a towel. The water streamed over the two of them, and showed the contours of them, showed their skin. Then, into the cold water, and Tommy saw the way her body arched with the shock of it. He was pleased, already, because it showed life, something like passion. Her body bent acutely, refracted at the water's surface.

Her skin was baggy, wrinkled, was as grey and black as old shark skin. I think she remembered a thousand previous baths, and Ern saying, 'Lie deeper in it, love, lie deep in it.' She knew how it stung, and how — after the bleach — it was true, her skin did seem fairer. She could look into its pores, and see tiny mine shafts leading into her. Her skin had been penetrated, and must have now been dead. Dead to some depth. The bones gone. She couldn't stand up.

Still, sometimes she moaned, and rose from the this or that water, up on shoulders and heels. Veins stood out on her limbs and neck like ropes.

'She's dying.'

She was wrapped in blankets, with cushions and pillows placed all about her. Tommy sat beside her, his arms around her, holding himself close as she stroked her swollen abdomen.

Then, on the drive, within a few hours of the coast, she seemed to recover. Sat up and held her boy close to her. She made him smile and laugh. And she swung her legs down to the ground and walked herself into the small hut Harriette lived in just past the edge of town.

Harriette could not help but flare her nostrils as she entered her own dark home. The air was stale. Topsy sat in a large soft chair, panting, and her skin seemed to glow with the heat she radiated. Her brow creased when she saw Harriette.

Harriette sat on the edge of the faded and shabby armchair, and Topsy fell against her. Harriette ran her fingers through Topsy's hair, and the younger woman's breathing slowed to match that rhythmic stroking.

As she caressed Topsy Harriette looked at Ern, and held his gaze. She was no young thing the white men chased. She saw Ern as a boy, like those who called at the camps; sometimes dangerous, but chiefly greedy and disrespectful and with no one to guide them. She waved a hand at Ern to send him away. He pretended not to notice, but Harriette saw that his mouth tightened even further as he left the room. Tommy, who had been standing behind his father, remained.

His mother fell and rose from the water.

When Ern placed the tub upon the beach, the sand screeched against the metal.

Buckets of water warming on a fire.

Ern hauled Topsy from the tub and stood her on the white beach sand. In that late afternoon night the steam rose from her like smoke. She had her hands to her head, and was stooped as if studying her feet on the ground. Her thin, wet clothing clung to her.

Ern took her to the ocean, and forced her to lower herself into it. Her head seemed to float upon the surface, as if her body had already dissolved. She looked at her boy, the land behind him.

Ern went to the fire he'd made on the beach. Stoked it up, and heated more water in metal buckets.

He took his wife from the cold ocean water to the heated tub, again and again.

Tommy saw his mother hauled from the water by her hair, staggering falling to the ocean, and then dragged back again. His mother rising and falling in steaming water, being cooked, being thrown into the ocean. Shivering and streaming on the sand.

Tommy sees her, lolling rolling about in the small waves. Her eyes one moment live things pleading, suffering, and then coloured shells as if the live thing has shrunk back within them. Ern still holding her by the shoulders, not realising at first. Small waves breaking, and bubbles forming in the foam as they break. Tommy can hear the small bubbles popping, and the foam is light and so full already of air that the gentle land breeze blows the white stuff back to sea, dispersing it. He sees the foam again, at the island's tip.

Topsy left her clear footprints in the sand, and a smear on the water's surface.

The boy watching is the man who one later day plucked me from that same ocean, and breathed the life back into me.

One of the few photographs I have of my father was taken when he was a young boy, and he is astride a shark which has been pulled up on the beach. The shark is on its belly, grinning at the camera and Dad has its dorsal fin in his hands. My father's feet don't reach the sand. The two of them — boy and shark — are both grinning, and although my father has considerably less teeth his grin is almost as big.

It was taken somewhere in the years after Topsy's death, and when Ern wandered away. Years when Harriette would take the boy to the beach, and sometimes there was a daughter and her white man with them. It would've been the women in the dunes, the men back around the corner of the beach in the pub. Any kids would be running along the shore, or throwing seaweed at one another, or playing hockey with the driftwood.

Did Tommy see something in the water? Something which materialised, a suggestion, a shimmering which became solid and then he felt its power, and the line was burning his fingers? He wrapped his shirt around his hands. Didn't sing out to anyone.

Half-an-hour, maybe more, the men, kids, they noticed and came calling out to him.

'Eh, Tommy. You got something there?'

Sweat in his eyes, his arms aching to the bone, he heard the call. He could see mostly, it seemed, sky. The blue of the sea, too, and the white beach in an arc echoing the sky's bend. All merging together, somewhere else. Just then, all meeting within himself.

He saw a couple of stick figures in the dunes, pointing at him, moving towards him. But they melted away when he tried to see them, and the line slipped further away from him.

Tommy was where the jetty met the sand, in the shallows, calling the shark in.

'No,' he snarled when someone tried to take the line from his hands. A small crowd had gathered around him. Men jumped back when they saw the size of the shark racing at them in the shallows. It turned, and headed for the deep, ripping the line again through Tommy's shirt covered hands, and he fell forward into the water, was towed a bit, before he got to his knees and elbows, and then to his feet. Still abusing anyone who came to help.

'It's yours Tommy. It's yours. It's his.'

The shark was motionless in the shallows when the publican pumped bullets into it. Later, when Tommy had recovered, it was the publican who took the photo of the boy astride the dead shark.

In the photo there's a fuzzy scratch of white. The fire in the background.

The fire crackled and blazed. My father's face was hot, his back cold. His body ached, his hands stung and the stars whirled around his head.

police report

Name: Harriette Coolman
Alias: —
Age: 62 years in 1946   *Sex: F*
H/C or FB: 1/2 caste   *Registered No. —*
At settlement: —
Parentage: ?
Widow. Husband was a white man. The woman lives in a hut on land leased to her husband when he was alive. No improvements have been made to the land since that time, although the hut is kept neat and tidy. The land is adjoining a water catchment area for a proposed dam for the town.

Mrs Coolman has her octoroon grandson Thomas Scat living with her and attending the school. Some local residents have complained at this. The boy is a reasonable student and could pass as a white boy. Mrs Coolman has not, herself, behaved in any way to bring her to my attention in all the time I have been in this town.

Mrs Coolman claims to be quadroon, and that Thomas Scat is one-sixteenth black.

I have not seen her consorting with other natives. However this town is usually free of them. I have recommended that she apply for an official exemption from the Act.

Failing this, the land can be taken from her without compensation.

Police Constable B Singer

the black bark of yate trees

Uncle Will, Uncle Jack, Grandfather Ernest, and myself;
we pulled into a track that led us a few metres off the
road and lit a fire. Occasionally a car tooted its horn and
screamed past. Perhaps it was a greeting, most likely it
was because of the fire. It was forbidden to light fires
because of the danger to the wheat crops which stretched
for miles and miles around us.

It was the furthest we had been together from the
house we shared, and it was a silent time. I thought we
had agreed that Uncle Will would tell me about his life,
from when Sandy Two died.

'No,' he said. And continued, a little. He had kept to
himself. 'And when I met Edie,' he said, referring to his
deceased wife, 'Ah, I was busy.'

He had never taken his children to see their
grandmother.

'Edie was a white woman, you know. Our own
children could have had trouble. Me too. No, I never

even told 'em and they never even asked.'

'Knew not to maybe,' said Uncle Jack.

I well remember that roadside stop, for its silence particularly. We had a thin fire going, and were in a grove of Yate trees. The ground was dark and cool beneath us. I remember noticing how the bark peeled back from the upper branches, so close above our heads.

never a dawg

'Never. Never a dog.'

Tommy watched his grandmother. He listened to her talking to herself, saw how she straightened her old body, raised her head.

'Never a dawg for them, as if I need any bits of paper, as if I want to run when they whistle. It should be enough for them I say I'm *quarter-caste*.' She snorted her contempt.

Harriette walked Tommy to the tiny school.

'This is my grandson.'

So Tommy received a new idea of himself from the weapons the others now used against him whenever they chose:

Nigger.

Boong.

Tarbrush in you, that's why.

White but a black heart.

He never said, No I'm not. He fought. And in the office felt the cane across his own hands.

'You've got to be better than this,' said the headmaster. 'You've got a chance.'

Harriette said, 'Yeah, you're one of us. Mine. You're as good as anyone.'

She told him the story of the curlew, and took him camping until eventually, after many nights, Tommy heard a haunting call, and what that call means to us.

'There used to be a lot of them too.'

Harriette taught him to fight. She sat in a chair, and Tommy aimed his blows at her hands. He jabbed lightly, and felt her hands give with the blows, and the fingertips touch his hands as he withdrew.

She was an old woman.

Which was what the police constable said to her also, when he came to tell her that the lease had expired. She was an old woman, and never any trouble so he could turn a blind eye if she could find somewhere else to live, but the boy ...

He recommended Sister Kate's, because it was quality schooling, and at least until they could contact the father ...

aunty kate

My grandfather was very generous to Aunty Kate. There were a number of children there, and it was a rarity for a white father to contribute money to her home, as Ern did. And he contributed more than was necessary for just the one son.

At least at Aunty Kate Clutterbuck's, it had been explained to Harriette, Tommy would get an education. He would get good food, a good bed, and a chance to hold his head high. To be as good as anyone.

When Tommy arrived at Aunty Kate's, firm hands pulled at his clothes. Those hands spoke of excitement, as did the voices; Uncles booming, Aunties shrieking, as if in ecstacy, their voices tangling and reaching higher and higher.
Look, oh look where the sun has not reached.
He is quite white.
Quite white.
Everyone says that.

And often, on the weekends, Ernest would be among those who arrived at Aunty Kate's to take the lucky children away for the weekend. It was, however, a rare thing for Ernest to take his own son — our Tommy — away with him.

Uncle Will and Uncle Jack were open-mouthed, staring at me. Old Ern, almost immobile, had closed his eyes. No doubt he wished he could close his ears also.

We were around another timeless fire. I hovered in its little light, smoke clinging to me like fabric, and my voice was shrill like the wind in a small space, or whispered in the different ways of waves, leaves, long grasses.

By now such behaviour seemed almost normal to the old men, even how — more and more — I took on the sounds of a place rather than the words. Although, when Ern opened his eyes, I saw the terror in them.

'I've heard some things about *Sister* Kate's,' said Uncle Jack.

Uncle Will slowly shook his head, no.

Ern kept his eyes closed.

I felt a little shame, then, at how I had treated him. Shame, even, for those occasions when I had cut him, taunted him, roped him in a chair and — holding a glass under his nose — never let him drink.

Dad ... Tommy met a sister at Aunty Kate's. He didn't know he had one, alive. Most of the other kids, they didn't know if they had mothers, fathers, brothers, sisters. Aunty Kate told many, sadly, that their mothers and fathers had died or did not want them.

But Tommy met a girl called Ellen. Just like his own dead sister had been called.

A lot of the boys were called Tommy; a lot of the girls Ellen. He thought it a strange coincidence.

At Aunty Kate's, at weekends and holiday time, they would all line up.

All line up for the visitors.

Line up, smile for the visitors, and they might take you to their nice homes. To the beach, for fish and chips and ice-cream too.

Tommy's father was often among the visitors, but rarely selected our Tommy to go with him. But sometimes a stranger would touch Tommy on the shoulder and ask him his name.

He might be taken into the city, or to the beach where he watched the sea flap against the shore. Tommy watched its thin edge lift, caught by the dry breeze. Each little wave feathered, and as it trembled and fell, Tommy saw the sliver of sunlight which raced before the closing water. It always escaped. Which made him see light everywhere, all around them. He could see light; ubiquitous, all but invisible.

Ellen, apparently, used to dazzle with her smile. Every time, the first one to see her took her. Tommy, initially, and even when he realised she was his (half) sister, was jealous.

White people, feeling very important and very generous, arrived in beaming couples. And quite often it was just a man on his own, shoes shining and tie tucked in, and sounding like Tommy in a lolly-shop fantasy: 'I'll have one of them, and one of them, and one of them, and one ...'

We spoke about it around our campfires. Thought it many times. Someone should have checked these people. They never checked, you know.

Ellen's used to smile. Tommy's did too. Fish and chips and ice-cream at the Royal Show!

You might stay one weekend, and the next time it's call us Mum and Dad. They look at one another, loving it, as soon as you say that. And if it was just the man? Call me uncle. Uncle. Uncle father doctor lover.

Stay one weekend with them, and the next they might be your foster-parents.

There were things I could not say around the campfires. I used to whisper such things to Ern, let him know I knew. Remind him that he did too.

Tommy was alone with his uncles.

You understand how I did not want to talk to Uncle Will and Jack about this?

Tommy was alone with his uncles. Just big boys a couple of them were. And the older man who had selected him at Aunty Kate's.

It was dark and hot on the verandah, but not so hot as outside. The sun stabbed through the lattice work, and slivers of it fell on the boards. They were whispering, kneeling.

'It's a game. You close your eyes and we'll put a lolly in your mouth. Don't bite it but.'

And one time it was not chocolate.

And it was a different voice.

'Suck on it.'

Suck on it.

Well of course Tommy didn't want to open his eyes. They were pulling his pants down and that.

Afterwards he got some white chocolate. One of them held his hand as they crossed the street.

'The girl is better, I reckon,' said one to the other.

'Whatshername? Ellen?' And they all laughed.

Next time they said suck it suck it, Tommy bit. And how the uncle howled.

At Aunty Kate's when they lined up, our Tommy kept his head down. He looked at the ground, watched shoes pass by, pause before him. Sometimes a finger under his chin, lifting.

'Look up!'

'He's so pale, isn't he? You would scarcely know. Oh, those eyes. What unusual colouring. They all have such beautiful eyes.'

Perhaps some were happy to sit in the baths of bleach. Some Ellens and Tommys wore a peg on their noses when they went to bed, and not because of any bad smell.

But, there's no denying what we smell here, my friends, my family. It is that familiar stench.

Then one day, a finger under his chin forced him to look up into the face of his father. Ern. The old man.

The car door opened as they walked to it. A new mother. She had opened the door, and now opened her arms to him.

'This is your new mother, Tom. You'll be living with us in the city.'

'But he's such a good-looking boy,' the mother said, turning to Ern. 'And you'd never know.'

Tommy's new mother was tall and had long yellow hair, dark at the roots. She smoked cigarettes, one after the other, and held the slender white cylinders between the tips of her two largest fingers. Her fingernails were hard and bright against the pure white of the cigarettes, and her knuckles deeply lined.

But other than this, all Tommy remembered of her was that she was the first of a series of women his father offered as mother. They never stayed, and Ern would be angry afterwards, and be away, and Tommy would return to Aunty Kate's, or some boarding school.

At one of these boarding schools there was an orphanage for *black* kids. They were kept apart. Tommy was always looking away. Why was he not with them, as he was at Aunty Kate's? Because of his skin colour? But, at Aunty Kate's they were all quite fair. Because of his father? Because of Ern?

In the school holidays the other kids would leave. Tommy would spend weeks almost completely alone, except for sport, when one of the brothers would allow him to join the kids at the orphanage.

Someone said they knew him. 'You a Coolman, eh?'

And when one of the children at an adjoining farm went missing, the brothers took several of the older boys down to the dam. It was school holidays, and so it was only the boys from the orphanage; and Tommy.

The boys were sent into the water, and told to dive and feel around in the mud with their hands. There was a boy missing, see. One of the farmer's boys.

They must have looked like cormorants as their heads came to the surface, sleek and shining. And black, except for that one, which was fairer. Fair hair, light brown skin.

The dam water was light brown also, and it was impossible to see anything once under it. The boys half-heartedly moved their hands about in the mud, hoping, no doubt, to not find anything.

But Tommy found something, and at first it felt like plasticine, or clay. It was firm, yet squishy. He came to the surface, took a breath and went down again. His hand traced a limb.

At the surface he waved a hand, but no one saw him, and he had to gather his courage to shout as he trod water.

Tommy was shivering. He was sick. He felt as if the water had contaminated him.

I know that I render Tommy as an anxious thing, introspective and shy. Not so. In reality he was a cheeky boy, with a swagger to him. He kept to himself, so far as any boy in a boarding school can.

He was at a boarding school where the names were those he'd heard of, of fathers and grandfathers who had not claimed their other children. Mustles, Moores, Dones, Starrs. These were the ones who took the land, cut and cleared it, sowed foreign seeds. The winners.

Tommy wished to be a winner.

But just now Rod Mustle had him backed against the troughs in the laundry.

There were gnarled mallee roots stacked to one side of them, on the other side a copper trough sat upon its fireplace.

'You stay at school in the holidays, don't you?'

'Me dad's working, he's away out bush.'

'The only ones staying on holidays are the *coons*.'

Tommy felt the trough at his back. Rod Mustle was old enough to have whiskers.

'You know old Harriette Coolman, don't you? What, she your grandmother? Aunty? You're an *Abo*.'

Rod was grinning and pushing him.

'You should be over with them. Your daddy don't want you.'

There were some others with Rod now, and Tommy was crouching, edging back to the cramped dark space beneath the troughs, and brandishing a mallee root he'd snatched from the pile. The boys were kicking at him.

Tommy moved at them to give himself room to swing and to keep them from grabbing a similar weapon for themselves.

Good. One of them was crying and hopping about clutching his leg.

Then Mustle was on the ground at Tommy's feet, and the other boys had their hands up before them, and were backing away from him. This crazy boy.

The brothers came running. They coaxed him out with cunning, soft voices. And then his ears, his very head, rang with their blows.

Tommy had another stepmother, and there was another maid. She must have been only a few years older than Tommy. Tommy would hear his stepmother calling to her.

'Ellen.'

And, 'We'll send you back, you know.'

'No. You'll have to take that up with the department. They bank the money for you. Rest assured, Ellen, it's for your own good. Now.'

The maid fell pregnant, and left, as did the latest

stepmother, although without the accompanying pregnancy. Ernest swore, and lashed at his boy. 'I should just dump you.' And I suppose it was at about this time that he began his little probings, in just such a lull between maids or wives. The same probings that he tried on me, but Ern had softened by then, and had not the steel in him.

Anyway, there was yet another boarding school. And Ern arranged for another maid.

In the school holidays Tommy boarded a train to Lake Salvation where the railway finished. He wore a school uniform, one from some long-ago school, and held out his ticket. Tommy would visit his grandmother.

Harriette's children rarely came to see her. A daughter in Lake Salvation would sometimes come, when her husband was away.

Harriette lived in a tent. It was a tent among a few others, just outside the tiny town. Their tents were out of sight of the road, but close enough to it when you needed a lift. Everyone, but the children especially, would run off the road and hide if they heard a vehicle coming. If it was the great black Maria that came cruising then you better stay hidden, because if they put you inside that you never come back.

There were other children living in the tents and bush shelters. Tommy went with them to collect water from the dam in a nearby paddock. Two of the men worked for the farmer there who'd bought the property from the Dones.

In summer the dam was muddy, and the children used old food cans to scoop water from the clear, thin layer on the surface. Then they poured it into bigger drums to carry back.

Harriette stuffed Tommy's good shoes with newspaper. She wiped the mud from them, and hung his school uniform from a nail.

They ran from the road, maybe a little too late, a group of them, the kids, walking along some miles from the camp. The vehicle stopped. The children were hiding in the bush, and they watched the policeman. He came striding in among the trees, straight for the one little girl too slow too innocent to get herself hidden properly. The policeman and her were just the other side of a bush and fallen log Tommy had hidden behind.

Tommy heard the struggling, the panting, the sobbing. He was a little boy himself, yet felt the shame of doing nothing. He pressed himself into the dirt. The policeman groaned, lifted himself to his feet. Stumbled back to the vehicle.

The girl lay as if lifeless. Tommy and another supported her, carried her back to the camp. The old people took her from them, thanked them.

What could they do?

Maybe it was just one of his whims, or because he wanted to finish off a job or see an experiment through ... Really, I don't know why; it is what I am writing for, to try and understand. Anyway, Ern was back in Gebalup. He stood at the front door of the house he knew and listened to someone tell him that no, no, no one of that name lived here.

They did not know where she had gone, and they looked at him with contempt.

He looked around Wirlup Haven, Gebalup. He went to the police station. The local Protector. His story was a difficult one.

He had left his boy where? With who? They looked at him suspiciously. They thought it was a disgrace, or perhaps they were embarrassed for him.

It is true to say that even though I write of him as a character in this long story, that I could never understand my grandfather. Even in the long time of his paralysis, and while he was under my care, and even while I tortured him and learnt his weaknesses, I could never understand him. And so it is hard to say why he came back to find his son, this one child from among all the others he sent back while they were still defined as part of their pregnant mothers.

He found Tommy among all those children who were now ill and vomiting from the muddy water they'd drunk. He took Tommy from among all those who were about to be sent to various missions and homes in an attempt to teach them how to become white people, or at the least to understand their place.

Harriette had once again slipped away.

Harriette went to where her daughter lived. The daughter, under the protective auspices of Constable Hall, had married a white man. So she was not a *native*, now. And she and her husband took Harriette in, continuing a pattern set by Harriette and her own mother. With good fortune, they thought, Harriette could escape being classified as a *native*.

She would lift her chin. 'I don't come under the Aborigines Act. I don't want their assistance. All I want is to be left alone. I am much better without their *protection*.'

And for Tommy there were all those years of just him and Ern, just as there was for Ern and I. There was a long procession of schools, as Tommy followed Ern as he travelled the state, building for government. Tommy cut the letters into his skin, and carved the words Mum, Love, Ellen, and then poured the ink into those words so that they would sting and stay. He used to wish that he was darker, somehow, so that he was not the man that his father was. Not destined to be such a one, so tight and hard and cruel.

This I understand too well. Once, I heard him say that he should have married a darker woman first up, a real dark woman. But there you go. And where would I have been then?

Dad used to wish that he was darker than all his sisters Ellen.

I went to see a woman called Ellen, once. My mother? An Aunty? I didn't know. Oh, this was after Ern had gone, after Uncle Jack and Uncle Will had died. I went alone. She recognised me, somehow. Said she'd heard of me. At first she wouldn't open the door.

Her hands shook as she held the door open, not inviting me in. 'The sun,' she said. 'I play bowls, and I get so burnt.'

Her hands were shaking.

'Yeah, your father,' she went on. 'He used to come and see me. He used to try and look up all his family. Really, but,' she said, 'I dunno why he should want to go back, after all that had happened. Why should he want to go scuttling back to *blackfellas*.'

She said that those wadjelas were her real parents. Because they were the ones who raised her, looked after her, brought her up.

'Their children were like my own brothers and sisters and look what they gave me,' she said, her eyes falling and her hands sweeping from breasts down, hands like a conjurer's, showing clothes, herself all dressed so prim and tight. 'And an education,' she said, speaking proper. Educated.

'And your grandfather did the same for you. Where would you be without him?'

What could I say? I stood on my side of the flyscreen door, and said nothing. I nodded. I kept a hand on the door handle, lest I suddenly rocket off into space.

It is the sort of experience that made it very hard for me to look up family. To find each of them, almost without exception, forgetful. Some were boastful, some were frightened, and all of them only partially alive. I don't know how my father managed to do it. I understand why he kept himself apart from everybody. I understand, but it is not something you choose.

The last time I saw that Ellen — aunty, mother, stranger — her mouth was wide open in astonishment at the sight of me drifting, blowing like a leaf in the wind away from her front door, across her front fence.

And why did my father seek to reconnect himself? Why do I?

When I was a boy, a little boy and too young — or so some might think — to be able to remember it now, my father came to collect me from his grandmother.

She was living in an asbestos and iron shack at Wirlup Haven, at that time a dusty and almost-ghost town which seemed stacked together of cast-off shells. The house she lived in had chicken wire stretching across the space between it and a skeleton fence. There was a rusty, leaking rainwater tank. Vines sprang from the ground and clawed up the wire, which sagged in places with passionfruit and melon. Vines reached out toward my father as we pulled to a stop.

Though not much more than a baby at the time, I swear to you that I saw how Tommy's grin linked with that of his grandmother across the valley of silence rendered by the ignition key. The car door slammed. The old woman called his name, and I felt the vibrations of her voice.

An old man came coughing out of the doorway behind her, and spat. The phlegm rolled in the dirt. Tiny red rivers ran from watery blue pools and through the yellow of his eyes. He was not a Nyoongar.

'Peter, this is my grandson. I've told you about him. He's Harley's father.'

'Yeah. G'day.'

'G'day.' The stooped man hawked, spat.

'I'm gunna marry a woman. She's pregnant to me,' my father said. He and Harriette watched Peter slump back into the house.

'It's a white woman. Not the mother of this one.' My father indicated me. 'But I've told her about him. I can take him.'

And as we drove away, my father and I, as we disappeared from her view, Harriette fell to the ground. She died before we were up to the speed limit of the open road. She died as quickly as that.

There is a photo of her holding my father and his sister. They are both very young children. She has her arms around both of them, and a dark hand grips my father by the wrist. Presumably Ern took the photo as some sort of trophy.

I thought that her death must somehow be my fault. My isolated father and I apparently turning our backs on her, my father — who had been so all on his own — was running to a white woman, going to make a white family, as Uncle Will and her daughters had also done.

Uncle Jack looked at me quizzically.

'Nah.' A long, drawn-out negative, to reassure me. Uncle Will was silent.

mother

It may be that a reader is wondering about my own mother, especially in such a story of men, with silent women flitting in the background; and I almost wish I were one of those pioneers with coloured ribbons to pull and bring the girls running. For different reasons, of course.

In my early drifting, especially when I was still finding my place, I often wondered about my mother. My biological mother. It was one of the reasons I went to visit my Aunty Ellen. There were very many Aunty Ellens, and how was I to know which might be she?

I confess to you that I lost the courage to keep inquiring that way. And for the many maybe-my-mothers, too, it was not easy to have a maybe-my-son turn up, knocking, inquiring, asking questions which led, snakingly, to answers they did not want to give or try to find. Not when there were other children clutching at them — some of them now grown-up and accusing them of this or that.

And other children means other fathers, and all the trouble that can bring ...

But I know of the mother, if not who or where she is now. My mother. Confusingly — but that is reality for you, how it will not fit the neatness a story requires — her name was Ellen.

She was another of Ern's domestics. Young, only a few years older than Tommy. Ellen. Her voice was soft, and — who knows? — perhaps it was she Mr Neville had in mind when he wrote;

> the young half-blood maiden is a pleasant, placid, complacent person as a rule, while the quadroon girl is often strikingly attractive with her ofttimes auburn hair, rosy freckled colouring, and good figure, or maybe blue eyes and fair hair ...

I suppose it was hard to keep a particular person in mind after all those women, all those boys, all those years.

> As I see it, what we have to do is elevate these people to our own plane ...

Ernest was working hard, still, as always. Thinking ahead, planning. He got home in the evenings, smelling of beer. This is long before such a word as 'networking' was in use. Tommy saw him in the mornings mostly, at breakfast. Ernest glared at eggs bacon toast tomato as the maid's knife sliced for him. Tommy observed how his father hid behind the steam rising from his cup, how his lips gripped the cup, and how his eyes followed the maid.

The maid, the girl, my mother — yes, Ellen was her name — kept to her room when she could. On Sundays, when she had the day off, Tommy used to go in there and open her wardrobe. He liked to run his hands through her underwear, and read her letters.

In this, at least, I recognise how I am so like my father. The business with the letters, I mean.

My father. His name was Tommy, and he was about, oh, sixteen years of age, or thereabouts, by my reckoning. And he was working with our Uncle Will. Uncle Will — in Ern's eyes — was a wonderful example of the sort of *absorption* which could be achieved with the right kind of help and encouragement.

My Uncle Will did not take his own children to see their grandmother, and his wife had emigrated from post-war Germany which meant her family was too far away. She and Uncle Will were making their own way, from a fresh start. Both of them with nothing behind them. There was equality, there was justice.

Uncle Will was shooting kangaroos for his living. He had dogs and rifles. He shot the animals, cleaned them up a bit and delivered them to another man who sold them in turn.

Tommy and Will had both shot their first kangaroos under the instruction of Harriette, sneaking on their bellies to where they could see the animal's liquid eyes. They had run with the dogs, and clubbed the cornered roos, evading the grasping arms and lethal kick. But this was different. Uncle Will had the use of a rifle with telescopic sights. It was an anonymous sort of slaughter.

Tommy and Will — my father and my uncle — found a hilltop above where the roos would come. The day was one of soft rain, the wind blew into their faces. They made a little shelter for themselves, and waited.

Each kangaroo loomed large in the shooter's eye. The shooter exhaled, squeezed the trigger; the animal dropped. The rest of the roos heard nothing. They bounded away a little, momentarily startled, but then resumed their grazing, uncertainly hopping around the increasing number of corpses which surrounded them.

These killers were unseen, unheard. The roos could not smell them, but detected only the peculiar scent of their family's blood coagulating. The shooters scanned the animals, sorted them, claimed those they wanted.

Perhaps the dogs became impatient with such hunting, resented their redundancy. Perhaps Tommy startled one of them, somehow. Whatever the cause, a roo-dog turned on him and, when Tommy thought about it later, seemed to snarl only after its teeth had sunk in. Its jaw enclosed his thin thigh, and it shook him so that he sprawled. Uncle Will swung the rifle like a club. A bullet, noisy and unintended, went whistling into the scrub. The noise — combined with the blow to its head — convinced the dog to let go of Tommy. Uncle Will hoisted the boy to his feet, and gave him his shoulder. The dogs slunk behind the strange-legged couple as they made their way to the car.

Uncle Will pulled up near the doors of the hospital. 'You'll be right, eh? I'll stay out here, just in case.'

Will watched the boy struggle with the weight of the heavy doors. The same doors Tommy would come crashing through years later, once again blood-splattered, and with a blue son in his arms.

Tommy awoke in the dark of night. His leg was throbbing with pain, and he needed a piss.

There seemed to be rods of pain connecting the holes

where the dog's teeth had entered either side of his thigh. Now, if they had not then, the holes seemed to meet. He was hot. He crawled from his room, and got to his feet using an upside down broom as a crutch.

The kitchen lino was cool under his feet, but it was also slipping away from him. He was at the centre of a moving spiral, and so, not surprisingly, as the broom slipped, was falling. Fallen.

He saw Ellen above him.

'I need a piss.'

He leaned on her. She waited at the door. Offered to help, and even with the pain he had to smile. They giggled as she helped him back to his room.

Ellen took the dressing from his inner thigh. His wounds were inflamed, oozing a clear fluid. She dabbed at them with her fingers. He found he was weeping. Silent tears of, what? Gratitude?

Tommy felt as if he was not there, as if he was not himself. Her hand brushed his swelling. He was throbbing, but not with the pain.

Ellen came to see him in the daylight, and Tommy found himself grinning like a child. Well, not quite a child.

'Shall I check again?'

'Oh yeah.'

He was wincing, but thought it should be he who asked am I hurting you, am I hurting you I don't want to hurt you and in fact they were both asking it of one another. Tommy saw that it was she who had the tears in her eyes, and understood his father.

'Your dad'll sack me I reckon.'

So when my father found Ernest pushing this Ellen forcefully into the mattress ... Well, they fought. There was anger there. Tommy remembering the ropes on his mother, remembering the many girls and women; Tommy knowing a lust like his father's, and, perhaps, love. He is my father, after all.

Tommy and Ellen ran. They went to Uncle Will, and kept going, and found Uncle Jack Chatalong on a reserve in the country. They went to Harriette, Tommy's grandmother. And, somewhere, I was born. Native Welfare caught up with Ellen, and returned her to one of the holding pens, the settlements, the refugee camps, the reserves, the missions, whatever it may have been called. Harriette held me for a little while then, and although it is possible that I have visited my biological mother I only know — for sure — the next mother. The one mother.

ocean, roads

I was conceived, I believe, on a beach somewhere around Wirlup Haven. And, although not born there, I fell into Harriette's hands.

But, no sooner had I begun to walk, to talk, than I was with a new mother, Tommy's wife. It was not Ellen. We were living in the house of Ern. And Harriette, the old woman, as hard and tough as an abalone shell and holding the spirit inside her, was dead.

The new mother, Tommy's wife? Well, Tommy was a young man, she was a timid and loving woman, smitten by him. When she became pregnant, Tommy might have taken the advice and money Ern offered, and gone away for a year or two — but for Harriette's words. About all the white men who had done that, had turned their backs on their children. How unjust it was. Already he felt he had let her down by not being able to help my mother, and having to burden his grandmother with yet another child to protect from the likes of Ern.

So that must have been why Tommy was so defiant, and said, 'I'm gunna marry her.'

'You stupid little bastard,' Ern said.

I was with Harriette and so I saw nothing of how, in the house of Ern, there was no privacy. How Ern would barge into Tommy and his new wife's cramped bedroom, as if to prove he owned the place. The new wife could not even sit on the toilet and be at ease. Ern would open the door, and walk in on her, and not say a word of apology. He would look, turn nonchalantly on his heel, and walk away without shutting the door. Although not one of a *coloured minority*, she was — he'd say — white trash.

And of course I saw nothing of how Tommy worked for the city, and I saw nothing of the trucks, bulldozers, police wagons rumbling through the rubbish tip where he was moving rubbish around in a tractor.

It was Tommy, not I, who heard the machines rumbling and snarling, and — scattered among that noise — the cries of human voices. He started the tractor, raised the bucket, and climbed into it so that he might see. He saw humpies bulldozed into heaps, and aflame, and people — Nyoongars — being pushed into the police wagons. He hadn't even known there was a reserve there.

The crammed police wagons filed by below him, and he tinkered with the linkages below the bucket, to fix his embarrassment. He saw a few who had escaped the police stealing away into the littered scrub.

Later in the afternoon he saw, atop one of the many mounds of rubbish which had been pushed together, a car body rocking. And the white flanks of one of his workmates backing out of it. The man turned and, pulling up his trousers, nodded at the derelict car body.

'I saved her for you, mate. She'd be related to you, wouldn't she?'

Tommy wedged the bucket and front wheels of the tractor into the incinerator. He smelled the rubber burning and left black marks upon the bitumen as he roared away.

And neither was I present when Tommy put Ern's house up for sale. I didn't see the *For Sale* sign spearing the lawn.

'When it's sold, I'll take you to see where I was reared,' Tommy said to his wife. 'Meet my granny.'

The real estate agent swore at Tommy when he couldn't produce the title papers. And when Ern, arriving unexpectedly, hit his son the agent was satisfied.

'You stupid little mongrel,' said Ern. 'You'll be lucky to get anything of mine. What do you think life's about? Just taking things you want?'

Tommy took Ern's blows, as I would years later, but Ern was stronger then and Tommy had less help than I would find.

I do remember a home in a hollow among peppermint trees. I remember the smell of those thin leaves, and the insects hiding in the bark.

A sandy track led to a small shaded patch which overlooked the ocean, and where men smoked cigarettes and waited. They talked softly, squinting in the blue smoke and broken sunlight as their liquid eyes scanned the sea for dark clouds of salmon moving in the broken blue and green.

Fish, solid and silver, writhed in the seine net which a

strong young Uncle Will and my boy father rowed around such a cloud. The two men had leaned into each stroke of the oars, the net's corks tumbling to mark the great half-circle of their wake, and surfed in on a wave which reflected the foam in its face. They leapt out of the boat as it slid before the bouncing, tumbling, white water, and my father's thin calves signalled for a moment as he lost balance, and then once again there was his dripping torso and wide-eyed face grinning, teeth bright. The net cramped the big fish close together, and the men's quick strong hands tossed them onto the beach, even as the net tightened, even as the tractors came grumbling to haul it quick smart from the sea.

Then the boy-father, my uncle, all of the men were skipping, tripping, running from where the net had condensed all this life, and the fish were churning the water because a great thing — 'Shark! Shark!' they called — shook and strained the net, which tore, loosened, and silver flashing fish spilled from it. Were gone.

Scales stuck to the men's hair and skin as they stood among fish, guts, blood. Scales which were like mirrors or even the sun itself, but fading, greying, flaking.

In such a mirror, say, I see a group of small children sleeping together.

Uncle Will said we went to stay with him. There's a photo of us. Mother, father, my brothers and sisters — a bunch of us — and me indistinguishable from them, save if you care to look for such things, if you are of a mind with my grandfather or my one-time self, then perhaps I am an nth darker, there may be something rounder in my features. But we are the same people, surely. How would you differentiate us at such an age?

My expression is tortured, for such a small child. It must be because I am squinting into the sunlight.

Squinting now, I see — as if in one of those scales, as if swirling and growing out of such a curling, grey mirror — a rough curtain, and a wardrobe behind which a man and woman move noisily in the darkness.

I think I woke crying and it must have been the mother above me in the darkness. A male voice — my Uncle Will's — 'Shut that bloody kid up!' and the mother's usually so timid hand hard across my mouth.

Is that why I have held my silence so long? Why I hesitate even now, thinking a shout must come from who knows where, and thinking that shout must be what is right, is far more authoritative than my own whispering, my own private snivelling?

I saw — I still sometimes see — a membrane far above my head, as if the stuff of one of those scales has stretched.

And I swear I hear screaming coming from beyond that membrane; or is it the call of gulls?

I am not swimming, but flailing, I am running in deep water, intent upon that surface above me. Ash falls upon it, and then the panic leaves me, and I resign myself to the tug and sway, and it must be my mothers fathers brothers sisters lovers floating in the growing darkness before my eyes, fading.

I am not an only. See, they float like me. There must be some ears this voice in my head speaks to. Must be.

So we fished. This is the 1960s, and there are many things happening in the greater world of policies and legislation, but down on the south coast there, my father and his

Uncle Will — both men only tenuously citizens of their own country, both men filled with pride and shame — lived in their tents with their sunburnt wives and children.

Barely hanging onto freedom, unsure who they were, they kept to themselves. Tommy took his new wife, the baby, the kids and me among them, to the pub. Shy — perhaps embarrassed by his pride — he pointed to a yellowing photograph on the wall. It was his own boy-self, straddling a shark on the sand of the beach.

We lived at Uncle Will's small property, just outside of the closest town, Gebalup. And it is from there that I recall the shout which shut me up. My aunty yelling. Uncle Will, sudden like that, in the dark of early morning.

There was a swamp among the white sand which used to call me; a quite different call.

It was definitely shouting and violence which shut me up, made me withdraw like a mollusc into its shell.

Tommy, his young and so timid wife with the children coming one after the other so quick. And that somewhat older one; myself.

We found a home — a shell to hold us. It was a timber-framed house, perched above the ground, and unfinished to the extent that only in the narrow passageway, kitchen and one other room was the flooring completed. Dad nailed branches across the doorways of the other two rooms at such a height as to discourage us from venturing into them. The floor joists spanning these rooms made a grid across the space from wall to wall and above the drop to the dirt below. Each floorless room seemed as if moored — but only just — to those joists.

I used to climb over the doorway branches, and balance on the spans of timber. It was quite a fall to the soil below.

I felt like that once again as I wrote this story of ours; as if I was poised in space, precariously supported. Particularly when I wrote of my father, with the very many gaps, the many things I did not know about him. I knew him when I was a child, and spent only a few days of my teenage years with him. The last time I saw him he tried to explain why he had let Ern take me away.

And then I killed him. My father, that is. Ern I helped keep alive.

Tommy got a job with the Main Roads Department which meant he was away from home for two weeks at a time. He used to bring home joeys which had survived their mothers being shot, or been rescued from the destruction of land clearing on a massive scale. We hung them in pillowslips in our warmest rooms, but they always died.

Once he brought home a pup to be a guard dog. It was a mongrel, he said. A dingo with just enough domestic dog in it to bark and yelp.

The yelping was very loud.

It was because the bitumen road was so warm, I suppose.

It was the sound of extreme distress, shall I say? Put it like that?

I ran out into the sun, and saw spatters of blood leading from the road, across the dry front yard, and to our rainwater tank. The tank was built on a thick circular wall of ironstone, and there was a small opening in the wall which led into a cave-like space.

The yelping was a howling now. A nightmare sound.

A car was stopped just past where the blood trail began. The car's brakelights went off, and the wheels of the empty trailer bounced as it accelerated away.

The mother was peering down around the side of the house. When the car left we went and peered into the space — that tiny cave — below the rainwater tank.

The howling, pale shape which we could barely discern in there must be our dog.

The blood on the soil was drying, and as each little puddle coagulated its edges contracted, pulling grains of soil to its centre.

On the Main Roads, Tommy started digging. Learnt about leaning on a shovel. He was bored, until they showed him how to use a grader. The blade pared back the earth, pushed a wave of earth to one side of the smooth tender ground it left behind it. The soil, the stones, lay in the sun, drying and fading. There were pegs stabbed in a line, in order to be followed and to show how deep to peel.

Tommy sat within the grumbling vehicle, and vibrated with it. He put the wheels on a lean, and yet he stayed perpendicular. A cigarette, hand-rolled as he drove, dangled at the corner of his lips.

A truck sprayed water, sparkling and profligate, dampening the wound along which it drove.

They cut and pared. They softened. They sealed with bitumen and brushed away the stones so that traffic might better rush along.

Rain bounced on the new road, and rushed away to streams running either side of it.

At night the guideposts reflected like the eyes of animals, and by day there were carcasses which stiffened and stank, but the posts remained, and only occasionally and stank, but the posts remained, and only occasionally teetered from their upright stance.

The men worked in gangs, and camped in iron huts. Their meals were prepared for them and at night they sat around the fire, drinking and talking.

'I could help you get along,' said the foreman, who knew Jock Mustle. There was a new gang being formed. An employment initiative. The new gang was to be made up of Aboriginal men, and Tommy could join them as Leading Hand.

The dog would not let us near it. Our mother knew no one, was too timid to ask, and we had no money for such a thing as a veterinarian.

We left food and water at the entrance to the dog's stone kennel, but it was some days before any of it was touched.

Dad came home on a weekend, and the dog limped out to meet him. It was thin, and black blood was caked between its back legs and across its stomach and chest. The car, or perhaps only the trailer, must have driven across its testicles while it lay sleeping on the sun-warmed road.

I suppose it fully recovered, I only know that it was still limping several weeks later when I met my grandfather for the first time, and went to live with him. But before that I had impressed my family with my ability to turn blue.

Yes, as perhaps befits one of a coloured minority, I turned blue, my limbs jerked, and I spat and tore at my siblings, whose arms, whose flesh and bones held me tight.

blue me

Perhaps it was hearing of this trace of blue which aroused my grandfather's interest in me above any other of those countless offspring of his. His curiosity about colour, about the remnants of it, the dilution of it. His interest in genetics. Perhaps it was this sort of detached interest; that of *the scientist, with his trained mind and keen desire* ...

I recall reading of a man who, sometime around the advent of electricity, received an electric shock and it was said that he turned blue, and remained so for a very long time. The mosquitoes were afraid to bite him, and the orgasms he experienced and delivered were ... Well, *he* attracted a lot of interest.

Who knows, my grandfather may have had some similar experience within his own family. He may have wondered if this blueness of mine was, to use his language, a *throwback* to an ancestor. Perhaps he had also read of the incident with electricity. All I know is that it certainly aroused his ... curiosity.

While I was ill and listless he investigated me most rigorously.

of water and ice …

At one time Tommy had the use of a good sized boat. I don't know how we got to have it. He had asked Ern for the money, but Ern never gave any.

He took me out onto the ocean with him, because I was the only one old enough to go, I suppose. It was a little before my drowning.

I cut mullet in two, and we baited the many hooks along a rope which my father tied to a series of rusting drums and left spread out across the ocean beside one of the islands. After a few hours we returned, and I remember leaning over the side with a knife to free stingrays too big for us to take aboard, and how the sharks piled up in the boat.

There's a Nyoongar word for island — kurt-budjar — which roughly translates as 'heart-land'. Out there between headland and heartland the sea was grey, and on this windless day it was thick and had a dull sheen to it and our little boat floated on the surface of regular, rolling mounds of energy. Sea birds, their wings tucked in, rose and fell with us, waiting.

We pulled closer to the island, and listened to the sound of sea exploding on granite. Whether headland or heartland, the land loomed impossibly solid and real as we moved into its shadowy protection. We heard the wind roar in blowholes, the salt water falling in heavy drops, and the birds calling as they wheeled and dipped and soared.

Closer to the mainland we trailed a lure, the boat moving slowly, and a gull swooped into our wake, then could not fly away. It moved heavily in the air, and made jagged lines of flight. I hauled it toward me, observing its struggle, the way I arrested it with the line, until I had it an arm's length from me, and the line was taut between us.

The motor vibrated in the boat's timbers, in me. We had to raise our voices to talk. If we talked.

Clouds touched the sea, and fine rain or mist moved around us; changing shape, reforming as we chugged our way through it. Rain, clouds, sea; all grey.

It came from the sea, and out of all that various and shifting damp stuff. It came out of torn clouds, came low above the sea, came with its long wings stroking, creating itself out of shreds of mist, fine ribbons of cloud, the so slow falling rain. A huge white bird, its wings cupping the damp air, appeared, was gone, back again, gone.

Land gently rose either side of us as we entered the harbour's channel, and the mist was clearing. Shrubs sprouted from smooth flanks of granite, water dripping from my eyebrows.

'Sea-eagle. Must be sick,' coughed my father.

All of us — the child I was thought this — all of us made of water, ice, drying in the sun's flame.

calling, and choosing

We were humming and rattling along, shrouded within a rushing wind just above the surface of the sealed earth.

For some reason Uncle Jack was with us. He often helped arrange that my mother take in very young children for a while, when their own mothers got into some difficulty or other. Sometimes, these children were related to my father through Ern's persistent efforts to breed us out, fill us with shame; all that rationalising to disguise his own desires.

We were all humming, singing; sometimes it was even the same song. The kids were all in the back of the old Landrover, either on the hard metal bench seats of its perimeter, or lying on top of the canvas and blankets which reached almost to the roof of the cab. There were a lot of us, perhaps that was why Jack was there. My father's wife was the only woman.

My father — Tommy — was in a good mood. Someone

farted, and everyone started teasing me, saying I must be going rotten. My father farted loudly, pulled the hand-throttle, and stuck his bum out the window as he was driving along.

'This is what you gotta do if you fart in the car.'

It looked a very uncomfortable position. Some of us went red in the face, wanting to attempt such a position ourselves.

We turned off the bitumen, and bounced and lurched in dust. All the windows were opened; dust in, dust straight out. We were speeding, and kept just ahead of the spiralling confusion of dust behind us.

Fence posts zipped along each side of the road, and stunted blue-grey mallee grew away in one dense coat, with here and there tufts of trees or growths of rock. In one direction clouds lowered themselves onto the peaks of distant ranges.

We turned into a sandy track, closed a sagging gate behind us.

'Mustle's property. Don't worry, I've sorted it with him.'

Now we drove slowly, and trees and shrubs each side of the road dragged at the vehicle's side.

It was mallee and dust and fence posts and we were ascending, I think, the most subtle of inclines. The track was sandy, and the vehicle slewed occasionally but less and less as we gradually slowed, adjusting to the terrain. Three emus ran before us on the sandy track; two parents, and a young one. They stayed on the track, running ahead and flicking sand as their long knobbly toes gripped and flung. They did their knock-kneed thing for us and then turned off into the scrub as they tardily realised how fast we were and that this path which was helping them run, helped us even more. Roos bounded through the scrub parallel to us, and met our gaze each time their heads looped above the bush.

Another gate. An old farmhouse, sagging chimney, windows bare and expressionless. A glimpse of sea?

We stopped at a boggy patch. It must have been a spring that made the ground soggy like that, a soak. The bush was closer, taller, leaves greener on flaking black bark. The shade was good, because we were hot and stale from sitting in the vehicle. The moist air was crowded with flying, biting specks. Dad fiddled with the wheels and checked out the car. He walked through where we'd drive. We had a drink of water, and a run around and a pee.

Us kids sat on top of the roof-rack as the Landrover crawled around the top of a hill. Our heads cleared the scrub, and we were looking down, down a slope covered with grey-blue growth, tight and coiled. Far away at the base of this long muscular slope, a pool of dark-sky-blue showed where the creek rested as it twisted its way to just short of the sea. The sunlight sank into the water, and reflected just the one heavy star back at us. It was shady down there, we could tell; cool and moist. We saw the white sand of the beach between river and sea.

There was a hut at the track's end. It was a very small one, only used in the salmon season, and built among shelves of stone in the lee of the hill and a rocky point which tumbled out into the ocean. I could see a couple of islands, far enough away to be dimmed by the sea haze.

The sand was soft and fine; it squeaked when we

walked on it. It was so glary in the middle of the day that it made you go inside yourself and people were just black shadows dancing. We splashed and swam in water that was as salty as tears. Crisp waves swung in from the point and folded themselves upon the rocks, upon the sand, around the children. The waves rolled us children to shore.

Once there was a young skeleton on the beach. I thought it was a shark because I could see bits of the dorsal fin with shreds of skin, but Unc said it was a dolphin and look, he said, here are its hands. Bits of skin and flesh still there.

They are friendly, dolphins. They smile. They loop and wave. They used to be like pet dogs for people, and herd schools of salmon to where they could be speared. A man would stand by a big fire, tap his sticks, and sing them in.

There was a big fire that night. My face got very hot, but only a few steps away it was cold again, and the stars lower. I was young enough to huddle in close with the others. The world seemed big, and out beyond the light was all cold fear and threat.

Dad was picking up the others, one at a time, and shaking them to the bottom of their sleeping-bags. Like a joey, he said.

'Eh, Tommy, don't do that to the poor little buggers.'

'Oh, we like it, Unc.'

'Well, I don't.'

He seemed angry, genuinely disturbed.

'I knew some kids got hung up like that all night.'

I wanted him to tell, but he wouldn't.

We dug ourselves into the dry seaweed high on the shore.

The mother came and and lay with her own children. I kept a distance, and arranged my seaweed cushioning so that I could look up into the far away but so close night sky, and also see the fire and the figures around it. I heard their voices, and watched them passing the beer bottle back and forth, the red fire glinting warmly on the glass as it moved from flickering black hand to flickering black hand. The firelight made their hands thin like bones, separated at each joint. They sat there; black skeletons bundled in baggy clothes, and the fire danced lower, lower.

In the morning there was a mist over the landlocked water. My father and uncle took me through the gap in the dunes to where the river waited. We stepped from the beach sand which barred the river's way to the sea and onto damp, firm ground fringed by reeds and paperbarks. The dog trembled with excitement, now and then releasing a tiny whimper.

We had a shotgun. The dog followed us, shivering its restraint.

Unc rested the gun in a tree's soft, paper-barked fork, and fired through the midges. At the bang the ducks lifted their wings, folded the air under them, and rose. The flap and flurry of wings faded with the gunshot, but one duck stayed, wing feathers whacking the water. Dad was naked and wading in among the reeds. He swam out to the bird. The dog started with him, but he sent it back and, before reaching the duck, slipped beneath the surface and we saw the bird suddenly go under the surface and Dad's head spring up in its place. He trod water, and held his arms high to break the bird's neck. The sun must have risen quite high, because

I remember how it shone on the duck's plumage.

We were building the fire again. Late in the day.

'This is where we come from,' Unc said. 'Once. From roundabouts here to a fair way east, Dubitj Creek way.' He pointed with a smouldering stick around the beach. The tip of the stick trailed smoke. My eye followed the curve of the beach, tracing the land south-east until it shrivelled into the distance of sky and sea.

A little arc of grey smoke, disappearing. Purple-tinted white beach, scraggles of weed, dunes, the sea glowing, the darkening sky. Cold.

Unc left one end of the net with us as he rowed away with the rest. I watched the net unfolding itself from the back of the boat. He went out, curved away to the right, and left the line of corks bobbing behind him. He came into shore again about fifty maybe a hundred metres around from where we remained, clutching the net. Then we all started hauling it in together.

Go into the water, grab rope, mesh, cork. Walk onto the sand with it and you can lean right over and not fall. But sometimes, it's nice to fall into the water, and then come up dripping, seeing your legs slide from the water, the long line of muscle, the bony knee. And go and do it again.

The net got heavier and heavier. The fish were calling to us through the ropes in our hands.

I have forgotten everything else but that weight, and the rope thrumming.

I did not speak of any of these things to my uncles as we drove along the coast.

Uncle Jack had worked on the same Main Roads Gang as my father. 'That's how he got a lot of his education as a Nyoongar,' said Uncle Jack. 'Elsewise it was only when he was a littl'n.'

When Tommy came home — four days each fortnight — we used to go camping. During the time Dad was away Uncle Will, or someone we called Uncle Les, used to come to chop wood and keep an eye on us. It was a neighbourhood of violence, which never touched my mother, whether because of the uncles I never knew.

Uncle Les, I found out in my adulthood, was another Nyoongar man stranded like my father; washed up, as it were, although not quite so alone. He lived with a family of black sisters and a white father, and my father spent a lot of time with one of the sisters. Perhaps they hoped Uncle Les would make an alliance with Dad's own white wife. But Uncle Les was very shy, as was my timid stepmother.

Uncle Jack explained it this way: 'I think, when Tommy went home, in town there, then he maybe didn't feel he was a Nyoongar no more. His wife was never too comfortable with Nyoongars. He was a split man. Because of the childhood he had. Like, if he'd been brought up with family, proper family, or even with any family. But all he saw was Ern pressing down on people like us.

'And brought up that way — his mother dead, no brothers and sisters to her, and kept away from us.

'Yeah, he was Nyoongar all right, even if he married a wadjela, even if he had a wadjela dad. Did you ever hear him sing?

'Around the campfire, get a few beers in him. And he sang at the end of year functions, a few times.' Uncle Will was nodding in agreement. 'A deadly singer. Like you.'

They both looked at me. Ern was staring, too. They wanted me to do my thing, to hover in the smoke, turn this way and that, and sing whatever it was I had taken to singing at such times.

I realised my father was very nervous, half-crouching to see into the mirror like that, and running his hands back along his scalp.

He had a bottle of beer beside him, and was singing snatches of song. Grinning to himself, at his wife and kids. Me too. It must have been the same week I have written of above.

What was he singing?

> *Trumby was a ringer*
> *A good one too at that,*
> *He could rake and ride a twister*
> *Throw a rope and fancy plait.*
> *He could counter line a saddle*
> *Track a man lost in the night*
> *Trumby was a good boy*
> *But he couldn't read and write.*

Oh, I sang this nonsense in the smoke, for three old men.

Tommy sang it in the spotlight, and loved it there. The light on him. He looked out over bodies dancing about, and the tables beyond them where so many blokes were jammed, getting drunk. Only a few Nyoongars. There was the law — even though it had apparently recently changed, minds and hearts had not — but who'd dare use that against him, anyway? He could be Italian, maybe Indian. Or just good-looking.

There was Will, on his own, in the crowd.

Tommy never felt ashamed, never really felt shy. Spoilt? Maybe he was a bit spoilt, because of those early years with his mum, and being brought up by his grandmother, whatever the troubles he might have had at the boarding houses and Aunty Kate's.

Tommy was singing. He could let songs fill him, and nevertheless transform them so they came out new, as if they were his.

People wanted to talk to him. He tried to be modest, but really, it was hard. He was swelling, blossoming with pride and with the attention he was getting. The women looking at him, giving him a smile, and their men just getting drunker, flush-faced and sullen.

It was the last song, this Trumby. A Slim Dusty song. They sang a lot of his songs around the campfires, but not this one. He had written the words on a large piece of paper, and placed it on the floor beside the microphone stand.

Tommy was so proud when he sang. Mid-song, this last song, he started changing some of the words. It was a song about someone not being able to read and write, and here he was, Tommy Scat, reading so well he was changing it even as he sang.

> *Tommy was a singer,*
> *As solid as a post*
> *His skin was black and his heart was white*
> *And that's what matters most.*

He couldn't change it quick enough. Only the first line.

Tommy kept his smile. He kept singing, but he was thinking of those words. He thought of how few of the men from his own gang, the Nyoongar gang, were here tonight. Lester, on guitar behind him.

His heart was white? He wished he hadn't said Tommy. He thought of his own not-black skin. How the first challenge was 'ding' or 'dago', and only later, if real malice was called upon, the other words where we would say 'Nyoongar'. And the colour of his heart, after Aunty Kate's, and with a father like Ernest Solomon Scat? He thought of his mother, grandmother. The real people, he always thought. Who I am.

He sang all the better. As if the only proof of who he was, was this.

> *Oft times I think how sad it is*
> *in this world with all its might*
> *that a man like Trumby met his death*
> *Cause he couldn't read or write*
> *couldn't read or write ...*

The crowd drifted away. The women who had smiled at him went home with the men they had arrived with. The musicians packed away their instruments. My father folded his voice within himself, I suppose, folded his lyrics up, packed it in. He sang in the bathroom at home, sometimes. When he was drinking, he always sang. And he sang in the car, when he was in a good mood. But he never again sang like that, never again put on a show of himself before that sort of audience.

My family, at the end of which line I dangled, learnt to read and write very early on. My great-grandmother signed her own marriage certificate. We have certificates, of marriage, death, birth. We got caught that way, on paper.

Harriette is there, apparently telling the inspectors pursuing her brother, Sandy, that she is not under the law pertaining to Aboriginal Natives, that she needs no exemption papers. See, she married a white man. Of course she tells him, *quarter-caste*. Says, *not half-caste*.

And then, what of me? A taint? It would be always enough to pull me into line, if needed, depending who I mixed with.

You can meet a death, just knowing the paper talk.

I worried, I considered myself. Taking on my grandfather's words, trying to save us that way. Saving us because I thought I could read and write so well that I should be able to find my way out of even here.

We had moved. This house had floors, and was at one edge of a state housing area, and at the bottom of the slope which ran from the school. Across the street from our house there was an expanse of soft-leaved bush surrounding a swamp, and beyond that you could see the blunt roof and high smoking chimneys of the superphosphate factory. To the east was the rubbish tip, beyond that the Natives Reserve.

Many of our neighbours were those attempting to negotiate that ultimatum delivered by the likes of my grandfather: 'Be a white man or nothing.'

We often had two or three younger Nyoongar children staying with us, apart from my three step-siblings. Uncle Jack would arrive with them in his arms. 'Tommy, you got a job, your missus is good with kids.'

On this occasion, there was just the one, Kenny, a boy about twelve months old. He was a chubby little boy, just learning to walk, and I — perhaps because I was the eldest, and he the youngest — took to him. His mother had got into some trouble or other, and was unable to care for him, temporarily. If he was related to us through Ern, or was even a child of my father's, it was never said. He was a dark-skinned child, a fact I mention here because — after what happened — it contributed to the grief my father must have felt, and the different pressures he came under.

Deep gutters of stone lined each side of our street. All of us kids used to play there, the littlest ones using it as a water slide.

The dirty tributaries rushing.

I walked in a little creek, it was a long day's drive from home. My father said he used to come here as a boy. Land-based whalers used to call here, he told me.

The water I walked in came from a spring, and usually runs in not much more than a trickle to the sea. I had little Kenny on my back; although I was so young myself, I liked to carry him around and he was a very small child. It was a winter's day, and the sea was all blue and black surfaces, slapped and chopped by a little wind. Kenny had his chin on my shoulder, and we looked into the creek, at my feet moving in it. There had been a lot of rain, and the creek ran in twisted cords and sinews of energy. It was brown with run-off, but I could see veins of silver within it, the like of which — only a child — I had previously only noticed in the whirlpool of water running down the drain of my bath.

I walked with the bush and the spring at my back, up to my calves in the creek, and feeling the push and pull of its brown sinews and fingers.

The little creek sprang from the bush and rushed across

the white beach as if it were made of thin ropes woven into a narrow horizontal plane, and Kenny and I looked through it to the wet, creamy sand which took and held the imprint of my foot. Kenny stood beside me, and I took his hand. The water was up to his thighs, and it was running fast.

When we reached the edge of the sea, the sand suddenly fell away. The rushing creek must've tripped me. I was tumbled and handled roughly; sand, white water, bubbles. I clutched Kenny to me, felt him struggle furiously and slip from my grasp, and then I saw the surface of the sea far above, the clouds and sky beyond that.

I could not swim. No one had ever taught me to swim. I tried to sprint along the sand, underwater, and reach the shore that way.

I ran. I did not think of Kenny. I jumped to the surface to draw breath, and tried to run further along the ocean's floor. Not far enough. Did it a second time. I thought I saw Kenny, limbs flailing, bubbles growing in a long line from his mouth to the surface. A surface which was higher again above me, like broken glass floating, and it took a long time for me to get there, that third time, to that membrane between myself and air, that sky. I sucked in air, water too.

I am dying. I was dying.

My father was fishing in a dinghy out behind a rock, which we called an island. He was out of sight of the shore, but not so far away. A few hundred metres.

He said it was the cry of the gulls that told him. He heard their crying, their screaming, their agitation. The brown rock he had anchored the dinghy behind was patterned with their droppings.

He started to row back to shore. He rounded the island, saw the mother running to and fro in the shallows, my brothers and sisters close together, looking out to sea. The mother — who could not swim — wading into deeper water. He heard her voice calling with that of the gulls.

The pastel bubble of my shorts floated between him and the shore. I was silent, suspended from that bubble.

Tommy dived into the sea, and afterwards said he saw his shadow among other dark shapes moving away. From the shore they at first thought, shark! but it must've been dolphins. He didn't see anything of a baby, of that child Kenny. Didn't even know what had happened.

He kicked off his rubber boots, slid from his jumper, and with one arm plucked and threw me into the boat. He thought he heard my bones break as I landed. My skin was split open.

Only on the shore did he understand that Kenny was gone. But I was not breathing, my heart only just there. My father breathed life into me, the others ran to and fro in the shallows. Blue and black flecked sea. Wet and pale flesh. The brown and silver-cored sinews running across the sand.

The mother, some of the children stayed behind, just in case, you know, the baby ...

A sister and brother held me, and we were flung together, apart, as the car slid on gravel corners, bounced through shrubs and up over the soft shoulder, wheels spinning motor roaring, and onto the sealed road. We were inside the wind, and bitumen rubber just touching.

I am pale enough to turn blue, and it was a blue light

which flashed and so it was a very blue me indeed whose limbs jerked, and who spat and tore at my bony, sharp siblings.

When the cop pulled past on his motorbike, and went to weave in front of us, Dad swung the car at him. Dim-wittedly, glaring through his adrenalin at the gesticulations, the contorted faces, the helmeted one slowly realised what was happening.

He went before us wailing, wailing; a racing vanguard for my nearly hearse.

I imagine my father with a boy-in-arms, kicking at the doors which swing wide and open. He and his boy are damp, scale and blood-caked, like two born from the sea. He calls down a corridor, shouting into the hospital, his voice splitting into many, branching this way and that to bring calm, competent people gliding toward us.

My father trailed them, trying to explain the decision he'd made. The son in his arms — but not breathing. The baby, gone.

Years later, Uncle Jack tried to explain to me what happened while I was still unconscious in the hospital. Some people were very angry, of course. They never found the body. How could Tommy just leave it like that? He was just looking after his own kid. He made the wrong choice.

Uncle Jack and some older people went to see Tommy and my stepmother, to try and help. They understood, too, how hard it was. But Tommy and his wife would take no more little ones to look after.

Uncle Jack also told me how, at my father's wedding — it

was in a registry office — the bride's mother had noticed Uncle Jack.

'Oh. Oh. Oh, of course, Tommy … ? Is he … ?'

'Don't be silly. They don't have *throwbacks*.' Yet another voice of authority, in the shape of the father-in-law, who had read Neville's newspaper articles; or perhaps even made his own contribution, seen with his own eyes.

The father-in-law said it authoritatively, and that had seemed satisfactory, but now; after the drowning, and thinking of their sister and daughter with that man, slaving for him, breaking up blocks of ice with an axe just to pack and send his fish, and he with his bastard from some other woman, and *coon* kids from who knows where, expecting her to look after them …

The mother's two brothers didn't even knock, they just came bursting in the back door, glanced at the branches nailed to doorways either side of the passage, and kept coming. The dog barked, limping in their wake and struggling to get up the steps.

'We've come to take our sister home, and the kids,' one blurted out.

'You can keep yours.' The other one — a sensitive soul — tipped his head in my direction.

The mother cried at them to go away, and come back when they were sober.

Tommy grabbed a tomato sauce bottle and smashed it on the table. I thought the red sauce particularly dramatic.

He brandished the jagged glass at them like a crazy man, and the sauce made an arc of thick drops and splattered across them. Tommy frightened all of us.

One of the brothers sprang forward, and Tommy slashed his forearm open. The real blood was so much brighter, ran so much more freely, than the sauce.

The brothers backed out. One of them kicked our poor dog down the steps again.

It wasn't much of a scene really, but — with the lingering sense that he'd betrayed people somehow, letting the baby go and saving me — all that must have made it that much the harder for Tommy, when Ern came for me. Ern and his scientific mind, wanting to see one experiment all the way through, to see irrevocable proof.

Tommy, in Ern's opinion, was unpredictable. Backsliding. Maybe with Tommy it wasn't going to work, not even with Tommy's kids even though he had married a white woman. But, the boy ...

He was clever at school (I was), he liked reading (ditto), drawing all the time (I do).

Tommy must've known, he knew what Ern was like.

He shouldn't have let me go like that.

'I didn't know,' he said, that last time I was with him. 'What could I do? I had a wife, four littler kids, it was hard for them. Ern had the money, the time. When he talked of a private school, and promised ... Everything was just too much for me.'

Tommy handed me over to Ern, and it was many years before we met again. I soon found myself understanding some of my father's long-ago critics; how he made the wrong choice, saving me.

last but one

It was the last time but one I saw my father. We didn't talk much.

We ran. I followed him and in that darkness I could not tell if it was his feet I heard thumping the hard sand or my own. He carried the fishing net on his shoulders, wrapped in tarpaulin. We ran along a narrow track, our footsteps a soft, fast rhythm, and the scrub around us unformed, coagulated darkness. It was a thin gleaming line, and we ran each twist and turn, crouching as low as we were able so that we would be hidden.

I saw my father through the billowing of my own breath in the cold air. We paused, and he was a strange, misshapen thing ahead of me, against the stars; the net bulging where shoulders and head must be, legs merging into what must be land. Then he was off again. The intricate rhythm of our hearts, feet, breathing. His breath came hard, now. If I was his size I could carry the net.

And then, in a patch of soft sand, he fell.

I was looking down on him from far above, and he was a thin figure, limbs akimbo, outlined against that softly glowing patch of earth. Net and tarpaulin splayed from one hand, smudging two pale lines which parted the lumpy darkness.

Then, up close. His breath a ragged and empty speech balloon.

So close, not touching. I could see the pores of his skin. And my father, he put an arm over me, drew me to him, and we lay warm against one another as the searchlight sliced the night above us.

I felt our warmth, saw and smelled the life of our mutual breath and heard, too, it slow and grow louder as the boat's motor faded and left us.

It was the last time but one I saw my father, and I had escaped my grandfather ... No, that is not quite right. 'Escape' is not the right word. I think it was simply that I had managed to ease away from my grandfather's control because — as much as anything — he was confident that he had succeeded with me. Had made me, finished with me. And he was distracted by business concerns, developing a working relationship with a new partner, Aunty someone-or-other.

I had gone to see Tommy, this time, in my teenage years, as part of a trip with my girlfriends.

My girlfriends? How tangled this story is, the explanations required, and I don't wish to speak too much about this, these others involved. In my ignorance, I was led by a girl and her adopted sister. They had been searching for, and found, the adopted one's mother. We had thought she would have Aboriginal family, and it turned out to be so. Her mother was descended from country in the north of the state, and had ended up with a Nyoongar, a man named Cuddles.

I had just learnt to make love with this girl and her sister. The three of us laughed together, could share silence. In our innocence we were happy for her, with her, and in fact her mother was delighted to meet her. She had other children, they all embraced. There were all these relations to meet.

The Cuddles family knew of my own father. 'Tommy Scat? He's a Coolman, unna?'

And my girlfriend's biological father? They didn't know. The Cuddles family said they hoped it was not Ernest Solomon Scat. The man had a reputation, they said.

Timid and timetabled — perhaps even sly — I nevertheless returned to my grandfather and confronted him.

'He can't be so bad,' I remember saying to the girls on the long bus trip back. I remember moving to defend him against their accusations.

I put it to Grandad — this Ernest Solomon Scat — that my father and I were the only ones he had claimed. Why?

I was his product.

The girls had left me with him. Of course. I cannot blame them.

'Your father?' Ern snorted. 'You're nothing like him. He's some sort of *throwback*, all right. I made you mine.'

I think I just yelled at him. 'Shutup. Shutup. Shutup.' Something similarly articulate.

'Get out.'

The old man got to his feet. He moved very slowly, but as fast as he could. I let him come to me.

He grabbed my hair.

'Ow.'

Swung a fist at me.

'Get out of it.'

I took hold of his wrist, loosened his fingers from my hair.

He was cursing and striking me. I skipped away, a couple of steps, and he stumbled and almost fell.

What could I do? Couldn't run; pride, you know. Couldn't hit back, felt it would be wrong to lay him out that way.

I grabbed his car keys, and found myself in the middle of my grandfather's front lawn, a series of fences one behind the other for as far as I could see, as if I was at the centre of some field of trick mirrors, yet not reflected at all.

There was dew on the grass. A streetlight held me, and it blazed and crackled in the moist night air. Grandad came at me, his fists bunched, arms swinging.

'I don't want to ever have anything to do with you, ever again. Not you, not any of your family.'

He said it. His business partner — the latest 'Aunty' — repeated it for him. His neighbours, leaning over fences and out of windows, said it. Shame shame be off with you.

I hate to remember this. How I was crying. It was the tears, I suppose, or something, but I looked up, and there was only comforting darkness, while all around me bounced thorns of light.

Grandad's fists struck me, feebly. I held his wrists in my hands and stepped back, and the old man fell. He was on his knees before me, still clawing, still trying to hurt me.

I went to help him to his feet, but he screamed at me like a child.

I could not strike him. I was too soft to put him down.

With my face in his I thought I might kiss him, thought I might scream.

I sprung away from him effortlessly, and in one bound was beside his car where it was parked in the driveway.

He was on his feet again, stumbling at me, gnashing his teeth, practically foaming at the mouth. His pale fists waving like lilies.

I watched his hands slapping the windscreen, watched him tug at the door I'd locked.

The car started, and I let it purr.

Grandad's pale and haggard face was pressed against the glass beside me. I winked at him each time I touched the accelerator, curled my lip and made the engine roar.

When I released the clutch the car lurched forward instead of back. Something crunched, I heard glass breaking. I laughed and whooped for the old man's benefit, and then reversed carefully.

I wanted to make the tyres smoke and squeal, and so it was with embarrassment that I kangaroo-hopped away.

My father.

I collected the girls and drove to see him once more.

My father raised his eyebrows when he walked out to the car. 'Flash. Aren't you the lucky one then?'

But he didn't want to talk, not just then. Not about his father. He didn't want to talk, I could tell.

He said we should go fishing, in an estuary around the coast which was closed to such practices. 'Doesn't apply to us though,' he said.

It was very dark when we got there. The moon was setting and we saw how high smooth cloud made a pelt for the sky. We walked into a tunnel of scrub, and suddenly it was so dark I could not see my father before me, or even a hand in front of my face. I was scratched, clawed, touched by something, but could see only the pale glow of the path at my feet.

We came out of the tunnel and the moon had gone, but the expanse of gleaming sand before us showed where the bush began again, but not detail or shape of any kind.

We entered the scrub once more, and this time the path was wider and the shrubs lower. I followed the sound of my father, and the vague, only sometimes human shape discerned against the gleaming, sandy track as it wound through an apparently homogeneous darkness.

My father carried the net upon his shoulders. It was folded into a metal tub and cushioned by a sheet of tarpaulin.

'We won't need long.' He knotted one end of the net to a paperbark branch at the water's edge. 'What about you swim it out, eh?'

The water rose, warm over my nakedness. I held the tub with one hand, using it to help me float, and fed the net out with the other as I frog-kicked away from shore. My father's crouching form melted into the darkness. I could only guess that it was a straight line I swam.

The cloud cover was dispersing, there were stars, and I tried not to disturb the surface of the water too much because of the violence it did to the sky's reflection. I was held, I floated, but the vision of swimming in the rippling heavens, and the warmth I floated in, conspired to disorient me.

I could count a few corks marking the net and saw what must have been white sand at the estuary's edge. Perhaps that was a couple of paperbarks defined by their pale, vertical lines and the absence of stars where their leaves would be.

My father whispered across the water to me. 'We got a couple already. Follow the net back.'

When I had wrapped clothes around my wet self, my father handed me a rope attached to the line of corks, and I felt the tremor as another life struck.

'We'll go back to the car, and …'

He fell silent, and across the little space between us I felt him tighten.

'Fuck it. Quick!'

He was hauling the net in. I sprang to help, was clumsy. We rolled the net up in the tarpaulin, I grabbed the tub and ran after him.

The sound of a boat's motor was clear now.

'Into the scrub.'

We looked out from among a tracery of reeds and leaves and thin limbs to where a light was bobbing above the water.

A spotlight, a launch.

The beam swept the low bush, and we ducked as it swung over us. The scrub and us must have appeared the same, even under the spotlight.

The boat's grumble was louder, then passing.

My father heaved the net back onto his shoulders, and we began jogging again, keeping well behind the boat.

The spotlight bounced in my vision. I heard my father panting. I was the younger.

'You want me to take the net?'

'Shh. Ditch the tub.'

I swung the tub around, released it, and continuing the motion, was running again.

The boat returned, and once more we hid. The boat was close, came closer, slowly. The motor fell silent, and we listened to the tiny bow wave die, the boat settle in the water, the small waves of its wake lapping the shore. The spotlight speared where we had come from.

'A tub.'

We heard them speaking. My father's hand was calm on my shoulder.

Once again it left us, and once again we ran. And then my father fell, as I have written.

He told me he was fine.

We made a fire deep in a hollow among the dunes, and cooked the fish. 'No good trying to get out now with the ranger snooping,' said my father. The small fire pulled us to it and, silent, we stared into the glowing embers of its heart. The impenetrable and spiky darkness of the dunes comforted us, as did the net of stars so close above our heads.

The embers shifted, the fish fell apart in our hands. We wiped our hands on leaves and our clothes, and when we touched the inlet, breaking up the night sky's reflection, star-fire followed our hands as we moved them in the dark water.

Our headlights shone on a circle of tyre marks behind our car — my grandfather's car.

'Been and gone,' chuckled my father. 'Hope they didn't get too tired waiting.'

The scent of the smoke, the images of fire, fish scales and close stars were still about me — more real than the soft dashboard lights — and so when the ranger's car parked across the road brought us to a halt, the sudden silence, the spearing torch, the contrast between my reverie and this sudden, silent darkness frightened me.

The ranger came at us along the beam of our headlights. Cold air rushed in, and our own lights were extinguished.

I handed the ranger the keys. We listened to his footsteps circle the car. Doors opened, and we got out while he searched beneath our seats. He found no sign of fish, no net.

'A lovely night,' said my father. 'We been walking under the stars, on the white sand. Listening out for night birds.'

The ranger did not smile. He turned away, releasing us.

'See ya,' called my father, cheerily.

He looked at me. 'Might leave it a few days before we go pick up that net, I think.'

He sang as I drove us home.

As we pulled over outside my father's house, the two girls came running and opened the back door.

'Let's get out of here.'

They had told Dad's family what they had heard about Ern.

'But you ...' said one of them, addressing my father. 'Why? You let him take Harley?'

'Yes. Why did you, Dad? Why did you do that?'

So my father stayed in the car, rather than going in to his family. And we talked.

I was driving. It was difficult to look at him, to look any way other than forward. We wore seatbelts, of course, so only our heads and eyes could turn. We should have stopped, embraced.

I looked ahead, at the road. He occasionally looked at me — I could see from the corner of my vision — but mostly stared out the window on his side. Tried to explain. He was young. He tried to do what was right. Obligations. Wanting what was best.

I drove badly. I saw the girls in the rear-view mirror. They also looked away from one another, stared out their own windows.

I kept driving. Dad was talking, rambling, trying to explain. He thought it was for the best. He was young. He did the fractions talk; *half-caste*, *quadroon* ... that sort of stuff. He talked racism, oppression, genocide. He talked defeat, isolation, loneliness. He talked of who he felt he was.

He was gunna retire from the roads, just go fishing for a living along the coast. As we must always have done, he said. Keep looking for relations, find out more and more about his place. He talked and he talked, and a lot of it made no sense to me, back then. He said maybe he should have got himself a different woman, a black woman, and had really dark kids. Maybe it wasn't too late.

And I just kept heading vaguely east. We hummed along, and night closed in. Headlights drilling into the dark before us.

My father pulled his seatbelt away and hunched over. He slid from his seat and onto the floor, and huddled there, taking less space than I'd thought possible.

We stopped, but didn't know what to do. He couldn't breathe, he felt numb. The silence beside the road, out there in the bush, in the night, was disturbing. Dad muttered at us that he was okay, but agreed that we better get him to a hospital.

I drove on, faster now, comfortable with the business of driving. Again, he unbuckled and slid from the seat. He seemed to have folded on himself, somehow, and was no more than a bundle of clothing from which one hand emerged, turning at the wrist in an ambivalent gesture. This way, that way; thumb and index finger offering alternate directions.

There was a sickening smell in the car.

I hated him. I wanted to kick him. I wanted to get him to a hospital. I wanted someone to save me. I was scared and so I drove faster, wanting to compress time and get there, now. I wished we had not come so far.

We were slipping along, gliding, and I followed a broken white line as it revealed itself to me, snaking this way and that under the headlights. Red eyes white eyes watched us pass.

In the rear-view mirror, a spot of light, and then darkness again as we dropped into a valley.

Next time it was closer, blue light flashing. We heard its wail.

I did not have the time to stop. The girls, as I asked, leaned from the windows and tried to indicate, by pointing and waving hands over their heads to represent a siren, that we needed an escort, that this was an emergency.

We did not know the car had been reported stolen. The police could not see my father. The pursuit car touched its front bumper against the back of our car, and nearly spilled the girls onto the road.

Then we were in town, with two, three, police cars at our back as we screamed and wailed around corners, the twisting streets. Houses and fences leapt away from us;

trees bent over our path. The car bounced over kerbs, fishtailed this way, that.

The explosion of one tyre going. Two. The car shuddered, convulsed. We were among the islands and concrete of traffic-calming devices. The motor and rims screamed, and there was a curtain of sparks between us and our pursuers as we ricocheted along the narrow way left to us.

Flames in the air, explosions, shrieking. I had my foot flat to the floor; the motor screamed and the spinning wheels' cry was shrill; we moved at maybe thirty k's an hour, slipping and sliding on a molten surface.

Sinking. We were slowly sinking.

Cops opened their doors, and leaned out to make faces of mock horror; they called to us, and threw things; cans, handcuffs, boots and notebooks. They were laughing at us. I swung the wheel this way and that, kept my foot flat to the floor, made the motor scream; and we bumped along like a slow dodgem car in that narrow space between kerbs.

My father's head flopped about, and his eyes were wide.

In the rear-view mirror, beyond the sparks, cop cars idled in pursuit, and the blue light intermittently washing over us all showed the girls repeatedly lost, repeatedly reappearing.

I knew that I would have to shout to make myself heard. But who could listen? My father had slid from the passenger seat, and shrivelled to a heap of clothes and a single raised hand.

There was that very bad smell.

The car stumbled over a kerb, fell through a neglected rail, and tipped, at the top of some stairs, to the sea below.

The car teetered on its front bumper.

There was no moon, no wind. I saw a black sky peopled with stars, above and below me and — somewhere — the smudge of an island.

A policeman grabbed the rear of the car, let go, and the car went up, over; so slowly, it seemed, bouncing down the steep slope. Figures flung from the windows. Free.

I was gone. I saw that same car bubble and hiss in the sea below me.

It was as if I were some creature caught in transition from shell to shell, upon the open rocks, the torchlight slashing closer.

You would think such things are endings. We all worried about that, in our different ways; Grandad, me, Uncle Will. At one stage, full of frustration and anger at my place in Grandad's story, I wrote END, CRASH, FINISH into his skin. I poured black ink and ash into the wounds, and tended them carefully so that the skin would heal and seal the letters stark and proud.

I read through his notes, and all I could do was work on his house by day, and tend him, treat him, tie him down and occasionally write a word or two in the way I have indicated above. 'Here,' I would poke and prod him, 'quite white where the skin does not touch. This soft skin.' And I sliced my words, not so deep, but just enough, as it were, to scar and tattoo him.

Thinking again of his plans, his words, I added the lines of ink. How the dirty tributary joins the great river.

I know it seems all endings, this. I supposed so, too, at the time and believed that I was writing only of death, of worlds ending, and I thought, too, that I must begin again.

There was the crash, where I was maimed as our dog had once been. There was the funeral, where I was chained, and later given into my grandfather's care.

There have been many funerals since then, of course. My grandfather's, for instance, where there was just my two uncles and I.

At so many funerals I have felt lonely, that it was I who had already been dead longest, that I myself represented the final killing off; the genocide thing, you know. Destroy memory of a culture, destroy evidence of a distinctive people, bury memory deep in shame.

Having survived genocide, what was left to me but to look, to think, to try to comprehend what led to this oh-so-near-to-death?

At that first funeral I felt sorriest, really, for myself; the more so when Ern took me in hand — so to speak — and furthered his investigations, and probing. I'm so grateful that Uncle Will came to assist, and returned with further help.

After Uncle Will's death Uncle Jack took me to meet some relations. He rested his arms on the top of the steering wheel as he drove, so that he was sort of hunched over it. As if it was some sphere around his heart he was protecting. He looked into a middle distance as he spoke, sometimes turning to me so that I could just see the other eye behind the bridge of his nose for a moment before he turned away again.

He'd worked with my father on all the roads we drove along. I built this one, he'd say, and the camber on this corner is ratshit. We sped along, the motor grinding below the sound of the wind.

The road headed inland. Sometimes we'd glimpse the

river, or catch sight of the smoky green of trees in a dip far across a brown and dusty paddock. We sped between some salt lakes which reflected the sun like dirty mirrors. The usual dead and dying trees. The raw sky, with blue intestines of clouds tangled where the sun was heading.

'You got family out this way.' Uncle Jack didn't look at me, but remained seemingly focused on the white line snaking before him. 'Maybe we'll drop in on 'em.'

It was a gravel track, and we slid on its corners. There was a gate, hanging from a post, and I struggled with it, trying to lift the wire over the post, and then — once the car had gone through — struggled equally to close it again. Uncle sat in the car, watching the rear-view mirror.

It was a sandy track, and we came to a sagging hut of asbestos and timber, with car bodies scattered around it. There were a few men sitting under a lean-to verandah and a couple leaning into the engine compartment of a car, with a light suspended from the bonnet above them. Its cord ran back into the house.

They looked at us as we drove up, nodded, and came over grinning to shake hands with Uncle through the window of the car.

'Tommy Scat? Oh yeah,' they said, after I'd been introduced. 'I know 'im.' I think they looked at one another. 'He was a Coolman, eh? You got a lot of people over the border, and ...' Uncle Jack interrupted them, and they got into the car with us and we were driving again.

I struggled with the next gate, and no one said anything about how long it was taking. Another car came from the other direction, slowly, because of the state of the track, and soft branches brushed it as it rolled dustily along. It accelerated as I got the gate wide enough for it to pass through, and two women smiled at me as they rushed by. My own reflection, also, open-mouthed. I recognised them all; the two women, and — of course — myself.

I turned on my heel and saw the men in the one car watching me, the other car continuing, leaving me. Its brakelights flashed red, and it stopped.

Children in the car turned their faces to me. Doors opening.

i say

You can imagine; castrated, *absorbed*, buggered-up, striving to be more than a full stop, to sabotage my grandfather's social experiment, to repopulate his family history ... *Can* you imagine how I felt, seeing these two women again? The girls — now women — the first two women, the only two women with whom I had ...

Well, as Uncle Jack put it, 'White seed in black ground. Black seed in white ground.'

Two women stepped from a car. Two children on the rear seat, turned to peer through the rear window. Two women, each side of the car, look at me.

Uncle Jack, the others, all watching.

Me.

Us.

I want to preserve the anonymity of those two women, in case my writing proves to be just another way in which I embarrass and discomfort people.

The two of them helped me grow from my bitter and isolated self; let me reconcile myself to what it means to be so strangely uplifted; one who hovers, and need only touch the ground lightly. They brought others to hear me sing, and it is not their fault if I am unable to bring together people from beyond our very small core.

They led me back to writing, after I had turned away from it because of the struggles with my grandfather's words. They did not want to be central in such a story, which they understood must be about place, and what has grown from it. 'Not us,' they said. 'Not yet. Our children, yes, but not us.'

And what did I want? What did I want, as I floated above the keyboard, my hands clumsily dancing with the alphabet? I wanted to make something of which both my children and ancestors can be proud.

The women and I ... This is no romance, it is not romantic love I speak. Negotiation, perhaps. We had shared experience, came to learn together. We shared responsibilities.

I think they saw I was harmless enough.

They smiled, laughed, teased me.

'Looks like him, unna?' One would say to the other, indicating one of the children. Or say, of a particular gesture or mannerism, 'Who's that remind you of?'

And in fact there were several children. Neither of the women would confirm if the children, or either of them, were mine. But it was obvious to me — even if remarkably coincidental — that the two I had first seen in the car were mine. I saw myself in both of them. And Uncle Jack told me I was right.

The women acknowledged that it was good for the kids to have a man around. Even such a man as myself.

I did not understand it myself at the time, but of course I was dependent upon them for some sense of a future, and of how I might simply be. I have no doubt that they were more pragmatic; I had a house, car, far more than I needed that way. Once they had adjusted to my one or two peculiar characteristics I was very easy to get along with. Was, in fact, very obliging. They sensed the measure of my dependence, and were flattered by it. So why shouldn't they join my uncle and I as we slowly moved a little further, a little deeper into our family history.

But now — having written such a very little of my people, both before and behind me — I would show you a place.

I wanted to visit Dubitj Creek with the children. 'Go alone,' said the women. 'No,' they laughed at me, doing a duet:
'Take the kids with you ...'
'We need a break.'
'They'll keep your feet on the ground.'
I was happy. Flattered, really.

Dubitj Creek is a national park, and we stayed in an approved camping spot. We walked a little, fished, read the plaque at the ruins of some homestead. We made a fire, sat around it in the chill night. This seems too simple, I know, but it is true. I felt at peace and as if belonging. I remembered places very like it, from my own childhood.

We slept among old and gnarled ti-trees. Magpies woke us in the morning, and danced away into a little clump of paperbarks which showed, in the way the flaking bark had not yet grown back over charred-black wood, the signs of past fire.

In the mornings the fine sand along the edge of the dune vegetation held the brushstrokes of sweeping grasses, and the delicate prints of small marsupials, reptiles and birds. The afternoon breeze lifted and swirled the same sand so that the creek and the base of the trees seemed indistinct and blurred as we approached them.

I was still a lightweight, but as I walked hand-in-hand with my young children, I noticed that my footprints in the sand were almost as deep as theirs.

There is a small granite headland which the sea wraps around, and banksia trees grow thickly on its slope. Fresh water seeps slowly from the granite, the south-west wind is kept away, and the banksia cones are like little heads looking out from between the serrated leaves.

When you're on that slope, among the banksia trees, yours does not seem the only head sticking up and looking this way, that way, everyway.

I awoke under the stars, and heard the chill cry of a curlew.

We were about to leave Dubitj Creek, but suddenly jumped out of the car to take a last walk across the headland to a place the maps name Dolphin Cove.

We came to a line across the granite where the lichen had not grown and, our feet choosing the way, we followed it. There was no real reason.

No, I am too offhand. There is a reason. Lichen does not grow on that thin strip of granite, because it is the path where, again and again and again, our people walked across the granite. And where they walked, year after year after year, the lichen did not grow. Lichen, unlike the rock from which it grows, is a very fragile thing.

But, it is true, I only half thought this at the time.

We weaved through shrubs, to the other side of the hill and a small beach only a hundred or so metres long, between our hill and the next granite outcrop. The beach faced east; its sand was talcum white, and squeaked at us when we walked on it, and the ocean was broken into many small surfaces by the wind, broken grey, black, blue, green. Waves collapsed heavily on the steep, wet sand. I intended returning by walking around the headland on the rock which sloped into the sea. No sooner were we away from the beach than we were among precariously balanced brown granite boulders and irregular, massive sheets of stone strewn about as if thrown and broken by some powerful force.

There were small crevices and caves, their entrances as smooth as skin. The rock sloped quickly to where the ocean must have been very deep, because its level merely rose and fell smoothly up the slope of rock as each swell swept past.

Something on the edge of my vision attracted me. Further around the rocks, a bird, hovering. A grey and brown bird, mottled and immature, it hung in the air, intent on something below it and, constantly adjusting itself, remained in position despite the blustering, shifting and buckling air which it rode.

I walked on that smooth and sloping rock. The sea on my right; to my left, massive boulders and shards of rock with small and wiry coastal scrub sprouting in every tiny place where there was a little soil, sun, and shelter from the wind. Even then I felt something particular about the place, reminding me of something, somewhere, some other occasion.

I stopped to wait for my children, and always there was that bird; dipping, rising, but remaining.

'That bird wants us,' I said. Was I talking to myself, or my children? Was I talking in such a way? 'That bird is trying to tell us something.'

My children were tired. I wanted to comfort them.

Another bird; did it appear from nowhere, or suddenly swoop *up*, as if out of the sea; as if out of the hole left when the sea recedes as it sometimes does where there is deep water beside sloping rock, and a powerful swell running?

It was a white bird with bright red at its beak. Mollyhawk, I called it. An adult. Flying low at the edge of the rock, its wing beats regular and powerful, it arrowed straight to where the younger bird was hovering, and then arced up to join it.

I looked to my children, and — oh, this was sudden, not at all a gradual or patient uplift — I was the one poised, balanced, hovering on shifting currents and — looking down upon my family approaching from across the vast distances my vision could cover — I was the one to show them where and who we are.

Uplifted, I was as I have always been; must be. From me came that long cry which has made so many shiver, and think of death.

And should you ever hear this, or see it ... Well, yes, it *is* terrifying. Uncomfortable. It is the sort of thing it is easier to avoid.

I told Uncle Jack and the others of what had happened,

and as I was speaking I found myself suddenly aware of how they listened. How they looked at me so closely, so attentive as I spoke.

'Those birds. That was the spirit in the land talking to you. Birds, animals, anything can do it. That is what Aboriginal people see.'

He and the women began encouraging friends and family to visit us. We lit a fire, and people would make themselves comfortable, and I would walk in that strange way I have to the fire, float above it, and ... sing.

Now, it may not be for me to put a name to myself, to who or what I am. Call me one of whatever you will of these; Wadjari, Kwetjman, Mirning, Runaways, Southern People, Coastal People, Shell People, Ngadju, Nunga, Nyungar, Noongar, Nyungah, Nyoongar ...

If I am one of the Runaways, then it means to runaway as in to withdraw. If one of the Shell People ...

A mollusc withdraws inside itself, and stays there, until it is safe again. So we ran away inside ourselves to wait; we withdrew. And a shell cannot always tell what life it holds.

Periwinkle, mollusc, abalone ... Shells grip granite rocks. It is hard to get those things away from the rocks and sea. It is very hard to get at them. Soaked in salt water, dried in the sun, the waves pounding again and again.

One of the shell people. One of those hard, and eroding slowly to the ridge of itself, eroding to the ridge on the sand dunes. Further back is where the plants grow. Here, there is white sand, granite, ocean. Here the shells stubbornly cling, birds hover, and the dolphins — like old dogs — herd the ailing sea-things into shore.

Call it what you will. I say Nyoongar.

not beginning

How necessary, then, is it to acknowledge, let alone discuss, some very-first-white-man? Well, to be *fair*, even if it took some time to arrive at me, there must have been some first-white-man involved. However, my grandfather was not first-anything, whatever he may have liked to think. He merely attempted to hasten things to their conclusion. The persistence, perhaps, of what he would have called the 'spirit of empire'.

A first white man is not the *beginning* of anything much.

Consider a sandy-haired man. One out of his country, and merely touching this one's shores, now and then, as if seeking replenishment. While John Forrest plodded, squelched, slipped; while the likes of John Forrest used various shackles to force us to lead him to water (Here, you must dig for it. Here, lift this shard of granite), this other man sailed upon salt water and shackled himself to the great things beneath it or to the very wind itself.

This Sandy-Mason-One helped bring the wire for the telegraph line. It was left on the beach, then strung up from post to post across the land.

One man coming from elsewhere, staying. Belonging. Why?

For a long time I puzzled over that, trying to understand. Why? Why such an anomaly? Why claim the children? Why marry the woman, and remain within her traditional country?

Few thought him a worthy man in his own time. But, he helped us read and write. He chose to put us on paper.

A strange gift.

There were a scattering of pastoral stations along the southern coast. The remnant of a last tiny whaling base close to one of them, Dubitj Creek. The land-based whaling industry was almost dead.

Whalers had touched this coast for years and years. It had become necessary to hide the women away. Sealers bashed out the brains of not only the seals. They plucked people from the shore, raped them, clubbed out their brains, dumped bodies in the sea.

They ate human flesh. And one man lay under the water for a very long time, his too wide grin shifting with the current, until the fish came and took him away. It was then, so soon, that we first began to go to the islands.

Sandy One Mason was in the whale boat. It was a lark, a one-last-time before they took the gear back to Frederickstown, or sold it to Mustle at the station. And Sandy One was close enough to see that what they said was true; a whale hides its face in its shoulder. And this one had its eye on him.

Someone threw, thrust, pierced.

A very last fling.

The rope suddenly alive; a loose coil spinning a straight line spearing the sky's shifting reflection. The rope sang its passion.

Flick. One man gone. A kink in the rope? Someone too slow with the hatchet, and the rope not cut. The boat diving, men sluiced out.

Sputtering to the surface they see the boat flip up — its dragging bucket gone — and skip away across the sea at a great speed. And there — impossibly — is Sandy One Mason still holding onto the boat, flapping like a rag doll and last in line.

The boat's speed! Silent, supernatural. It became small, and then disappeared beneath the surface.

As I said, Mustle's pastoral station crouched on land about this place. Remarkably, written records assure me that it has snowed along this coast only the once, ever, and that it was at about this particular point in our history. But I am not surprised by any of this, really; not the claim for singularity, not the reality that it was so very cold. It is like ice dreaming, and of course there is always a storm. Squalls. Hail. And there are variously sized and delicately shaped flakes of white, ephemeral except where they are by chance tossed together in some shelter.

The sea spews you up into the chilling wind, a deep and numbing cold.

In the uplifted state provided by my grandfather, such a scene reminded me of Phantom comics. An ancestor is washed ashore, 'four hundred years ago'. But it was only one hundred years to when I began this great fat bunch of words. Like the Phantom, after a fashion, I have my chronicles, my secrets. But I'm no phantom. I'm no phantom.

And as a child I always identified with tubby little Guran, anyway. The harmless, grinning apologist. And, yes, some may still see me this way.

I suppose this is what made people wary, when they came to my little performances. I was so pale, there were strange scars marking my burnt and wrinkled skin, and yet I had that way of hovering, and of singing ... Those who met me were further puzzled by the fact that — away from the performance — I was so meek, so weak.

Who is he? What family? From where?

Can he be trusted?

But once again I digress. The mind of a child. No sticking power. Some atavistic fault, I hear someone say, in the character of the narrator.

Something more than one hundred years ago, Sandy One Mason is washed ashore.

It was the same south-westerlies that drove him now, on land as they had at sea. He had some dim sense of fire, of sticks rhythmically tapping, but his rational mind told him that it was too close to where he had come from — the water — and so, blind, he followed an opening in the land and let the wind take him into scrubby dunes, where it moaned and insinuated itself into the very curves and whorls of him, upsetting him again. He faced into the wind — a measure of his determination (once, my grandfather's eyes lit up when I read such a thing to him) — and fell down the slope.

Water flowing there, a narrow expanse of it, warmer than the air but salty still. And the wind has gone, is kept away. The shrubs at the creek's edge seem frozen, rearing back in surprise, as if startled to see him. He hears the firm white sand squeak at his hands and knees, and becomes aware that his skin is loose and wrinkled, suddenly the wrong size for him. Gradually — but realised all at once — there is warmth, and company.

He finds himself among creatures he recognises. Dull eyes, and long narrow snouts. The fragile tinkling of a pair of bells. An occasional bleat torn away, disappearing.

He thought it was afternoon but then suddenly the clouds, the sky, dropped; and it was dark. The wind inside and outside him. He was shivering, wind-whipped. The sheep huddled together, and he huddled with them, those with bells allowing him close.

He was moving again at first light. A grey, woolly light. Crawling, shivering, touching his cheek to the earth and resting when he could. The edge of the creek, which is swollen with the rain. Everything shivering in his vision. The trees in this what-might-be-a-valley dancing, swaying with the madness.

Suddenly, no wind. Cold; and he felt nothing. A sheep beside him had fallen and the spear in its side knocked against him.

He was on his feet, and following the two men who carried the sheep away. They were in a hollow in the land.

He followed those legs moving beneath kangaroo skin cloaks. In the now painful quiet he fancied he could hear his own feet stumbling. The men looked back once or twice, saw that he was still following them.

Up a short rocky slope, across granite. There was a fire, and people surrounding it. He listened to their voices, and wanted the kangaroo skin and that fire. The whole world shook in sympathy with him and his vision.

The scent of meat on the fire. Mutton. Whale flesh? They were looking at him, must have been speaking about him. Laughing at this shivering, weaponless, naked him. He was on all fours again, stupid and staring, waiting — just like one of the sheep — and wanting to turn his back on them but he could not help thinking of those spears. There was fire, and food.

He lay down not caring, deranged and confused and blown in with the wind like one from the world of the dead.

He tasted mutton, stayed by the fire in the cave opening, and pieces of cloud began to fall. He saw how the snowflakes drifted and, touching the earth, disappeared. Oh, except for some that eddied back into a small drift beside the mouth of their cave. He took some in his hand, tasted it.

I'd say they noticed his smile, his resigned confusion; the look of one dreaming and accepting.

He saw clouds racing across the distant sky and also right close in front of his eyelashes; and that the granite a few body lengths away was dark with rain. He was warm, dry and close to the fire. He was among.

He ate. Slept.

Must've felt their warmth, perhaps their nakedness, and it was these things that played through his wind-addled thoughts as he dozed.

When he awoke the slope was in deep shade, and little of the morning's warmth remained, although there was a small fire either side of him, and a kangaroo skin, soft and grimy from long use. He saw all the sheep, not far.

Next daylight he was led, following the sheep, to where a new homestead was being constructed. Stone

461

walls first, and very small openings for windows.

Fanny and some others — I don't know who else — had gathered shells from that edge of the rocks where the water is very deep, is blue and black, and even when there is a swell running the sea barely reforms itself, but simply rises and falls on the granite slope. They walked down the rocks, collected shellfish, saw the sea coming, quickly stepped higher. A graceful dance with the sea, really. To their right, and behind, was where the whale had stranded itself. Some of its skeleton still there.

Now they crushed the shellfish, piece by piece, and dropped small quantities into the water. It was a patient exercise; and they were hoping to make a groper appear from the deep, the way you can; make it slowly appear, and come circling closer and closer, to eat almost from your hands.

The whale boat, which had been making its slow way toward them, was close enough to require them to leave. The women turned from the sea.

There were men — at least three or four white men — standing among the huge broken rocks where the sloping sheet of granite became scrub. They must have landed the other side of the hill, and walked over.

This scene was one the women knew and feared. There appeared no escape.

The men stayed where they were, able to cut off any retreat.

The boat arrived; two men in it.

Fanny recognised one. Had been told. Trapped like that in a closing space, she walked straight at where the boat bobbed in deep water beside the rock. She heard the oar's blade scrape and scratch the granite.

Fanny walked at the boat, and now its hull nudged the rock. She brushed a man's hands aside, stepped light and quick into the boat, and put her own hands on Sandy One Mason's shoulders.

Maybe it was something about the way the sun lit his hair, maybe she saw a youthful, ancestral hero, but she went straight to him, and she grabbed him. She looked boldly into his eyes, wanting to take him on, this one among others closing a trap.

The men laughed. 'Looks like Sandy's all right.' And when the two of them — my ancestors — got out of the boat, because after all Sandy was all right and he may as well stay here now, it was all the easier to get others in.

It was crowded, that boat, and they were all moving about too much. It was crowded, but only a few hundred metres from shore …

My ancestors could hear the screaming as clear as that of sea birds. Quickly, the two of them ran away.

At least Fanny and Sandy acted, and did so with some dignity. Whereas — pursued — I was frightened and ignorant. I killed my father, almost killed my children and their mothers, and found myself in darkness, scrabbling up rocks and looking straight into the torches of my pursuers.

It is not always so easy, to speak from the heart. It is not an easy choice, and it is not so easy to find your way out from the heart. And neither is it necessarily a subtle thing.

Sandy One Mason was among those stalking the women, yet one turned to him, and stuck with him. It limited the violence, solved some immediate and pressing problems. She saved herself, and she saved him.

Fanny recognised him by his blond hair, that Sandy One. It is something to do with what Uncle Jack said, some of those places we came across; something about some blond ancestral hero.

She later saw me looking for her, and came to save me, too.

Anyway, those two ancestors turned back toward the mainland. Turned their backs on what happened on the ocean that day.

The pastoralist, Oliver Mustle, wanted Sandy to stay, help work the station. The *blacks* were only trouble. Mobs of them had appeared from who knows where — it was frightening to see so many — to feast on a whale which stranded itself at Dolphin Cove, and now they were all away again.

Mustle noted that his new shepherd, Sandy Mason, had quickly acquired a companion. Sandy gave — and she took — the name *Fanny*, and put it on paper. It was the same name Sandy's own mother had used, and Fanny accepted it. She knew of his mother.

There are others of her names, or her father's, which have been variously preserved on paper. Father's name: Wonyin, Winnery. Her name: Pinyan, Benang.

None of these make sense to me now, although there is a Nyoongar word, sometimes spelt, benang, which means tomorrow. Benang is tomorrow.

Sandy One and Fanny took the sheep out, for months at a time, to where there was good feed and water, and away from the narrow-leafed poison bushes. She taught him, prepared a camp each evening, found and cooked food.

Sheep moved slowly behind them across a plain of waving grass, and this after days of scraggy saltbush plain which, on his own, Sandy would not have tried to cross; he would have veered away and not come so far north.

The sheep grazed greedily, their eyes focused on the grass just beyond the end of their snouts.

Following Fanny's pointing finger, Sandy One saw a small ridge rising from the plain. Soon, standing upon that same ridge they saw, between the distant shrubs and trees, pieces of pink sky. But some of it was so low. And there, below them, a large piece of sky rippled as birds moved across it although — it was true — these particular birds flew with their wings folded and heads upright.

That bony ridge my ancestor's feet gripped was the highest part of a low, rocky outcrop which, its crevices pink and brimming with the dying sky, stretched into the distance.

All that water and, in the distance, great red rocks.

Sometimes they saw smoke from small fires, and waited to be approached. Benang spoke to the people, and Sandy stood weakly behind her, making soft sounds in his throat, pushing his lips out.

The water shrank, and the pools in all the whorls and crevices of the granite diminished, so that the land showed less and less of the sky within its self. But still, when they looked close, it showed their reflections. A man's bearded face, and then a girl's gliding in behind it, grinning, and spitting to break up the image.

They slept in a shelter of mallee branches woven and laced over a burrow in the ground. It was a nest they entered in darkness. And what was he being called? A penguin? A bird becoming a fish, flying in water? And she a curlew? Wilu? Wee-low? Is that what was said?

Returning, for the shearing, Sandy One told too much. Trying to impress, he said the wrong words at the wrong time to the wrong people. Always a danger. Soon there was a pastoral lease taken where that water was, and you could follow waterholes all the way to the goldfields, and back again to where, within a few short years, there would be a tavern and a place for Christmas *sprees*.

Of course, all this did not come without a lot of work; even my grandfather's notes admit that, but they assure us that:

> *Natives like working to help their white boss, and do not think of it as work. You could hear their laughter and chattering from a distance. They were all together, and worked for only a few hours at a time, in shifts throughout the day. Picking and shovelling, carrying the soil in a sack held at each side by sticks inserted in the material. A man would be at each end with the handles in his hands. They enjoyed the sense of industry.*

Well, as I have been at pains to point out, I am a very fair man. I know that the early pastoralists worked very hard, and so did their employees. But those pastoralists must have had some moments of satisfaction, too. Even, I trust, of pleasure. After all, they had been given the land for free, were able to use government rations to train themselves a workforce. As cultured people, they even gave themselves the delights of theatre, and of performance — witness the sprees — and the often associated delight of dispensing justice.

Mustle, as did so many others, held trials in his homestead. People were chained up on the verandah, and given their chance to speak in whatever English they may have had. Mustle liked to wear a wig on these occasions, to use the proper legal language, and make his impressive voice boom.

A gavel striking our wood; rap rap rap. Tap tap tap. Hollow sound of wood on wood. Already there were coloured ribbons hanging from the wall, and old Mustle sat there with the coils of a silver wig falling over his shoulders. He was enjoying himself, was grinning to an audience which contained, beside his own brother, a Moore, a Starr, and a Done. There was enjoyment, certainly; but it was malicious, and angry, and the laughter was cruel, even its restraint.

'Send them to the islands.'

Sandy One, because of his skill with boats — he had been whaling, after all, and his mother was the child of a sealer — was enlisted to take the schooner back to Wirlup Haven, from where he could return with a wagon load of goods.

Fanny was with him, and the wind lifted the boat, and as they skimmed by the islands they saw the station boat rowing away from the island, and that a fire had been lit on the island the boat had so recently left.

blooms its heartbeat

Once he was on the island, the scrub was set afire.

The black smoke rolled with the wind, the fire crackled, and even from the boat they could see the flames glow and gather and leap.

The name is Wonyin. (Or, something like that ... You understand, the difficulty of this, all I have is a misspelt name on a certificate.)

Jogging down the south-west slope of the island, Wonyin sees the ship's sail, itself like a cloud, drift in between him and the headland.

He reached the great granite boulders; black, and slippery from the sea's drenching although today it is relatively calm. Nothing like the usual swell, but the sea throws itself against a rock shelf, and falls back again, hissing. He feels the fire racing at his back, feels its heat ...

And is wrapped within the smoke, and amongst a flurry, a stampede, of soft footed animals rushing and scampering; tamar, wallaby, goanna … Scorching heat, and a great wind at his feet.

Sandy and Fanny, sailing, skim by the seaward side of the burning island. A larger swell passes beneath the boat and then, looking back through the smoke rolling out to them, they turn and see the great moving hill of ocean break over the granite and, partially transformed, rise higher. It hangs, and they hear the further boom of a blowhole. Small channels of grey ashy froth run down the rock, and the heads of small animals bob about in the sea.

The vegetation where the fire had reached was black and still steaming from its drenching.

The salt bleaches our skin. The mist hangs above the rocks where the big sea blooms. Blooms. Booms. Booms its heartbeat.

continuing ...

Sandy and Fanny sailed on to Wirlup Haven, and were left there to make their way back in the wagon. Payback, Fanny thought, but then was the further killing at Gebalup and they had to journey even further, to put us on paper.

Sandy One, perhaps returning to the practice of the sea and the salty taste of the knowledge his mother and grandfather had given him, sailed to and fro between Frederickstown and our home.

But for Fanny it was too much to be on a wind-tossed, water-swept boat, wishing to at least keep the land in sight. It was difficult adjusting to the constant knee-bent shift and stagger of standing above the waves, and to the shelter of tarpaulin only. She could not be always sailing, skimming to and from the edge of land, and only sometimes swooping into its shelter and perhaps a message on the beach.

Their children were all born in her home country, and then Sandy took them to Frederickstown to learn to read and write. There was a mission school where Sandy One had been educated as a boy.

Sandy thought it was the thing to do, the way to save them. He said, we're teaching them to read and write, teaching them all ways. They both knew Fanny had things to teach them, also. And to teach her man. She returned to the camps of Kylie Bay, travelled old trails. Was watchful. And Sandy worked the boats with the ex-whalers, and visited her regularly.

Sometime she might have sailed back to Frederickstown with Sandy. Did she huddle at the town's edge? Or walk its streets? Visit her children? She did.

My family were reunited, and gradually, we edged our way home. There was roo-shooting, there was simple living from the land, and the following of old ways, even while they were carrying goods from the coast to the pastoralists. 'This is the way it must be now,' Sandy had explained to her.

I know that Sandy One Mason was glad to have Fanny Pinyan Benang Wonyin with him, and glad to return to country rather than remain forever floating upon the sea's skin.

It was never random, it was never just wandering, it was never wilderness. I think it was more like my own wondering, even as I made my way through my grandfather's papers, looking for traces, for essences, for some feeling of what happened, for what had shaped it this way. Fanny led her family through a terrain in which she recognised the trace of her own ancestors, and looked

471

for her people. She brought them back. I would like to think that I do a similar thing. But I found myself among paper, and words not formed by an intention corresponding to my own, and I read a world weak in its creative spirit.

There is no other end, no other destination for all this paper talk but to keep doing it, to keep talking, to remake it.

For Sandy and Fanny it was companionship, it was reminders that somehow this was the same story despite the surface confusion. Even where strange animals had stripped the land to its essentials, to bone, to the bare contours of the land, it just made you turn inward all the more, to the bones of yourself.

We have always been surrounded by others. Needed to communicate with them, and yet be wary and watchful.

In strange country, where no clear voices remained, she turned inward, sometimes brightly blossoming out to those few she saw, still springing from the land. And blossoming, too, at the growing response in her fair man.

Flowers, fragile, nod in the dry wind.

They learnt to stay away from the goldfields, from the crowds, the noise and stench and stirred-up earth. It was there that, with Sandy away, those men stopped Fanny and the children one day, even though they were on a wagon, and took Harriette. The child born from that was lost in the goldfields, and came back to haunt them, came back coughing, lungs again bubbling black stuff and blood, bowels oozing. They saw how its smooth, soft skin had erupted in pustules, and — being a baby — it could not walk, but drifted in its dream motion toward them, and away again.

It was many years later, with the children grown, that they met with the Coolman twins and Sandy tried to commit them to paper and his family. Sandy and Fanny pursued Patrick, who had left taking their daughter Dinah with him.

They found Dinah at one of the Mustles' homesteads. Campbell Mustle, at Dubitj Creek. She had been kept there, working. There were rope marks on her wrists. But now Mustle's wife had come to stay. Cammy told Sandy that one of the red twins was working for him, and was due back soon. It was many years since Wonyin's exile, and they had avoided the place since.

Even as they left the homestead the wind was growing, gathering itself. A strange and resentful wind, it worried at them, put dust into their eyes, made the animals nervous. It came from the sea off the bight, and so they set off with it at their backs. It would have been better not to go, but the Mustles had to get there.

Mr Mustle and his wife sat at the front of the small cart. His wife had been at the station for some months now, and needed relief, so he and his good wife intended going on to Frederickstown by steamer from Kylie Bay. Mustle noted that his employee's *lubra* and *half-caste* son had — at the last moment — slipped onto the back of the cart. It was too much of a load really, but he let the matter pass; he could eject them along the trip if he wished. And three sets of hands would mean the cart would be loaded and returned so much more quickly.

The cold wind was insistent enough to make their teeth ache. It started to rain. My family huddled together in the tiny space available on the cart until Mustle had Sandy and his son hold a large oilskin over Mrs Mustle. The oilskin flapped, and at times the wind cracked it like a gunshot. Fanny turned her face up into the rain from where she sat on the jolting floor of the cart, at the feet of her men. She swung her legs around, and slid from the back of the vehicle. It was going at a fair pace, and she stumbled a bit as she touched the ground and left the track they had followed.

The horse and cart continued through the rain with its four passengers. That wind! Even with the rain being driven before them it was very difficult to see anything. Things formed and reformed as you got closer. But it was a good horse, and Mustle decided to trust it. Time was limited. He could hardly complain of rain, it was needed. Campbell Mustle was considering whether to get Sandy One to replace him on the seat, so that he and his wife could shelter more fully. It would be only a temporary indignity, leave them rested for their time in Kylie Bay where they would cast their vote against federation, and spend the inevitable social time with his brother's family. They were rolling through the bed of what was an only occasional creek, and the Mustles were dreaming of various *Entertainments* in the parlour, when one wheel rose over a fallen balga trunk, and the cart tipped.

Cammy Mustle left the vehicle first, and flew higher than the others. For a moment it seemed that he was intent on immediately ascending past the spiteful clouds, but the lack of sunbeams and the persistent, beating rain defeated him. He was an inordinately long time falling, seemed almost to drift down and the rain rushed by him. Sandy Two, lying on his back on a stumpy mallee bush, the rain playfully tapping his face chest belly, saw the white man flying above him. Fanny, standing a little off the track to observe it all, saw the same man go up up up, and then return with the curve of the sky. His downfall culminated in a sickening sound. He landed like a spear; head first, body straight and quivering. Then, slowly, he tipped and slammed onto his back.

Fanny went to her son first, and then to the sobbing white woman while Sandy One bent over the silent one. They arranged the couple side by side in the shelter of the upturned cart. Mrs was screaming, afraid to touch her own man.

They would have to send the boy for help, decided Sandy. He could ride to the Mustles at Kylie Bay. Sandy sent Fanny back to the homestead to let the workers know. She would have to be seen to be helpful, he quietly said to her. 'Cry,' he said. 'Look upset.'

Away they went; Fanny trudging one way, a strip of oilskin wrapped about her, and Sandy Two going the other with his thin legs gripping the big horse's stomach.

The youth rode with the rising wind. The world was grained diagonally, and individual drops of it clung to his eyebrows. His clothes were heavy. Often he passed so close behind the dunes that he felt — even within the rain — the salt of the sea, and heard the surf mumbling fitfully over the fretting wind, his breath, the rhythm of the horse. Once or twice the rain cleared from around him, and he looked down as if from a great height at the sea shifting the white sand about, and worrying at the granite outcrop beneath him. Cold water everywhere.

Kangaroos, at peace in the driving rain, watched him pass. If he rode them he might be faster still.

It was dark.

There were fires at the camp, but the homestead was

silent. Sandy Two scratched around, and asked the old fellow sleeping on the verandah to wake the bosses and tell them what had happened. A pale, already expressionless face falling with the rain, and the woman soundlessly shrieking.

The old fellow was shaking his head, and pushing the boy away when the boss's young son, Andrew Mustle, came onto the verandah from the outer darkness. He adjusted his clothing as he listened.

An older man arrived, and lit a small flame to expand the space around them. Sound was muffled, and the old man — Willie Mustle it must have been although in that light and shifting space it could have been who knows what? — made Sandy say it all again.

'You're Sandy Two are you?'

There was a boat with a sail. In the darkness Sandy Two thought of his father's and mother's stories of boats, and he saw the sea torn and ripped and bleeding white. The wind was turning, and they sailed away from land with it, and then returned, thumping and breasting the waves, and so it went on until eventually they came into the shelter of a headland, and the sea relaxed. Sandy Two leapt from the bow as they had told him, but leapt too early, and had to clutch again at the gunwale as the boat drove on. Andrew Mustle grabbed a fistful of hair and held him above the water.

In the pale light they could see purple lines marking the contours of Mrs Mustle's face. The Mustles took the unconscious man to the boat — there was no time to waste — and despite the weather, they must get him to Kylie Bay, transfer him to a bigger boat and send him on to Frederickstown. They'd take the boy also, and leave Sandy One with Mrs Cammy until they could send help.

476

Fanny materialised from the drizzle and sat beside the weeping woman. She leaned her back against the broken cart and thought of a loose bundle of flesh slumping from side to side as the boat tacked, and a skinful of bones vibrating as the little boat fell into each sharp, dark valley.

Her boy on board.

Sandy Two was shaken, uncertain; he always remembered that trip with fear. An oddly angled and diminished swell moved between the islands, and a strange wind shifted to and fro there, brushing the sea's grey surface in contrasting directions. The granite wall of an island seemed akin to the sea itself, the bruised sky was solid. He heard his mother cry; winged voices called to him, and — leaning over the edge of the boat — Sandy Two began emptying himself.

Vomit sprayed his face as they re-entered the wind. Another swell exploded against the island, became some great irrepressible entity, rising rising even as the wind whipped it and the deep earth pulled it down.

Now the wind drove them, filled the sail with its power and gave the boat life. The little boat leapt and leapt and seemed to stumble, would have wallowed but for the stretched-tight sail holding them just above the surface. Their eyes clung to the gloaming shape above before them which would not let them rest.

Sandy, drained as if to his essence, wondered if they would ever turn the boat, ever be capable of making it stop. They might eventually find themselves becalmed, drifting and — waking up in sunlight, crusty with salt — turn to the islands thinking of water, to drink to drink.

On one of those islands there is a salty pool the colour of

blood. Even today you can lift things from it which might have been pieces of timber, or rods of iron, but which — salt encrusted — look like thin limbs.

The red twin Patrick and Dinah had moved on already.

There was no place for Sandy and his brood at Mustle's station now, the new manager wanted nothing to do with them, and chased them off.

At Badjura Station a new manager looked at my family blankly. 'No, there's no Pinyans Benangs Wonyins no Winnerys here no more.'

Sandy had not moved from his seat on the wagon.

Asked about work the manager said, 'No.' There were more than enough men wanting work, that was what was worrying him, not the plight of some jumped-up little *gin*-jockey hauling some books and his family behind him. Who knows how many others might turn up next.

A bunch of books. An empty cage. A couple of kegs for water, some food. A *gin* and a *half-caste* boy. Probably a few tools, and a rifle. A horse and camel hauled the wagon, and although the manager was curious as to how the fellow got the animals to work together, he did not want him staying any longer than necessary. He wanted them on their way, as he did each roo shooting party which wandered in now expecting hospitality as their right, and half the time with the *blacks* carrying guns same as white men. There should be a law about it.

Someone said, 'Pat Coolman? Yeah, him and Daniel were heading for Done's lease. There's gold there.'

Fanny worried for her daughters. A world gone? The children remained.

A world gone? Changed. The telegraph line, railway line,

wheel tracks everywhere. Rubbish, and bad smells. Trees gone, grass grazed to the ground, the earth cut, shifting, not healed and not yet sealed; vegetation left too long without flames and regeneration. Dust coated the leaves. So many places seemed empty or had new inhabitants. Fanny and the two Sandies once dined on cat, a descendant of a crate of animals dumped inland and expected to feed on the pioneering rabbits. There were plenty of rabbits now. Cats, too.

Her people huddled in groups, dressed in the rags of white people. They held out their hands to strangers, and were herded about like sheep and cattle, though less well fed.

Fanny and the Sandies were heading back to Wirlup Haven and all the death they had left scattered there.

They got to the Forty Mile Tank all right. They had carted that way years ago, but this time, with just the old cart and a horse and camel hitched to it and searching for somewhere they could live, Sandy One saw it with new eyes. Beating the dust from his clothes he took a long look; it was barren as far as he could see.

On the plains around him there were no more pink flowering gums, no trees of any kind. They'd seen no roos, no emus; even a knowing eye could find very few signs of the little animals that should be there.

There were men with rifles at the hoof-churned waterholes and at the condenser tanks.

All in all Sandy felt like giving in. He'd just about had enough.

And anyone could see that the people slumped together in one another's shade were not well. They sat at a distance from the store, having been shooed from its verandah by the woman there, whose hands had fluttered like pale moths in the heat as she hastily dispensed rations. Her husband had run off to the 'fields, and here she was, again, running the business.

Sandy One offered to help, but she hissed at him, and refused him even as much as she'd handed out to the others.

'Let's eat the camel,' he muttered, as he crouched and came in under the wagon.

The three of them sat in the shade, a good distance from the store and those who remained behind it, some of whom periodically tried to lift themselves from the ground, before once again resigning themselves to the comfort of their shadows.

'We're gunna end up no better.'

They saw a thin woman leave the hut where the tank's caretaker lived, and walk over to those behind the store.

Sandy One crawled out into the dying light, hitched up his trousers, and swaggered over to the caretaker who was methodically dealing with the locks of his hut.

When he returned Fanny and the boy were out from under the wagon. The fire showed only their faces, their eyes teeth floating in the air. Sandy was heavy with grog, and roaring as he entered the firelight.

His tongue must have been bothering him again. The boy knew his mother would be able to see its red and inflamed tip within that bleached beard, darting between yellow teeth and cracked lips. It could be fiery, that tongue, like the very heart of a flame.

The old man got his rifle and disappeared into the darkness, shouting about charity, about stolen land, about gold and miners and cockies; shouting bitterness and betrayal. People should be looked after.

A mad bellowing began even before the rifle's explosion had faded. Sandy Two thought the stars should fall with such sounds, but then he heard the crackling of the fire, and even — it seemed — of the stars burning.

There was a dull thud as the camel fell. His father was the sound of footsteps moving to the flickering fires behind the store, was a voice calling them to come eat his food for there was too much for him on his own.

Kylie Bay was ahead of them still when they came across the camp close to the track. There was very little water, no shade. The dusty wind dried the skin, the moisture in the eyes and tongues of the people crouching there.

Closer to town they read the sand, and again heard the story. Boots and hoofprints had scuffed and dug. There were black flecks, and twigs and grains of sand had been curled together as the spilt blood dried. Quick bare feet stepped away, returned a little later and, repeatedly stamping, circled the site.

Next was a salty red pool, and they were approaching the government water tank, and — yet again — that very bad smell. The returned body of Johnny Forrest, namesake of the Premier. Grandchild of the Premier who had promised much, but forsaken his family.

At Kylie Bay camels lay in the sandy street, and were loaded with stores for their journey to the 'fields. There were less than there had been just a few months ago. The place had grown first a homestead, then telegraph office, police station, store, pubs.

Here and there, our own people, begging.

At Kylie Bay once more, Fanny, and Sandies One and

Two went to the police, to speak of justice, and ask for rations. At least for the wife and boy, said Sandy One. He explained his situation, how they had fled. There was so little life, there was no food, no water. Murder everywhere.

The police asked if he had any daughters. About fourteen or fifteen years old was a fine age.

The Coolman twins? Yes, they were at Gebalup.

My family camped just outside of Kylie Bay. That night in the camp a woman and her baby died. She was not much more than a skeleton, as was the child at her breast.

Gebalup was a flock of tents scattered over the shrub-scraggled slopes, and a little creek where men panned for gold.

A policeman had set up his tent beside the hessian and timber store. Cans of food were heaped in the shade of a lone salmon gum which was part of the store's structure.

The storekeeper had heard of Sandy. His father had spoken of him.

'I'm a Starr. Henry Starr,' and he held out his hand. Sandy Two stepped up beside his father as the two men disengaged.

'You working, Sandy? You carting?' asked the young storekeeper, ignoring the upstart boy's raised hand, and simultaneously appraising the woman.

'Hello. We don't get many *darkies* around here anymore,' grinned Starr.

'No,' said Sandy. For a moment he saw the young man falling toward him. 'You shot the rest,' he wanted to say, but his tongue gave him trouble, again, and all that came was a slur of words to which young Starr merely nodded politely.

'I had the ration contract for them, too, in Kylie Bay,' said Starr. 'Not without some trouble getting it, I can tell you.'

Sandy Two saw that the walls of the store behind Starr moved with the breeze. Legs of bacon hung in the space above his head, and chickens roosted here and there, clucking and ruffling their feathers against the gloomy heat of the tent.

Starr advanced Sandy some supplies, on credit, on account of their long relationship. He thought Sandy might want to do some carting for him, for them.

'Dad's got a property, by the coast. Half a day away, just west of Kylie Bay. Everything comes in from there.'

They were growing fruit, in a little valley. 'There's water, and it's cool.'

'Sandy Mason? Well,' said the elder Mustle to young Starr, 'his father was a shepherd for us, west of here.'

And his mother?

'A *gin*, a *half-caste* from hereabouts, Dubitj Creek. You remember old man Williams, the sealer? No? He used to camp at Dubitj Creek, came across from Tasmania, and he grew vegetables to trade with the whalers, and he used to guide them in through the islands.

'That was her father, that's old Sandy Mason's grandfather. So, anyway, I know who Sandy One Mason is. He's a *nigger*, really. It pays to keep track of these people, I've found. And the son? Yes, I reckon there's a regression there all right. He is not with us either. I wouldn't trust him.'

Sandy One, our first white man?

Sealers shot the men, kidnapped the women, bashed

the children. Sandy One's mother was conceived in rape, born on an island, and — snatched from her mother — was little more than a child when she was thrown from a boat and into the arms of the convict shepherd who walked her to Frederickstown. A good white man, he schooled her and their boy.

Sandy One, our first white man?

Sandy drove for his sons-in-law who had set up business carting for the mines, and the pastoralists. They had his daughters with them.

And so, some weeks later, our very first Travelling Inspector for Aborigines met up with some of my family. It seems it was the Travelling Inspector for Aborigines who first caught them, first sentenced them to a page. He fancied he had a great power, and never more so than when — leaving his horse, cart, and *native* boy — he took to his bicycle and, not quite touching the ground and with the wind at his back, skimmed along the camel pads. He ascertained things at a glance, swooping into a succession of towns, settlements, stations, camps. Each evening he dutifully condensed it all into long looping lines of ink.

It must have been somewhere in the southern goldfields, a tiny mining settlement long past the edge of what would become the wheatbelt, that he met my family. It must have been not so far from Gebalup, that little part of home, where the railway lines pointed and never reached, and where the trembling telegraph line curved by, not stopping. It was not so far from where the police constable would soon say, 'No, there's none. There never was many, except maybe at the station, at Mustle's station. But that was before my time.'

The inspector wrote them down thus:

I saw the following: a woman, about forty years of age, with a half-caste baby, and a half-caste youth. They were well dressed, and, as usual, dodging about among the houses.

Fanny had seen him first, anyway. Looking down a glary and dusty space between hessian, canvas, corrugated iron, she had seen that small, bandy-legged man who flapped his arms and held his head to one side.

She clutched her grandson to her breast and called out to her son, 'Sandy'. They hurried. A fast walk, legs moving from the knees down only so as not to draw attention to themselves. They ran when they could.

Together, they glanced down another dusty corridor, one walled with the words of flour bags, metal containers pressed flat, and the many labels — Lucifer Matches Kiwi Polish White Washer Velvet Soap Mrs Williams Pink Pills for Pale People Seigels Syrup Bile Beans ...

Looking for me, between even such walls of words as these. I can feel it.

And there was Sandy One beside the dray, once again cursing and stamping his agitation. Fanny and her son stepped into the unwalled space and the inspector came gliding by them; quiet, fast, and just a little above the ground.

He was standing with Sandy One, talking with him as they arrived.

Fanny did not look at him, nor speak. She sat in the shade of the dray and held the infant close. The boy moved into the space between her and the two men, and

485

leaned on the shaft of the cart, ready to spring to its seat.

The stranger, this watcher, was a small neat man. He wore a cane hat, and a moustache that gleamed and curved like the handlebars of his bicycle. He didn't let go of the machine.

'Yeah, I married her.' Sandy One reached across, and put his hands onto the bicycle. 'Reverend Burton. He's got one of these, as well. He married one of my daughters, too, to someone else; to a white man, I mean.'

Fanny could not help but feel her children beside her, all of us; even those who remain unaware of her today.

Sandy had hold of the machine's metal moustache. He pushed it a little, feeling the wheels roll easily on ball bearings and air. He picked it up.

The inspector looked at the woman and boy, his trained mind slicing, delineating, making sense of what he saw. *Full-blood*. The boy *half-caste*. But surprisingly fair. And this fellow talking to him? A *blackfella* all right. As the baby must be.

Sandy One looked into the other man's eyes, daring him. 'My boy,' Sandy One said to the Travelling Inspector, tilting his head to his grandson, Will. Fanny held the child tight, closer. Sandy One looked up at his son, Sandy Two, who had now climbed to the summit of the wagon's load. Sandy One was about to take a risk, to try a new strategy on the inspector. He indicated the boy, said, 'He was the first white man born in ...'

The inspector raised his eyebrows at Sandy One, who didn't finish the sentence. The inspector smiled, but not enough to offend. He didn't want to make fun of any man, not to his face.

The inspector laughed freely as he recounted the story over a meal, some days later, to the young Police Constable Hall, the Resident Magistrate William Mustle, the Mining Warden Done, and company.

'Of course, theoretically, that fellow — Sandy, you say? — had a point. His claim for the boy may be valid, at least by the letter of the law as it presently stands — we expect it to change, by the way — providing the grandson doesn't associate with the family, and keeps away from his own mother.'

The police constable told the inspector, washed and relaxed after his day's exertions, 'We don't get many Aborigines here. They don't come here much, not anymore. There aren't any that *belong* here, not now.'

The company nodded thoughtfully at these well chosen words.

'Though there are some at one of our stations,' added the Mustles. 'A small family, perhaps the ones you met with. They work there. And we bring in the wild ones each year from the outer stations, for shearing. The sheep, not them!'

'Yes, indeed!' said the inspector. And, yes indeed, behind his laughter he did have some concerns about the use of rations in exchange for employment, and about white men cohabiting with Aboriginal women. But he had already presented his opinions on these matters to the Mustles.

The inspector was pleased. He had trimmed his short whiskers. He looked at the white boater he held in his tanned hands.

'We expect legislation soon,' he said. 'It will enable us to protect and save them from contamination by whites. We will be able to force them to stay in designated areas.

They seem more of a problem further inland. Why, in the goldfields ... in the north of the state ...'

The inspector had been making notes each evening for weeks. He summarised his findings for them.

Unfortunately, he had found it a similar story in most places. The *blacks* had been horribly spoilt by contact with the whites. His mind parted people like a scythe. Oh, he was rigorous.

Most of the *blacks* were absolutely useless. The goldfields was worst. They hung about the town the greater part of the day, cadging tucker. Sometimes the women did a little work — if they obtained liquor in payment.

He had poked around — busier than you would believe! — and found numerous cases of venereal disease. Doubtless there were others. But it was not easy to get them to own up.

He had been surprised at the impudence of some of them, even half-naked they held their heads up to him, seemingly unaware of their degraded state.

They intimidated the public.

And it was not as if people objected to giving a little food, but ... well, giving water was a different thing. Water was a very expensive item on the 'fields.

The inspector, like his informants, found the very idea that the public should be obliged to supply the *natives* with water offensive. He suggested that a condenser be placed at one of the salt lakes, one of those a good way out of town. If the rabbits advanced this far — which seemed likely — the *natives* could catch and bring them in to exchange for water from the condenser. Something must be done to make them earn an honest living.

'They must be kept out of town, otherwise they will certainly not attempt to hunt for their own food. Not when they can get it simply by begging.'

But he had also written of how, in most areas, there seemed a dearth of game, a lack even of vegetation.

This Mustle's place was not so grand as some of the others, although even they had those coloured cords hanging from their ceiling.

'We're pulling back the land we've got,' the one said. His brother nodded. A wife was in the other room.

'We've got mines, now, after all. And we'll hold onto land along the river.'

'What can we do?' They talked to Sandy — they hoped — as men who shared a common past, and have sympathy. It was not like it used to be, twenty years ago, Sandy would remember.

'That government man here, a travelling inspector for the Aborigines Department, of all things. He reckons he'll put a stop to us issuing rations. We've got this last shearing season to get through,' they said. 'Then they're out. All of them, on all the other stations as well; Kylie Bay, everywhere …'

Perhaps the brother remembered Sandy One's family, because he added, as an afterthought, not quite sure how they stood; 'Well, most of them …'

Sandy would know how it is, wouldn't he? The families; all those relations.

Once again, a brother interrupted, and led the conversation over what was a sticky patch.

'You remember how it used to be? If they didn't get a daily dole of flour they entered our paddocks and speared our sheep. They cost us. They cost us eighty pounds a year. They are on the land, and someone has to feed them.'

'Or they did it at our expense,' said a brother, leaning forward.

Sandy was silent. It was unusual for him, but he had this continuing trouble with his tongue.

'Why should we maintain any of them — at our own expense — when a fund is set aside, from our taxes, for them?'

They told Sandy they had written to inform the Chief Protector of their opinion, and of the incompetence of this inspector who had been traipsing about on his bicycle and horse and cart and costing the government — taxpayers — God knows what.

'The constitution prescribes for a tax to provide for them, the *natives*, and our *natives* should receive their fair share. That bloody inspector. If they refuse us rations, refuse us flour then we shall simply be compelled to turn a number of unprofitable *natives* adrift. Let them apply to the local magistrate for their maintenance.'

They asked Sandy to cart for them. They had the dray and the beasts; horses, donkeys, 'Even a camel if you prefer,' they joked. 'Cart ore to the coast; sometimes wool from the soak, where they're sheared. You could bring fruit and vegetables back, for the town. There'll be a town here before you know it.'

If he preferred, Sandy could help with the sheep. 'Black shepherds are worthless, unreliable. Even rations won't get them here, let alone do the work that is required. It's hard to make them work for their keep.'

'If we must pay our workers, let it be a white man.'

It was like they shared the one head, these men, the one intelligence.

'The past is the past,' they continued. Sandy was watching the sky, behind their heads, bleeding. But it was too early in the day, he thought. His tongue was numb again.

'The past is the past,' one of them — both of them? — intoned. Sometimes it was the one, sometimes the other speaking at him but it was all one sentence and even if his tongue was as nimble as it had once been he would not have been able to interrupt them.

'Your children, they're all of them white, aren't they Sandy, really?' The two heads were grinning at him. 'You claimed them, you raised them.'

One of them glanced at the door beyond which his wife sat.

'We didn't. That's the only difference.'

'And that boy, Sandy. He looks like you, I can see you in him.'

It was true, Sandy felt a power the boy gave him.

'You're a character, Sandy. You're an original, we need you around here.'

'Look. Come and work for us. And your son? Count him in. If he's good enough for you he'll do us. We'll make it worth your while. What do you say? We need good men, with everyone still after gold — they're mad — we need men we can rely on. What do you say?'

Through the doorway, Sandy saw what I only read about much later. He saw Mrs Mustle, with one of her sisters-in-law, beckon one of her old and crippled slaves to the door. She had the old man tilt his head back, and she tipped the tea dregs from her fine china pot down his throat. The women leaned together on the closed door, weak with laughter.

Despite his stinging tongue, despite everything, Sandy formed the word for agreement easily. No stutter, but a consonant hissed softly. It is a strange and sibilant tongue this one I share with, among others, he and the inspector.

And what else do I share with Sandy One? This man who for so long I assumed was a white man, and wondered at why he should register and educate his children, marry the mother, do all these things and be such an anomaly, for a white man in such times. Strange things for a white man to do, still stranger — maybe — for a Nyoongar.

Sandy One found himself, like me, bereft, bleached, all washed up. His memory? Nothing! Yet he had returned. Had to act.

Sandy One was washed up, rolled in the beach sand.

It is a powerful place he was washed into and upon. It is so powerful that when I first went back there the birds spoke to me. Looking east we saw, through the sea haze, a headland far across the bay.

It was very cold when the dolphins brought Sandy One to the fire on the beach, where one man stood, singing and tapping sticks. There were others hiding there, waiting to spear the salmon the dolphins herded in. But this time there were no salmon, because the dolphins had brought a sick whale with them. It had a spear in it, and a rope at the end of which was tangled a sandy-haired man. He seemed like he was asleep, and the rope was wrapped around his arm.

That blond man was washed up here in this place now called Dolphin Cove, and he knew nothing. He didn't know what was going on. He lay down and was rolled in the white sand, and he crawled to the creek. His skin was all loose and wrinkled and pale, as if it did not fit him, as if he had shrivelled within it.

Like myself, caught up in a long and most unbecoming process, he had returned.

Fanny must have known it, been told.

Whether they were the dead returned, or not, they brought death with them. And the world changing all the time. After all it was she — variously named in the documents as Pinyan, Benang, Wonyin, Winnery — who became, simply, Fanny Mason.

Her people. Then came the whalers and sealers. Bits of the islands detaching themselves, and bearing these mostly white skinned ones ashore. Those skins the colour of ... skins like the sky, sometimes; like clouds, with the sun on them.

In the sun, those sails like bleached skin, billowing, blowing to us in the sea breeze.

As a little girl, for a long time she was among those kept out of sight. But there were fewer and fewer available to give such shelter.

Let us disregard those shot, brain-bashed, stolen. Forget those poisoned, those chained and force-fed with salt until they led the way to water.

Forget whalers, sealers, explorers, assorted adventurers.

Fanny Benang Mason saw her people fall; saw them trembling, nervous, darting glances all about them. Some became swollen, felt themselves burning up. Their skin — too hot to touch — erupted in various forms of sores. People itched, and scratched the skin away, and writhed on the ground with their arses raw from so much shitting, until eventually even that ceased and there was only an ooze of mucus and blood.

And always, again and again, even in Grandad's sources, but never underlined. *They shot a lot.*

Children, becoming white, gathering at the woodheap, learned to work for indifferent and earnest fathers.

Yes, the birth of even an unsuccessfully first-white-man-born-in-the-family-line has required a lot of death, a lot of space, a lot of emptiness. All of which I have had in abundance.

And also — it must be said — some sort of luck. I mean in that I am still here, however too-well disguised.

Uncle Jack said to me, 'To start with, what you are is a Nyoongar.'

Sandy One was no white man. Just as I am no white man, despite the look of me and the sudden silence — the temporary laughter and disbelief — of distant nephews nieces cousins grannies when they see me come gliding in above the fire. I hover in the campfire smoke, and hum with the resonance of that place.

Those nameless women from my past invited friends and relations to come visit, see me perform.

Some talked tourism, business possibilities — an abhorrent thought, I need not tell you. Grandad would have loved my involvement in any version of his bed-and-breakfast establishment.

Such talk came to nothing, anyway, because there was so much fluctuation, and so very slow an increase in the number attending my performances. I caused embarrassment, and made many people uncomfortable.

Yes, I am something of a curiosity — even for my own people.

We thought it strange, but possible, that we might reach more of you this way; from practised isolation, and by scratching and tapping from within the virtual prison of my grandfather's words.

I have written this story wanting to embrace all of you, and it is the best I can do in this language we share. Of course, there is an older tongue which also tells it.

Speaking from the heart, I tell you that I am part of a much older story, one of a perpetual billowing from the sea, with its rhythm of return, return, and remain.

Even now we gather, on chilly evenings, sometimes only a very few of us, sometimes more. We gather our strength in this way. From the heart of all of us. Pale, burnt and shrivelled, I hover in the campfire smoke and sing as best I can. I am not alone.

I acknowledge that there are many stories here, in the ashes below my feet — even my grandfather's.

I look out across the small crowd, hoping it will grow, hoping to see Uncle Will's children, and those of his sisters, and theirs in turn. And my father's other children? There is smoke and ash in my skin, and in my heart too.

I offer these words, especially, to those of you I embarrass, and who turn away from the shame of seeing me; or perhaps it is because your eyes smart as the wind blows the smoke a little toward you, and you hear something like a million million many-sized hearts beating, and the whispering of waves, leaves, grasses ...

We are still here, Benang.

Acknowledgements

This is a work of fiction even though some of the characters are based on real people, and its landscape upon real land.

The words attributed to A O Neville, and in italics on pp 11, 132, 160, and 399 are from his book, *Australia's Coloured Minority: Their Place in Our Community* (Sydney: Currawong Publishing Company, 1947), which was a continual — albeit perverse — source of inspiration. The words in italics on pp 26–9 and 47–8 are close paraphrases from the same source, with the exception of p 29 which is from an interview with A O Neville in the *Daily News*, 2 March 1932.

The quote beginning the chapter on p 157 is from a speech A O Neville made at Parliament House, Canberra, in 1937 and which I read in the Aboriginal Legal Service publication *Telling Our Story* (Perth: 1995).

The dialogue on pages 74, and 121–2 is based upon submissions to the Moseley Royal Commission (1934) and letters in the file of a member of my family. The words in italics on p 150 are from Neville's submission to the same Royal Commission.

The italicised words on pp 324–8 and 334–6 are taken from internal correspondence of the then Aborigines Department, and particularly A O Neville's correspondence with the first superintendent of Carrolup Native Settlement, Mr Fryer.

Neville's part of the dialogue on pp 38–40 is not literal but is based upon his letters in the file of a member of my family and phrases and attitudes occurring elsewhere in his writings and the letters I have him writing pp 63–5 are compiled from a range of very similar letters of his.

I am very much indebted to the then Aboriginal Affairs Planning Authority for helping me locate particular files of both the Aborigines and Native Welfare Departments, and to the J S Battye Library of West Australian History in Perth for their assistance, and have taken inspiration from a range of local history notes and sources particularly covering the Ravensthorpe, Hopetoun, Esperance, Balladonia, Thomas River and Point Malcolm areas of Western Australia. An exception among all these local histories is a Nyoongar social history, *Yarra-mo-up, Place of the Tall Yate Trees* (Canberra: Australian Government Publishing Service, 1996), by Roni Forrest and Stuart Crowe.

The text in italics on pp 183–4 is a very close paraphrase of an entry in the *West Australian Royal Historical Society: Journal and Proceedings (1954)* Vol IV, part VI, pp 6–7. I have changed a couple of sentences and omitted the names. The 'quote' in italics on p 359 is derived from the same source.

The phrase in italics on p 14 which concludes the chapter is from Western Australian Parliamentary Debates, 28, 1905: 315, and I am indebted to Anna Haebich's *For Their Own Good* (Nedlands: University of Western Australia Press, 1988) for this reference.

Some of the dialogue on pp 484, and 487–90 is based upon phrases in *Reports on Stations Visited by the Travelling Inspector of Aborigines, Perth* (Perth: Government Printer, 1901) and the departmental notes contributing to that publication.

The phrases in italics on p 365 and some of that on pp 45–6 are from an archival document, 'Our Southern Half-caste Natives and Their Conditions'.

The teapot incident on p 491 is inspired by one described on p 47 of Rica Erickson's book *The Dempsters* (Nedlands: University of Western Australia Press, 1978).

I have also paraphrased or quoted newpapers: *Sunday*

Times, 1927, on p 20; *West Australian*, 1928, on p 39; *Wagin Argus, Dumbleyung, Lake Grace Express*, 1933, on p 137; *Phillips River Times* (an advertisement), 1901, on p 248; and *Albany Advertiser*, April 1914, on p 292.

Esperance: Yesterday and Today (Perth: Service Printing Company, 1973) by S Rintoul, and *Ravensthorpe: Then and Now* (Perth: Imperial Printing, 1977) by A W Archer directed me to some useful sources.

Humphrey McQueen's *Social Sketches of Australia: 1888 — 1975* (Melbourne: Penguin, 1978), informed me of the man who turned blue after an electric shock.

The verse Jack Chatalong recites on p 277 is from Banjo Paterson's 'Frying Pan's Theology', and acknowledgement is due to Castle Music and Joe Daly for the portion of the lyrics of the song, 'Trumby' on p 423.

I would also like to acknowledge the encouragement of the following publications: *Telling our Story* (Aboriginal Legal Service, 1995); *For Their Own Good*, Anna Haebich; *Sort of a Place Like Home*, Susan Maushart (Fremantle Arts Centre Press, 1993); *Mister Neville*, Pat Jacobs (Fremantle Arts Centre Press, 1990).

Will Coolman's historical writings and the story of the curlew are based upon some fragments written by my own Uncle Will Coleman, and which I remember reading in my youth. The names correspond somewhat, but I never knew him so I am sure the reality and the book diverge.

This novel is in part about reclamation from the printed page and so I would like thank the *Noongar Dictionary* (Noongar Language and Culture Centre, Bunbury, 1992), compiled by Rose Whitehurst, for giving meaning to the name, Benang, which I found in some departmental papers concerning an ancestor of mine. I think *Nyungar Anew* by Carl von Brandenstein (Pacific Linguistics, Australian National University, 1988) is an insightful and interesting book, and although it is controversial and undoubtedly eccentric I am grateful for its discussion of aspects of Nyoongar, and in particular of the word *twertawaning*, which is one word, among others, for dolphin, and which may be literally translated as something like 'dog-like', 'old/past dog'. Thus I was led to use the dolphins as I have in this story.

This leads me to a final and most important acknowledgement. The above two works have their 'informants', many of whom have passed away, and some of whom I have not met. I would like to sincerely thank them, albeit in this distant way. Similarly, I would also like to express my gratitude to a number of people with whom I have been associated over the time I have been writing this book, and — not wishing them to share any criticism it may attract or to use their names to imply any greater credibility than what I possess as an individual — I can only hope that by this novel, if not in person, I can thank them adequately and help create more space into which all our stories and voices may grow.

Finally, as my wife and mother advise, I would like to dedicate this book to the women in my life.

Another great book from
Australia's finest small publisher

FREMANTLE ARTS CENTRE PRESS

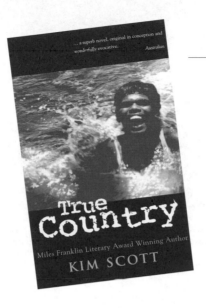

TRUE COUNTRY

Kim Scott

An exploration of unforgettable realism
With straightforward prose, which is often poetic in its
energy and rhythm, Kim Scott captures the ambiguities,
the troubles and the rewards which accompany the brutal
and the delicate nuances of relations when particles of
one culture pass, as if through a *not so fine* sieve, into the
heart of another culture.

Elizabeth Jolley

RRP $19.95

ISBN 1 86368 323 2

First published 1999 by
FREMANTLE ARTS CENTRE PRESS
PO Box 158, North Fremantle
Western Australia 6159.
www.facp.iinet.net.au

Reprinted 2000 three times. Reprinted 2001.

Consultant Editor Wendy Jenkins.
Production Coordinator Cate Sutherland.

Typeset by Fremantle Arts Centre Press
and printed by South Wind Productions, Singapore.

National Library of Australia
Cataloguing-in-publication data

Scott, Kim, 1957– .
    Benang: from the heart

    ISBN 1 86368 240 6.

    I. Title.

A823.3

The State of Western Australia has made an investment in this project
through ArtsWA in association with the Lotteries Commission.

Publication of this title was assisted by the Commonwealth Government
through the Australia Council, its arts funding and advisory body.